The VERMILION SEA

ALSO BY MEGAN CHANCE

Glamorous Notions
A Dangerous Education
A Splendid Ruin
A Drop of Ink
The Visitant
Inamorata
Bone River
City of Ash
Prima Donna
The Spiritualist
An Inconvenient Wife
Susannah Morrow

YOUNG ADULT FICTION

The Fianna Trilogy

The Shadows
The Web
The Veil

PRAISE FOR MEGAN CHANCE

For *Glamorous Notions*

"The plot is intense and dramatic, and it is always edifying to experience Chance's scene-setting where she revels in minute detail to embed her characters firmly in time and place. The author writes superbly and never fails to weave a powerful story."

—*Historical Novels Review* (Editors' Choice)

For *A Dangerous Education*

"Long-buried secrets, agonizing choices, dangerous obsessions: This thought-provoking historical mystery is destined to become a book-club favorite. Its timely emphasis on women's autonomy (or lack thereof!), not to mention its twists and turns, will keep you reading all the way to its unpredictable, but fully earned, ending."

—Christina Baker Kline, #1 *New York Times* bestselling author of *Orphan Train*

"Chance's knack of introducing quiet menace into her novels pulls the story along at break-neck speed. I couldn't let go! Highly recommended."

—*Historical Novels Review*

"A powerful and thought-provoking story that is impossible to put down."

—Kristin Hannah, *New York Times* bestselling author of *The Four Winds* and *The Nightingale*

For *A Splendid Ruin*

"A thoroughly enjoyable read highly recommended for fans of Suzanne Rindell, Melanie Benjamin, and Greer Macallister."

—*Library Journal* (starred review)

"This is a spellbinding page-turner of a book."

—Kristin Hannah, *New York Times* bestselling author of *The Four Winds* and *The Nightingale*

"A wonderful sense of menace: duplicitous characters, family secrets, and cliff-hanger chapter endings."

—*Historical Novels Review*

The VERMILION SEA

A Novel

MEGAN CHANCE

LAKE UNION
PUBLISHING

This is a work of fiction. Names, characters, organizations, places, events, and incidents are either products of the author's imagination or are used fictitiously.

Published by Lake Union Publishing, Seattle

www.apub.com

EU Product Safety contact
Amazon Media EU S. à r.l.
38, avenue John F. Kennedy, L-1855 Luxembourg
amazonpublishing-gpsr@amazon.com

ISBN-13: 9781662533501 (paperback)
ISBN-13: 9781662533518 (digital)

Cover design by Faceout Studio, Spencer Fuller
Cover image: © Sudha Peravali / ArcAngel Images; © Allexxandar / Shutterstock

Printed in the United States of America

This one's for my dad, C. William Chance,
with much love.
Thanks for all the adventures, Dad, especially
on Hueva del Mar, Tigger Too,
Hushwing, *and* Hellbitch.
All of them were memorable, some of them intense.
Fortunately none resembled the voyage depicted here.
Mostly.

Chapter One

San Diego, CA
June 1925

Billie McKennan hurried from the laboratory, hastily dusting her hands on her trousers, blinking in the bright San Diego sun. The summons from the zoo director had been urgent—urgent enough to interrupt her examination of the algae recently fouling the sea lion dam. It was unlike Tom Faulconer to be so insistent. In the year that Billie had worked at the zoo, he'd never called for her like this. She wondered what she'd done wrong. She couldn't afford to lose this job; it had been hard enough to get it.

The zoo visitors were out in force today. Men in their straw boaters and summer suits, women with their light dresses quivering in the faint breeze, children racing about in delight. For June, it wasn't too hot, a perfect day to tour the zoo. While a small contingent gathered at the sea lion dam, it wasn't the main attraction. Faulconer had recently brought in koalas from Australia, and they'd been drawing crowds. It was, Billie hoped, a harbinger of greater things to come for the zoo. Though Billie was only an assistant zookeeper, she hoped the success of the koalas would open the director up to other ideas.

Don't get your hopes up, she told herself. In fact, she should assume that she'd failed. Already June, and she'd heard nothing about the expedition she'd applied for. She shouldn't want so much. She was bound to be disappointed. Yet after the last two years, she needed some luck, and this was the opportunity of a lifetime—why shouldn't she get it? Why shouldn't she want it? She deserved it. Maybe today she'd go home to her dingy bungalow to find a letter waiting. Maybe. She'd known when she'd chosen to pursue marine biology that it would be difficult. Her professor father had discouraged her. *"You're so smart, Billie, but for a woman . . . maybe choose something easier. I hate to see you make your life so hard."*

"*It won't be hard for me*," she'd told him. *"I'm going to change the world, Dad. Watch me do it."*

So yes, here she was, setting the world on fire. Billie laughed softly to herself. An assistant zookeeper who could barely afford her rent. The best thing about her bungalow was that it was within walking distance of the zoo. Despite the ads saying a car was "within the means of millions," it wasn't within her means. Her neighbors were getting refrigerators, but she still had an icebox. At least the bungalow had electricity. The prosperity promised by the magazines and the radio and the politicians had not yet made its way to her. Instead, she—who had won awards in college, who had been considered brilliant *for a woman*—was constantly mocked by stubborn algae and obstinate sea lions.

A roar echoed from the lions' grotto, a flurry of birds squawked in protest, and Billie brought herself back to the present moment, and Tom Faulconer.

There was always a bustle around the director's office, and today was no different. Everyone wanted something from Tom Faulconer. Well, not Billie. At least, not today. She paused at the door, her anxiety rising as she wondered what he wanted from her.

She set her expression to pleasantness, and knocked. At his "Come in," she entered.

The zoo director sat confidently behind his desk, which was littered with books and papers and a stuffed animal koala. "Ah, Miss McKennan," he said with a smile. "Please, take a seat. How's the dam algae?" He laughed lightly at the homonym.

Nervously, she sat. She didn't believe he'd summoned her to discuss the algae in the sea lion dam. She sent him a weekly report, and he knew the status very well. His question was simply indicative of his attention to detail. She smiled as best she could through her nerves and said, "I expect to have it under control shortly." She searched his good-natured face, but the light reflected off his glasses, and she gleaned nothing. "Is that why you called me here? Is there some problem?"

"No, no." He waved her words away. "I've every confidence in you regarding that. The thing is, I've got a rather strange request, but perhaps you already know about it. I got a call this afternoon from James Holloway's representative."

Billie's heart jumped.

"Have you been hobnobbing with the rich and famous, McKennan?" he joked.

She tried to smile, but she was too anxious. There was only one reason for Faulconer to bring up James Holloway to her. Only one. "I got word of his planned expedition, and I thought . . . why not us?"

"You know what they're calling it, don't you? Holloway's Folly."

She had heard something like that, but Billie had no idea why. Why would anyone call it such a thing? The Holloway expedition was set to explore the Gulf of California for the month of July. No one had the money and resources to undertake such a thing the way James Holloway did. The Gulf was a little-explored area. There hadn't been an expedition to collect specimens in the Gulf of California since the US Fisheries had explored the lower Gulf in 1911. The California Academy of Sciences had only collected on land when it had sent an expedition out a few years ago. The waters of the Gulf teemed with life; it would be a prime area for picking up new species or variations—any scientist's, any *marine biologist's* dream. It was certainly hers, and now—if she was understanding correctly—it seemed it was within her grasp. It would be a triumphant return to the career that had been stolen from her.

She didn't want to ask questions that would spoil it. "If it brings the zoo a marine exhibit, I don't know why it would be folly."

"I didn't ask for a marine exhibit, McKennan."

"The zoo needs one."

"Who would administer it? You?"

"Yes. Why not?"

"You're a woman and an assistant zookeeper. You've only been here a year, and might I remind you that you've published nothing?"

Billie bit her tongue to keep from responding. For two years, she'd managed not to respond to this jibe, and she was sick to death of it. She'd finally taken a positive step toward rebuilding her career, and she refused to regret it.

"I'm a good marine biologist, Mr. Faulconer. I can do what needs to be done for an excellent exhibit. But are you saying—"

"Yes. James Holloway has requested your professional skills to gather and catalog marine specimens in the Gulf of California. He says he's taking two scientists, and your talents are perfect for his needs. The salary he's offered is quite generous, and he's offered the zoo an incentive to release you for the month or so of the expedition. I don't mind telling you that it's a generous incentive, and frankly, though I can't afford to lose you for a month, I also can't afford to refuse his offer."

"I . . . see. So . . . you're saying you've agreed." Billie tried to stem a wave of pure elation.

"I thought you'd appreciate the professional opportunity," Faulconer said. "You're a talented naturalist, McKennan, though I confess I'm surprised a man like Holloway chose you for this expedition."

"Maybe he'd heard of me," she said brightly.

Faulconer gave her a skeptical look. "How would he have done that?"

"Well . . ." She didn't want to say that she'd written to Holloway the moment she'd heard the rumor of his expedition, or that she'd practically begged for the spot as the marine biologist aboard. That he'd chosen her, out of all the naturalists who must have wanted it . . . She couldn't quite believe her luck.

Faulconer shook his head. "He's not known as a particularly progressive man," he said, almost to himself.

"He's done a great deal for San Diego."

"That he has. But he's a builder and an investor and . . ." He trailed off as if he couldn't think of the appropriate word to say in mixed company. "I was surprised when I heard he'd taken an interest in museums and science, though I suppose I shouldn't have been. But generally his interests are more . . . ah . . ."

Hinky. Hinky was the word he wanted. As in suspicious, weird, a bit crazy. Billie couldn't come close to listing all the fancies James Holloway had drifted to, but whatever the man pursued, the whole world seemed to know it. The millionaire had suffered lung damage after a bout with the Spanish flu, and since then he'd been seeking a cure in every crazy bunco one could imagine. He'd pursued spiritualism and had traveled for months with the faith-healing preacher Aimee Semple McPherson and for a while had adhered very publicly to Kellogg's bizarre health crazes and was said to have believed one could exist only on air and . . . too many other mad conceits. Now, he'd apparently turned to thinking about his legacy by setting up museums named for him, which was fine with her, because it meant that what he wanted was her presence on a cruise in the Gulf of California to establish a marine exhibit at the San Diego Zoo, and Billie was willing to overlook his eccentricities and dubious reputation.

"Of course we're happy for the investment, though what we will *do* with the collection I have no idea. Maybe we'll lend it to the California Academy of Sciences."

"No." Billie could not keep the vehemence from her tone, and when Faulconer looked at her in surprise, she said, "I'm doing this for the zoo, Mr. Faulconer. When the Australian animals arrived, we had no place to put them, and now look how the public loves them. I ask you to think of the number of visitors a marine exhibit might draw."

He sighed. "Koalas are cuddly. People tend not to feel the same way about *fish*."

"The sea lion dam draws crowds," she pressed.

"Yes, it does. Children love to bark at them. Very well, I'll consider it. But do keep to your schedule, McKennan. You'll leave someone in charge of the algae?"

"Of course, sir," she said. "I hope to have it taken care of before I leave."

"Good. Good. Count yourself lucky, McKennan."

Lucky. She had studied at the Pennsylvania College for Women and at the Marine Biological Laboratory in Woods Hole. She had published—*co*published, which was the problem—how many articles? She had worked as a research assistant at prestigious academies, and then disaster, and now look at her. This zoo job was far below her skills and her education and her experience, but she had spent six months wondering if she would get a job at all, and so . . . *Yes, count your blessings. Lucky, damn it.*

⸻

July 5, 1925

The afternoon she was to meet Holloway's yacht, Billie made her way to the pier at Point Loma, where there waited an enormous ship with a white-painted wooden hull and a looming red funnel above a deckhouse and a perching pilothouse, a canvas canopy and what looked to be yards of portholes. Billie stared in stunned amazement. She had expected . . . well, not this. The yacht had to be at least two hundred feet long; it reminded her of the presidential yacht she'd seen in newsreels—the USS *Mayflower*—the kind of ship used in diplomatic worldwide missions. So awe inspiring and immense that it took her a moment to notice the man in a green uniform standing on the dock waiting for her.

Or at least, waiting for *Mr.* McKennan. Billie had forgotten, in all the flurry of getting ready, that of course James Holloway was expecting a man. He had addressed her as Mr. in all their correspondence, and she had never corrected him. It wasn't that she'd meant to be dishonest, exactly. It was more that . . . well, yes, she had meant to be dishonest. She had used her initials, W. F.—for Wilhelmina Faith—on purpose. She had already spent so much time fighting the prejudice against women scientists, and she'd just wanted to get past the initial vetting. But then, well, it had simply been easier to go along. She'd meant to tell him eventually, but the time never seemed right, and so here she was.

Billie's nerves flared. She tried to ignore them. When she approached with her bags, the man looked past her, rocking on his heels. She stopped, waiting for him to acknowledge her. He smiled and gave her a questioning look. "May I help you, miss?"

"This is the *Eurybia*?"

"Yes, miss."

"Then I'm expected aboard. I'm Billie McKennan."

The man blinked, obviously surprised. "You're Mr. McKennan?"

"Well, yes. That is, I'm Miss McKennan. Billie McKennan. I was told to be here at two p.m."

The man's brow furrowed. "I was told I was waiting for a scientist."

"Yes. That would be me."

The befuddled man attempted to regain his composure. He reached politely for her bags, and she released them with relief. They were heavy. "This way, Miss McKennan."

She followed him up the gangplank. He set her bags down in front of another uniformed man and said, "Take these to Miss McKennan's stateroom."

The man stared at her and said, "*Miss* McKennan? But they've put her with—"

"That's gotta change, don't it?" snapped her greeter. "You'd best talk to Boyd."

Now Billie realized that her little omission about her sex might be more complicated than she'd anticipated. She had never believed that James Holloway would find the surprise to his liking, but she'd had faith in her ability to convince him. She had the best of credentials, she told herself, even if she couldn't claim some of them. She was an excellent marine biologist. She deserved to be here.

Still . . . she'd seen the expressions on too many men's faces when they'd been introduced to a female naturalist, and she'd felt their resentment and dismissal often enough to wonder what the hell she'd thought she was doing by keeping her gender from a man she'd spend a month with aboard a yacht in the middle of the Gulf of California. She would be lucky if Holloway didn't send her packing. Straight back to the zoo.

"This way, miss," said the man who'd brought her aboard.

He chose you, she told herself as she followed along the passageway skimming the deckhouse to the stern of the ship. But now she remembered Faulconer's puzzlement over that fact and asked herself what she had been too excited and relieved to ask before.

Why had James Holloway chosen her?

Thanks to past circumstances, she couldn't make use of half her qualifications, and neither could she fully explain the reason for their exclusion. Not only that, but Faulconer had said that Holloway was bringing only two naturalists—an expedition of this size should have at least five. Billie had given none of this any thought before, but now the questions rushed through her mind, too late. Not that she would have turned the opportunity down anyway.

The passage opened onto a deck with—unbelievably—a player piano. There was a huge, square, cushioned wicker lounging platform, and a small group of people gathered around a cluster of wicker furniture and a built-in wraparound settee. Mostly men—correction, all men, but for one elegantly dressed blond woman.

Billie's uneasiness grew. She struggled to hide it as the man led her to them and announced, "Miss McKennan has arrived, sir."

They'd been talking; they stopped.

"*Miss* McKennan?" A blond man she recognized as James Holloway turned, an odd-smelling cigarette in hand. Billie had seen his picture in the papers: good looking, a bit weak chinned, but otherwise a man who commanded attention with his golden hair and blue eyes. Eyes that seemed tired, she thought. Skin pallid. Too thin in that way that said he'd lost weight in illness. "You're W. F. McKennan?"

"I am." She infused her voice with confidence. "Wilhelmina Faith. Most people call me Billie."

Holloway pulled on his cigarette, regarding her with something like—was it displeasure? She couldn't tell. She felt the others staring at her, but she held Holloway's gaze. That is, she did until he turned away to someone else in the group and said, "Did you know this?"

She followed his glance.

Roland.

It was a shock. The last person in the world she expected—or wanted—to see.

Roland Ely. He looked no different than when she'd seen him last. Well, he seemed calmer now, which only irritated her. Dark haired, hazel eyed, the most charming herpetologist at the California Academy of Sciences, and a bum of the first order.

He met her gaze, briefly, unemotionally—what did she expect?—and then said to Holloway, "You wanted a marine biologist. You got one of the best there is."

His compliment made her want to laugh, but it would be too bitter, so she didn't.

"But . . . a woman."

Roland nodded. "She's as good as a man."

She could not even look at him. *Better.* She was better than most of them.

Holloway harrumphed, and took another puff on his cigarette as he turned back to Billie. "It's a surprise, I'll grant you that."

"I appreciate the opportunity, Mr. Holloway. I assure you, you won't regret it."

He laughed shortly; it brought a raspy choke from his chest, which he pounded with the flat of his hand. "I hope not, Miss McKennan. Anyway, I suppose it's too late now." He introduced the others, who were all in their late thirties, Billie guessed. His wife, Victorine, obviously once a great beauty, bolstered now by artistry and clothing. Her dotted georgette looked so expensive even Billie, who had little eye for fashion, couldn't help but see the money in it. Oliver Stanton, the vice president of the Holloway Foundation, who appeared athletic and good natured, with sandy-colored hair and the kind of easy grace that made him seem as if he'd just stepped out of a Fitzgerald novel.

James gestured to Roland. "And of course, it seems you know Roland Ely. How *do* you know each other?"

"I think all the scientists in California have at least heard of each other," Roland said before she could answer.

She wondered what he would do if she told the truth just then. She wondered why he was hiding what they were to each other—no, better to say *what they had been*. They were nothing to one another now, and she wanted to keep it that way. She had no idea why he hadn't told Holloway who she was and put an end to her presence on this ship the moment he had the opportunity. She didn't like that he hadn't, not the fact that it meant she now owed him a debt nor the fact that she had to guess at his motives. What the hell did he want from her now?

Because he had to want something. There was not an altruistic bone in Roland Ely's body. She had spent two years trying to recover from what he'd done to her, and now, just when she was starting to pull herself up again, here he was. She wanted this expedition so much, but had she known Roland would be her colleague on this ship . . .

She might have preferred burying herself in algae at the San Diego Zoo.

Chapter Two

"I'll show you the lab." Roland took Billie's arm, leading her away from the others.

She tensed at the touch, but knew him well enough to be sure there must be a reason for his pretense, so she waited until they were out of sight before she jerked her arm away. At the top of the stairs to belowdecks, she demanded in a low voice, "What the hell are you doing?"

"Showing you the lab," he said.

"You know that's not what I mean."

He glanced behind them and then led her down the narrow stairs. "Just hold your temper for half a minute, okay, and I'll explain."

"Why didn't you tell him? Damn it, Rolly, if you think you can just walk all over me again—"

"Quiet. You're here because you're good, Billie. You have a million reasons to be mad, I know, but just . . . not yet."

Billie bit back her words with effort as he took her into a corridor paneled with dark wood, narrow and claustrophobic, where she heard the noise of machinery beyond the wall.

"That's the engine room. The boilers are beyond that, and the generators, and then the crew quarters." Roland pointed the opposite direction, down another narrow, dark corridor. "The staterooms are down there, but this is what I want you to see." The stairs made a U-turn, then grew almost impossibly narrow, and she followed him into abject darkness, nearly falling into him when he stopped abruptly to switch on lights.

"The forward hold has the darkroom. The photography equipment is there. I'll show it to you in a minute. One of the staterooms has been converted into a lab. But here's the main show."

The ship's aft hold. Dank and shadowy, with a ceiling low enough that it nearly brushed Roland's dark head.

The engines started up, loud here, the hull vibrating into Billie's feet. They were on their way—any fears she'd had that they would send her packing disappeared, and so she could fully appreciate the space, which had been converted into a storage area for equipment and collected specimens. Shelves of stacked jars of all sizes, glass observation tanks piped and pumped for circulating ocean water, a refrigerating chamber, barrels of Epsom salts, formaldehyde, denatured alcohol, and chemical kits. Boxes of gloves and glass slides, string, scalpels. Piles of shovels, long-handled nets, trawling and dredging nets, barrels, flashlights. Galvanized nesting trays, glass trays, a microscope . . . everything she needed.

As well as one thing she didn't understand: a very large tank that took up a good portion of the hold. She estimated it at ten feet long, probably five wide, and four deep.

She'd heard the tales of giant manta rays in the Gulf. Of swordfish and many kinds of giant sharks. Of whales. This tank was too small for any of those, and there was no reason to put one of those majestic creatures in a tank in the hold of a yacht for study anyway. They would be photographed, killed, and dissected. But the tank was too large for octopi or anemones or fish or holothurians or ctenophores or sponges or gastropods.

She looked at Roland. "What's that for?"

He shrugged casually. "You never know what we might find."

She knew his every nuance. Billie laughed. "You've always been a terrible liar. I should have known the moment I saw you that there was something going on. Why are you here, Roland? On this expedition?"

"To collect for your zoo."

She knew that innocent look too. "Oh, don't make me laugh. Why are you really here? I can't believe you didn't decide to bow out the moment Holloway brought me on board."

"Well, actually . . . I was happy when he hired you." Roland smiled the smile that had softened her a hundred times before.

Billie made a sound of disbelief. "Who do you think you're talking to? Listen, Roland, I want you to hear me when I say this: When I find a new species, it's going to San Diego, do you understand? Not to the Academy. It's going to be named by me, and it's going to be studied by me, and I am going to be the one who publishes the paper. Me. It's going to have *my* name on it. Only mine."

Roland's face tightened. "I told you I was sorry for that."

"Not sorry enough to ask them to print a retraction."

"I did ask them. They did print a retraction."

"Two months later, in a tiny note on the very last page, and they didn't change it on the article."

"How is that my fault? What were they supposed to do, Billie? Reprint the magazine?" He looked impatient.

"Yes!" she snapped. "It was important to me. I worked for a year on that research."

"It was an accident to begin with. I sent it in with both our names on it."

"You sent it in with our initials."

"R. *and* W. Ely. I can't help that they misread it."

"How convenient, then, that your middle name is Walter."

"We've discussed all this before."

"I never get tired of it," she said. "It was mostly my work. I let it go when it was only the Academy papers. But *Nature*—a *national* publication—"

"It makes it hard for you to claim it when you've gone back to your maiden name," he pointed out. "The scientific community knows we were a partnership. But they don't know who Billie McKennan is."

"You'll forgive me if I didn't want to be an Ely anymore. I wanted to be myself again."

"Is that what they're calling it nowadays?" he asked mockingly. "Is that some kind of Freudian mumbo jumbo? I hear divorced women are thought to have a touch of the scarlet about them—"

"You are horrible." Her hand itched with the urge to slap him. She curled her fingers hard into her palm.

Roland took a deep breath. "I'm sorry. For all of it. Really. I've tried to tell you that over and over again—"

"Oh? I haven't heard from you since our divorce was final."

"I was pretty sure you didn't want to hear from me."

She didn't dispute the truth of that. "Let's just say I'm smarter now. If you didn't tell Holloway about our past because you thought you could take advantage of me, let me assure you that you're wrong. I have no intention of letting that happen. I'm here for *my* career this time."

"Billie, when James said he'd hired a marine biologist and that it was you, I didn't see any reason to tell him anything. I didn't know why you wanted to join the expedition, but I figured you must have your reasons. I didn't want to ruin it for you. I *don't* want to ruin it."

"How generous," she said acidly.

He shrugged. "That's the truth."

She regarded him, looking for something in those hazel eyes to tell her otherwise. She didn't see a lie, but that didn't mean anything. "I don't believe you."

"I was surprised you wanted to be a part of it, to be honest."

"I wouldn't have been, had I known you were involved."

He laughed lightly. "Still the same Billie."

"It's not that I don't respect you as a scientist. It's that I don't respect your motives. Why are you here? What's that tank for? Tell me the truth—does this have something to do with the Society?"

The Empedocles Society was a club that Roland had belonged to—and perhaps still did. She might have got past Roland's small instances of downplaying her contributions, the lack of mention in his talks, the omission of attribution in grant proposals—though it rankled, it was common practice among senior scientists when it came to assistants, and she had been not only his wife but also his research assistant. But in the end she could not excuse his involvement in the Society. Named after some obscure Greek philosopher-doctor, it was, Roland had told her, a "discussion and debate" club where the members delved into philosophical and scientific tenets over liquor and dinners far into the night. But she'd heard other things. Rumors about secret rituals, weird Frankensteinian experimentations, cloaks and incantations, dabbling with ancient grimoires. Roland had denied them, but she knew him too well. Her ex-husband was ambitious and a little too smart. Intrigues like that would appeal to him. When he offered their research on sea snakes and their venom—a potent neurotoxin—to the Society in hopes of securing a patron to fund an expedition they'd planned to Sinaloa, Billie had been horrified.

"What possible use could powerful, rich men have for snake neurotoxins, Rolly?"

"Don't be ridiculous. There are scientists in the club too. And I'll be there to make sure everything is copacetic."

She'd felt betrayed and furious, and the *Nature* debacle had been the last straw.

Now, Roland looked at her as if she were speaking a different language. "The Society?"

"Are we playing this game? I didn't give up my mind along with my married name. I assume you're still a member."

"I—"

"Please, Rolly."

"You've never understood about them," he protested. "The philosophy—"

"Is *bunk*, and you're an intelligent man. Is Holloway a member too?"

"You know the membership is secret."

"So he is." Billie looked again at the tank, the scores of supplies. "I hope you know what you're doing."

"Don't worry about what I'm doing. Worry about yourself. Get your specimens and write your papers."

She met his gaze. The excitement in his . . . Where had she seen it before? It made her nervous in a way she couldn't define. Again she wondered why Holloway had brought only two naturalists for such an extensive expedition—and one of them Roland. She was suspicious now, and she didn't like it. "Why are there only two of us on this cruise?"

"James had trouble finding anyone else who could take a month from their job."

"To explore the Gulf? No one could take the *time*?"

Roland nodded, but he wasn't looking at her. "Yeah. Everyone's so busy these days."

Billie regarded him incredulously. "I can't believe no one jumped at this."

"There are a lot of people on the lecture circuit. Companies are hiring researchers."

"Don't lie to me. They're calling this Holloway's Folly. Why?"

Now Roland met her gaze. "Who's calling it that, Billie? That's baloney."

He made her feel ridiculous for saying it too. Ridiculous and too suspicious. That way he had of looking at her. *"You don't have to be so serious, Billie."* Usually followed by a quick kiss and a smile. The memory made her falter, because he was wrong; she did have to be serious. She couldn't get caught up in something shady. He knew this. She had no leeway, given her sex. She couldn't afford to be viewed as frivolous.

"Don't try to put one over on me," she said.

Roland let out a breath. "Just trust me, Billie."

She laughed again. "Oh, I know better than that."

"This time you can," he said. "I promise."

After a tour of the stateroom lab and the cramped but serviceable forward hold, with its platform above the ship's storage that served as a darkroom and photography studio, Billie finally found herself alone in her stateroom. It was pretty but simple: a berth over a set of built-in drawers, with a curtained porthole above; a dressing table with a mirror; and a narrow closet. She expected to spend most of her time collecting or in the lab, and her stateroom was as cozy as she could have wished with its chintz bedcover and curtains and bird's-eye maple. Dark and close enough that it felt as if it held her tight in its embrace.

The attached bathroom was a very pleasant surprise. It was tiny, everything nearly on top of everything else, but it had a bath with fresh- and saltwater taps—she'd never expected a bathtub!—and a drop-down sink with a mirror and a toilet, with black-and-white linoleum tile and fresh white towels with a green stripe across the bottom bearing the name *Eurybia* emblazoned in blue. It was as nice as the finest hotel bathroom, though without much room to maneuver. Billie glanced in the mirror, disturbed to find that strands of her red hair had escaped her cloche to straggle about her face. She hoped she hadn't looked like that when she'd been arguing with Roland. The last thing she wanted was for him to think he'd impacted her in any way, and she didn't like looking as distressed as she felt.

Carefully she lifted off the hat and adjusted her hair, tucking the loose strands back into their pins. When she reached for the cloche again, a movement caught the corner of her eye, something in the mirror behind her, but when she turned, she found nothing there. How could there be? There was barely room for her. Still, it left her strangely unsettled. She felt as if someone had been watching her, as impossible as it was.

She went back into the bedroom. The movement of the ship was both harder to discern and more unsettling here below, where she could see nothing to orient herself. She drew aside the curtain over the single porthole, which helped. The creaking timbers and the rumble of the engines were reassuring as she unpacked. She hadn't been sure what the trip required exactly, but she knew she'd need clothes for mucking around in tidelands and dissection rooms, trousers and shirts, a light jacket and a sweater, sturdy boots for exploring, rubber boots for tidelands. A bathing costume. She had also packed a simple skirt and shirt and heeled shoes in case they had to go into port somewhere and she had to look like a respectable woman.

Generally her hope was to work—and now not to fall into the habit of becoming research partner again to Roland. She'd told Faulconer at the zoo the truth: She wanted a marine exhibit for the zoo, and so she would get specimens people liked to look at, brightly colored parrotfish and angelfish, hopefully a sunfish. Sea stars and anemones and octopi. But her secret goal was to establish herself as an expert on the Gulf, to write a paper of her own on its diverse biology. She hoped to find new species or new variants and to publish her own research, her very own. Nothing that anyone could take away or claim as theirs. She refused to let Roland make her part of whatever his plans might be.

She had just finished unpacking and was arranging her lotions—her one vanity—on the dressing table when a knock came at the door. Billie stiffened, half expecting Roland, but when she answered the door, she found instead a young woman with dark hair and eyes.

"Mr. Holloway sent me to tell you there are cocktails on the aft deck," the woman said. She seemed distracted as she curiously glanced past Billie into the stateroom.

"Oh. Thank you."

"Will you need my help?"

"Oh, no, I know where to go. I'll meet you up there. I'm Billie McKennan, by the way." She held out her hand.

The woman stared at her hand as if it were disembodied. "Yes, Miss McKennan. I meant: Do you need my help to dress?"

"Oh. Oh . . . you mean . . . you're a maid." Billie wasn't sure why, but the young woman seemed a bit discomfited. Perhaps she'd said something wrong. She'd had few dealings with help.

"I'm Maud."

"Maud. Well. Um. No, thank you. I think I'll wear what I have on."

Maud frowned. "They dress for cocktails and dinner here. I don't think—"

"Thank you for your offer, Maud," Billie said. "Please tell Mr. Holloway I'll be there shortly."

She shut the door before the maid could disagree. Billie hadn't packed clothes for socializing; it wasn't what she came here for, and she had no interest in it, but now she'd been summoned. There was nothing she could do about it.

Billie took a deep breath and sat down at her dressing table to fix herself up as best she could. A bit of lipstick was her one concession, though even that felt like an awkward gilding. Time to discover what the Holloways expected of their resident woman scientist, as far as entertainment went. Perhaps she would simply sit there and look stupid, and hope they would stop inviting her to things like cocktail hour.

Well, she thought, *hope springs eternal.*

Chapter Three

The others gathered in the sitting area of the aft deck, Roland included. The player piano was anchored onto the deck, but still it rocked with the movement of the ship as it played "I Wish I Could Shimmy like My Sister Kate," and a stooped, balding man dressed in a dark suit busily mixed drinks. He looked at Billie when she approached and said, "Corpse reviver, Miss McKennan?"

"Can you make a Manhattan?" she asked.

"With pleasure," he said. "I'm Pollan, miss. Mr. Holloway's valet. Welcome aboard."

It was like being in the bar at the Emperor Hotel, where she had gone once or twice with friends, except there was a breeze, and the hazy afternoon light softened the high, ranging hills of the coast into a purple-gray sfumato, and really it wasn't like the hotel at all; it was actually quite surreal to stand on the deck of a ship swaying beneath her feet, the piano playing while a valet handed her an expertly made Manhattan that sloshed in the glass even though she stood still—a cocktail she was to drink with her ex-husband, who looked strangely at ease where he sat with a couple of millionaires.

Bizarre, Billie thought as she went toward them, trying to steady herself with the boat rising and falling through the waves. Maud had been right; Billie was severely underdressed in her trousers and blouse. Victorine wore a gown of lavender chiffon with light sleeves that gently fluttered; James Holloway and Oliver Stanton had changed into white cuffed trousers and blazers, James Holloway's a gentle stripe and Oliver Stanton's a staid navy. Even Roland had changed; his tweed trousers and a vest with a geometric pattern showed how he had come up in the world—no longer a lowly herpetologist, but the friend of a rich man, *and* he'd got another promotion at the Academy, too, she remembered, somewhat bitterly. Thanks to *Nature*'s republication of the *Hydrophis platurus* article by R. W. Ely—oh, wait, that should have been R. *and* W. Ely.

She took a sip of her drink and pretended not to notice the way they all took in the linen trousers and blouse that she'd come aboard wearing.

"Did Maud not intercept you, Miss McKennan?" James Holloway asked.

"She did." Billie took a seat, choosing not to comment on why she hadn't changed.

Holloway lit one of his cigarettes, inhaled deeply, and coughed. The cough expanded, lower and deeper in his chest.

"Should you be smoking that?" Billie asked in concern. "Doesn't it inflame—"

"It's belladonna and stramonium," Roland said. "With potash."

She frowned. "Yes, but that cough . . ."

"You're not a doctor," he said.

"Oh, but James is not listening to doctors now," Oliver Stanton noted acidly. "So maybe he'll consider her opinion."

Billie sent a quick look to Roland, who didn't meet it. Obviously she'd hit a sore spot.

James Holloway cleared his throat. "Thank you for your concern, Miss McKennan, but my lungs were damaged some years ago—the Spanish flu . . . perhaps you've heard? The cigarettes help more than anything. I'm considering other options as well."

Stanton gave him a sharp look. "Are you? The options of more charlatans?"

"How can they be worse than the charlatans who abused me with morphine and adrenaline?"

"You can't ignore *science—*"

"He's not ignoring science, Oliver," Roland put in. "You're putting too narrow a definition on it. Science is as much about new discoveries as it is about the world we know. Breakthroughs happen when we push the boundaries, not when we respect them."

How often had Billie heard that from him? Too many times. A too-easy justification for dangerous procedures. She couldn't keep from saying, "What boundaries are those? Please tell us, won't you?"

Roland threw her an irritated glance. "Of course I don't mean ignoring scientific precepts."

"No, I didn't think you did." But she didn't keep the barb from her voice.

"But one needs an open mind, yes?" Holloway looked straight at her. "You do have an open mind, don't you, Miss McKennan? I had hoped it when I hired you, though to be honest, I couldn't much tell from your sparse résumé."

She wondered why he'd hired her if he found her wanting. It was all she could do to keep from throwing an accusatory glance at Roland. "Call me Billie, won't you? Yes, I agree, my résumé was sparse, but there's a good reason for that, Mr. Holloway. It's all in the past, however, and I don't badmouth my fellows. As a woman, I'm sure you must understand how I'm taken advantage of in scientific circles. Why, I'm sure Roland can tell you of other women scientists he knows who have suffered as I have."

Roland smiled easily and said, "I've seen it happen."

She wanted to hit him, but instead she looked back at James Holloway. "I assure you I've an open mind. I chose science because as a child I was fascinated with nature. So much life, even in a droplet of water. I'm still captured by it. Every single day."

Mrs. Holloway leaned forward so eagerly her drink sloshed over the edge of her coupe glass. "What of things you can't see?"

"There are many things you can't see except through a microscope," Billie said. "But they're there."

"No, no. I mean . . . energies," Victorine Holloway said.

"Like what they're discovering in physics, you mean?" Roland said.

Oliver Stanton laughed. "No, she doesn't mean that. Here we go. Let's see whose theories Miss McKennan thinks are crazier. Victorine's or James's."

Victorine Holloway only gave him a bland look, but Billie felt the tension. Best to tread carefully. To Mrs. Holloway, she said, "Energies?"

"Spirits. Ghosts. What does science say about that?"

"I confess I haven't studied it," Billie said, not wanting to offend either of her hosts. She remembered the rumor that Holloway himself had once dabbled in spiritualism, and wondered how ardently his wife followed his enthusiasms. "I don't know anything about it."

"Do you believe such things are possible?" James Holloway asked. "Or are you one of those who deny there might be other realities?"

Once again, Stanton laughed.

Holloway ignored him. His gaze was uncomfortably intense when he looked at Billie. "Well?"

"I believe in things I can prove," she said.

"A follower of Descartes." Holloway sat back with satisfaction.

"I'm not a philosopher, Mr. Holloway—"

"James," he said.

"James. If I can see it with my eyes or a microscope or measure it, then I believe it." Billie took a great sip of her Manhattan. "If I can test it and prove it, then I believe it."

"Billie's a good little scientist," Roland said.

"You should know," she said before she could stop herself. Then she noticed the others staring at them. She gave them a smile, and took another sip of her drink. In an attempt to deflect, she said, "What is your role on this expedition, Mr. Stanton?"

James laughed shortly. "We've all been wondering that."

It was not a joke, Billie realized by the way it landed. Another tension.

"We're going to be together for a month," Oliver Stanton said, ignoring James's comment. "I think we should agree to call each other by our Christian names. As James told you, I'm the vice president of the Holloway Foundation, Billie. The Foundation is financing the expedition. I'm here as its representative."

"To make sure I'm not foolishly spending my own money," James said. "Doing the things I want to do with it."

"We've known each other since college days. The three of us." Oliver indicated Victorine, who smiled thinly.

"She was Ollie's girl first," James said. "But now Vic's mine all mine, aren't you, darling?"

"Oh, most assuredly," Victorine said, though . . . did Billie catch a quick glance between Victorine and Oliver? She wasn't sure. What she was sure of was that the war could not have had so many land mines. No wonder they tried to numb themselves with cocktail hour. She felt the need to be somewhere else. "You know, I'm quite worn out. If you'll excuse me . . ."

Victorine looked up in alarm. "Oh, but dinner is nearly ready to be served."

"I think I'll take it in my room, if you don't mind."

Her hostess looked ready to protest, but surprisingly, Roland came to Billie's rescue. "We've had two days on board to get accustomed to everything. The sea air can be exhausting, and Billie's been here only a few hours. It's a lot to get used to."

She sent him a grateful glance.

"Of course." Victorine smiled. "Please let me know if you need anything? Should I send Maud, or . . . ?"

"I'll be fine," Billie assured her.

She hurried away as quickly as she could without it appearing unseemly. A month with these people. It was bad enough to have to deal with Roland; she didn't know how to manage the conflicts of these others, whom she didn't know at all.

Don't manage them. She just needed to do her job. Keep to herself, focus on collecting and cataloging. Remember her goals. That was why she was here. This was the opportunity to make a name for herself. To revitalize her career. She didn't care about spiritualism, or Holloway's health, or the Holloway Foundation. Holloway had agreed to six scheduled collecting locations, and beyond that she had access to whatever they discovered dredging and trawling. She meant to make the most of all of it. As for the rest . . . she wouldn't be rude, but she wouldn't get involved either.

She went past the deckhouse, with its main and dining saloons that she still hadn't seen, and went belowdecks, where it was stifling, hot and close. The drink sloshed uncomfortably in her stomach, which growled because she hadn't eaten anything at all today, nervous about her impending departure. The closeness of the companionway and the pitch of the ship didn't help. She needed to get something into her stomach, but she refused to sit through dinner with those people. She paused. Roland hadn't said where the galley was, but she could ask a crew member. Some toast would help.

The crew quarters were on the same deck as the staterooms, she recalled, but forward of the engine and boiler rooms. The stairs and passages were so narrow that her shoulders rubbed either wall. She passed the closed doors of the crew quarters, and the smells of oil and musty fabric and sea grew stronger, as did those of sweat and food and coffee. She stumbled upon the pantry, and then the galley and the small mess hall that opened off it. Heat from the kitchen emanated as from a steamy blast furnace. The tiny room, full of hissing and bubbling and clattering, was big enough only for the cook who sweated over the stove while a scullery boy stood at the edge of a sink full of peelings, half in the doorway. The fan there did almost nothing to alleviate the heat from the oven and the stove. Shelves lined the wall behind the stove up to the ceiling. The cook spooned sauce over something in a sauté pan. The smell of meat and herbs and heat seared Billie's nostrils.

She hovered next to the scullery boy. "Hello. Excuse me, if I might—"

The cook and the boy turned so abruptly and with such aggression that the words stopped in Billie's mouth. She backed away.

"I—um—I'm Billie McKennan. A . . . um . . . guest. I wondered if I might have some bread?"

She heard mutterings behind her from the mess, and glanced over her shoulder to see a few of the crew sitting on campstools around a drop-down table, with a closed drop-down berth above it. Their gazes, too, were disbelieving, as if she'd fallen from the ceiling.

She began to feel that just by being here she had done something very wrong.

The cook jerked his head at the boy, who frowned at her but put some bread on a plate—only bread, nothing else—and gave it to her with reluctance.

"Thank you." She tried to smile. The boy had already turned away. The cook returned to spooning sauce over whatever smelled so good.

She stood there awkwardly, embarrassed and uncomfortable. The crew at the table went back to talking as if she'd disappeared. It took a moment before she recognized the language they spoke. It wasn't English. The two in the corner spoke Italian. She and Roland had had Italian neighbors in San Francisco years ago, and the cadences, the gestures, were familiar. But the others at the table engaged in an entirely different conversation in Spanish, which she understood—mostly. Many of the workers at the zoo were Mexican, and with that, and her time in San Diego, she had picked up enough of the language to be conversant.

She heard the word *fantasma* first, which meant . . . "ghost"? Then *ella es el monstruo*, which made her pause.

Billie stopped in the middle of turning to leave. Her ears pricked to attention.

"We shouldn't be here," one of the men at the table complained in Spanish. "Cortez is a bad place. It is a bad time of year."

Cortez? Billie wondered if she'd interpreted correctly, then remembered that was the Gulf's other name, what the Mexicans called it. The Sea of Cortez.

"It's just a story," the man beside him said as he drank his coffee.

"You hope it's just a story. But Cortez is a dream place, and dreams have monsters."

Then the two of them looked up, having noticed her just standing there, listening, and in embarrassment, Billie took her bread and left.

Monstruo. Fantasma. Monster. Ghost. That bit about the Sea of Cortez being a bad place at a bad time of year. They'd just been telling stories. But the corridors of the ship seemed to close ever tighter; it was darker than she'd first perceived. The lights weren't yet on—how did you turn on the lights—

Almost as if thinking made it happen, the companionway lights switched on. Billie jumped—and then jumped again, startled, when Maud appeared before her.

"Oh, God, you frightened me." Billie pressed her hand to her chest. Her heart raced.

Maud glanced down at the plate of bread in Billie's hand. "You aren't going to dinner, Miss McKennan?"

"No, I—"

"You didn't go to the galley yourself to fetch that?"

"I did. Why?"

The maid's expression of disapproval chastened Billie. "You shouldn't do that. They don't like guests in the crew quarters."

Billie tried to laugh. "Yes, I did get that impression."

"There's a bell for service in your room."

There was something about the girl—was it insolence, or something else? A frankness, a lack of subservience? Maybe that was how servants were these days. God knew everything else had changed. That direct, dark stare . . . whatever it was, Billie found it off-putting. "I'm not used to being waited on."

Maud said, "You don't want to be a problem."

"A problem?"

"For Mr. Holloway, miss."

Billie felt the words as a warning. "No, of course not," she managed. "I'll just . . . go to my room." She eased past the maid. When she got to her stateroom, she turned on the light and set the plate of bread on the dressing table. Then she closed the door behind her. The sun had set; the blue of evening looked dark and misty outside the porthole. The shadows seemed to reach out from the bathroom, and the creaking groan of the ship pierced the hum of the engines.

Billie shook her head as if she could shake those things away. *You are a scientist,* she berated herself. *Act like it.*

Chapter Four

In the morning, Billie woke early and washed and dressed, anxious to explore everything Roland had shown her yesterday, the lab in the aft hold, the refashioned stateroom lab, and the darkroom / photography studio that had been set up in the forward hold. She also wanted to check the trawling nets and the supplies without being under Roland's watchful gaze, and to take a good look at the strange tank he'd been so dismissive about. She hadn't noticed if it was piped for water or had an air pump. Was it meant for live things or dead ones? What secret and obscure research project had the Empedocles Society funded now?

James had told her there would be no collecting on the west side of the peninsula—they wouldn't waste time where others had already been—and though Billie would have liked to gather specimens, she had no real reason to argue, and it would save time getting to the real prize of the Gulf of California. So for now, they were only cruising, and it felt like what she imagined a vacation must be. She'd never taken one, nor had anyone she knew. Pleasure cruises were for the rich, and that was certainly the world she'd stumbled into now. The kind of world one saw only in movies or read about in novels, an escape from the culture and political wars impossible for working people like her. Here, where the fog burned off the water in wispy streams, and the coast of dark-colored hills and sandy beaches reaching into deep blue water was both rugged and sublime, it was possible to forget that the world felt like it was burning. There were no bitter arguments over morality or women's proper place or immigration, evolution, or religion. Politics felt far away. The flying fish jumping and soaring alongside the boat knew nothing about deep social tensions or inflation, and for the moment Billie wished she didn't either.

From the aft deck she heard a quick, deep voice ordering, "And one and two and three and four," along with faint grunting. She walked around the deckhouse but stopped at the corner when she saw Oliver and James and Roland in athletic shorts and shirts, exercising to a droning record.

Quickly she backed away, out of their sight. They would be embarrassed to be caught in such a state of undress in front of a woman—at least Oliver and James would. Roland would probably find it amusing, or decide to tease her. In fact, watching him now while he did push-ups in that sleeveless shirt made Billie think of things she did not really want to remember—God knew that the physical aspect of their relationship had never suffered, and it had been a very long time . . .

She turned and hurried back to the railing and the flying fish, struggling to bury those memories. She would have to avoid the aft deck in the mornings, but then again, once they were on the other side of the peninsula, Billie expected to be too deep in work to think about the aspects of Roland Ely she missed, few as those were. How easily he managed to make himself at home among Holloway's crowd. Like yesterday, during cocktails. He was gifted when it came to ingratiating himself among those who could help him. Where he'd learned that, she didn't know. He'd grown up with academic parents, just as she had.

She felt someone come up beside her and tensed, afraid it was Roland, but when she turned to look, she saw it was one of the crew, a tall man who looked to be near her own age of thirty-two. He gave her a small nod. "*Buenas días, señora,*" he said, and then frowned into the distance as if searching for something.

Billie said good morning in return, and then, in Spanish, she asked him what he was looking for.

He gave her a curious look. She didn't know if it was her Spanish or the fact that she spoke to him that surprised him. "We will be in the Gulf soon," he said in Spanish—it was not an answer. "Have you been there?"

"No. Have you?"

He shook his head and raked back his shaggy dark hair. His frown deepened. "I have fished the waters off Baja my whole life with my family. But I do not know the Sea of Cortez."

Billie remembered the snippets of conversation she'd heard in the galley. The talk of the Gulf's reputation. "You look worried."

"It is known for being unpredictable. There are many stories, and this ship is strange to me. I wonder now if I should have taken this job."

"Oh." She looked at his uniform, the green livery with the *Eurybia* crest. "You've never sailed on this ship before?"

"None of us have, except the captain," he said. "We were hired only a few weeks ago, when the regular crew went on strike."

"They went on strike? Why?"

"I do not know." He gave her a thoughtful look. "You are a scientist, yes?"

Billie nodded. "Billie McKennan. My specialty is in marine biology."

He regarded her doubtfully. "A real scientist?"

"Yes, sir. I have a degree and everything."

"But you have come on this . . . expedition."

"Yes."

"And you are a woman."

The same old questioning. The same old doubt. How annoying that it existed in every language. "Yes. Why? Do you think a woman cannot do a proper job?"

His forehead wrinkled. "Do you understand the stories of the place we are going? Have you heard the rumors?"

"Rumors of what? I've only heard what you just said. The Gulf is unpredictable. It has a bad reputation. Maybe . . . I overheard the crew say something about a monster?" She laughed lightly at the absurdity. "What else? What should I know?"

The crewman stared at her for a moment, and then he shook his head and looked away. "I do not know what you should know. I do not know what *I* should know."

Billie found it strange and a bit confusing. She didn't know what to make of the sailor's talk, or what to take from it. "Are you afraid?"

He let out a small laugh. "I think it is a good thing to always be a little afraid, *señora*. But I will do my job as well as I can, and hope for the best."

"What is your job?"

"I am assistant engineer," he said proudly. "Matías."

"Very pleased to meet you, Matías," Billie said. "If you are the assistant engineer, then I do not see any reason to fear."

This time he laughed out loud. He indicated the sky, God, a universal prayer that she understood: *From your lips to God's ears.* "I hope you are right, *señora*."

He saluted her and walked away, leaving Billie bemused by the conversation.

"There you are, Billie!" Victorine came languidly down the stairs from the pilothouse, her dress of pink silk caught by the currents of her movement, making her look as if she descended weightlessly to the main deck. "Do come with me and have some coffee while the men are flexing their muscles, will you? I detest the smell of sweat."

It was almost the last thing Billie wanted to do. She made a vague gesture toward the forward hold. "I wanted to get to the photography studio . . ."

"And do what? Can't it wait?" Victorine was at the door of the deckhouse. "Please. We're the only two women aboard, you know. We really should get to know one another."

"Not the only two."

Victorine raised a questioning brow.

"There's Maud."

"Oh. Maud. Yes. Yes, of course." But Victorine's dismissiveness said that the maid didn't really count. She opened the door and ushered Billie inside, and when Billie went, Victorine beamed so genuinely that Billie felt reluctantly glad she had.

Victorine crossed the narrow companionway, past the stairs that led belowdecks, to the main saloon, kept curtained and dark, with a large built-in hutch, a dark-green carpet with an acanthus design, and rosewood furniture covered with woven blanket throws. She motioned to a skylight painted with a storm: dark clouds, dashing waves, and rays of sun breaking through the clouds to turn the waters green and translucent blue. "A nod to the ship's name," Victorine said. "Eurybia, the goddess of mastery over the sea. This was my brother's favorite room, though honestly I've never liked it very much."

"Your brother?" Billie asked.

"The *Eurybia* was a gift to him from my father," Victorine said. "My family owns Coustan Shipbuilding."

Coustan Shipbuilding. Famous the world over. The Holloways had more money than Billie had originally imagined, and she had imagined quite a lot. "I see," Billie said. "Does your brother have an interest in science?"

"Oh goodness, no."

"Then it was kind of him to let James refit the ship for the expedition. It was quite a favor."

"Not really." Victorine's voice went soft and sad. "Emile died two years ago."

"I'm so sorry." Billie felt she'd misstepped terribly, but Victorine didn't seem fazed; she sailed from the main saloon into the dining saloon, which wasn't as gloomy; the drapes were tied back to let in the light, and the design on the skylight here was a calm sea at sunrise, the upholstery on the chairs a sky-blue silk. Victorine motioned for Billie to take a seat at the table, set now for six, though the chairs against the wall showed a capacity for ten. Billie sat, noting the mirrored surfaces everywhere reflecting the sea light coming through the many windows overlooking the main deck.

Victorine went to the button on the wall—the service bell. One of the steward's assistants arrived almost immediately in answer. "We'll have coffee, please," she told him, and then when he rushed off, she sat across from Billie, folded her hands before her lovely chin, and gazed at Billie with her perfectly shaped blue eyes. "How did you sleep? I understand they put you in the chintz room?"

Named, no doubt, for the chintz upholstery and curtain. "Fine," Billie said.

"Nothing . . . troubled you? No dark dreams?"

"None at all. The rocking of the ship—"

"Yes, it's very soothing." Victorine seemed somehow disappointed by Billie's answer. "You're certain? We usually leave that room unoccupied. You'll let me know if it becomes . . . uncomfortable, won't you? I won't have it said that I'm a bad hostess. I hope Maud is satisfactory?"

"I hardly know," Billie said with a small laugh. "I've never had a maid in my life."

"I find her a bit strange." Victorine spoke confidingly. "My usual maid gets terrible seasickness, so Maud is a substitute. Like everyone else on this cruise."

"What do you mean, like everyone else?" Billie asked.

"I think she practices some kind of folk magic." Victorine didn't seem to hear Billie's question. "She's always muttering prayers or spells or something. She doesn't seem to like the ship either, but maybe it's only that she's not used to it yet."

Billie had no idea what to say to that, and for the moment she didn't have to say anything, because the assistant returned with a silver coffee set, bone handled, art deco styled, and all embossed with the *Eurybia* crest. He set the tray before Victorine, who said, "Thank you, George," and proceeded to pour.

"Black, please," Billie said.

Victorine made a face, but passed a cup of what was already lukewarm coffee to Billie before she added what must have been half a pot of milk to her own. "I saw you with that sailor this morning. What were you talking about?"

"You said Maud was a substitute like everyone else on this cruise. That's what Matías said, too, that none of the crew had worked on the ship before but for the captain."

"Captain Rogers." Victorine nodded. "He's been the captain on our yacht the *Mariana* for years. We were lucky he could come. He's a lifesaver, especially now."

"There was a strike?" Billie prodded.

Victorine stilled. "Is that what the sailor said—Matías, is that what you called him?"

"He's the assistant engineer."

"Yes, there was a strike. Oliver refused to negotiate with them. He felt we were already spending too much money. James refused to cancel the expedition. Instead he hired whoever would take the job. Rogers felt they were all competent enough."

"Matías said he'd never sailed the Gulf of California before."

"Do you imagine that will be a problem?" Victorine asked.

"I don't know," Billie said honestly. "I'm not an oceanographer."

"You're a marine biologist." Victorine met her gaze, and it felt probing, intrusive. "A good one, too, I understand. What makes a woman like you turn to science? You're very pretty, you know, with that hair and your skin. You could easily have married."

Very blunt. Billie wondered if her hostess always spoke so directly. She told the lie—or the half truth, anyway—that she had told too often the last two years. "Not all of us want to turn our whole lives over to a man."

Her hostess laughed shortly. "No, I suppose not. Some of us just fall into it. I suppose . . . well, I suppose we just don't see any other way."

Victorine rose. She looked sad of a sudden, as melancholic as the main saloon had felt. Her mood changed the feel of the dining saloon, too, from friendly—albeit chillingly so—to strange and alien.

Then, without another word, Victorine walked out, leaving her untouched coffee, and an unsettled Billie, behind.

Chapter Five

Billie made the rounds of the refurbished lab and the forward hold and found everything perfectly to her liking. It was almost as if someone who knew her had set them up to her exact specifications, and she had the disquieting sense she knew who that person was. Everything was simply too perfect—even to the order in which she liked her pencils positioned. That Roland should remember that kind of detail made her nervous. That he should actually *arrange* it thus made her more nervous. It meant he wanted her to be happy, and that meant he wanted something from her. The fact that he hadn't told her what that was roiled her stomach the rest of the afternoon.

And that tank . . . what the hell was that tank for?

As the afternoon wound on, she grew tired of asking herself the questions and more tired of avoiding him, and she went to her stateroom. But the little room that had seemed so comfortable the night before now made her feel cramped and restless. She felt again as if she were being watched. Billie told herself it was only because she wasn't used to the crew being constantly underfoot—she could hear them no matter where she was on the ship, the strangely echoey, muffled sounds that seemed to come from nowhere and yet were everywhere at the same time. Creaks and bangs, ringing and vibrating shakes, shouts and calls, whistles and bells. Unending. There was never silence, and for a woman who treasured silence, it grated after only a day, and the little room made it worse. She felt hounded.

She didn't want to stay there, but she didn't want to be with the others either. Only a few more days until they reached the Gulf, and then her work could begin, and she would be busy enough to avoid all of them but Roland. Once they had worked together very well, but that was before she'd known to watch out for herself. Now . . . well, she would figure out how to manage that when she had to.

Billie was in the middle of deciding whether she could find an unoccupied saloon to hide in and read the latest *Proceedings of the California Academy of Sciences*—she had to stay abreast of the latest studies, even if it irked her to sometimes see Roland's name in the contents—when a knock on her door made her wonder if a time would ever come during this cruise when she would stop freezing at the thought of her ex-husband at her door.

"Yes?"

The door opened, and Maud stuck her head around the corner. As she had the last time she'd appeared at Billie's door, Maud took in the room warily. "Mrs. Holloway asked me to see to you for cocktail hour."

"Is this an everyday thing?"

"You don't want to go on deck and have drinks and watch the sunset?" Maud came fully—and obviously reluctantly—into the stateroom, bearing a bundle of mint-green fabric that glittered with beading.

Hearing it put that way, Billie felt sanctimonious for refusing, especially when just that morning, she'd been musing about the rarefied world she'd suddenly found herself in. She sighed. "What do you have there?"

"A dress Mrs. Holloway wants you to wear."

Such presumption caught Billie unawares. "A dress? My clothes are perfectly fine."

"She says they're not, miss," Maud said matter-of-factly. "She wants you to dress for dinner, and she has plenty of clothes she says will fit you from when she was eating too much."

"Excuse me?" Presumption with an insult. Billie's irritation pinched. "Is she saying I'm fat?"

Maud said only, "I think she brought her whole wardrobe. It took me a whole day to unpack her."

"I do not need to wear her clothes!"

The maid held up the dress. It was gorgeous. Sleeveless, with a dropped V-neck, in mint-green silk that turned to matching mint-green chiffon at the thigh. The entire gown was beaded in dark-green leaf patterns. "This is one of her standbys."

"*That* is a standby?"

Maud gave her a look that reflected Billie's own skepticism. "She won't be happy if you don't wear it, miss."

"I'm a guest, not . . ." *A servant.* Billie broke off just as she remembered she was speaking to a maid.

Maud laid the dress on the bed. "Isn't Mr. Holloway paying you to be here?"

"As a scientist, not an entertainer." But even as she said the words, Billie felt the squeeze of them. Maud wasn't wrong, was she? Billie *was* being paid to be here. She was an employee, and it wasn't just Victorine who had made it clear that she disapproved of Billie's trousers that first night—so had the others. Hadn't Billie just been thinking about Roland's ease in fitting in?

Too, the dress was beautiful.

"Fine," Billie said.

Maud made a sound—disdain, disagreement . . . Billie wasn't sure—and said, "Will you need my help to dress?"

Billie eyed her. "Victorine says you're a substitute for her regular maid."

The girl said nothing.

"How long have you worked for the Holloways?"

"One week," Maud said steadily, with a direct, unflinching stare. That stare made Billie itchy, but she also saw something else in it—a challenge, a dare that told her Maud would not be taken advantage of, and it reminded her of herself.

"Mrs. Holloway says you don't like the ship."

"I don't." Again, direct. "I wouldn't be here if I didn't have to be."

Billie took that to mean the young woman needed the job. "I hope Mr. Holloway is paying you well, then."

To her surprise, Maud's face hardened. "Mr. Holloway gets what he wants. All of them do. Do you need me for anything else?"

The comment, and Maud's obvious wish to be gone, took Billie aback. "No, thank you. You can go."

Maud left with lightning speed, and once she was gone, Billie turned to the fragile-looking dress on the berth and forgot the maid as she marveled at the workmanship of the beading, the delicacy of it. This was a *standby* dress, a dress Victorine chose when she had "eaten too much," though honestly, Billie did not think she was *that* much bigger than Victorine. Taller, yes. Bigger boned.

She changed quickly. The dress fit well enough, a bit tightly at her breasts, and if it didn't skim her hips as it was supposed to, it didn't cling either. The fabric was light and wispy, soft and ephemeral as it brushed against her legs—it had been a long time since she'd worn anything like this, and never anything so fine. She went to the bathroom and pinned up her hair, but she couldn't get a good look at herself in the small mirror above the sink, no matter how she twisted and turned. The mint color had always become her; she had to thank Victorine for seeing that.

Billie put on lipstick and twisted again before the mirror until she again felt that uncomfortable sense of being watched. She was only wasting time now. Oddly, the dress made her anxious. She had brought only one good pair of shoes, black leather with a single strap and a Louis heel, and though they didn't really match well with the mint green, they were better than her rubber boots or crepe-soled shoes.

Billie put them on and went above deck. The warm breeze wrapped the flowing chiffon around her legs nearly the moment she reached the deck. Beyond, the high tablelands rose from the edges of sandy beaches and rolled into undulating hills turned dusky and purple with late-afternoon light. The water was an astonishing blue-green. Her heels made a clip-clop sound on the wooden planks, an off rhythm to "Yes, We Have No Bananas" playing jauntily on the piano. Victorine's laughter came to Billie as she approached the twinkling lights of the canopied sitting area. Once again, Billie felt struck by a sense of unreality. This could not be her, on this ship with the tinkling music and the laughter and the smell of gin and whiskey and the faint floral scent of Victorine's perfume wafting to her on a salt-laden breeze.

She was so busy feeling surreal-struck that it took a moment before she realized the talk and the laughter had died and the others were staring at her—all four of them—as if she were some curse crawled from King Tut's tomb. "What?" she asked, looking down to see if there was a stain on her skirt, or if she'd put the dress on backward.

"Look at you," Victorine said softly. "My, how lovely you look, Billie. That color was made for you."

"Well done," James said, clapping his hands.

It was both humiliating and gratifying. Billie very purposefully didn't look at Roland as she felt the heat come into her face, and wasn't sure why—because she was afraid to see his admiration or because she was afraid she wouldn't? Either thought required more introspection than she was ready for. "Thank you. And, Victorine, thank you for the loan." She walked quickly to Pollan, who very efficiently had a Manhattan waiting for her. She took a great sip and then went to join the others, sitting next to Oliver, who said, "You're quite the Sheba, Billie. Why keep such a light under a bushel?"

She smiled tightly. "You're very kind."

"I'm serious." Oliver's brown gaze searched hers. "It's obvious that you underestimate yourself. Why, my guess is that you wouldn't have to rely on making a living if you chose not to. You could be well married."

"But I love my work. I don't think marriage is for me." She very carefully kept from looking at Roland.

"Well, you haven't given it a try, so how would you know?" Oliver sipped his whiskey.

"Have you?" she asked.

He looked flustered. "No, but . . ."

"I think it tends to be more beneficial to men than to women."

Victorine laughed.

James said, "Not if a man appreciates living within his means."

"I'm not the one spending two fortunes on cures." Victorine spoke lightly, an obvious tease.

"Au contraire, my love. Take the splinter from your own eye. Your séances aren't free," James teased back.

Billie couldn't tell if there was bitterness beneath his banter.

"You can only blame yourself for that," Victorine said, shaking back a loose blond tress with an elegant motion. "You were the one who introduced me to the Golden Gate Spiritualist Church."

Oliver groaned. "The two of you are giving me a headache. I see the account books floating before my eyes."

James laughed. "Your favorite pastime is dreaming of those account books, Ollie, and scheming of ways to take full control of them."

"How you overestimate me, my friend." Oliver smiled thinly and turned again to Billie. "A woman like you can't really enjoy spending her days bent over a microscope."

Roland let out a snort of amusement, and Billie could no longer avoid him. His gaze was low and slow, measuring in a way she couldn't read, but one that still made the heat come again into her face. He'd dressed today in buff linen trousers and another stylish vest, not the same as before, with his shirtsleeves rolled to expose his forearms.

"What do you find so amusing?" she asked.

"Nothing." He shook his head.

"You seemed to think Oliver's comment funny. Did you have some insight about women scientists?"

Victorine swirled her coupe glass with its pale liquid and frowned. "What is that perfume you're wearing, Billie?"

Irritated, not taking her eyes from Roland, Billie said, "I'm not wearing any perfume."

"Are you sure? It's very . . . familiar."

Roland swallowed his drink in a gulp and went to get another.

Victorine said, "Doesn't anyone else smell it? Oliver, you're closest. Smell Billie."

"Excuse me," Billie said at the same time James said, "Are you smoked, Vic? What a thing to say!"

Oliver said, "As delightful a suggestion as that is, I'm afraid even I find it a bit forward."

Victorine turned to James. "It's so strong. It smells like . . . why, it's cedar. It's that scent Emile used to wear. Don't you smell it? Truly?"

For a moment, Billie had no idea who Victorine spoke about. Then she remembered. Emile, the brother who had died.

James gave her a gentle smile. "Seriously, Vic, how many of those corpse revivers have you had?"

"Well, I can't believe no one else can smell it." Victorine frowned. "It must be coming from shore."

"No cedars on shore," Oliver said, looking over his shoulder at the passing landscape. "Doesn't look like much vegetation at all."

"I understand they grow oranges and lemons. Maybe it's lemons you—" James broke off with a cough that worsened quickly. Billie frowned as the others simply watched him hack without doing anything to help him. But then the cough eased. James said in a raspy voice, "Where are my cigs?"

"Right here, my darling." Victorine reached for a package lying crumpled beside him. In only moments, the foul floral-chemical smell surrounded them.

They had told Billie that the cigarettes helped him. Billie didn't believe it, and believed it less when James went into another coughing fit at the first drag. But again, the others did nothing, as if it was a common thing.

Roland returned as the piano segued into "Baby Won't You Please Come Home." Billie thought he seemed disgruntled; the ease that had possessed him that first night was nowhere in evidence. Twilight came quickly, and the light was already fading, the sky taking on a deep lavender cast, looking darker beyond the small bulbs strung beneath the canopy. James's stinking cigarette smoke hung in a fog beneath the canvas. Billie's Manhattan worked upon her, turning her languid.

Victorine rose abruptly, surprising them all. She rocked on her feet, swaying either with drink or with the motion of the ship. She set aside her corpse reviver with a deliberateness that said it was probably the drink, and went to the rail. James watched her with vague interest. Quietly, he said, "Anyone else smell that cedar?"

Oliver shook his head. "You know how much she misses him."

"It's been two years."

"They were very close." James considered his cigarette. "Maybe it was a mistake to bring her on this cruise. This ship . . . it's bound to bring back memories."

Billie remembered what Victorine had told her. "It was Emile's ship?"

James made a sound of soft despair. "Yes."

"It's where he died," Oliver said.

That Victorine had not said. Billie couldn't hide her shock. "On board?"

James nodded. "So you see . . ."

"You couldn't have stopped her," Oliver told his friend. "She was insistent."

The two of them fell into silence. The song on the piano finished. They remained quiet while the scroll changed. The rumble of the engines and the rush of the water against the hull suddenly seemed very loud. Then the music started again. "I'll Build a Stairway to Paradise."

The song sent another little shock wave through Billie. Even more so when Roland rose unexpectedly and put aside his drink. Like Victorine, he, too, swayed—drink or the ship? She didn't know—but she thought it was probably the drink when he stepped toward her and held out his hand.

"Dance with me," he said.

What she would have said: *For God's sake, Rolly, no.* But that was too intimate. What she should have said, *Absolutely not,* was too strident to say beneath the watchful gazes of James and Oliver. The truth was that she had no ostensible reason to say no, beyond her own resistance, which would only raise questions, and it would embarrass him, and the drink had loosened her just enough, and . . .

This song.

She would berate him later. For now she only tried to appear nonchalant and let him bring her to her feet. He pulled her into his arms and waltzed her a few steps away from the others, then into a half-baked foxtrot—not really a dance step at all, but they had danced this way before. They didn't have much room to maneuver on the deck anyway. He held her too close; she pulled away to a more reasonable distance. She smelled the gin on his breath.

"What exactly are you doing?" she murmured.

"This is our song, don't you remember?"

It was not their song. They didn't have a song. Having a song was such a romantic notion, and she was no romantic. But she couldn't deny that the song had meaning, or that it threw her back into a memory, or that the memory was a good one. A day celebrating his promotion from junior to senior herpetologist, which had turned into an evening at a dance hall, dancing until the pink and gold of morning pearlized the sky above the pillows of fog filling the San Francisco harbor. "I'll Build a Stairway to Paradise" had crept from the sleepy pianist through the open doors to the dewy lawn, its notes punctuated by the calls of sea lions from the harbor. They'd danced without shoes. She'd ruined her silk stockings—her only pair.

She remembered every touch and every look of that night, mostly because it was an interlude during a troubled time, and it was less than a year later that everything had seemed so irreconcilable between them, and even now it was difficult to understand how things had changed so quickly.

Now she only said, "Oh, Rolly."

His hand tightened on hers. "You do look beautiful tonight."

"Thank you." Even to her own ears, her voice sounded stiff.

He started to sing, softly, for her ears only, bits and pieces. "'I've got the blues . . . Up above it's so fair . . . '"

"Please stop," she said.

"Why?"

"Because I don't believe you anymore."

He slowed. The music sped on.

"You can't seduce me again." She heard her own lack of conviction.

He laughed softly, shortly. "I love it when you pretend you're conventional. For God's sake, why not? Who would know out here, in the middle of nowhere? That was always good between us, wasn't it?"

"That's not why, and you know it."

His eyes looked dark in the darkening twilight. "Then why?"

She met his gaze. "Because you're not telling me the whole truth."

"About what?"

"What's the tank for, Roland? Why are you here with James Holloway? What is it you're hoping to find out here?"

He stopped and tried to pull away. She clenched her fingers around his hand, holding him in place, until he had to jerk his hand loose.

"I'm trying to help you, Billie," he said.

~

That night Billie lay in bed and stared at the low ceiling. They were at anchor, and the *Eurybia* settled, rocked, creaked. The generators hummed. With the curtain closed over the porthole, the darkness in the little room was complete. She should have slept easily. She could not. Billie's skin felt too tight; her blood raced through her veins. If she turned on her side, she heard her heartbeat pounding in her ears. If she lay flat, her nerves twitched. On her stomach, she felt her hair prickling the back of her neck.

It was because of Roland, she knew. The damned song, the memory, his touch. All so familiar and unwanted. Yes, *unwanted.* She thought she'd reconciled herself to their separation—permanent now, decreed by the courts—and yet seeing him again had raised the doubts she still had in rare and vulnerable moments. In that way, she supposed she understood Victorine, who still smelled her brother's cologne even though he'd been gone two years. There were times when Billie, too, thought she saw Roland from the corner of her eye, sensed his shadow or his walk, or heard his voice even when he was five hundred miles away in San Francisco, and she was bent over a microscope (as Oliver had said), trying to come to terms with a new life. How memories gripped. What authority and power they had, how they made the betrayals that much harder to understand, so she second-guessed and questioned herself still.

She was better off without him. There was no doubt about it.

But what were those whispers she heard now as she let herself relax finally into sleep? The tiny voices probing the edges of her mind, trying to get in. The watchful intuition that never let her forget every bad decision she'd ever made, every mistake—or that told her this trip might be the worst one yet.

Chapter Six

The third day out, Billie was surprised to see the *Eurybia* approaching the shore. She had not known of any scheduled stops so soon.

"Boyd wants to fill the water tanks," Oliver told her. "There's a good stream at Todos Santos, and Vic wants to see the old mission here."

"What old mission?" Billie asked.

Oliver made a face. "Santa Rosa or something. Who knows why?" Oliver blew smoke toward the bluff banking one side of a river flowing into the sea. "If you want to get off the ship for a bit, this is your chance. I think you should. Have a bit of fun."

She'd barely got used to the ship, but Billie wasn't going to refuse the sandy beach before her or the clear river cutting past the rocky point dotted with cormorants. Especially when she saw a motorcar—a black Model T touring car—being loaded onto the launch.

"Where did that car come from?"

"Stowed in the hold. I'm surprised you haven't seen it before now. James never travels without it. You might want to dress for town. Not sure how the natives will react to a woman in trousers." Oliver winked. "They might not let you into the mission."

Billie didn't care about the mission and kept staring at the car, stunned by the ostentation and the luxury. She hadn't seen the car in the hold, nor would she have expected to see a car on a yacht, but maybe it was something the rich did all the time. How would she know? She took Oliver's advice and dressed in the skirt and blouse she'd brought—a rust-colored knife-pleated crepe, and a blue-and-rust paisley overblouse. She wore the strapped heels.

When she went to board the launch with the others, she was glad she'd done so, because they had dressed up too. Victorine especially looked elegant, her hair covered with a thin silk scarf instead of a hat. Victorine and James got into the front seat as if it weren't at all remarkable to ride in a car aboard a launch traveling over a lagoon of crystalline water. Billie caught Roland's gaze. When he rolled his eyes, she knew he found the whole thing as crazy as she did.

At a stone pier, two crew members started the car and rolled it off the launch. On the sandy beach a beat-up truck was parked, with a man sitting idly on its running board. He pushed his worn hat back to stare as the Model T chugged over the sand. Billie could only imagine what he thought to see an elegant black car bearing five people dressed in linen and crepe, jaunty hats, Victorine's silk scarf trailing in the air. Oliver and Billie and Roland squeezed into the tight back seat. James sat in the driver's seat with Victorine beside him.

The car wheels spun in the sand, sending a flock of cormorants into a frenzy, squawking all around them.

James called out to the man in the old truck, "Where's the road?"

Wordlessly, the man pointed. James jerked the steering wheel, which would have sent those in the back seat slamming into each other had they not already been jammed tight. The Model T bounced and jounced over the beach. Billie didn't see a road until suddenly it appeared, narrow and dusty, following the bank of the river.

She leaned to say in Roland's ear, "Did you know about this?"

He nodded. "A short detour."

The valley was beautiful. Fields of sugarcane stretched on either side. The Sierra de la Laguna rose rocky and blue in the near distance. Palm trees dotted the fields in the breaks between the sugarcane. The sun beat down on the black top of the car, heating the inside so that Billie, wedged between Oliver and Roland, felt sticky with sweat. Even with no wiggle room, Oliver seemed to claim the space between them in an unnervingly intimate way. Now and again, as the car jolted uneasily over the rutted road, he put a hand on her knee and quickly removed it as if he meant only to keep his balance, but it made Billie uncomfortable. Fortunately, it wasn't a long trip. Todos Santos was only a few miles away, right on the bank of the river, a collection of adobe-and-brick houses, some with wooden awnings. The motorcar raised more than a passing glance. People on the streets stopped to stare. Those in a crowded market pointed and called out to their neighbors. Men sitting at outside tables at a small cantina squinted into the dust the car raised.

Finally, James pulled over to ask a man with a burro for directions to the mission of Santa Rosa. The man looked confused; Billie had to translate. He smiled and showed them the way. "You cannot miss it," he said.

It was true, they couldn't. The old mission was simple and square, with an arched doorway decorated by white pillars and a cornice and a square, tiered, wedding-cake-like tower on one side. It seemed peaceful and quiet, the plaza in front of it quiet too.

James stopped the car before it. "Well, here we are."

"This is what you wanted to see?" Victorine asked. "May I ask why?"

"I thought it was you who wanted to see it," Oliver said.

Victorine laughed. "Oh, for heaven's sake, no. I gave up Catholicism a long time ago, Ollie. You know that."

"I thought you might want to light a candle for Emile," James said.

Victorine looked at him as if he had gone insane. "For *Emile*? He hated the priests more than I did. James, have you got sunstroke? Is this really why we came here? So I could light a candle for my brother's soul? Even if I did, the very last place I'd do so would be in some old mission in some godforsaken Mexican town."

Billie had only known the Holloways for two days, but the goofiness of all this felt typical. Billie said, "I need some air."

Both Oliver and Roland scrambled to open the door. Oliver was faster. Billie nearly crawled over him—was it her imagination, or did his hand brush the back of her thigh? She stepped on his foot in her haste to get out.

"Sorry," she said, relieved to be out of the car. Dust from the journey had settled on her skirt. She brushed it off and stared up at the single window above the door, with its red accents. It was pretty enough, but she was thirsty now, and the vegetables at the market had looked good. "Now what? If no one wants to go inside?"

But Roland and James exchanged a quick glance. "I think you should find the chapel and light a candle for Emile, my darling," James suggested to Victorine. "It couldn't hurt."

Victorine frowned and got out of the car, shaking out yellow crepe and adjusting her scarf. "The spirits know when one is insincere."

"Oliver can go with you."

"Oliver is going to the cantina we passed," Oliver said, emerging. "Anyone care to come with me? Billie?"

She was thirsty and had no interest in the mission. "Count me in," Billie said.

"I'll go too." Victorine grabbed her purse. "If you're so bent on saying a prayer for Emile, James, you can do it."

"Roland?" Billie asked.

She was surprised when Roland shook his head and looked uneasily at James. "I think I'd like to look through the mission."

It was so unlike him that Billie laughed. "You'd like to look through a *mission*?"

"I've heard a great deal about it."

"You've heard a great deal about a mission in a town we haven't heard of before now."

"Speak for yourself. I've heard of it."

"Really?" Billie eyed him skeptically.

"The last time the Academy did an exploration in Baja, they stopped here. Lots of snakes and lizards."

Now she knew he was lying. Partly because he wouldn't look at her. Partly because she'd never known Roland to be the least bit interested in religious iconography. "So . . . correct me if I'm wrong, but you're not looking for snakes and lizards. You're checking out a mission?"

He nodded. "I hear there's a famous statue here."

"Ah. Of who?"

"The saint, of course. Who else?" He scowled in obvious irritation. "Why are you questioning me, Billie? What do you care if I want to look at a mission? Go have a drink and let me be."

Definitely lying. James stared at the ground as if he'd spotted something fascinating in the stone plaza.

Oliver cleared his throat. "Fine. When you're done, meet us at the cantina."

"Do not light a candle for Emile, James," Victorine directed. "He'll only take offense. I don't need anything else to keep me from contacting him."

James waved her away. "Of course not."

Billie threw a last look at Roland as she followed Victorine and Oliver away from the mission. He frowned at her, but he and James hurried up the red steps of the building as if they could hardly wait to get inside. Why? There was something else going on here, and that question distracted her as they walked the narrow road to the cantina, and continued to distract her when they reached the small tavern, enough so that at first she didn't notice the way the men there looked at her and Victorine. They took a seat at a tiny table. It wasn't until Oliver bought them each a drink—no ice, of course, a shot of something strong smelling and clear—that Billie noted the hostility in the stares they got.

When Billie noticed it, she said quietly, "Let's sit outside."

"But it's so hot," Victorine said.

"I don't think they welcome women in here," Billie told her.

Victorine glanced around. "Oh." Her eyes widened. "Oh, yes, you're right. Let's move."

Quickly they took a small table beneath the wooden awning. The sun blasted through the cracks in it and slanted beneath, and Billie sweated even in the light paisley overblouse. Her hair, pressed to her hatband, was wet. The dust from the road dulled her shoes.

"What is this?" Victorine asked, holding the drink up and wrinkling her nose. "It smells fatal."

"He didn't say," Oliver told her. "They're all drinking it. It doesn't seem to be doing them any harm."

Victorine took a tentative sip. "Oh, it"—she choked—"it burns a bit."

"Cheers." Oliver gulped his down, then bent over coughing. When he settled, he said, "Good God. I think I need another one of those."

Billie took a sip. It tasted slightly sweet, and it did burn, and it was strong. She tipped it back and swallowed the whole thing and heard the gasp from the men watching at the table beside them. She turned to them and smiled, raising the empty glass. *"Está bueno."*

One of the men laughed. Another one picked up his glass and raised it to her. Their hostility dissipated.

She nearly jumped at the touch of a hand on her knee. Oliver. He smiled at her. She tried to move away, but couldn't in the small space.

He squeezed and said, "Another?"

Billie nodded eagerly, just to get him away, though now she felt the drink coursing through her, warming her insides. Perhaps another one wasn't a good idea. Oliver went inside to the bar.

Victorine glanced around. "Why do you think we're the only women here?"

Billie shrugged. "It would be the same in half the bars in America. If there still were any bars. That were legal, I mean."

Victorine looked thoughtfully into her half-full glass. "Those stupid women."

"What stupid women?"

"Those temperance women. It's their fault, you know. All that protesting and moralizing. Maybe women should never have got the vote."

Billie could not believe Victorine had said it. "You don't mean that."

"Oh, I do. What use have women for politics anyway? I don't."

"Of course you do."

"I suppose you were one of those suffragettes."

Spoken with such disdain. Billie worked to keep her temper. "I marched for woman suffrage, yes." Just moved to San Francisco to work at the Academy. Taken by her new home and its possibilities and the women she hoped to meet there. Days away from meeting Roland. Billie remembered that march well, the thrill of it, the hope for change. Before she'd comprehended that she was the only woman in her department. That her role as an assistant meant that her male coworkers hardly considered her except as a drudge, and that having the vote couldn't change attitudes or traditions that had been in place forever. "Think of it this way, Victorine: What would you do if the government decided that your spiritualism was devil worship, and outlawed it?"

Victorine frowned. "They wouldn't do that."

"Wouldn't they? There are plenty of people who believe that your 'energies' are wicked. What if they convinced the rest of the world? What if all these people trying to get schools to teach creationism win? How long before they come after religions they don't believe in?"

"I . . . That won't happen."

"I hope not." Billie fingered her empty glass. "What about you? What did you do about Prohibition?"

"What did I *do*?"

"Did you protest? Did James vote for it?"

"No one voted for it," Victorine scoffed. "They made it a law."

"Sure people voted," Billie told her. "They voted for their representatives in the legislature, and those men voted for Prohibition."

"James doesn't vote," Victorine said smugly.

"Then in essence, he did vote for it," Billie said, curbing her urge to sneer. "Because he didn't vote against the men who did. But I guess that's fine for you, isn't it, Victorine? Because you're rich enough that you can get all the liquor you want, whenever you want. You can hie off to Baja to drink in a cantina or stock your yacht with enough booze that you can all get smoked every day. But the rest of us, well . . . I guess it's only regular people who have to live with Prohibition. So you don't have a beef, really, do you? You've got everything you could ever want."

"That's not true." Victorine's voice rose. She shook her head so violently that one side of her scarf fell from its pins. "That's not true at all. You don't know anything—"

"Here we go." Oliver returned with the drinks and set them on the table, pushing a glass each to Billie and Victorine. "I think I've developed a real taste for this stuff."

The sound of the car's engine broke through the talk. Billie looked up the road just as the Model T came into view. It stopped in front of the cantina, and Roland bounded out. In a moment, she took in his obvious discomposure—or was it panic?—as he searched for them. When he saw them, he rushed over.

"We need to go," he said.

"But we just got our drinks!" Oliver protested.

"We need to go now." Roland took Billie's arm, pulling her from the stool. "Come on."

She was so surprised, she went along. Oliver swallowed his drink, and he and Victorine hurried after. James drove off almost before they'd got into the car, leaving a dust cloud in their wake.

"What is it?" Victorine shouted over the sound of the engine. "What's wrong? Why do we have to leave?"

"Best to make a quick departure," James said with an uneasy glance behind them.

"What the hell did you do?" Oliver asked.

The car careened over the road too quickly, barely negotiating the curves of the riverbank, throwing her hard into Oliver. Billie straightened and looked over her shoulder, but couldn't see much out the small, dust-covered window of the back. No one seemed to be following them, though James drove as if someone were. Fast and jerky, so that by the time they reached the beach, she felt nauseated.

James jumped out of the car and shouted orders to the crew members lazing on the beach. They had already loaded the barrels of water the steward wanted onto the launch. James hurled himself aboard and left it to the crewman to drive the car over the beach—with them in it—and over the stone pier onto the boat.

It wasn't until they were unmoored and off that Billie realized how tense Roland had been. He leaned out the window to look behind them, and then relaxed.

"What was that all about?" she asked quietly.

He shook his head, a *not now* gesture.

Victorine said, "We were having a perfectly lovely time."

Which they weren't. She and Victorine had been arguing. Now, in retrospect, Billie remembered the look on her hostess's face, the quick luminosity of Victorine's eyes. Almost tears? *"You don't know anything."*

Well, maybe not. Maybe Billie's lecturing had been a bit too much, but the whole day had been too much. A car on a yacht, Oliver's advances, Victorine implying that she never bothered to vote. Billie felt unexpectedly overwhelmed. It felt sometimes as if her life was only one big fight, and here was Victorine Holloway, drinking whatever she pleased and bemoaning the temperance women who had made her life so hard.

It was enough to give one a major headache, which was what Billie instantly had.

Or maybe it was the fact that nothing today made sense. When they reboarded the *Eurybia*, Billie searched out Roland. He was in the lab, bent over a chart of the Gulf. He looked up at her soft close of the door.

"Not now, Billie," he said.

"What were we doing there today?" she asked.

He hesitated. She saw his brain working, trying to come up with a lie.

"I know you haven't suddenly developed a passion for missions," she said.

"Maybe I have."

"Sure. Who was the saint inside?"

"The saint?"

"You went to see the statue, didn't you? Ah—you didn't."

"I did, in fact. It was Pilar. Pilar the Virgin."

She laughed. "You're praying to virgins now? You need that much help?"

Roland chuckled. "I don't have anything to say to that that won't make it worse."

Billie stepped over to the table where he sat. "I had to listen to Victorine tell me she was angry at temperance women even though James didn't bother to vote, and she isn't interested in voting, but life is so difficult for her, so please, Rolly, give me something else to think about tonight—and no, none of that. I'm not flirting. I want to know why you had to go to that mission today."

He released a deep breath. "There was someone there I wanted to talk to."

"About what?"

"About James's health."

"You went to a mission about James's health. *You* did?"

A pause. She saw him understand there was no point in lying.

"Okay. He wanted to ask. I went along."

"Who was he asking? God?" Billie searched Roland's face. "Is James praying now?"

"You could say so." Roland folded the chart. "Anyway, it didn't matter, because the man he wanted to talk to wasn't there, and the only person we could find told us to get out before he called the police—or whoever the law is in Mexico—and threatened to fine us for entering the port without paying the fee or whatever . . . I don't know, he spoke bad English. Suffice to say I understood well enough to get the hell out of there."

"I see," Billie said, though she didn't really. Yet she didn't see a lie this time. The reason for going to Todos Santos might not be what Roland said, but what had happened there was true enough.

"Anyway." He rose. "It was a waste of time, but you look pretty. I think I remember that skirt?"

She shook her head. "Only if you've been following me. I bought it last year."

"You've always liked that color."

She said nothing. It surprised her that he remembered, though she supposed it shouldn't.

"Let's go get a drink," Roland said. "It's cocktail hour."

"I don't know if I want another drink," she said. "That stuff in the village . . ."

Roland grinned. "Made from sugarcane. A local specialty."

"How do you know that?"

"I know more than you give me credit for, sweetheart," he teased, but his heart wasn't in it, she could tell. He seemed tired and worried, and what had happened at the old mission of Santa Rosa today—the virgin Pilar notwithstanding—had troubled him. He might have told her the truth, but he hadn't told her everything, and Billie sensed that there was a world of difference between those two things, and that the difference was important.

He took a deep breath, distracting her from the thought.

"Hey, Billie—you . . . um . . . you should stay away from Oliver."

His comment surprised her, and annoyed her too. So he'd noticed Oliver's attentions. It gave her a little satisfaction to know it. Not that it mattered or that it was any of his business. "Should I? Why is that?"

"He's no good. He's been angling to get control of the Holloway Foundation for years. James keeps him close to keep an eye on him. Oliver tries to influence Victorine, too, and she's impressionable. You don't want to get near that."

Billie laughed shortly. "Really. How involved you seem with all this. Aren't you worried for yourself?"

"I know what I'm doing."

"I see." She couldn't keep the acid from her tone. "How does Oliver feel about the Empedocles Society?"

Roland smiled, but the warmth didn't reach his eyes. "Just a friendly warning, Billie. Take it or leave it."

"A friendly warning," Billie repeated flatly. "How nice to know we're friends."

"Aren't we?" he asked.

"I wonder what you believe a friendship is, Rolly," she told him. "If you think it means I'm going to take everything you say at face value, you've got another think coming."

"Billie—"

She didn't wait to hear more.

Chapter Seven

The next morning, Billie was halfway up the stairs to the deck when she heard the faint strains of the exercise record—the men were already up and about, doing push-ups and laps—and the thought of possibly running into a scantily clad Roland was more than she could manage. Instead, she made her way to the galley for coffee.

It was early enough that the mess was full of crewmen, all of whom stared at her with obvious unfriendliness. Billie belatedly remembered Maud's comment that she shouldn't be here, and that she should ring the bell for service. The scullery boy she asked for coffee nearly shoved the cup into her hand. The crew's low grumbles weren't quite low enough to keep her from catching a few words. *Bad luck. No good for her to be in the galley. What is she doing here?*

Billie left quickly and went to the makeshift photography studio in the forward hold. She left the hatch open for light, holding her coffee carefully as she went down the narrow stairs to the platform over the storage area. The camera, tripod, table, and trays waited at the ready, the lights set up. She had nothing to do in the studio, but here she could be alone for a time, and drink her coffee without the risk of Roland or Victorine or Maud or anyone else finding her. The sound of water rushing against the hull was easier to hear, the splash and the speed. The dredging and trawling nets swayed gently where they hung from the railing surrounding the platform. Below, something rocked.

She had just sat down when she heard another kind of movement. A swishing sound, a live sound. Rats, she thought, but then a light switched on. Billie leaned to see over the platform, past the nets. It was a crewman—an older man, short and burly with close-cropped hair. She thought she'd heard someone call him Tomás, and say that he was an oiler.

Billie pulled back and quieted, hoping that he hadn't seen her, but of course he must know she was there. The hatch was open. She wasn't surprised when he called up, "*Señora.*"

Billie looked down again. Even with the light, he was in shadowy dimness among the barrels and boxes. She had to move to get a better view through the nets.

"*¿Si?*" she called back.

"You should be careful," he told her in Spanish.

"Oh, don't worry. The platform's quite steady."

"That is not what I mean," he said. "Monsters are not only in the sea."

How strange. How oblique. She said, "Okay?" and he nodded as if he'd made his point, slung a coil of rope over his shoulder, and disappeared. But he'd ruined her peace. Billie finished her coffee quickly and left the hold.

She nearly ran into Victorine, who stood near the hatch on the forward deck, staring out at the sea with its veil of fog. The woman seemed not to see Billie at first, and Billie would have slipped away, but what Tomás had said perplexed her, and she let the hatch close a bit too hard, and Victorine turned with a start and gave her a distracted smile.

"Good morning," she said. "I was looking for you."

The air felt damp and slightly chill, and where they stood at the bow, the breeze from the ship's progress was strong, but Victorine didn't seem at all cold in her short-sleeved, pale-yellow-dotted crepe de chine, with a tiered skirt banded in pink, though it looked better made for a spring parlor with a fire than for shipboard.

"I was in the photography studio." Billie had no idea why Victorine might search her out. After yesterday, Billie assumed the woman would rather avoid her.

But Victorine touched her arm with anxious intimacy. "I wanted the chance to explain. Have you seen those photographs of spirits?"

Billie frowned at the abrupt change of subject. "Um, I don't believe so."

"I have a collection of them. You'd be surprised how well they capture the essence of the one who's passed."

"Do they?"

"I want to get one of Emile, but you can't get a picture if the spirit doesn't make contact, and he never has. I've been to so many séances looking for him, and . . ." She trailed off despondently. "You think I'm silly and insensitive. You think I don't see . . . but that's not true. It's not true at all. I'm too sensitive. It's why this is so hard for me."

Billie didn't know what to say.

"Emile was the only one who understood. James tries, but he's a man."

Billie frowned. "Wasn't Emile a man?"

"Yes. Yes, but he . . ." Victorine paused and glanced away as if trying to find the right word. "He was sensitive too. He wasn't just my brother—he was my best friend. We were only a year apart, you see. Close to twins. That's what everyone said. We were nearly twins." A deep breath. "I don't understand why he won't come to me. I thought—I thought perhaps I'd done something to displease him, but I can't think of what that might be, and if he won't tell me, how can I know?"

That Victorine grieved was obvious, but Billie hardly knew her. What did one say to such pain except the barest platitudes, which she imagined Victorine had heard a hundred times. Billie had never lost anyone important to her, and so now she grasped at straws. "It must comfort you to be on this ship that he loved." Then she remembered what James had said yesterday, about the *Eurybia* being the place where Emile had died, and thought she'd probably said the wrong thing entirely.

But Victorine brightened at her words. "It does. It does! I just wish I knew if he was at peace now. It torments me, not knowing."

Billie frowned. "Why would he not be at peace?"

"The way he died, of course." Victorine tucked a loose blond strand behind her ear and glanced at the passing shoals, where the roll of waves breaking was a line of white against the blue. "He took his own life."

Now what did one say to that? "I'm sorry" was all Billie could come up with.

"He came home changed from the war. He and my father argued about his taking over Coustan Shipbuilding. Emile was never cut out for business, but Daddy wouldn't listen, and the war made everything worse. Emile became . . . distant, I guess you would say. James would tell you he was touched, and I suppose he was, but the things I heard—didn't you hear them too? The terrible things about the war?"

"Yes," Billie said softly. "I heard them too." The mustard gas, the shelling and the snipers, the bloody trenches and the land mines. Fields of disease and death. A childhood friend of hers had come home scarred both physically and mentally, unable to return to work. He was in an asylum now. She didn't tell Victorine the other story she knew: that Roland had worked for the US government during the war, exploring antidotes to biological warfare after the Germans tried infecting Allied horses and donkeys with glanders and anthrax. He rarely spoke of it, but it had led them to their sea snake research. Like everyone else, Billie had grown used to a "since the war" way of thinking. Everyone she knew wanted to forget those years. They wanted escape and change. All the men were dead, and their gods with them. What had they all died for, and why did so many people insist on bringing those old, obsolete gods back?

"Still . . ." Victorine looked thoughtful. "I have so many questions for him. I had thought the ship would be the perfect place to find his spirit. It's why I came on this cruise. Oliver doubts I can contact Emile, but he has an accountant's soul, and sometimes it's quite barren."

Interesting, Billie thought. Maybe Victorine wasn't as malleable as Roland believed.

Victorine went on, "James doesn't believe Emile can still be here, but why not? Why shouldn't I try?"

Billie nodded, wanting to be done with the conversation. It was enough to know that Emile Coustan had died upon this ship. That he'd committed suicide. She really wanted nothing more to do with the whole thing.

"Have you felt him?" Victorine continued almost desperately.

"Felt him?" Billie was confused.

"His presence? His spirit? Did you smell his cologne the other night as I did? The cedar scent? Have you smelled it anywhere else? In your room?"

"Why would I smell it there?"

Victorine looked impatient, as if she were trying to explain to a particularly stupid person. "Because your room was his room."

Billie stared at her. "What?"

"Well, it wasn't his room, not really. He owned the ship, so the stateroom was his. But that night . . . the night that he . . . that night, he was in your room because the ship was full. Daddy was on board, and James and I, and several guests. Emile gave me and James the master stateroom, and he took the chintz room, and then he . . . he . . ."

The truth dawned slowly, and then it slammed into Billie. "Are you saying he killed himself in my room?"

Victorine winced. "Can you not say it so . . . badly."

"But you're saying—"

"Yes. Yes, it was his room that night. It was where he . . . his funeral bier, I suppose you'd call it."

Billie was too stunned to speak.

"Do you feel his presence? Perhaps you see things moving, or hear voices, or . . . It could be so many things. It's hard to say how his spirit might manifest. Surely you've heard of such things."

Billie shook her head in disbelief. "You must be joking."

"Oh, no, I'm not joking in the slightest."

"I can't believe I'm having this conversation." Billie turned to go.

Victorine touched her arm, stopping her. "There's something else, Billie. I'd like to try to contact my brother's spirit. I believe the veil is thinnest in your room, and that he might answer if I tried. But it would mean a séance—"

"In my room?" Now Billie was incredulous.

"It was Emile's room first. It *is* a liminal space. You don't have to be present, of course, when I call him. In fact, if you don't believe, or if you're skeptical at all, it would be better if you're not present, and there's so little space anyway. But I would need use of your room."

"Then what?" Billie asked. "What happens after you call him?"

"Hopefully, his spirit would come. It's my most fervent wish. I've been trying to contact him for two years."

"And then?"

Victorine floundered. "Then . . . I would want to speak with him again. I have so many questions. You must understand, I feel so lost without him, as if I'm missing part of myself. We shared so much, and I need to know why he took his own life, what caused him such unhappiness. If I'm very lucky, he would stay for a time—"

"Stay?" Billie could not help the sharp pitch of her voice. She felt increasingly as if she were in a disorienting dream. "You're saying there would be a ghost in my room that you would want to talk to whenever you felt the need."

"Yes," Victorine agreed. "But only at your convenience, of course, and Emile was a very gentle man. Very accommodating—"

"No," Billie snapped. "No, absolutely not. I'm very sorry for your loss, and I understand you're grieving, but I'm here to do a job, Victorine, and I've had enough goofy for today."

She started to walk away.

Victorine called out, "What if I had a séance in the saloon? Would you come? If the others were there too? The spirits are drawn to life forces."

Billie kept walking.

~

But she could not walk far enough to get away from Victorine or the idea of a séance once her hostess had it. That night at cocktail hour, as they sat watching the sun dip below the horizon, Victorine brought it up once more.

"There it is again," she said, sitting up so quickly that she nearly spilled her entire drink. "Cedar! Do you smell it?"

"Vic," James protested.

"Emile's cologne," she said. "Do you think that means something?"

"What could it mean except that you have a vivid imagination?" Oliver said. "Don't be a bunny, Vic. This was his ship. It's hardly surprising. Maybe there are traces of his smell still on pillows or something."

"Two years later?" Victorine asked incredulously.

"There was a great deal of refitting," James said.

Billie tended to believe it was as Oliver said—Victorine's imagination, as well as wishful thinking—so she was surprised when Roland said, "There might be something to what Victorine feels. We're discovering new things every day. The world of the unknown is vast. There may be other universes—I mean, the very structure of the atom is in question. It wouldn't be all that surprising to find that people leave behind traces we can't see. We don't know." Billie turned to give him an incredulous look. Roland shrugged in response. "We don't. Can you deny it?"

"That's hardly a scientific response," she said.

He took an irritatingly unperturbed drag on his cigarette. "What would be a scientific response, Billie? We don't know everything. It's only in exploration that we find out."

"You see?" Victorine said eagerly. "I would like to find out. I think the scent must be a sign. I think Emile's spirit is telling me he's here, that he wants to make contact."

"For God's sake, Vic," Oliver said.

"Or it's the sillage of his cologne, left two years after his passing," Victorine challenged. "Which seems highly unlikely, don't you think? I'm willing to admit you could be right, but how will we know if we don't try?"

"Try what, exactly?" Billie asked uneasily, remembering Victorine's suggestion of a séance in her room. Billie had refused it; surely Victorine wouldn't try to force her into it.

But of course Victorine said, "A séance."

Billie protested, "I told you—"

"Not in your room. You're right. It's too small, and I don't know that we need to. I've thought about it, and I've smelled his cologne in other places on the ship. It doesn't have to be in the room he died in."

"The what?" Roland straightened.

"He took his life in Billie's stateroom," James informed him. "In the bathtub. Took some chloral and drowned himself."

In the bathtub. Billie would have preferred not to know that.

Roland sounded aghast. "You're sure it was . . . it wasn't an accident?"

"It was quite deliberate," James said grimly. "A terrible thing. We were all aboard when it happened. Honestly, we didn't plan to put anyone in that stateroom. Billie was supposed to share yours until we discovered she was a woman."

Roland lifted a dark brow at Billie, accompanied by a knowing little smile. "The best-laid plans . . ."

Billie ignored him.

Victorine went on as if she'd heard none of the discussion about Emile's death. "The saloon was his favorite room. He loved the skylight. We could hold it there."

"Whatever you like, my darling," James said.

"I guess it could be amusing." Oliver swirled his glass and looked down into it. "Something to pass the time."

"Well, you can count me out," Billie said.

"Why, are you scared?" Roland asked.

"Scared of what?"

"Spirits. What else?"

She laughed. "Why should I be afraid of something that doesn't exist?"

"Oh, come on, Billie, you don't know that for sure. Show me the paper that says they don't. Show me the proofs."

Billie glared at him. "There's nothing like that. You know it perfectly well."

"Actually, the Society for Psychical Research has written many papers," Victorine said. "I've issues of their journals here if you'd like to read them—"

"Real scientists?" Billie persisted. "Real experiments?"

"How does one quantify the unquantifiable?" Roland asked lightly. His gaze met hers, challenging, a dare. "Where's your spirit of adventure?"

It had been a joke between them, a line he'd teased her with often during their marriage. She had already crossed so many boundaries in a world where women broke more and more taboos every day. She drank, she was a scientist, she wore trousers, she'd slept with Roland before they'd married. She had dared so many things already. He used the jibe to remind her whenever she grew too serious.

She hadn't heard it since she'd left him, and it surprised her how much it still provoked her. It surprised her more when she heard herself respond. "Fine. Why not? Nothing like a little hokum to while the night away."

"You can't go into it with that attitude," Victorine scolded. "If you're skeptical, the spirits won't come."

"Don't worry," Roland said. "Billie's curiosity will win out. It always does."

It was a compliment, Billie told herself.

⁓

They assembled after dinner in the main saloon. Victorine asked Maud to light candles, which glowed on the hutch and the end tables. Maud and Pollan had moved what furniture wasn't fastened down into a makeshift circle and drawn the curtains. The room, which Billie had found melancholy before, was even more so now. It might have been romantic with the candles, but instead it felt crowded, gloomy, and claustrophobic.

The wind had come up; the *Eurybia* rocked in the chop, making the pictures hung on cords and the drapes in the saloon swing in a nauseating way. Victorine ordered them all to their places. James and Oliver in the armchairs. Victorine in a dining room chair brought in specially so she could sit in the middle of the circle. Roland and Billie were seated together on the settee. Once they were all assembled, Victorine said, "Now we must all hold hands. No one can break the circle once it begins, do you understand?"

"I've done this a hundred times, darling," James drawled.

"The instructions are for the others," she said. "Maud, Pollan, keep an eye on the candles, please. I don't want them rolling and catching something on fire."

The two servants stood against the doorway to the dining room, trying to keep their balance against the jamb as the ship pitched.

Victorine seemed to vibrate with enthusiasm. "Oh, I know he's here—I think I can already feel him. Quickly now! Everyone—everyone take hands!"

They all did. Billie was between Roland and Oliver. Oliver's hand felt soft and smooth, that of a man who didn't work, obviously. Roland's was familiar; strong fingers, blunt nails. The touch sent a warmth through Billie that she tried very hard to ignore. She turned her attention to Victorine, who instructed them to close their eyes. The woman began to hum—an old song that Billie recognized. A hymn or a carol . . . The words came into Billie's head: *Lully lullay, my little tiny child* . . . Victorine's voice grew stronger and louder, and then James's rose to join hers, still just humming, then moving to "La la lala . . ." No words at all, just the melody, until it abruptly stopped, the couple seemingly knowing exactly the moment to quit in unison.

Roland's hand tightened on hers. Billie let her own hand go limp. The sickening motion of the ship eased. Billie opened her eyes. The others still obeyed Victorine's orders, even Roland.

Victorine threw her head back—she looked as if she were in ecstasy—and sang out, "We ask the great unseen force to remove all obstructions that keep the spirits from communicating with us. We ask this in all sincerity and honesty, and we will do our part to help them transcend the heavenly ether of the spirit realm to come to us. We ask the great unseen force to help. In thy power we put ourselves and our trust. Emile, come to us!"

James repeated, "In thy power we put ourselves and our trust."

Ridiculous, all of it.

"Emile! Emile! Come to us!" Victorine called. "Emile, please—I know you are there. I feel you. We all feel you. I have received your signal."

The ship rocked again. The candles flickered. Behind her, Billie heard a small gasp in the silence that followed Victorine's words—Maud.

Victorine began to sway. It was strangely hypnotic; her motion telegraphed through Oliver's arm, signaling Billie to sway as well, to push Roland into it, not quite subconsciously, but still, Billie was part of the circle's motion.

"Emile . . ." Victorine took a great, deep breath. The darkness seemed to press against the candle flame. No, it could not be. It was all suggestion, Billie knew. It was a trick of her mind.

"Emile, I sense you are near," Victorine whispered. "Make yourself known. Show yourself."

Silence for a long moment but for the ship's creaking, the engine's rumble.

"Emile, my brother, come to us."

Was it Billie's imagination, or did the air feel as if it were gathering? Oliver's hand was uncomfortably moist in hers.

"Emile, I feel you! Emile, I—"

"Stop! Stop!"

The panicked, distressed voice seemed to come out of nowhere, surprising them all. Billie jumped, dropping Roland's hand and Oliver's. Victorine started so violently that she lost her balance on the frail dining room chair. She went over backward, crashing hard to the floor, knocking the breath from her lungs.

"Vic!" Oliver was at her side immediately. "Are you all right?"

"Who was that? Who said 'Stop'?" Victorine struggled to sit up, batting away Oliver's too-helpful hands.

Billie turned to look at Maud, who stood at the doorway, grasping some kind of pendant around her neck. The maid's eyes were wide and frightened. Her lips moved silently in some kind of muttered—prayer? Billie didn't know. What she did know was that the *Stop!* had come from Maud.

"Maud!" Victorine snapped.

"I'm sorry, ma'am." Maud looked frightened, almost white in the near darkness. "I'm so sorry, but I couldn't . . . I . . ."

"Dammit! Look what you've done!" Victorine grabbed Oliver's offered hand and got to her feet, obviously furious. The tension in the room had snapped, replaced with the woman's anger. "Emile's gone. Who knows if he'll return. I felt him! Didn't you all feel him?"

Billie shrugged when Victorine's gaze landed on her.

"Roland?" Victorine asked. "Oliver?"

Oliver shook his head.

Roland exhaled. "We can always try again."

Always pandering, Billie thought.

"You felt him, too, didn't you, my darling?" Victorine asked James.

"I think so," James said slowly. "Maybe."

Victorine spun toward Maud. "What exactly were you thinking? Now we'll never know, will we?"

"But didn't you feel it, ma'am?" Maud said quietly. "It wasn't kind."

"Not kind? It was my brother! My brother's spirit was here."

"*Something* was." Maud's voice quivered.

Oliver righted Victorine's chair, and Victorine nearly flung herself into it. "Well, you've ruined it for all of us. Why don't you leave us, Maud. Honestly, I don't think I can stand the sight of you just now."

Maud rushed out with a small cry. Billie wondered if she should go after her to convince the girl that the whole evening had been a game. Creepy, yes, but the ship was creepy in and of itself, and the candlelight and windy night had only made it worse. Too, Victorine's certainty had taken whatever silliness might have existed from the ritual, or whatever one called it.

But before Billie could rise and follow Maud, Roland did. He made no excuses; he just left, to Billie's intense surprise. Why exactly would Roland go after a maid? What could he intend?

Victorine let out a frustrated sigh, distracting Billie. "I know I felt Emile there."

"Another time," James said. "Pollan, the lights, if you please."

The valet turned on the lights. James blew out the candles on the table next to him.

"That was quite the thing," Oliver said. "I think I'll go have a cigarette on deck. Anyone care to join me?"

"I think I will." James rose. The two men went out the door into the night, leaving Billie and Victorine alone.

Victorine stared at one of the still-lit candles as if she meant to burrow her gaze into its flame. "I would let that girl off at the next port if I could."

"She was only afraid—"

"She kept Emile from showing," Victorine snapped. "I want her gone, but James would never permit it."

It seemed an odd thing to say. "Why not?"

"She's his insurance policy."

Another odd thing. "What do you mean?"

"Her family owes James a debt of some kind. I don't know. Something important. Anyway, he won't let her go." Victorine rose and swiftly snuffed the candle with her fingers. "Now how exactly will I contact my brother?"

Billie grappled with everything Victorine had just said. A debt. Something important. An insurance policy. James Holloway seemed so strangely ill and ineffectual on board the ship that she'd forgotten the rumors about him—at least, the rumors beyond his afflictions and his varied descents into quackery. The claims that he'd conned some of his business associates, for one thing. The accusations that he'd come by some of his riches through unfair means. Victorine's comment about Maud reminded Billie of that, and reminded her of what she tried not to think about—her own association with James Holloway, and Roland's.

Instead, she said, "Why don't you let your brother rest in peace, Victorine? He's gone. Why not just celebrate that he lived and resign yourself to his passing?"

Victorine gave Billie such a vicious glare that Billie jerked back in surprised defense. "Have you ever lost someone important to you?"

Lost. A difficult question to answer. Billie floundered.

"Don't pretend to understand my grief," Victorine said. "You couldn't possibly."

She went out to the deck, slamming the door behind her.

Always so dramatic, wasn't she? Billie heard a sigh behind her, and looked over her shoulder to see Pollan still there. He gave her a small nod of acknowledgment. She nodded back and bent to put out the last candles, but he said, "I'll take care of the rest, miss."

She left the saloon gratefully and went down the stairs to belowdecks. She had never been so glad to escape company, but as she approached her stateroom, there was Roland, coming toward her.

"The others are on deck smoking," she told him.

"Are you okay?" he asked.

"Why wouldn't I be okay?"

"You just learned that your room is a—I don't know what to call it. What do they call it when someone bumps themselves off in a certain place?"

"I don't know that there's a word for that, but I'm fine."

"Are you sure?" He waggled his eyebrows suggestively. "You can spend the night with me if you want."

Billie rolled her eyes. "How generous of you. How very altruistic."

He grinned. "I don't want you to be scared."

She leaned close, tapping her finger against his chest. "Look at you, such a knight in shining armor. You seem to be all about saving scared women tonight. I don't know how you can have room for both Maud and me."

His grin faded. "I just—"

"Of course you did. Good night, Rolly."

Her room was only a few steps away. She eased past him, unable to keep from brushing him as she did so, and opened the door, slipping inside. She closed the door firmly behind her and waited until she heard his footsteps down the companionway, then went to lock it, but there was no key. She would ask Maud or one of the crew for one in the morning.

Billie slipped off the dress Victorine had loaned her—again, Victorine's insistence already a habit—and prepared for bed. The wind had died again, and she found the gentle creak of the ship soothing. She hung the dress—a champagne chiffon that was not as becoming as the mint green—and put on a nightgown, then crawled between the damp, clammy sheets. She was exhausted; the evening had been a trial. Tomorrow, they'd reach the Cape and round into the Gulf of California proper the day after that, and her work could begin in earnest. She wanted to be rested and ready for it. No more wasting time on séances and cocktail hours.

She closed her eyes, expecting weariness to overcome her quickly. Instead, the room felt too still. The sounds of the ship, which had served as a lullaby the last few nights, were gone—it was blackly silent, as if the room had absorbed all sound, even that of her own breathing, and the moment Billie had the thought, she wondered if she was breathing at all, and the rhythm of her breath tightened; she couldn't regulate it again, couldn't bring it back into her chest, into her lungs. She felt as if she were suffocating. A weight, a press, the darkness—

She knifed up, choking. The stricture in her chest broke, but then the champagne dress—a pale, glowing shadow in the darkness—swayed violently where it hung on the wardrobe door. The ship was still. There was nothing to make it sway. A stifled cry—her own—and the darkness gave way; the movement stopped.

Somewhere, something clanged. Someone banged on a pipe. Timbers rasped. She heard voices coming from the engine room, low, muttered sounds. The sounds of night. Billie lay down again and closed her eyes and remembered a time when she was twelve, and she'd gone into the woods near their house in Pennsylvania late at night. She'd heard an owl, and then a scream that sent terror racing over her skin in shivers, that sank into her bowels. The scream had been cut dead in an instant, and she had run for home, certain that whatever had screamed was chasing her.

The next morning, she'd gone back. She'd found a rabbit claw, the remains of the rabbit's head. The owl had hunted it, and the scream had been its capture. She had taken the skull home and defleshed it. She'd kept it for a long time, but now she couldn't remember what had happened to it.

There was an explanation for everything, she knew, and then she faded into sleep.

Chapter Eight

When they reached the southernmost point of the peninsula called the false cape, Billie was ecstatic. Another day and they would be on the east side, and it could not come too soon. They arrived in the late evening, passing a wrecked steamer that the ship's searchlight lit eerily, so it looked like something from a horror novel. The abandoned ship, half sunken, its paddle wheel and funnel exposed and darkened by the elements, only made the furious crashing of breakers on the beach sound more ominous; Billie could easily imagine the *Eurybia*, too, cracking apart on the rocks.

"Don't worry, Captain Rogers has a good sense of it," James said jovially.

"The lighthouse is unreliable," Roland said to her under his breath. "Keep your fingers crossed."

Billie couldn't help her tension. This was just the beginning; everything she hoped for started with the Gulf, and she didn't want it to be the end too. They were lucky; as they rounded the false cape, the lighthouse beam punctuated the darkness; there would be no wreck of the *Eurybia* tonight.

Cape San Lucas proper was marked by rocks, and even in the darkness Billie saw the formless shadows of the Friars, the two great, high rocks noted in the *Coast Pilot*, glanced by the ship's lights. No pier light, though, and so they anchored outside the cove. The Cape was busy with other yachts, with fishing boats and native canoes; still it felt strangely remote and lonely, as if there were no one else around. One more thing to give Billie an otherworldly feeling; one more thing not to like.

In the morning, however, the headland came into view with breathtaking beauty. The rocky hills, some of them white with guano, the archway to the east where the ocean rushed forcefully through, the sandy strip of beach. Billie longed to go there. The steward, Boyd, and two of his assistants planned to go ashore to the village for supplies the next day, and she wondered how she could convince them to take her along. It wasn't one of her agreed-upon collecting stations, but the thought of doing some research and getting away from the others for a while was too tempting to resist.

Victorine and James already occupied the aft deck. James read aloud from what they called the *Eurybia News*, a collection of news from the wireless that Pollan put together for them every morning. Clarence Darrow, the prominent and controversial defense attorney, had arrived in Tennessee for the upcoming Scopes trial—or the monkey trial, as people were calling it, where a schoolteacher had been accused of breaking the law in Tennessee by teaching evolution; elsewhere, a professor claimed to see microscopic proof of evolution taking place, the details of which Pollan hadn't bothered to include; trade was up, and authorities had discouraged financiers against a new outburst of speculation, which James muttered angrily about; and an anti–Ku Klux Klan protest against a planned Klan meeting had been banned from the Capitol.

Billie didn't care to listen to James read the rest. The news was too depressing. She decided to go to the laboratory for the hundredth time, and she was halfway there when she heard the screams and the shouts coming from the crew quarters.

She ran toward the noise, bumping into Roland in the companionway. His hair was wet, as if he'd just come from the bath, and he frowned at her in concern and said, "You'd better stay here."

Billie ignored him and raced with him toward the screams, which came from the pantry, just off the galley. Some crewmen blocked the entrance. Roland pushed through them, while Billie told them in Spanish to move back. At the opening to the pantry, she stopped short in surprise, as did Roland.

It was a tiny room, lined with shelves full of foodstuffs. Backed into a corner, Maud crouched, looking like a wild thing, her dark hair falling into her face and her eyes huge. Facing her was Matías, the assistant engineer who had told Billie that the original crew of the *Eurybia* had gone on strike and refused to sail. He stood only a few inches from Maud. He gestured warily to her, speaking slowly, as if to a scared animal.

"Come now, *chica*. Come. Put it down."

It was only then that Billie saw Maud held a knife. A sharp, wicked-looking thing.

"What's going on here?" Roland asked.

The crew broke out in confused explanation, too confused for Billie to interpret. Roland looked at her. She shook her head and waved her hand for quiet. "What are you doing, Maud?"

"This animal tried to attack me," Maud said.

"No. No," Matías explained helplessly. "Not true."

"You did!"

"You screamed." Matías looked over his shoulder quickly, then back to Maud as if he expected her to lunge at him. "I came to see."

"Maud?" Roland asked.

The maid looked at him with an unveiled relief that sent a twinge of irritation through Billie. "I did scream, but he came in here and threw himself on me."

"To protect her!" Matías protested.

"From what?" Billie asked. "Why did you scream?"

"Put down the knife first." Roland motioned for Maud to lower the blade. "Come on now. No one has to get hurt. This sounds like a misunderstanding."

"*Si*," Matías said with relief. "I mean her no harm."

Maud looked warily at Matías, and then at Roland. Slowly, with a nod, she pulled up the hem of her uniform and slid the knife back into a sheath just above her knee. Billie couldn't help feeling a prick of admiration that again turned to annoyance when Roland said, "Good girl. Now let's hear what happened."

"I came to get Mrs. Holloway some sugar," Maud explained. "Then I saw the shadow."

A murmuring among the crew. Billie heard a low rumble, no real words, and she felt a sudden tension. "I think you all must have jobs to do," she told them in Spanish. "Go back to work."

They hesitated. One of them said, "We wish only for our own safety, *señora*."

"Why do you think you're not safe?" she asked.

Again, a low murmur, an exchange of glances.

She frowned. "What is it?"

"Cortez," said one of them.

"I told you," said Matías. "These waters . . ."

"What's he talking about?" Roland asked.

"There are stories about the Gulf, I guess," Billie said, and then stopped when she saw something come into Roland's expression, a flash, some knowledge. He knew something about the stories, she realized. Something about why these men might be wary of the Gulf of California.

"Not just that," said another man, nodding to Matías. "Tell them."

"They do not like the thing the other night," Matías said to her in Spanish. "The ghost-calling. There are rumors about this ship already. And now she"—he pointed to Maud, who watched him with big eyes—"she speaks of shadows. There are enough men on this ship who talk of curses and haunting. They believe the stories. She will only make it worse."

"What did he say?" Roland asked.

Maud spoke to Matías. "I am not telling stories. I am telling the truth. I saw something evil."

Maud understood Spanish. Billie wasn't surprised. "You are frightening them."

"I cannot help what I see," Maud said. "Talk to Mrs. Holloway. She's the one calling spirits."

"What?" Roland asked.

Billie didn't switch to English. She would explain it to him later. "She did not call a spirit that night. You stopped it." She turned to the men. "Maud stopped it."

"She spoke of a shadow today," one of the deckhands said.

"I—"

"No." Billie shut Maud down quickly with a warning look. "We will have no more talk of shadows. This was all a misunderstanding. Maud saw something that frightened her, and Matías was trying to help, and she mistook it. That's all this was. Now let's go back to work and forget it, yes? All of you."

They silenced. Then a general consensus, nodding, grumbled *sís*, and the crowd dispersed.

Matías looked at Maud. "You cannot frighten them this way. It will only cause trouble."

"I didn't mean to scare them," she said softly.

"Tell me if you're afraid, and I will help you, yes? I will not hurt you, girl. I can be your friend. But do not do this again."

Maud nodded, obviously only partially reassured, and Matías left. Roland looked at Billie questioningly, and she translated for him.

Roland touched Maud gently on the shoulder. "You're okay?"

Maud took a deep breath. "Yes, thank you."

"Then I'll go up and see to the others. Who knows if they heard all this. Can you . . . ?"

The question was for Billie, and she understood it. Could she mend things with Maud and make sure the girl was calm. When he left, she asked the maid, "Is that what really happened, Maud? Everything is as you said?"

"I thought he was trying to attack me."

"But he wasn't. You see that now?"

"Yes. I see it."

"And this shadow you saw . . . ?"

Maud went quiet. That obstinance again, or . . . no, something that was less easy to solve. Resistance. Billie was unsurprised when Maud met her gaze and asked, "Did you feel it in your room that night?"

It was as if the maid knew about the terrible silence, the press. The swaying of the dress. But how could she? They had just been tricks of Billie's own mind. Suggestion due to Victorine's antics. Nothing more. "I don't know what you're talking about," Billie lied. But she felt that Maud saw the lie, that the young woman knew.

Maud's half smile settled oddly—no, it unsettled. Uncanny. Unnerving. "Are you part of it too?" she asked softly.

"Part of what?"

Maud looked as if she was trying to decide how much to say. "You know him from before. Mr. Ely."

"Yes. Why?" Billie couldn't help that little prick of—it wasn't jealousy. Possessiveness, maybe? Why was Maud asking? What did she mean by it?

"How well did you know him?"

Billie stiffened. An impertinent question coming from a maid, though it was more that Billie felt an underlying reason for the question, probing interest. She thought of how quickly Roland had rushed to Maud's defense. How it had annoyed her. She shouldn't care what romance Roland decided to pursue these days. "We're colleagues, that's all."

Maud's expression didn't change. Still questioning. Still wary. Not reassured, which wasn't what Billie expected. The maid nodded. "Colleagues. You're a collector too."

Puzzling. Billie nodded.

When the maid pushed past Billie to go, Billie didn't stop her.

Sun blasted through the windows of the laboratory, heating it so that the little fan whirring away in the corner struggled to lend even a breath of relief, but Billie diligently arranged and rearranged her equipment, not wanting to go on deck and talk to any of the others. She had done all the prep she needed. Now she was only wasting time, but it was worth it to be alone.

When the door opened, she looked up in irritated surprise, which became only surprise when it turned out to be Oliver Stanton. Of all those on board, she expected his visit the least.

"I hope I'm not interrupting something important," he said, closing the door behind him. He wore tan trousers and a brown-and-white striped boating jacket, and looked every inch the casual rich man, athletic version, his sandy-brown hair a bit windblown, his chiseled face tanned from the sun.

"Not really." After Todos Santos, Billie could fathom only one reason for Oliver to seek her out, and so she said nervously, "Am I needed on deck?"

"Not at all. I had a few questions for you."

"If it's about Maud, or the spirits Victorine frightened her with this morning, I have nothing to say. Ask Roland."

"Maud?" Oliver looked confused. Then he laughed lightly, revealing straight white teeth, a dimple. "Oh, the maid. No, no, it's not about that. Vic is a little goofy about this Emile thing, I admit. Hey, you've got quite the setup here."

"Hmmm. I'm hoping to need every bit of it."

"Does it trouble you that your colleague is from the Academy of Sciences?"

"What do you mean?"

"Well, he's not from the San Diego Zoo. What interest can he have in collecting specimens for you instead of the Academy?"

Billie considered Oliver bluntly. "You'll have to ask him that."

"I did. He said he was here to collect for the zoo, and if there were specimens you didn't need, then the Academy would take them."

It sounded like Roland. Like Oliver, she didn't believe her ex-husband, but that was between her and Roland. "Then I suppose that's what he means to do."

"You haven't discussed it with him?"

"My interest is in marine specimens, Oliver. Roland is a herpetologist. He can have all the lizards he wants."

"I see." Oliver looked thoughtful. She regarded him warily as he roamed the room, taking in the reference books, the beakers. He reached out to touch a jar.

"Be careful. That's chromic acid."

He snatched his hand back. "Oh. Sorry."

"What is it you really wonder, Oliver?" she asked. "I don't think you're here to ask me if Roland and I get along as colleagues, or if I trust him not to steal my specimens."

"Do you? Trust him not to steal your specimens?"

"There's a tacit agreement among scientists," she informed him. She didn't say that Roland had broken it before.

Oliver nodded. Again, thoughtfully. "We're really here to gather specimens for your zoo? You don't have any other agreement with James, do you?"

Implicit was a question that echoed her own. What was James really looking for—and, by extension, Roland? But it offended Billie that Oliver might think she had ulterior motives. "If I did, why would I tell you?"

"That's the thing. That's just it. I'm the head of the Holloway Foundation, and it's funding this trip, and it just seems hinky to me that we're paying for a marine exhibit for the San Diego Zoo when James has shown no interest in the zoo or in fish or ocean animals *ever*.

Why? That's what I keep asking myself. Why? Why? And do you know what I come up with, Billie?"

"He has a new interest? Another hobby?" Billie suggested.

Oliver shook his head. "The original *Eurybia* crew went on strike shortly before we were due to leave."

"I heard that they weren't offered enough money," Billie said. "I heard that the Foundation refused to pay."

Oliver snorted. "It was only partially up to me. Yes, I would have refused to pay them, but they wouldn't even negotiate. There was no amount of money that could convince them to go. Do you know why? Because they'd heard a rumor that this trip was sponsored by the Empedocles Society. You know it?"

The damned Society. Its shadow seemed to hover over everything. She remembered her questions of Roland, the way he'd evaded them. "Yes, I've heard of them."

"The crew believed that we were collecting not for the San Diego Zoo, but for Empedocles. They accused us of procuring creatures for experiments. Putting shark heads on octopuses—"

"Octopi," she corrected automatically.

Oliver looked momentarily perplexed. "Octopi. Giving porpoises human feet. All kinds of ridiculous atrocities. What do you know about that?"

Damn Roland. Billie struggled to hide her rising temper. "The Society's been accused of such unethical experimentation in the past. But I don't know anything about that being part of this expedition."

"You're sure? You're not working for them?"

Billie laughed shortly. "They don't admit women. Surely you know that."

"Yes, but—"

"No, I'm not working for them. I find everything about them abhorrent." She nearly spat the last word—too vehement; she'd taken Oliver aback. She worked to calm herself. "I would not."

Oliver nodded. "James has said nothing to you about searching for anything other than . . . I don't know . . . starfish, or whatever."

The tank. The stories about the Gulf. What was it she'd overheard in the galley? *Monstruo. Fantasma.* "He hasn't."

"Nor has Roland?"

"He certainly hasn't," she said. "What do you think James would be looking for?"

"A new cure," Oliver said grimly. "I think he's brought the Empedocles Society in and he's searching for something to do with one of their crazy theories. I don't know what it is, but I think he's finally done it and gone mad. I mean to save him from himself this time, if I have to take over the Foundation to do it. I'd like your help."

"My help?"

He nodded. "I've tried to bring Victorine around, but she's too consumed with this Emile nonsense lately. You seem to have a good head on your shoulders. We could be allies and"—a suggestive smile—"maybe more than that? I've heard plenty of stories about redheads, and God knows the cruise is long and, frankly, boring."

He moved closer. Billie stepped back. "I . . . um . . . I'm not sure what I could do."

"Be another set of eyes and ears. Help me gather proof that James isn't in his right mind. I'd need you to bear witness before the Foundation board, of course, at the right time. I'd tell you what to say. You wouldn't even have to think."

He came up to her, too close, and reached out to cup her cheek.

Billie jerked away hard, banging her hip on a nearby cupboard in her haste to escape him. She grimaced in pain. "I don't think I'm cut out for spying, Oliver, and I'll be far too busy for any . . . um . . . extracurricular . . ."

His hand, suspended in midair, dropped to his side. His expression hardened. "Of course, if you find my attention distasteful . . . I assure you most women don't."

She noted his anger, and Billie knew well how troublesome angry, rejected men could be. She tried to smile, to backtrack. "That's not it. It's only that I've worked so hard for this opportunity. As a woman scientist, I . . . I can't afford to mess it up."

"Ah yes, a good little scientist." He quoted Roland's earlier words with scorn. "Well, I won't disturb you further, then."

She sagged with relief when he left, but she cursed herself for not handling him better. He'd surprised her, and she knew that despite her efforts, she'd made an enemy, and one whose impact she couldn't begin to guess.

Chapter Nine

Whatever Billie thought of Oliver, his theories stayed with her. She hadn't suspected James was looking for a new cure—but given his past and well-reported obsessions, it made sense. She had suspected this trip had something to do with the Empedocles Society from the moment she'd known of Roland's involvement. She wondered how to broach the subject with Roland in a way that wouldn't result immediately in a lie or an evasion.

The next morning, she grabbed the opportunity to go ashore with Boyd, the steward, and his assistants—maybe something would come to her as she roamed the beach.

She came on deck to find Oliver and James arguing while the steward patiently waited.

"What else do we need?" Oliver demanded. "Why should we make a stop at all?"

James sent a pointed glance to the steward, who said, "Beef, sir, and poultry. We should take every opportunity for water."

Oliver ignored him. "You're spending too much on supplies. No beef. We can eat fish. There's plenty. The sea can be our larder."

"This has all been figured into the expense. Boyd is right. We need to replenish water whenever we can, Oliver, and you know why? We drink it. I suppose even you might grow tired of whiskey." James caught sight of Billie standing there awkwardly. "What is it?"

"I'd thought . . . I'd like to go along."

Boyd gave her a skeptical look. "The *Coast Pilot* says the village is small and poor. It's not for tourists, miss. It won't be a long trip."

"I just want to look at the beach," she said.

The steward looked to James. "I'll need Mr. Holloway's say-so to take a woman alone."

James chuckled, and Billie bristled. "I'm not a possession, you know. I can make my own decisions."

"I'll go with her," Roland said, coming up behind them.

She had not known he was anywhere near, and his volunteering vaguely annoyed her.

James said, "If Roland goes, I don't see why you can't."

"I don't need protecting," she said.

"How do you know?" Roland asked. "Are you familiar with how many smugglers and brigands there might be on this coast? We're not in America anymore. Besides, James won't like losing his marine biologist before we've even started."

"No, I definitely won't," James said.

She made a face at that, but she wanted badly to survey the beach, and it might give her the chance to get some honest answers out of Roland, so she assented. It wasn't as if she had much choice anyway. It was three of them—and no doubt Oliver would weigh in too—against her. She couldn't go without a man to accompany her, and she feared that if she pushed further, Oliver would volunteer too.

As the skiff was readied, Billie gathered her bag with a net and some jars, her sketchbook and a bucket.

They lowered the skiff over the side, and Boyd and his assistant George, a crewman named Aldo, and she and Roland boarded. Aldo tried to start the outboard motor, which choked and stalled, coughed and started, then died. A long stream of cursed Italian, and the whole process began again. This time, the motor purred. Aldo made a sound of satisfaction, and they pushed off from the *Eurybia*. About four yards away, the purring became high pitched, then screeched and sputtered. The engine died.

Aldo cursed and tried to start the engine again. Nothing. Again. A choke. He pounded on the housing. Again. The third time he hit it, the thing started and stayed started, and they sped through the lagoon to the sandspit, where Roland helped the others pull the skiff to a safe place beyond the waves.

As Boyd and his assistant went on their way to the village, Aldo waited with the skiff, and Roland and Billie set off toward the eastern end. The rocks seemed to vibrate with black cormorants nesting in the nooks and crannies, setting off from the heights, streaking the crags with gray-white stripes and patches of guano. From somewhere close came the barking of sea lions. Waves beat upon the sand. But Billie's hopes of tide pools were disappointed; there were none. Plenty of seabirds, and some seaweed that had washed up with the waves, which she examined for larval fish or snail eggs and worms and tiny dead shrimp. She put the wads of limp vegetation in a jar for examination later, but she didn't find much else. The sun beat down, but the wind kept it from getting too hot; it whipped her hat from her head and her hair loose from its pins and into her face, and the sand into a fine mist at their feet. The bag full of equipment pulled heavily at her shoulder; jars clinked gently within. The bucket bounced at her calf.

The beach was empty but for the two of them and a few sea lions lolling about, who either ignored them or rolled into the sea to avoid them. The silence between them felt thick, but it wasn't silent at all. The beach was full of sound.

"So," Billie said finally, searching for a way into the question Oliver had planted firmly in her head. "How did you meet Holloway, anyway?"

Roland sighed and looked up at the sky. "Why does it matter?"

"Did you meet Holloway at the Society, or before?"

Roland said nothing.

"Please don't try to pretend that's not where you know him from, or that the Society isn't involved in this whole expedition. I'm not the only one who suspects it. Answer my question. Please."

"It was all about the same time. There was a . . . dinner. A club thing—the Bohemian Club, you remember it?"

Yes, she remembered the Bohemian Club. Where the richest and most powerful men in San Francisco met and played. An old club, founded in the nineteenth century.

"The night you spoke there," she said, remembering. A science-themed evening. Roland had been so very excited to be invited. They'd had to borrow a suit for him, because he had nothing appropriate for such an event. He'd been shaved and primped within an inch of his life. She'd been so proud of him. She'd bought him a special cologne. "It was that night?"

He nodded.

"You never said anything about meeting Holloway then."

"Would you have remembered if I had?" he asked. "Would you have known who he was?"

"Of course." But . . . maybe not. She had been so busy with their research then, and truthfully she had never cared much about who was on the social register. That had been Roland's obsession.

"Well, yes, it was that night. Someone there mentioned Empedocles. I decided to look into it."

He had not mentioned that either, Billie noted. Keeping his secrets even then. "Was it Holloway?"

"You know I can't reveal who's in the club," he chided.

"Very cute."

He shrugged. "I'm telling you the truth."

"Okay. So . . . the two of you are in cahoots. How is the Society involved in this? Why are we out here?"

Roland laughed. "We're collecting specimens for the San Diego Zoo. James told you the truth."

"Hmmm. Just maybe not the whole truth."

"Now, why do you say that? For God's sake, give me that bag. You're sweating." Roland took the bag from her shoulder and put it across his own.

They had reached the cluster of rocks, which loomed high above them. A group of cormorants swirled low and raucously. The sea breeze took on a tinge of rot, seaweed in the sun, or maybe birds' nests. The sound of rocks falling interrupted them; Billie looked to see two men, both with heavy bags, climbing down, hats settled low over their foreheads.

Roland put a hand on her arm. When she looked at him in question, he nodded toward the men and said urgently, "I need to talk to them."

"About what?"

"I'll be right back."

He started walking toward the rocks, and Billie hurried after him. The men stopped guardedly at the bottom of the outcropping when Roland called out, "Excuse me! *Pardon!* Can I talk to you a minute? *¡Un momento!* Billie, some help, please."

Billie caught up with him and smiled at the two men, who didn't smile back. In fact, they looked almost hostile, which Roland ignored. He gestured with his hands. "Um, could we . . . ask you a few questions? What's that word in Spanish, Billie?" He gave her a pleading look, and with a sigh she stepped forward.

In Spanish, she said, "Excuse us, but we're scientists from California doing a study on the Gulf. Would you mind if we asked you a few questions?"

The men looked at one another. One of them, the older, shrugged.

"Ask them if they know any local legends," Roland said quickly. "Ask them if there are any about sea creatures like a black demon or the *antorcha del mar*, or . . ."

The rest of Roland's words trailed into nothing, because the moment the men heard *antorcha del mar*, their eyes widened in alarm, they muttered between themselves, and they rushed away. Roland hurried after them, but the younger man raised his hands, waving him off, and the men only increased their speed. It was clear they would say nothing and wanted nothing to do with any of Roland's questions.

Billie watched them go and didn't try to follow them. She heard one of them mutter *monstruo*. The same word the crew had used. *Ella es el monstruo.* But today, from these men, it had a different intonation. It felt different. Billie tried to figure out why.

Roland turned around, obviously frustrated, and came back to her. "What the hell? What happened? They didn't even wait for the questions."

"They knew what they were about," she said quietly. "The minute you said *antorcha del mar*, they knew. They didn't want to answer questions about whatever it is. They were frightened. What is it, Roland?"

"Frightened?"

"*Monstruo*. That's what they said." Now she understood what felt different about the way these men had spoken. When she'd heard the crew use the word, it had been disconcerting, but still, they'd said it the way one told ghost stories around a fire. Tales told to raise the hairs on the back of your neck. These men had acted as if it was more than that. They acted as if it was real.

"What's the *antorcha del mar*?" she asked. "'Torch of the sea,' that's what it means. What is it?"

"A story." Roland's frown grew. "Just a story. A legend."

"Is this why you're here? Is that what you're looking for?" she prodded. "Is this what the Society's involved with? Some legendary creature? Why?"

He kept walking, and she followed him.

"Roland," she pressed. "Roland, tell me."

"I've said too much already."

"You haven't said enough," Billie snapped impatiently. "Do you really mean to keep this a secret the entire cruise? Do you think I won't find out? What's going on?"

They rounded another group of rocks, onto a bit of beach completely cut off from the water by a wall of craggy brown rock, and the faint tinge of rot in the air turned into a heavy miasma of sickening, nauseating putrescence. Cormorants and seagulls mobbed a pile of something on the beach. Buzzing flies swarmed it. Whatever it was, it was the cause of the stench.

"What's that?" Billie asked, momentarily distracted from her questions.

She was halfway to it before she heard Roland's "Be careful!" but he was right behind her. The birds scattered reluctantly as she approached; the flies didn't. The smell was almost overpowering, but when she saw what it was, she forgot the stench.

A pile of sharks. About five hammerheads, with their weirdly elongated skulls, the eyes on either end mostly pecked away by the birds, leaving fleshy hollows. Two were more rotted than others, crawling with maggots, but the others looked as if they hadn't been there long, and they were intact, except . . . they were slashed between the pectoral and pelvic fin.

Billie stepped closer. Roland came up beside her. He frowned and leaned in, reaching into one of the cut sharks with his bare hands, pulling the wound apart. Flies buzzed angrily and flew up into his face. He brushed them away with his forearm. "Its liver is gone." He frowned and groped at another carcass, pawing through wriggling maggots. "This one too."

Billie put down the bucket and looked at the sharks. She reached beneath the one nearest her, feeling the sandpapery skin, the edge of the slash, the glop of inside. It was the same. No liver.

All five were the same.

Finally they stood back and stared at the decomposing pile.

"Why?" she asked.

Roland shook his head. "I don't know. Maybe one of the crew can tell us."

"Maybe it's a delicacy," she offered.

"Maybe," he said, but there was something in his voice that made her look at him, something that made her think: *This excites him.* "What do you suppose those men back there had in those bags?"

"You don't think . . ."

"I don't know," he said. "But you said those men were frightened. You said they called the *antorcha del mar* a monster. What do frightened people do to keep monsters away? They make sacrifices."

"To *gods*. People make sacrifices to gods," Billie said. As usual, he went too far. "Those bags could have held anything. You're making quite an assumption. Roland, for God's sake, you're talking nonsense. What is an *antorcha del mar*?"

He hesitated, but that light in his eyes didn't fade. She saw him thinking, considering, but his excitement got the best of him, as always. "It's a fish."

"A fish."

"A fish that can live both on land and in the sea."

"Not a fish, then. It's an amphibian. But . . . there are no true saltwater amphibians. Or am I wrong? Are you saying you've found one?"

He shook his head. "No. It's not an amphibian. Not that we know, anyway. It's a fish, apparently. And a legend. Everything we've heard indicates it might be the missing link."

"The missing link?"

"The evolutionary link, Billie."

Billie stared at him in astonishment. The idea of such a fish was absurd. A *fish* that could breathe on land and in the sea? How did it breathe—through its skin? Had it lungs? Such a thing would be an evolutionary freak. A rare discovery. So rare as to be . . . impossible. That kind of rumored creature, if it were thought even remotely to exist, would lure scientists from all over the world, especially now, when the upcoming Scopes trial in Tennessee had brought evolutionary theory to the forefront of everyone's mind. Such a fish would demonstrate the link between life's beginnings in the sea and its transition to land, and . . . well, it would be a sensation. If any scientist believed it, they would already be looking for it.

Which meant Roland was hallucinating, or someone was lying to him. He was chasing a story.

"Do you have proof of this?" she asked slowly.

Roland took a deep breath. "Proof? A hundred stories. That's why we went to the mission at Todos Santos. A man there claimed to have seen it. He was long gone, unfortunately, but when we asked about it . . . Well, I told you how they chased us out. It was the same kind of fear we saw in those men just now." He gestured to the sharks. "And now . . . missing livers. Maybe."

Billie laughed shortly. "That's not proof! You can't be such a fool. You really should be more discerning, Rolly. What are you pursuing next, vampires?"

"Vampire mythology had a basis in the vampire bat."

Billie sighed. "You know what I mean. Why does Holloway care about this torch of the sea?"

Roland glanced away. "He's very interested in evolutionary science."

She slapped his arm to make him look at her. "You are such a liar. This has the Society written all over it."

"Billie—"

"So here you are, chasing stories all over the Gulf of California. A man who once studied lizard venom for antidotes to biological weapons."

"Where do stories come from, Billie?" he asked. "They have to come from somewhere. Cause and effect."

"Another stretch. Some stories are just for fun, Rolly. Like"—she grabbed at what she'd been thinking only minutes before—"ghost stories. Some stories don't have meaning."

"But some do. When something doesn't make sense, look for the thing in it that does. Nothing's completely irrational in the end. You know that, too, if you just let yourself believe it. Let's get back. I want to talk to the crew."

"It's not you who will be talking to them," she reminded him. "It's me. You can't speak Spanish."

He gave her that earnest puppy dog look that had convinced her of a hundred things over the years they'd been together. "Then I need you to believe me when you ask them," he said. "Please, Billie. For me. Treat this seriously."

She hesitated. She didn't want to look like an idiot, but then again, maybe there was something to this. Roland was ambitious, yes, but he wasn't stupid—or at least not usually. She didn't know how to explain his willingness to overlook the crackpots in the Society, but that was an aberration she'd never understood. Those men they'd talked to today had been truly frightened. She didn't want to admit it to Roland, but that fear worried her. Billie was too much a scientist to put much faith in stories, yet she was on edge after Victorine's séance, and after yesterday, when that séance had turned into the fracas in the pantry between Maud and Matías. Billie knew better than to just push that tension aside. Fears had a way of turning deadly sometimes, whether they were real or not.

"Yes, of course," she promised. "I'll treat it as a genuine scientific inquiry."

Chapter Ten

By the time Billie and Roland returned, a humid breeze stirred. Now that Billie knew why James had organized the expedition, she noticed James's avidity when Roland approached. The man obviously anticipated news. Or perhaps he saw Roland's excitement.

"What did you discover?" he asked without even a greeting.

"A pile of dead hammerheads with their livers missing," Roland said.

"Livers missing? Why?" James asked.

Roland reached into his pocket for a packet of cigarettes. "I don't know for sure, but I have theories. We'll see if the crew knows anything. Some of these men are fishermen, aren't they? Also I think we should start dredging."

"I'll give the order," James said, grinning.

"Dredging for what?" Oliver asked, throwing Billie a glance.

Billie grimaced. "I'm going to change. I smell like dead shark. You should do the same, Roland."

"I will," Roland said, and then turned back to James, and they began discussing shark livers while Billie walked off.

"Oh, wait, Billie, please!" Victorine waved from where she stood at the rail, looking over the side.

"I've really got to change—"

"Five minutes," Victorine pleaded.

It was the last thing Billie wanted to do, but she went to Victorine, who said, "I've been meaning to ask you: Do you really think Maud saw something at our séance?"

This again. Billie sighed. "No."

"She told me this morning I'd raised something evil." Victorine laughed nervously. "Which is ridiculous, don't you think?"

"Yes." The smell of dead shark filled Billie's nose. She also itched from sand and sweat. "I don't believe it."

"You slept well?"

"I had nightmares, but that's all."

"Of course. That's natural, I suppose. I'm sorry. We should never have put you in that room, but there's really no place else now that the other's been turned into a lab. I suppose you could sleep there, or . . . or share Roland's—" Another nervous laugh. "I kid. Of course I don't mean it. I don't think there's a berth left in the crew quarters—oh! Maud's room is meant for three—"

"I'll be fine, Victorine, really."

"You'll tell me if . . . if you feel anything or note anything . . . unusual."

"Like what?"

"Unusual cold. Or the feel of a presence, like someone is watching you. Things that move without volition, or voices. Whispers. They like to whisper."

Billie tried not to think of dresses swaying violently or strange dark silences, or the fact that she had indeed felt watched in that room. "Yes, I'll be sure to let you know. Now, if you don't mind . . ."

Victorine frowned. "There it is again—do you smell it?"

"Cedar?" Billie asked wearily.

"Yes! You do smell it!" Victorine stared out at the water. "Oh, look!"

Billie followed Victorine's gesture and saw a great long shadow, sinuous and smooth, water rippling above it, there and then gone, a shark, no . . . "A swordfish," she said.

It was huge, one of the largest she'd seen. It swam out, a far distance now, its dorsal fin slicing the water, far enough to almost disappear, and leaped into the air, shedding droplets that made rainbows in the sun, arching its great body in a kind of flight.

She heard the shouting on the aft deck. Some of the crew had seen it too. The great fish dived into the sea. How beautiful it was, how majestic. Billie caught her breath as it leaped again into the air, and then dived and raced toward them, the fin blurring with speed, so much power, and she realized then that it was headed right for the ship.

"No!" Victorine gasped.

The ship rocked at the impact—not hard, but the fish was huge, and the *Eurybia* felt the blow of its sword. The ship slowed to a dragging stop. Captain Rogers raced down the stairs, concern on his face, just as the deckhands hurried over to see what had happened. Roland rushed to where one of the men had grabbed the hook resting at the rail, and Oliver and James followed.

"What is it?" James asked.

Victorine went to him. "It's a swordfish. You should have seen it, darling. How it flew. It was beautiful. Then it rammed the ship."

He gave Billie, who stood right behind his wife, a puzzled look. "Why would it do that?"

Several crew members lowered a ladder over the side, the one with a hook halfway down, trying to get the fish loose. Billie watched as Roland and the others worked. The fish would be a wonderful start to her collection, but for some reason Billie couldn't raise any enthusiasm for it. It had been strange to watch it attack the ship, but beautiful, too, and to see it now, its sword stuck in the timbers of the hull, depressed her in a way she hadn't expected. She knew it was dead before she saw the stream of its blood through the water, before she heard Victorine's quiet little "Oh, how sad. I'd hoped we could set it free."

Captain Rogers came over to them. He called over the side, speaking rapidly in Spanish. One of the crew below answered.

"Well?" James asked. "What happened? What are they doing?"

"They're going to caulk the hole," Rogers said. "They're bringing the fish up for the scientists to dissect. We'll have the rest for dinner. You're to have the sword, Commodore." The captain clapped James on the shoulder with a grin. "Quite a trophy for you."

"We should have it taxidermied," Oliver said. "Now *that* would be a trophy."

When the steward's assistant set the plate with the slab of swordfish before them, Oliver took a bite and said, "I have gone to heaven, I swear."

"Delicious," James said. "I've never had fish so good."

"Charles Simmons had one on his wall, remember, James? It was half the size of this one." Oliver forked into the swordfish steak with gusto. "It should feed us and the crew for a few days at least."

"It was a monster." Roland sipped his wine.

Billie remembered the way the swordfish had come at the ship. The *intention*. It had as much as committed suicide. "All that's left now is a photograph. And some tissue samples in jars."

"And this delicious meal," Oliver said.

"I wonder why it decided to ram us," Victorine asked.

"They do that often here. That's what the first mate said. Though he crossed himself when he told us that." James's laugh turned into a little cough.

"Probably a legend about it," Roland said.

"Like the legend of the *antorcha del mar*?" Billie asked deliberately.

The room went silent. Victorine busied herself with her fish. James raised his gaze to Billie's. Oliver drank his wine, and then looked around the table as if just realizing that no one spoke.

"What did you say? The *del mar*? What?"

Billie took a forkful of fish and dragged it through a pool of lemon-and-caper sauce. "The *antorcha del mar*. The torch of the sea."

"The Gulf is full of strange things, I understand. There are plenty of stories," James said. "But stories contain the grain of truth. We've learned that again and again."

Billie said, "I see you and Roland find much to agree on."

"What are we talking about here?" Oliver asked. "What's the torch of the sea?"

Victorine put down her fork. "It's a fish, Oliver. James's latest obsession—oh, stop giving me that look, James. You would have told him eventually, and it seems that everyone knows but Ollie. Why keep torturing him?"

Billie saw the way Oliver tightened. "Is *this* why we're spending a fortune? A fish?"

James sighed. "Not just any fish, my friend. This is a legendary fish. A mythic fish."

"Myths are not facts, James," Oliver said. "It's easy to spend one's life chasing after stories. And wasting fortunes on them."

"What are facts, after all?" Victorine asked. "You might as well ask what truth is."

Sharply, Billie said, "Are you saying facts can be disputed?"

"Not disputed, necessarily, but which ones are we to believe? For example, people say that spirits can't be contacted, but I myself have seen that they can, so what are we to do with that contradiction?"

Billie shook her head. "I don't believe it's been proved that spirits can be contacted."

Victorine said, "Oh, but they tend not to show when there are disbelievers present. No one believed in the platypus either. They're very difficult to find in the wild, and so absurd that no one thought they were real. But they are, aren't they?"

Billie frowned. "Yes, but—"

"I smelled my brother's cologne again just before the swordfish attacked the ship. Do you remember, Billie? Another sign. I just wish I knew what it meant."

"Damn it, we're not talking about Emile now, Vic," Oliver burst out. "We're talking about some damned—I don't know what it is. Some torch fish. What the hell, James?"

James coughed and reached for his wine.

Roland cleared his throat. "It's not a 'torch fish,' Oliver. It's the *antorcha del mar*. It's said to be a fish that can live both on land and in the sea."

"Is that possible?"

"Theoretically, no," Billie said.

"But legends persist anyway," Roland went on. "They have for years. We believe there must be truth behind them. If the fish exists, it would be a huge boon for evolutionary science. As you know, James is very keen on discovery—"

"I know no such thing," Oliver said. "What I know is that James has been the victim of every con man spouting miraculous cures from here to Timbuktu, and this can be his only interest in it. Who told you about this thing, James? What sick lunatic is spouting baloney this time?"

"Calm down, Ollie," James said.

"Vic, tell me you don't know anything about this!"

Victorine sighed. "James will do as he wants, Oliver. You know that. Will you take all hope from him?"

"Ha! You've just admitted it! James is searching for another cure! What is it this time? What does this fish provide? Who's selling him this story now? The Society? It is, isn't it?"

Billie threw a glance at Roland, who carefully avoided making eye contact.

"You know what the board will say to this," Oliver warned.

"I know what you'll tell them," James said. "Who will convince them better, I wonder, when I tell them that the cure I seek is sea air and balmy weather. Adventure. The lure of knowledge. Pure philanthropy. It does me much good to know I can be part of exploration that gives so much to the future." James put a hand on Roland's shoulder and gestured toward Billie. With his other hand, James raised his glass. "To science!"

Roland grinned and toasted. "To science!"

Billie snorted. The two of them looked like a still from a newsreel. She could almost see the headline: Millionaire Philanthropist and Scientist Find Missing Evolutionary Link!

How happy Roland looked. She knew that expression on his face, that relief of tension that brought out his charm and his charisma. He'd been worried that this legend would slip through his fingers, she understood, but those men on the beach today had reinforced his belief that he was on the right track. It made Billie both happy and sad. Happy that he was finding his dreams within reach. Sad that she was no longer really a part of them. She had once been so much a part of that quest for him, just as he'd been part of hers, and they'd planned so many more projects for the future. It seemed both familiar and strange, to be on this cruise with him now, both of them working for their careers, but not really working together, because how could she really help him when she didn't believe in a myth? Not only that, but how could she be sure he was helping her, whatever he said? He'd broken the trust between them. It would not be easy to fix, and she wasn't sure she wanted to.

She'd been staring at him, lost in thought. He caught her gaze and smiled.

That smile . . .

She had to force herself to look away.

Chapter Eleven

The night was balmy and calm, with the moon playing peek-a-boo behind the few shifting clouds, silvering their billowy edges and then easing out again. James brought out champagne to celebrate that dredging would start tomorrow, thanks to the frightened men on shore who'd given Roland a reason to think the mystic fish was close. Captain Rogers, who looked to Billie like every blond Viking she'd ever seen in a history book, but dressed in a well-tailored uniform, brought James the sword of the swordfish.

"En garde!" James pointed it at Oliver and danced around like a drunk Musketeer, nearly losing his balance on the swaying deck. "Now I have you, villain!"

Oliver grabbed the end of the sword and recoiled. "Ow! That thing is sharp! Let me see it!"

"They use it for defense," Billie told him. She heard the slight slur in her voice. She should stop drinking, but the champagne was lovely and fizzed deliciously against her lips, and the night was gorgeous. Where there were no clouds, so many stars played in the sky it dazzled. She felt she could stay there and watch them all night. Once again, that sense of unreality hit her. This trip was bizarre, true, but it was also true that there had never been a time in her life when she could have imagined being on a yacht in the middle of the sea on such a night, and yet . . . here she was. The smell of Holloway's cigarettes polluted the briny air. Victorine started the player piano, though Billie would rather have listened to the soft slap of the ocean against the hull. But now "What'll I Do" was playing, and Victorine and Oliver danced while James coughed, and Roland—where was Roland?

Billie sat up on the chaise, trying to keep from spilling her champagne. There he was, over at the rail with . . . with Maud. Billie took another sip and leaned back again, and then thought, *Maud?*

She looked again. The maid stood very close to him, and the two leaned over while he spoke and pointed to something in the water. Billie couldn't hear the murmur of their voices over the music and Victorine's giggling. Billie watched as Maud started to leave the railing, and Roland touched the young woman's arm, stopping her so she turned back again, and . . . and disturbingly she felt a prick of—what was that? Jealousy? Absurd. She hadn't seen Roland for more than a year. She'd had nothing to do with him. She rarely thought of him—*Liar*—no, she mostly didn't. Sometimes when she felt lonely or maudlin. Their relationship was over. If he wanted to talk to a maid, that was his business. It had nothing to do with her.

But then Billie remembered the way he'd gone after Maud when she'd broken up the séance, how he'd touched Maud's shoulder in the pantry and asked if she was okay. His concern over the scream that had sent him running. He'd told Billie to stay behind. Why? So he could play the hero alone? Well.

Billie turned back to her glass and drank the rest of it. She rose clumsily, dodging Victorine and Oliver, who danced like deranged puppets, to go to the bar, where Pollan poured her more champagne. Billie didn't go back to the chaise. Instead she leaned against the piano, which vibrated with the clanging of its keys, and watched Roland and Maud. Billie saw the maid smile. She saw the way the young woman looked up at Roland. The way he looked down at her. The moon broke through the clouds again and lit them both in silver. They looked striking together, Billie had to admit. Both so dark. She felt a bit sick at the thought.

Maud said something, and Roland put his hand on her shoulder, just as he had in the pantry, and the girl paused and smiled and then walked away, leaving him alone at the rail. Roland turned back to the water, limned by that moonlight trail.

Billie felt suddenly too hot.

Oh dear God, she was such a bunny. Billie laughed softly to herself and took another sip of champagne. The thing to do was to go down to her stateroom right now. She'd had too much to drink, and the night was beautiful, and she had been alone for what felt like a long time. In the morning she would be herself again. *Don't go to him. Don't speak to him.* Those were the orders in her head. She knew to follow them. And so instead she walked to the railing. She said, "More champagne?"

Roland held out his glass. It, too, sparkled in the moonlight. "I've still got some."

"I saw you talking to Maud."

He made a motion, the water below. "I was showing her this."

The moonlight on the water, she thought. *How romantic.* But it wasn't moonlight. It shifted, moved, splashed against the ship. Iridescent and beautiful. Like living, moving stars suspended in the sea.

"Bioluminescence," she murmured.

"I think she thought at first it was some kind of witchcraft," he said. "She's afraid of the ocean. She lost two brothers to the sea."

"What did you tell her?"

"What it was. Millions of organisms. I told her you would show her through the microscope. It seems such an ordinary explanation, doesn't it, for something so pretty?"

"It's not, though. It's pretty fantastic that they can do that."

"That's my Billie," he said, and she heard an admiration in his voice that reminded her of times before. "Making the ordinary remarkable."

She laughed shortly. "Or the remarkable ordinary. I think I remember you saying that once or twice."

"You were never ordinary," he said softly. "Not ever. Do you remember the time in Sacramento . . ."

The words shocked her. That he'd said them. That he would say them now. That he remembered. But no, how could that shock her, when she remembered too? She could barely say, "For God's sake, Rolly, I was . . . not myself."

He turned to look at her. "It was one of the best nights of my life. I think about it all the time."

She felt the heat move over her entire body. They'd been camping by the river, looking for salamanders for a project of his, and the night had been gorgeous and warm, like this one, and they'd brought a flask of some moonshine that he'd got from some friend, which was so rough and nasty it felt like it burned every taste bud and scoured her throat going down, but it had done its work well. They'd made love in the open and had to scramble naked to the tent when they'd heard noises in the brush, so loud and raucous they were sure it was a crowd of drunken people, but it turned out to be marauding raccoons. She had laughed so hard she couldn't breathe. The next morning she'd awakened in Roland's arms with dried mud on her skin, and his hair had been so full of twigs he'd looked like a scarecrow.

Billie swallowed. *Leave right now. Say good night.* Except that she didn't want to. He ran his hand down her arm, and she shivered in response. He said, "I've missed you."

It was over then. She knew it. She knew it when she didn't pull away. She knew it when his words seemed to race hot through her blood. It was all she could do to remember the people on the deck behind them, to say, "Don't do that."

"Don't do it at all? Or don't do it here?"

Billie said nothing. He knew exactly what she meant. She saw it in his expression, lit by starlight. *Here. Don't do it here, where everyone can see.*

"Well? What do you say?" he asked quietly, a whisper. "Tell me you've missed me too."

"Yes," she answered, though it was stupid to say it. She knew it was stupid. "Of course I have."

She felt the way he stiffened. She heard the catch of his breath.

He glanced beyond them, to the others. "I'll go first. Meet me in my room."

She didn't even think *No*. Not a hint of a warning. She watched him go and turned back to the phosphorescence and thought, *Yes, why not? Why the hell not?* She wouldn't sleep anyway for wanting him. She drank the rest of her champagne and heard James coughing behind her, and the music changed to "Mandalay," and James called, "Billie! A dance!"

She was hardly aware of turning. She thought she said, "I'm too tired. I'm sorry, James, but I'm turning in. Good night!" She hoped she sounded normal, instead of possessed by a desire that tightened every muscle.

Billie set her glass on the deck and went down the stairs. Slow, slow, anticipation burning. The *Eurybia*'s motion felt part of her; she pushed herself from one wall to the other, a little bounce, a dance. Roland's door was cracked, and she opened it to find him waiting there, unbuttoning his shirt. She stepped inside and shut the door behind her.

"Lock it," he said hoarsely.

She turned the key, pulled it out, and dropped it to the floor with a thin clank.

Roland said, "Come here."

Billie only smiled. Her dress was not her own—it was one of Victorine's, this time blue. She undid the buttons on the back as far down as she could and slipped the sleeves over her arms. She shimmied it from her hips and let the georgette pool on the floor. In her knickers and undervest and stockings she went to one of the two beds in the room and sat on the edge of it, and then she spread her legs and said, "*You* come here."

He made a sound in his throat that stole her voice, but then he was there, kneeling between her legs, pressing to her. He wrapped his arms around her waist, and she bent to kiss him, opening her mouth as if she could inhale him. Yes, she had missed this. She had missed the taste of him and the warmth of him and the scent, and she gasped when he undid her vest and his mouth was on her breasts and she arched against him. When he slid his fingers up the leg of her knickers and into the very heart of her, she forgot everything else between them and celebrated only this, the part of them that she had never wanted to give up, the part that had always and forever been good—no, she amended, when they'd finally shed their clothing and he was inside her, and they rocked against the rhythm of the ship so she moaned her pleasure against his mouth, better than good. She could admit this now, dizzy with desire and champagne. He had transformed her.

⁓

She woke with a headache and his heat against her back and a sense of merciless foreboding. It took her a moment to understand—less than a moment to grasp, more than a moment to absorb—where she was, what she had done. Her mouth was dry; her tongue felt heavy, her skin grimy with a film of sweat. Billie tried to lie still, to calm her now-panicked breathing.

"I know you're awake," he said.

"I'm not," she insisted softly. "I'm deeply asleep, and this is a dream."

"It's not."

"I'm not going to ever admit we did this."

Roland sighed. She was on her stomach and he was half on top of her, his arm over her naked back, and this position, too, was familiar. He rolled off. "This is what I think. I think you should move your things into my room—"

"No, Roland. Are you crazy?"

"You prefer your murder room?"

"It's a suicide room. No one was murdered there."

"How do you sleep knowing what happened there?"

"Better than I'll sleep here." She started to sit up and push aside the covers. Roland stopped her.

"I'm serious, Billie. Why not? We'll tell the others what we are to each other—"

"What we *were*." She lay back to look at him. "This is not going to happen again."

He laughed. "Okay."

"It's not. I mean it."

"Your ability to refuse a good thing has always been a wonder to me."

"Because I see the consequences and you don't."

"What consequences are those?"

"Nothing's really changed, has it?" she asked. "I was drunk last night, but I'm not this morning. I remember too well our problems."

"I've apologized." Roland propped himself up on his elbow to look down at her. "I'll apologize again."

"It takes more than that, I'm afraid." She met his gaze, even though she didn't want to. What she wanted was for him to understand—to truly understand—the importance of what she said next. "I'm afraid of you, Rolly."

He frowned, obviously confused. "Afraid of me?"

"You took advantage of me more than once. How do I know you won't do that again?"

"That was a long time ago. I know better now. I've learned."

"That might be so. But I'll need a little more proof than an apology and a night in bed."

"Okay," he said agreeably. "Tell me how. I'll do it."

She pressed her hand to his chest, curling her fingers into his chest hair. "You changed when you joined the Society—no, don't argue with me. You did."

He put his hand over hers and tried to laugh. "That's bunk."

"Are you still a member?"

"Yes, but—"

"What if I asked you to give it up? To quit the club and walk away?"

Roland was silent.

"You see?" She pulled her hand from beneath his and rose.

"No, wait, Billie, don't go. You've just sprung this on me, and—"

"And the fact that you even have to think about it, that you can't just say yes, tells me everything I need to know."

"You don't understand," he said urgently. "You don't understand what this means, Billie. It's not just the Society—it's this expedition. The two are entwined. I can't just walk away now. Not until this is done."

She looked over her shoulder at him. "Until what's done? Until we find a fish that only exists in stories? You're admitting the Society is involved in this—how? What is this really about, Rolly?"

He sagged back against the pillow. "Science. It's about science."

"I see." His answer disappointed and disheartened her. Mostly because it told her that nothing had really changed; in a contest between her and his ambitions, his ambitions would always win.

Billie grabbed her knickers and her undervest from the floor and slipped into them, then the dress. She hoped she could get to her stateroom unseen—or at least unseen by anyone who might remember that she had worn this same dress last night. She went to the door.

Roland said, "Don't go. Please."

She said only, "This won't happen again, Roland. Don't expect it," and opened the door, stepping into an already hot and cramped companionway. She started to her stateroom, longing for a bath and hoping to wash away her regret. Another stupid mistake—how many times must she make the same one when it came to Roland? This time, she would not repeat it. Once and done, she promised herself fervently. No more.

The ship shuddered in the way she had come to associate with slowing and stopping, and Billie heard a flurry of alarmed shouts from the upper deck. *Ignore it.* She wanted that bath. She wanted to change. But then Aldo nearly jumped down the stairs from the deck. "*Signora*!" he exclaimed in obvious relief when he saw her. "You must come! They ask for you!"

Billie had her stockings balled in her hand and couldn't imagine she looked anything other than someone who had just rolled out of bed and thrown on the dress she'd worn last night. The morning was turning into one of her worst nightmares.

"What is it?" she asked.

"The others call it *agua de sangre*," he said. "Mrs. Holloway has fainted."

Water of blood, Billie translated silently. She had no idea what he meant, but that Victorine had fainted obviously had him concerned. There was no help for it; she left her stockings outside her door and followed him above deck.

There, Oliver knelt next to what looked like a newly revived Victorine, who glanced about in confusion. Victorine clawed lightly at a string of pearls wrapped about her throat. Billie looked beyond them, beyond the rail, to the water. It was indeed the color of blood. A deep vermilion surrounded them. A red tide. Microorganisms.

"Billie," Victorine murmured. "What do you see? What color is the water?"

"It's red," Billie said.

"Blood," Victorine said. "It's a sign, isn't it?"

"A sign of what, Victorine? It's not blood. It's crustacea. Tiny shrimp. Microscopic."

Victorine frowned. "Shrimp?"

Billie nodded. "Or an algae bloom. I won't know until I look under a microscope. It's a natural occurrence, not a sign. Are you all right?"

"I heard a voice." Victorine grabbed Oliver's hand tightly. "Bay of the Dead. That's where we are, isn't it?"

Billie glanced at Aldo, who said, "Los Muertos."

Which did translate to "the Dead."

Oliver sighed. "You heard Billie, Vic. It's only shrimp. There's no meaning in it. Nothing to frighten you. It's not any kind of a sign."

"A natural occurrence," Billie repeated. "Aldo, would you mind getting a bucket full of water for me? I'd like some samples."

The sailor bowed his head in acknowledgment.

"It seems coincidental, doesn't it? The Bay of the Dead at the same time we come upon red water. Did you hear what the crew called it?" Victorine's voice was high and sharp. "Blood water."

"Because it's the color of blood. No other reason." Billie turned to go.

Victorine said, "Are you having trouble sleeping, Billie?"

Billie stopped. Another allusion to the spirit in her room, no doubt. She tried to keep her expression neutral when she said, "No, not at all."

"I assumed you had, as you're still wearing yesterday's dress."

"Oh . . . I heard the shouts, and I grabbed the closest thing."

"Hmmm." Victorine did not seem convinced. "Just for the future, then: You really shouldn't sleep in chiffon. It's very delicate. You could tear it."

Billie smiled against the speculation in Victorine's eyes. "Of course not. I never would."

Chapter Twelve

The next day they anchored off the coast of Cerralvo Island, Billie's first collecting station. She couldn't get to the skiff fast enough. At last, to do what she'd come to do. They were going to start dredging but hadn't yet, and the only things she'd managed to examine were the swordfish, the seaweed she'd gathered, and whatever she'd managed to net and capture from leaning over the side—including the ciliate infusoria turning the water red yesterday. She was spoiling for some real finds.

Not only that, but she was glad to get away from the ship, from Victorine's spirits and fainting spells—whatever that had been about—the tension between Oliver and James, and Billie's own discomfort with Oliver. Had she been able to leave Roland behind as well, the day would have been perfect. But being busy was only a partial antidote to her regret over the night they'd spent together, and she could only do so much to avoid his searching gaze.

Even so, Cerralvo Island turned out to be all Billie had hoped for. Crystalline water, rocks laden with sea life, so many specimens it was all she could do to limit herself. But the best, the most amazing thing, was the sea cucumbers. She found them only a few yards underwater, black and unlike any she'd ever seen. Billie was sure they were a new species of holothurian. The moment she spotted them, the idea of the paper she'd write, the acclaim, the attention . . . she nearly trembled with excitement as she collected them. The pinnate oral tentacles, the papillae . . . she hadn't seen any like that before. It was either a new species or a variation.

She was trudging back to shore and had paused to take up some spiny starfish when a boom startled her into almost dropping her bucket.

Water and rock rained down just beyond her, scattering into the clear water. A dead parrotfish landed with a splash in front of her. She grabbed it and glared into the near distance, where Roland and a few of the crew tromped along the boiling water near the shore. He was dynamiting. It was a standard collecting procedure, but she hadn't had a chance to explore those rocks yet, and the fish that had been feeding around them were fleeing, schools of them racing by her feet.

She readjusted her bucket and net and hurried over to him. "What are you doing?" she demanded the moment she was close enough.

Roland looked up. "What does it look like?"

"I thought you were searching for lizards."

He squatted down, picking up a handful of broken shells, holding them out. "Do you want these?"

"Rolly! I wish you'd let me have a chance here first—"

"This is the kind of place the *antorcha* might be," he said quietly. "When it's on land."

She glanced around at the now-destroyed rock, the dead and scattered parts of fish and other creatures littering the water. "You really think it would be hiding in such close quarters?"

"I don't know where it would be hiding. That's why I'm looking here," he said, then called to the skiff captain, who stood on a ridge rising from the water. "Aldo, not there! Closer to the edge."

"No, don't—not yet, I—"

Too late—the charge blew. Billie ducked as water spouted into the air.

Roland said, "Besides, these charges aren't strong enough to do anything but expose its hiding place."

"And blow my specimens into pieces," she chided.

Roland sat back on his heels. "Those men at the Cape, remember? And Todos Santos? They were frightened. That means the creature must be close. Hey—" He reached out. She recoiled so sharply he sighed. "I was only going to say you're getting sunburned."

Billie frowned at him and adjusted her broad-brimmed straw hat, but it wouldn't matter; the water reflected the sun upward into her face; her pale skin would burn no matter what she did, and she would end up with more of her despised freckles than she had already. "I found a new species of holothurian," she said, holding out her bucket. "At least I think so. I won't know until I get home, of course, but it's promising."

"Congratulations. Did you get two?"

"One for you and one for me?" she asked sarcastically. "No. All for me. You'll have to find your own."

"I've got bigger things to look for." His gaze swept to Aldo. "Anything?"

Aldo called back, "An eel!" He held it up, limp and shell shocked.

"Give it to Billie!"

"No more charges," Billie told him. "If the fish was here, you've probably scared it away."

"The water's so clear we'd be able to see it scurrying."

"Not now that you've muddied it. If you don't mind, I like to see things living before I start killing them."

He saluted her, a tease, a blinding smile. "Aye, aye, captain. We've got another hour. Get what you can."

"I need more time than that."

"I'll have Aldo gather what's floating."

"In one piece, Rolly. *One piece.* You've never been careful enough with the charges."

"I rarely need them for snakes and lizards."

"Then get snakes and lizards," she said.

"I'm looking for something much more important." He gave her a suggestive look and lowered his voice seductively, the voice from the night before. "You could help me, you know. Why don't you?"

Damn her, she felt its effect. "Don't," she warned.

"I'm serious, Billie. You want to resurrect your career—"

"With you, who wrecked it to begin with?"

"Trust me."

"Prove I can." She walked away.

They boarded the skiff to return to the *Eurybia* in the late afternoon, and Billie was more than happy with everything she'd gathered. She hadn't found anything new beyond the holothurians, but those alone were amazing luck for a first day out.

The outboard motor stalled half a dozen times on the way back to the yacht. The engine sputtered so violently at one point that Billie thought water had got into it, and then she noticed the water had grown choppy. Billie looked back at Cerralvo Island. A haze seemed to blur the mountainous land—or no, it was more as if the landscape shifted and changed before her eyes. The island seemed farther away than it had been only a moment ago, though they hadn't moved.

Billie blinked, and the island righted itself. Only a mirage, then, but what was not a mirage was the way the breeze had roughened, as well as the sea, which had darkened as well. The motor stalled again, and the waves slapped the sides of the skiff, splashing over the sides. She was already wet from the day of collecting, so she didn't care about that, but Roland frowned as if he read her mind. "Looks like a storm coming in."

Aldo hit the outboard motor with the flat of his hand, muttering in Italian.

The crates and barrels filled with specimens rocked with a sudden larger wave.

Aldo kicked the outboard. It grumpily growled to life. The wind rattled the water, chopping hard so that the skiff bounced as it approached the yacht. Billie kept a steady hand on the crate with the holothurians. She was relieved when they finally arrived. Wind rocked the boat and grabbed the rope when Aldo threw it for the first mate on the deck of the *Eurybia*. The rope fell into the water; Aldo gathered it up to throw again. This time the first mate caught it. He pulled the boat in, spun the rope around a cleat, and offered a hand for Billie as she came up the ladder.

She turned back to see Roland struggling with one of the barrels. The skiff rolled with the waves. "We'd better get that out quickly!" she called down.

He nodded and called for Oliver, who was on deck, along with the first mate, and they went into the skiff to help. Billie stood by to corral them. Roland lugged a barrel to Oliver.

Billie called, "Be careful with that!"

Irritably, Roland called back, "Why don't you prep the lab and leave this to me?" The wind rocked the skiff so it banged against the yacht. One of barrels tipped; Roland caught it before it fell.

The wind had risen hard and quickly. It yanked Billie's hat from her head and sent it skittering across the deck. One of the crew snagged it just before it went overboard. Worriedly, Billie looked up at the sky. "You're going to need more help!"

"Get a few more crew, will you?" Oliver shouted from the skiff.

Billie hurried to the pilothouse and asked Captain Rogers to send a few other men down, and then went back to her post, though she wasn't much use, and all she could do was worry. But the engineer and other hands arrived within minutes to drag up the supplies and specimens. The wind grew more forceful. The sea splashed over the sides of the skiff. Oliver scrambled out and up the ladder, and Roland and the engineer fought with a barrel that seemed particularly heavy.

Overhead, the skies darkened. Billie craned her neck to look up at the racing clouds. A strong gust blew over the wicker chair near the searchlight.

A cry from below, followed by a splash. Billie jerked around to see Roland throwing himself at the side of the skiff after a crate sinking into the water. "The holothurians!" she shouted, but then she saw that no, it wasn't the crate Roland grappled for.

Someone was in the water. A man. Sinking, bobbing, desperately clawing at the waves.

"Grab my hand!" Roland shouted, crawling half out of the skiff. One of the other sailors took hold of Roland's suspenders as he tried to grab the man who'd gone overboard. He had one of the man's hands, struggled to keep a grip, and cried out when the man slipped from his grasp and into the churning dark water. "Where is he? Where the hell is he?"

The wind howled. Another wicker chair skidded across the deck.

Roland wrenched loose of the man who held him and dived over the side of the skiff into the water.

"Roland!" Billie screamed.

"No!" one of the crew shouted. "*Tiburones!* No! No!"

Sharks. Billie's panic turned to horror. "Roland! Roland!" She turned back to the deck and screamed at Oliver, who stood there watching helplessly. "Do something!" But she couldn't look away for long. Roland dived beneath the surface, disappearing just as the man before him had disappeared. In the skiff, Aldo grabbed a rope and scrambled to the side, searching the sea.

Roland emerged again, breathing hard. "I can't find him!"

"Get out!" she shouted at him. "Goddamn it, get out!"

Aldo threw him the rope. It slapped against Roland's shoulder.

Roland glanced up at Billie briefly, and she knew what he would do. When he ignored the rope and dived again into the water, she yelled, "Damn it, I'm going to kill you, Rolly!"

Aldo shook his head and pulled the rope back in, ready to throw it again. "Come in, stupid!"

From the deck, a crewman shouted, "*Tiburones!*"

"What's he saying?" Oliver asked.

"Sharks," Billie said grimly. She gripped the railing so hard she couldn't feel her fingers.

Roland popped from the water.

"Get out!" Billie yelled. "There are sharks, you idiot! Get. Out!"

"I can't just leave him!"

"He's gone, *amico*." Aldo threw the rope. This time Roland caught it. "He's gone."

"He can't be gone," Roland protested. "He was right here. He's got to be right here."

Oliver yelled above the wind, "Come in before you die too!"

"Listen to him, Rolly!" Billie shouted. "Listen to him and get in the damn boat!"

Roland ignored them both and dived again. This time, he stayed submerged for an impossibly long time. When he emerged again, Billie realized she'd been holding her breath.

"Now, Roland!" she shouted.

"*Now!*" Aldo called urgently, offering his hand.

Roland swam to the skiff and hoisted himself in. The water whipped violently. There was no sign of the man who'd gone overboard.

"Who was it?" Captain Rogers yelled down. "Who went overboard?"

Roland sat back and closed his eyes. Water dripped from him into a puddle in the skiff. Then he looked up at the captain, who was leaning over the rail. "It was the engineer. Ángel."

Captain Rogers groaned. "Are you sure? Ángel Veracruz?"

Roland nodded. His voice cracked as he said, "I had him. But I couldn't hold him. I tried. I . . . It was like something pulled him away."

"The engineer. Christ."

The look on Captain Rogers's face alarmed Billie. It was just one step short of horror.

Just as quickly as it had begun, the wind died.

Chapter Thirteen

Billie didn't look up from the sorting tray when the hatch of the aft hold opened and Roland came down the stairs from the deck. She kept her gaze on the creatures she'd spilled into the tray. Anemones, sea stars, crabs fighting each other.

She said, "I wish it was easier to get the anemones to open up. They persist in staying closed. I know they're trying to protect themselves, but—"

"Billie."

She turned to look at him, surprised to see he was still soaking wet. "You haven't changed yet?"

"I was talking to James. Then I thought I should talk to you right away. The crate we lost had your holothurians."

At first she thought he must be joking, but his expression told her he wasn't. Her disappointment came fast and sinking, followed just as quickly by resolve. "Well, that's easy enough to fix. We'll just go back. There were dozens where I found those."

"We're not going back."

"You can't be serious. We've just left there. All we do is turn around and—"

"We lost the engineer, Billie. You know, the man who knows how to run the engines."

She remembered the look on Captain Rogers's face, and felt it herself, despair turned to horror. Billie was confused as well. How could they go on without an engineer?

"James has decided to continue. The fish is the most important thing, and as you just saw, the weather is changeable and unpredictable. Without an engineer, well . . . we have to make do with the assistant engineer, and the captain is unsure how capable Matías is. So . . . we won't be taking a chance and going back, and we won't be making all the stops you want."

It took her a moment to understand what he was saying. "Wait a minute . . ."

"We'll go to Espiritu Santo, because it's near. And Tiburón. Not sure about Estero de la Luna because Rogers isn't sure about—"

"Wait a minute," she repeated. "Wait just a minute."

"Things have changed, Billie."

"No. No, that's not fair. It can't—"

"Think of it this way: If we find the fish—"

She threw the tongs at him, and felt a great burst of satisfaction when he flinched. "A fish that might or might not be real! What has it to do with me anyway? I'm sorry the engineer is gone. It's terrible. But this isn't what I signed on for."

"It's not my decision."

Billie hated feeling helpless, and she felt horrible on top of it, arguing this after a man's death, because a man's death had created circumstances that she had to at least try to fight, though it felt so trivial in light of what had happened. But it wasn't trivial to her. It couldn't be. Her career depended on this trip. "You could influence it, though, couldn't you? You could convince him—"

"I can't, Billie." He spread his hands, that puppy dog look again. *I'm sorry, I can only do so much, I tried.* "Listen, I promise I'll help in any way I can."

"I've heard enough of your promises." She turned back to the sorting tray, unable to hide the extent of her disappointment. What she would do now, how she would make up for the loss . . .

"You'll get a few of your collecting sites, just not all of them."

"Three instead of six. It's not enough."

"There's still the dredging. We'll find plenty, and I'll talk to some people and make sure you get published—"

"I do not want your help." She emphasized each word through clenched teeth. She would have to make do. She had no other choice. "I'm done with male scientists. I'll do it on my own. In *my* name."

He was quiet. Then, very softly, "At least you don't want me dead. That was nice to know."

She parted two crabs engaged in deadly combat. "I'm changing my mind about that right now."

He unbuttoned his shirt. "I can't much blame you. But I did try."

"I would rather have that crate of holothurians."

Roland peeled off his shirt and laid it over a stool, revealing the upper half of his sleeveless union suit, which was plastered wetly to him.

The dark hair of his chest peeked over the low collar, and to Billie's horror, she felt the heat of desire even through her frustration and disappointment. The night they'd spent together intruded, flashes that made her voice too strident when she asked, "What are you doing?"

"Taking off my shirt. I'm soaking wet, and the salt's starting to itch. It's too hot in here."

"Can't you do that in your stateroom? It's indecent."

"It's indecent?" Roland raised an eyebrow at the absurdity of her protesting his partial nudity, after the things they'd already done.

"You're trying to tempt me."

"Am I? Is it working?"

Billie let out a breath of frustration. "I told you, it was a mistake. No more."

"I see. I throw myself into shark-infested waters trying to save our engineer, and I don't even get a reward."

"Such a hero you are. Did you even see a shark?"

He frowned and shook his head. "No, I didn't see a shark. In fact, I saw nothing down there. It was strange. The water was clear as day earlier, wasn't it? There were all those jellyfish just this morning. We could see to the bottom. But when Ángel went down, I couldn't see anything."

That *was* strange. "The wind must have stirred everything up."

"Hmmm. Maybe. Don't you think it came up too quickly for that? And it wasn't like the water was silty. It was just . . . dark. Like it had turned black." Roland's frown deepened. "Honestly, I've never seen anything like it. And there was something else. Something . . . I don't know."

"What do you mean?"

"I had a good hold on him. But I couldn't see him. And then it was . . . it was as if something *pulled* him away."

Billie stared at him, trying to decide if he was joking. He looked just sheepish enough that she decided he was not. "Something pulled him? Like what? What could that have possibly been, Roland? Your giant squid?"

"Ha ha," he said humorlessly. "You're never going to let me live down *Twenty Thousand Leagues Under the Sea*, are you?"

"I'm never going to let you live down making me read it. So what was it?"

"I don't know. I thought . . . a current, maybe. But it didn't feel like that. I've been trying to figure it out. It just doesn't make sense. Maybe a shark had him and I couldn't see. But it was something."

Roland's account intrigued and disconcerted her. The scientist in her knew, just as Roland must, that there had to be an explanation, both for the black water and for the pull he'd felt, but she couldn't help remembering the talk of the crew about the Gulf being a bad place. Along with the memory came a sense of—what was it? Warning? Something must have changed in her face, because Roland said, "What is it? What are you thinking?"

She shook her head. "Just that maybe there's something particular to the Gulf that the crew might know."

Roland considered her. "You're not telling me something."

"As if there aren't a hundred things you aren't telling me."

"What are you keeping from me?"

"Nothing really. Those stories about the Gulf you're always mentioning. The other day I heard the crew say the Gulf was a bad place. And the *antorcha del mar*? They called it *monstruo*. The same thing those men on the Cape called it."

"Monster—isn't that what you said it meant?"

"There was more to it than that. They said *ella es el monstruo*. *She* is a monster, Rolly. Whatever this monster is, she's a girl."

Roland scowled. "Are you sure you didn't mishear?"

"I know it might be hard for you to believe that a female could be dangerous, but trust me, I know what I heard."

"What else did you hear?"

"That was it."

Instead of looking alarmed, Roland looked pleased. "Then we really are on the right track."

Billie couldn't help a laugh of dismay. "You truly are goofy. If this fish is the monster they're talking about, don't you think it would be better *not* to pursue it?"

"I never thought you were a coward, Billie."

"I never thought you were an idiot. No, wait, that's a lie. I have thought that many times, including today. Really, Roland, what exactly does the Empedocles Society want with a monster fish? You might as well tell me the truth so we can stop with this farce of scientific discovery and a boon for evolutionary research."

"But that's what it is, Billie," he said, all innocence. "I can't tell you what isn't fact. Do you want me to make up some esoteric ritual just to please you?"

Billie let out a groan.

"Just keep your eye on your prize, Billie," he said. "I promise you'll get your own research out of all this, and your career will be more brilliant than ever. But now we'd better change for dinner."

"I need to get to this." She gestured to the sorting tray.

"All work and no play makes Billie a dull girl," he said with a smile, that charming smile again to make her forget whatever she might be angry about, whatever discomfited her. Billie hated that it still worked, that it still charmed, even as his words stung with familiarity. "*All work and no play*," he'd used to tease, and she had always said back what she said to him now.

"That's not fair. Women have to work twice as hard as men just to be ordinary."

"Come to dinner, Billie," he said, and went up the stairs.

But neither his smile nor his words took away her discomfort, or her sense that the crew understood something about this place that she should be paying attention to, even as Roland's ambition dismissed it.

~

Dinner started off tense and became more so as the wine made the rounds. There had been no cocktail hour, Billie discovered; the engineer's death had wrought an uncomfortable propriety, and it seemed everyone felt the need to at least pay lip service to mourning a man they hardly knew. Cocktails and music seemed inappropriate.

Wine at dinner, however . . . well, apparently that was something different. Not that Billie objected.

"That poor man." Oliver poured more wine into his glass and took a great gulp.

"I'll send a stipend to his family," James said. "More than he would have been paid."

"That's a lovely gesture," Victorine agreed.

"He wasn't that good an engineer," Oliver said. "You don't have to. It's more than they expect, I'm sure."

Billie winced at his callousness. "Surely they deserve something."

"Truly, Oliver, that was uncharitable," Victorine chided.

"He was already paid too much, given his experience. The crew allotment is outrageous." Oliver drank again.

James said, "Well, his family will be well compensated anyway. Fishermen tend to be away from home so much they probably won't even notice he's gone."

Victorine said, "My darling, you shouldn't say such things. He's dead."

Oliver snorted. "Why? Might his spirit be listening? Is it hovering 'round? Hello, what's-your-name, do you mean to haunt us?"

Billie reached for her wine and sent a pleading glance at Roland, who pretended not to see her.

"For God's sake, Ollie," James said.

"His name was Ángel," Roland said.

Victorine looked nervously about the dining room, and Billie tensed, waiting for the woman to stiffen and start spouting spiritualist nonsense. "You shouldn't mock, Oliver. His spirit could be here."

James poured more wine and tore a piece from a roll, which he methodically ripped into pieces that fell onto his plate, meaningless destruction. "Shall we ask our scientists what they think? What about you, Billie? Where do you think our good engineer's spirit is now?"

"Wherever you like to believe it is," she answered.

"You won't get Billie to answer that question," Roland commented.

"Why not? Doesn't everyone have an opinion about where our souls go when we die?" James asked.

Oliver said, "Not everyone likes to talk about it."

"Or be mocked for it," Victorine put in pointedly.

"Which is it for you, Billie? You don't like to talk about it, or you have mockable theories?" James presented his question with a tease of a smile.

"Tell them about your father," Roland urged her.

"Don't tell me you, too, had a terrible father," Victorine said.

"No." Billie reached again for her wine. "He taught me and my brother, and he was very thorough. You can never win an argument with someone determined to make a fool of you, he used to say. So there's no point in participating."

James laughed. "I see. It's not the theology that's the problem."

"No." The conversation only increased Billie's unease.

"You're much smarter than I am." Victorine smiled thinly. She raised her glass. "Here's to those who know when to hold their tongue."

James raised his glass. "Would that more of us had the wisdom."

They drank to it, but Billie felt the tension in the toast, and the undercurrent of anger and resentment, and wished to be downstairs with her anemones, and wondered how and why Roland had aligned himself with these people. But of course she already knew the answer to that. The Empedocles Society. Ambition.

Victorine asked, "Are we continuing, then, even with such an inexperienced assistant engineer—what was his name?"

"Matías," Billie said.

"The captain says that he's been watching and attending the engineer, and feels the man is capable of taking over," James said.

"Then we should be able to make all my collecting stops," Billie noted.

"I am sorry about that." Though James didn't look the least bit sorry.

"That wasn't our agreement."

"Billie," Roland warned quietly.

"No, it wasn't. But I must ask you, Billie—would you prefer to be wrecked on some desolate shore in this vast Mexican wilderness instead? Because that remains our other option, given the inexperience of our assistant engineer," James said.

"Who you just said the captain believed was capable of taking over," Oliver pointed out.

"Capable is as capable does. Let's see a raise of hands: Who likes the thought of being capsized while trying to navigate some harbor so Billie can procure sandworms? Quickly now? Ah, I thought not. You see, Billie? You lose this round, I'm afraid." James drained his glass and poured another.

"Then maybe we should turn around," Victorine said.

She seemed nervous, Billie thought. Ill at ease.

James looked at her in surprise. "What?"

"You heard me. Turn around. The trip is beginning to feel ill-omened, wouldn't you say?"

"I agree with Vic," Oliver said.

"We're continuing on. Rogers agrees."

"The captain will do what you say because you pay him," Oliver said. "Please think about this, James. Most of the crew has no experience in the Gulf. I'm worried about our safety. The San Diego Zoo hardly requires us to risk our lives for an exhibit, and you are chasing rainbows."

Billie said, "Now wait—"

"You always were the prudish sort," James said to Oliver, ignoring Billie.

Oliver frowned. "Prudish? What are you talking about?"

"In school you were never willing to take a risk. Always running from anything remotely dangerous—"

"I played on the football team!"

"I remember you were always on the bench because of some injury or other—"

"That was the coach's decision, not mine." Oliver's face flushed.

Billie squirmed.

"Please, James," Victorine said in a soothing voice.

"I am *not* stopping this expedition because you and Oliver are being namby-pambies," James practically shouted at his wife. He began to cough and clutched at his wine, managing to swallow some and contain the fit. "We are not turning around."

Billie felt relief touched with dismay. She needed whatever specimens she could get. Without her research all she had was an ignominious return to the zoo. If all she had was three collection stations and the dredging, she would make it work, even if the thought of continuing with these tensions exhausted her.

"There is a great deal we can achieve on this trip," Roland remarked in the silence that followed James's fiat. "It would be a shame to stop out of an overabundance of caution. The captain thinks we're fine."

The fish, Billie knew. *It's all about the* antorcha del mar.

"Of course you would say that," Oliver snapped. "You've a 'great deal' to gain as well, haven't you? What do you care about the danger to the rest of us as long as you manipulate James into getting you what you want—and what is that exactly? Fame? Your rich patrons hungering for your services? You and your *colleague*"—here, Oliver flashed an accusatory glare at Billie—"defrauding the Holloways? Thankfully I'm here to keep that from happening."

"I have a feeling you have plenty to gain yourself," Roland said lightly, fingering the stem of his glass. "Why are you here, Stanton? Is it really to help James, as you say? Maybe to help him into an institution under your control?"

"How dare you!" Oliver half stood.

James jerked on his arm. "Sit down, you idiot." The action turned into a great cough.

Abruptly Billie felt a pressure in the air that had nothing to do with the storm that had passed or the gloom of the engineer's death. Roland's words about the darkness of the sea and something pulling Ángel from his grasp came into her head as if they'd been forcibly shoved there. She felt a chill, though her skin was sticky and too warm; she felt almost sick with the wine and the stress of the day.

The lights flickered and went out.

Chapter Fourteen

The ship echoed eerily with the crew's disembodied voices in the engine and generator rooms, and the creaking of the directionless ship. The anchor went down; the clanking rumble of the giant chain echoed, too, yet all of it felt weirdly silent without the hum of the generators or the thrum of the engines. Every voice sounded too loud. The air was hot and stifling, the darkness profound. Billie made her way down the stairs from the dining saloon. The narrow companionway felt narrower—and darker—than ever as she went to her stateroom, placing her hands on opposite walls to guide her.

When she opened the door, a soft light greeted her—candlelight. Bent over the candle on the dressing table was Maud.

"What are you doing in here?" Billie asked. "Why are you in my room?"

"Preparing it for the night," Maud said calmly.

Did she usually do that? Billie didn't know. She tried to think of what Maud must do to prepare a room for sleeping—change the towels? Was there usually some difference in the room each evening?—but she could think of nothing she'd noticed. Still, she could not definitely say there wasn't, and the evening had been tense, and the darkness of the *Eurybia* was unsettling.

"Well. Thank you for the candle."

"You're welcome."

"What's that smell?" It was woody, earthy, not unpleasant, but Billie could not put a finger on it.

Maud pointed to a small salver beside the candle that Billie had never seen before, where a thin tendril of smoke curled upward. "Incense. The room smelled musty. I thought this might help."

"Oh. I see. What's in it?"

"I'm not sure. My *abuela*'s mix. Perfumes, cedar bark—"

"Cedar?" That explained Emile's cologne that Victorine kept smelling. "Have you burned it in other places than here?"

Maud nodded. "My own room. But here needs it much more." Her eyes seemed very dark, her expression very serious. She turned to go.

Billie stopped her with "The other day, you asked me if I was 'part of it.' Do you remember?"

Maud turned back to her. "Yes."

"What was the 'it' you thought I was part of?"

Maud looked as if she didn't want to answer.

"Please," Billie said.

"The Empedocles Society," Maud said softly.

The words surprised Billie even as she'd expected them. "How do you know about that? Are you . . . do you . . . ?"

Maud laughed, short and bitter. "My brother."

"Oh. Oh, I see." But Billie didn't see, not really, because as far as she knew, the Society was for rich men, and Maud was a maid, her brothers fishermen. The dissonance so jounced that in the space of Billie's inability to absorb it, Maud whispered, "Good night, miss," and disappeared into the darkness beyond.

Once Maud was gone, the dim light from the candle seemed not enough to hold off the dark of the room, which seemed to press more here than in the hallway, where it had been deeper. Billie no longer heard the sounds of the crew; even the ship's creaking didn't reach her.

She rolled her shoulders to rid herself of tension. Then she took the candle into the head to wash at the sink. But when she turned on the tap, nothing came out. The saltwater tap was only a little better. A trickle of water to stain the basin, very rusty looking—or no, red. Red water from the faucet, pooling now in the basin. Billie cupped her hand beneath it, collecting it in her palm. Water full of *ciliate infusoria*. The ship had passed out of the patch of red, but maybe they had hit another one. Yes, they must have. It was strangely reassuring to see something that made sense, though she didn't know if the pumps brought water directly from the sea into the pipes, or how any of the plumbing in the ship worked, and she supposed anyone else might find red water coming from the tap creepy, especially because the darkness beyond the candlelight seemed to be gathering in intensity—that couldn't be. It wasn't possible. But it felt . . . threatening.

Billie opened her fingers and let the water fall, turned off the tap, wiped her hand on the towel, and grabbed the candle. She was tired; the day had been long, and she'd never been prone to such flights of fancy. She hurried back into the bedroom, unable to keep from glancing over her shoulder to make sure the darkness didn't follow her, but of course it did. It was all around her. It was darkness, and the candle was her only light, and it pooled around her and cast her in shadow.

She undressed quickly. As she pulled on her nightgown, she heard a clanging sound, like a wrench on a pipe. Clang clang clang. Rhythmic, not loud. As if it were right overhead. Then the sound of water running. Billie frowned and tried to see into the darkness of the bathroom. It was coming from there, she was almost sure of it, but she'd shut off the tap; she was sure of that too. Still . . . steadily running water.

Her heart pounded in her ears. The clanging abruptly stopped. Ridiculous. She took up the candle again and went into the head. Water poured into the bathtub from its freshwater tap, which she hadn't touched. She hadn't touched it since the day before, when she'd bathed. It hadn't been running moments ago, but now water cascaded into the tub. Billie wrenched the tap, turning it off. When she had, the saltwater tap came on, pouring a stream of red water. With a curse, she turned that one off too.

She felt a breath on the back of her neck, stirring her hair. Cold. Icy cold. The candle flame flickered violently.

Something—someone—was behind her; she felt it. But she heard nothing. No movement, no breathing. She only felt the presence. She only felt the breathing.

Billie rushed from the bathroom. She shut its door firmly behind her and then remembered she'd left the candle there, and she had to go back for it, and now there was nothing, nothing odd about the room at all, all the taps silent, no breath, no cold, nothing strange about the darkness. The smell of the incense, of cedar, filled her nostrils, suffocating. She smashed it out and thought of Roland down the hall, warm and tempting. Reassuring.

Firmly, she put him from her mind. He was a disaster waiting to happen.

You've let Victorine's nonsense unsettle you, she told herself. *It's nothing. You know it's nothing.* It was only the lack of light, the talk of monsters and stories. Maud's reference to the Society. Being a scientist didn't mean one didn't pay attention to things that went bump in the night. There was an explanation for everything, and she would find it.

In the morning, when there was light.

Billie crawled beneath the covers and then pulled them over her head as if she were eight years old again, and hiding from the boogeyman under the bed.

Billie woke to a sudden sound, the flash of light. The generators had started up again. The light easing past the curtain at the porthole said it was very early morning. Once she was awake, she couldn't get back to sleep, so she got up and dressed. Her room felt stuffy and close, with the lingering heavy scent of incense, and she wanted to be out in the fresh air. She wanted to put last night behind her.

There was no one up top. The decks and the chairs were slick with dew, and wispy trails of fog clung to the water. They had anchored near a long, low rock covered with the fat brown bodies of sleeping seals. The morning was too quiet, the sea calm and still. It was hard to imagine the wind of yesterday, or that a man who'd been alive at this same time yesterday morning now lay in the depths of this sea. *"It was like something had pulled him."* She'd believed Roland when he'd said it felt different from a current, and the blackness of the water . . . the blackness of her room . . . that solidity . . . that cold . . .

Too many odd things. Just as she had the thought, she saw a group of ships heading toward them, sailing ships, their masts forming ladders into the sky, the sun playing off their sails in the oddest way . . . and in an instant a flock of pelicans took their place. A mirage, unsettling. This place lent itself to a strangeness that made her uncomfortable. Give her straight lines, logical results, things she could prove, that stayed in one place.

She heard a slip of sound and looked down to see a porpoise skimming through the water, and then another. Two of them playing beside the boat, and then a third, beautiful, dodging each other as if they were in a game of tag, the water streaming from their slick bodies in ripples. Billie was caught by them, by the Gulf's unpredictability, its quick-change moods, from mirage to storm to stunning beauty, from unsettling strangeness to playfulness. Was she haunted or bedazzled? She hardly knew. She felt mystified mostly, undone and awestruck. Maybe this was what the crew meant when they talked about the Gulf.

She was so consumed by her thoughts that it took a moment before she noticed that a member of the crew had come to the rail.

Tomás, the oiler, who had given her that warning in the forward hold, who had told her to be careful, that monsters weren't only in the sea.

He nodded to her and then looked down at the porpoises. In Spanish, he said, "Beautiful, eh?"

"They are," she agreed.

"Will you want one for your studies?"

She did, but it was hard to look at them now, so joyful, and think of killing one, and there was something in his voice that told her that he didn't want her to, and the day was so young yet, so pretty and peaceful.

He said, "They cry like babies when they are hurt. It is bad luck to kill them."

His words took her aback. "Oh. I . . ."

"None of us will help you do it. There is too much bad luck on this ship already."

Billie didn't know what to say. Finally, she settled for "Why do you say that? You mean the engineer's death? The winds came up so quickly."

"They sometimes do in this place. Not just that. Many of the men think the ship is cursed. Haunted by an unsettled spirit."

She didn't want to ask if they knew about Emile Coustan. If they didn't, her question would only make things worse. "Have you seen evidence of that?" she asked, ignoring for the moment the things she'd experienced. "What proof do you have?"

Tomás held her gaze. "Do you not feel it? Strange things happen in that room where you stay. I have felt it myself. No one likes that you stay there. A man took his life in that room."

So they did know. "What kind of strange things?"

He shrugged. "Water turning off and on. Red water. Whispers."

Billie's own uneasiness pricked. "The red water comes from the salt taps. From the sea."

"Yes, but it does not always come when we are in the blood water. It comes when it is called."

The tone of his voice sent goose bumps over Billie's skin. "Called by what?"

Tomás stared down at the porpoises. "The sea itself has a spirit. You know this, yes, as one who searches its secrets?"

Billie considered that. Certainly the sea had its moods, and yes, it kept its own secrets, ones she had spent a lifetime trying to unravel and understand. She had never thought of it as a spirit, exactly, but his words described the vast collective of it as well as anything. "I guess that is true."

"Sometimes it is best to let secrets be."

"Do you think so? I disagree. There is so much to learn, Tomás. The sea is full of knowledge. I believe it holds so much that can help the world."

"What if what it holds harms instead?" he asked. "What if there are some things that should be left alone?"

She turned to him. "You mean the torch of the sea. It cannot be real, can it? Nothing like that exists. How can it exist?"

Tomás's mouth tightened. He took a moment before he said, "This part of the Gulf is mysterious and dangerous. You can choose to believe or not, but not believing does not make things less true. Legends come from somewhere, yes?"

James had made the same argument. So had Roland.

"Is there a reason for the natives to be harvesting shark livers? Hammerhead shark livers?"

Tomás paled. "Who told you this?"

"No one. I saw them myself. A pile of sharks without livers on the beach at the Cape."

He glanced away. "That is a warning."

"A warning of what?"

He hesitated. "I can tell you this: If you continue on this quest, the crew will have their say."

"You mean . . . a mutiny?"

Captain Rogers came out of the pilothouse and shouted an order at Tomás before the oiler had a chance to answer her. The man hurried away with only a grim glance.

"Good morning, Miss McKennan!" the captain said as he came down the stairs. "A beautiful day, isn't it?"

It was, but Billie was too preoccupied to answer, and when James and Roland and Oliver came together on deck, clad in their short athletic pants, ready for morning exercises, it was all she could do to greet them. Her mind spun with Tomás's words. She couldn't dismiss them.

James went to start the phonograph. Roland caught sight of her and came over.

"Couldn't resist taking a peek at our exercise, could you?" he teased.

She glanced at him, too distracted to take in his state of undress.

He frowned. "What is it? What are you doing up here so early?"

"I woke with the generators," she said.

He glanced over the side. "Porpoises! James, look! Porpoises!"

Oliver hurried over. "My God, how splendid. James, where are the rifles?"

Billie looked at him in confusion. "Rifles?"

James called out, "In the saloon!"

Oliver ran to the saloon in the deckhouse. The phonograph started, and the record announced: "We'll start with push-ups. Everyone down for a count of twenty. Ready? And . . . one . . . and two . . ."

James ignored the record's instructions and rushed to the rail. He peered over at the porpoises. "What fun!"

Billie looked at Roland and said, "I don't think—"

"Don't you want a specimen?" he asked.

There were more of the *Phocoena* now, dozens of them, jockeying each other beside the ship, glorious in the morning sun. She thought of what Tomás had said about them crying when they were hurt. "Oh, maybe later. I . . ." She trailed off when Oliver returned with the guns.

He handed one to James and another to Roland, who offered it to Billie. She shook her head, and he gave her a questioning glance, but he didn't take it up either.

The other two began to shoot, aiming at the animals in the water. The pops of gunfire, the pings of the bullets hitting the water, Oliver and James laughing.

"Almost got that one!"

"Ah! Close! Just missed!"

Roland didn't play; instead he watched her with a puzzled expression.

James whooped, "Got it!" and Billie heard a cry, a humanlike scream, and she looked over the rail to see one of the porpoises trailing blood.

A cry like a baby's. Just as Tomás had said.

James gestured to one of the crew polishing brass. "Hey, you—yes, you, man, grab the hook, will you? Help us get this thing aboard!"

The man froze, one hand poised on the rail.

"Well, come on now. Hurry! Before it gets away. It's wounded!"

Wounded, not dead. Billie watched with her heart in her throat as the rest of the pod circled it, easing it away from the ship. Protecting it. They were protecting it. She looked at Roland, who was watching, just as she was.

"What's wrong with you?" James nearly screamed at the deckhand. "Get the damned hook!"

"He won't help you," she said. "They think it's bad luck to hurt them."

"Bad luck?" James stared at her in obvious exasperation. "For God's sake, everything is bad luck to them!"

"Never seen such a superstitious bunch," Oliver said darkly.

"I don't know," Billie said quietly. "Maybe they're right. Listen to it."

She felt Roland's stare like heat, and knew she had confused him further. But now the ship was pulling away, the porpoises herding their wounded member, too far now to catch, the trail of blood dispersing into the vastness of the sea.

James put his rifle down. "I think I'll have a word with the captain."

"You need to be careful, James," Billie told him. "The crew doesn't want to be here as it is."

James ignored her. Roland said, "How do you know that?"

"I talk to them, Rolly," she said.

"Have you asked them about the shark livers?" he asked.

Her discomfort over Tomás's words flooded back. She turned to him. "Yes. This morning."

"And?"

"Tomás was frightened when I mentioned it. And, Rolly, when I asked him what it meant, he said it was a warning."

Roland's entire body seemed to go electric with excitement. "A warning of what? Did he say?"

She shook her head.

"Let's get the dredging nets out." He started toward the forward deck, where all the equipment waited. It was hard to doubt the existence of the *antorcha del mar* in the face of such excitement, or in the face of Tomás's obvious fear. *El monstruo.* Billie hurried after.

Chapter Fifteen

Dredging brought up mostly jellyfish and shrimp, larval fish and sea worms, but of course no *antorcha del mar*, not even a hint of it. They arrived at Billie's next promised collecting station the following day. Espiritu Santo Island was long, volcanic, many peaked, and rising from blue water so clear that it was easy to see schools of fish swimming in its depths. Manta rays cruised everywhere, the tips of their wings piercing the surface—impossibly wide between, impossibly huge. Eighteen, twenty, twenty-five feet across. When the *Eurybia* approached, the creatures sped away. They were so fast, Billie marveled at them.

So did James. When one of the rays leaped from the water to expose its white belly, seeming to fly several feet as its whiplike tail spun water out behind it, he cried, "I want one. I must have one. We have harpoons on board, don't we?"

"Let's just try to shoot one first," Oliver said excitedly.

"They're too fast."

"Look at how they hover," Oliver disagreed. "One clear shot is all I need."

The animals were magnificent, and Billie saw the glances exchanged by the crew when James asked for a harpoon, and she knew they felt about the rays the same way they'd felt about the porpoises.

"Not today," she said gently. "I need to get some collecting done before I spend time dissecting a manta ray."

"You won't be dissecting the one I get." James looked affronted. "I'll want it stuffed."

Once they were on the island, Billie put the manta rays out of her mind. The water was warm, but she didn't dare take off her rubber boots. These waters were full of dangerous things. The sea urchins had sharp and poisonous spines, anemones stung, crabs aggressively attacked, and one might encounter an eel with its clutching pharyngeal jaws and infective slime, sea snakes, and who knew what else. Her fingers already bore numerous cuts and slices from the barnacles on Cerralvo Island. But it was exciting, and it made up for the weirdness of everything else. She loved the feel of the sun reflecting off the water into her face, and the burn on the back of her neck where her hat did not reach, and the surprise when she turned over a boulder covered with sand and algae to reveal a hundred little animals beneath, a community of sea creatures.

Such excursions had always been the way for Billie to forget whatever worries might be troubling her; all of it disappeared as she gathered chitons and limpets, the thick, ruffled clams, the green-black sea cucumbers that weren't the same ones she'd found on Cerralvo, but maybe . . . piles of black sea stars that wriggled in knots when she brought them up. She took more than she needed, because these creatures often cast off their parts when she tried to preserve them and it was hard to keep them whole. Snails, flatworms . . . She was away from the others, shin deep in the water among the rocks, and she preferred it that way. Alone, with no one—no Roland especially—to distract her. She could fully concentrate on what she was seeing, on her first perceptions. Observation was the most important of all a scientist's skills. She liked to be slow and methodical. She liked to focus her thoughts.

The sea urchin before her was gorgeous, with needlelike blue-black spines that seemed to waver with the motion of the water. The damn things could sting like the dickens. Billie took her metal prying bar, slid it beneath the urchin, and stepped forward on an algae-covered rock to lever it loose. Just as she did, a shout came from onshore—Oliver, who had come to watch over the crew, pointing to a manta ray that had soared from the water near the *Eurybia* anchored beyond. Billie glanced up. Someone pushed her hard from behind. She lost her footing, crying out as she went down into the water, one hand sliding along barnacles, the other planting hard, completely, irrevocably, into the needle-spined urchin.

Pain was instantaneous, fiery and terrible, unlike anything she'd known. Her hand, her arm felt on fire.

Oliver splashed through the low tide to her. "What is it? What happened? Are you hurt?"

"Yes, I'm hurt!" she snapped. "I'm hurt! Goddamn urchin. Who pushed me?" She grabbed her wrist tight, holding her injured hand, bristling with spines, steady. It didn't help.

He knelt in the water beside her. "Okay. Okay. You'll be fine. Come on, I'll help you to the shore."

"Oh God. Damn damn damn. You have to get the spines out. But . . ." She bit her lip, trying to stem the currents of that burning sting, then lowered her head, rocking back and forth. Her vision blurred with tears. Her hat fell off. She didn't reach for it, didn't care. She thought she saw Oliver grab it.

The sound of faint splashing behind her, growing louder. "What the hell—Billie?"

"I don't know what happened," Oliver said. "I heard her yell, and—"

"Someone pushed me is what happened," Billie snapped.

"Move," Roland said bluntly, taking Oliver's place. "Get me the forceps in the kit on the beach—and the scalpel."

"The scalpel?" Oliver squeaked.

"Hurry. There's vinegar in there too. Bring it."

Oliver splashed away.

Roland pried her fingers from her wrist. She cried softly as he looked at her hand. "What did you do, try to pick it up?"

"Of course not! I *told* you. Someone pushed me."

Roland's brow furrowed. "Pushed you? Who would do that?"

"I don't know. I didn't see. They shoved me from behind."

He glanced about. "But . . ."

"But *what*?"

"No one was near you."

"Someone pushed me, dammit!"

"Okay, okay. Damn. You know you picked a poison one."

She could only nod.

"Come on. Let's get you back to the beach."

"I can't move."

"Yes you can." He put his arm beneath her shoulders and lifted her to her feet. She reached for the bucket with her other hand.

"Leave it," he said gruffly.

"The tide . . ."

"I'll send one of the crew to get it. Come on. We need to get those out of you as soon as possible."

That she didn't argue with. She staggered with him out of the shallow water, onto the beach, where Oliver met them with the items Roland had requested.

"How many are there?" she asked once Roland deposited her on the beach.

He squatted beside her, considering her hand somberly. "Fifteen? Twenty?"

"Oh God, Rolly."

"Don't worry. We'll be in La Paz tomorrow. If things get . . . bad, there's got to be a doctor there."

"What do you mean, if things get bad?" Oliver asked, hovering.

"*Diadema mexicanum*," Billie managed.

"It's poisonous," Roland provided tersely, brandishing the forceps. "Give me the tweezers, too, will you? The spines are barbed. That's why I'll need the scalpel. And the vinegar."

Oliver exhaled. "Shouldn't we take her back to the ship?"

"Why, is there a doctor there?" Roland snapped. "I can do this as well as anyone."

The burn was excruciating and not letting up. Billie ground out, "He knows how."

She closed her eyes when Roland went in. She felt the pressure, the slight twist, the jerk. Billie tried to choke back the scream. Impossible.

Roland's other hand tightened on her wrist. "Shhh, shhh. It's all right. One gone."

Oliver looked around nervously. "Can you keep her quieter? Someone will hear."

"What if they do? Who's around but us and some natives?" Roland asked. "I'm going again. Ready?"

Billie nodded, but she couldn't really be ready. The next one hurt worse—the piercing sting of it stabbed clear into her shoulder. She swallowed the scream on a garbled choke.

"Couldn't get the barb out with that one," Roland said grimly. "You understand me, Billie?"

She did. For every barb he couldn't get out, he'd have to use the scalpel. Vinegar and hot water could help to dissolve what was left of the spine, but the longer it stayed there, the longer the toxin had to do its work. She tried not to think about what that meant. Had anyone died from a sea urchin's poison? It would take more stings than this, wouldn't it? Fifteen spines? Twenty? She tried to remember if she knew of symptoms besides swelling, numbness, blisters, maybe necrosis.

Roland knew. There had been that friend of his long ago, hadn't there? Was she remembering correctly? Or had that been a jellyfish sting? God, she couldn't remember.

"Roland," she said.

"Quiet. I'm going to keep on. As fast as I can. Okay?"

She gulped her question and nodded.

"You want to bite on something?" Oliver asked. "Maybe the rope?"

She might have laughed had her hand not felt like it was ready to burst from its skin. A tight, burning, blistering sausage. Oliver pressed rope into her other hand, and obediently she put it between her teeth. It tasted of salt and sweat; it was gritty with sand, coarse and splintery.

She bit down, but it didn't help much. Two more spines, and the world began to spin through her tears. One more after that, and she wanted to vomit.

Roland said, "I won't think less of you if you . . ."

She didn't hear the rest of it. The horizon shifted, and so did Roland.

Billie was barely conscious on the ride back, and the next thing she knew, she lay on the lounging platform on the *Eurybia*'s aft deck, and Roland was saying, "Don't move her. Is there any aspirin?"

Billie heard Victorine's voice as if it came from far away. "There's a medical kit in the saloon. Maud, will you fetch it?"

"And please, some isopropyl alcohol from the lab? There are several large bottles of it. I only need one. And a bucket of vinegar."

"Give her some gin to numb her a bit," James suggested.

Roland sat beside Billie. She closed her eyes, unable to do anything but focus on the pain of her hand. She heard him fumble with something, and then he eased his arm beneath her neck. Billie muttered a protest.

"Drink this," he told her. "As much as you can, okay? I'm going to have to cut for the barbs, but if you drink enough gin, maybe you won't feel it so much."

She couldn't imagine his cutting would hurt more than the original pain, but obediently Billie drank. If the gin dulled the pain of the scalpel, it couldn't help but dull the pain of the urchin spines. Roland wouldn't let her stop gulping; not until she choked did he take the bottle away, and she heard the concern in his voice when he said, "I don't think that will be enough."

Billie brushed his hand away.

He persisted. "You need to drink more, Billie. Please."

Obediently she did when he held the bottle again to her mouth. More and more, and already the gin did its work; she began to feel languid. She was glad when Roland took the bottle away and eased her down again onto the platform. She heard James say, "My God, look at that one! Ollie! Get the harpoon!"

A manta ray, no doubt, but Billie no longer cared. She heard the ruckus of Oliver and James readying the harpoon. She heard Victorine say, "Must you? It's so majestic." Closer, Billie heard Roland's fumbling. His thigh felt warm and reassuring against her shoulder.

A loud sound—a bang, a rattle—"Got it!" James's crow of triumph. "My God, don't lose it!"

"They've got so much pull," Oliver said. "Those things must weigh—what do you think, Roland?"

"About two tons," Roland said distractedly. Billie felt him take her hand, but it was an out-of-body touch. She felt but did not feel, encased as she was in a drunken warmth. When he pressed the tip of the scalpel carefully into her hand, the pain was there and not there, sharp enough that she jerked, but not of her. Roland tightened his hold on her hand. "Billie?"

She couldn't answer, couldn't rouse herself. When he cut again, and once more, she felt both conscious and not—the drag of the buoy trailing the harpooned ray through the water filled her head, the slap of the line, the splash of the great fish as it tried to evade the pain of the spear . . . those were things she heard. Billie opened her eyes. The world was a great smudge before her, the canopy breathing above—*in and out, in and out*—and Victorine's face a pale smear.

"We're running out of line!" James cried out.

"Don't worry, we'll tire it out," Oliver assured him. "It can't dive with the buoy attached."

Billie saw it in her mind's eye. The ray diving down and down, the buoy bouncing on the water, holding it back, the rope a blur of motion through the blue, the great fish's pain . . .

Roland cut again. Billie heard her own breath ratchet. She felt the pressure now, but not the pain. Growing pressure, harder and harder, deep and deep, and then a *snap!* as if a line had gone taut. The air shivered and broke. James cursed.

Oliver said, "It's too damn heavy for our lines."

Billie shut her eyes.

"What happened?" Victorine asked.

"It got away," James said with a sigh. "They're too big and too strong."

"I guess you should leave it be, then," Victorine said.

"We'll get a thicker rope next time."

"That's it," Roland said. The clanking drop of the scalpel into a tin pan.

Relief swept Billie, but she couldn't have said if it was because he was finished or because the manta ray had escaped.

Victorine's voice, once again, seemed to come from a fog. "Is this with Billie terribly serious, then?"

Roland said, "I hope not. The urchin was a poisonous one, unfortunately. Billie's not usually careless. It was an accident, obviously."

"How long before she can use her hand again?" James asked. "Have you spoken to her yet? We're going to need her help."

Something about those words niggled at Billie, but she couldn't grasp what it was. It loitered in the fog of gin, refusing to cohere, and along with the words came drowsy visions, not quite dreams, swordfish battling one another in the fathomless waters, scores of them—how odd. Swordfish tended to travel alone, and why were they fighting? What were they doing?

"Really, James," Victorine scolded.

"I don't know," Roland said. "We'll see how long it takes the swelling to go down. I think I got all the barbs."

"She looks feverish," Victorine said.

"It may take days. When we stop at La Paz, I'll have her see a doctor. There's a hospital there." Billie felt Roland lift her hand again to submerge it in liquid. She let it float limply. "I had a friend once . . . necrosis . . ."

"We still plan to stop at La Paz to give the crew a day off?" Oliver asked. "What's necrosis?"

"Tissue death." Roland spread his fingers to illustrate. "He lost his hand."

They all went silent.

Billie felt cold as Roland rose. "The vinegar has to be changed out for hot water every half hour or so."

Maud said, "I'll take care of it, sir. I'll ask the cook to heat some water now."

"Hey, look at this—we got some of the manta ray after all. There's a big chunk of it on the end of the harpoon," Oliver said.

Billie heard the sound of something heavy thudding to the deck, the drip of water and rope. The swordfish in her dreams gathered to watch her. The waters were dense and cold and full of whispers. Tomás was right. Secrets of the sea. There was so much here to know—the swordfish were beautiful, but they were chilling too; there was nothing benign about them. They were almost . . . threatening.

James whooped. "Aldo! Have the cook fry that up. We'll have a feast tonight. Look at that. It's a chunk, but I'll bet it's hardly a flesh wound on that thing."

Billie wanted to see. It was too hard to open her eyes, and the dream called her. It made her listen, it made her watch. The biggest swordfish, huge and strong, gathered its strength, aiming for the *Eurybia*. She tried in her dream to warn it. *Don't do it! We'll only cut you apart and eat you!* But it was coming anyway. *It is coming.*

"Wh—what's coming?" Victorine's voice in her dream, quiet, in Billie's ear. "Billie, what's coming? What?"

How funny that Victorine should ask. It was as if her words banished the dream. There was nothing now in the ocean but blackness. The same dark Roland had told her about when he'd lost Ángel. A penetrating black daring Billie to enter it, to press on.

She fell deeper into her dreams.

Chapter Sixteen

Billie's sleep whirled with murmurs. *Un barco fantasma.* A ghost ship. Haunted. All around it the waters of the Gulf tossed and twisted it about, and those waters tried to get in; they swirled and crashed against the ship's sides; they threatened. *Leave this place. You're not wanted here. Go.* The words were a buzz in her head, a constant throb in her hand and a terrible thirst that finally forced Billie awake.

She opened her eyes to see Maud asleep at the dressing table, her head buried in her arms. Billie got out of bed on shaky legs and went to the head quietly, trying not to wake the maid. But she was awkward with her bandaged hand stinking of vinegar, and lightheaded. Billie turned on the freshwater tap, fumbled with a glass on the shelf above the sink, and gulped down two full cups of water before she was satiated, and there was Maud waiting for her when she came out.

"Miss McKennan! You shouldn't be out of bed!"

"I shouldn't be in bed," Billie answered, grabbing on to the doorframe with her good hand for purchase. "I'm fine. My hand hurts like the devil, that's all."

"But your fever—"

"Gone." Billie touched her forehead. "But I could use some aspirin."

The maid reached into a dresser drawer and pulled out a tin. "Mr. Ely left these for you."

"Roland was here?"

"He seemed very worried."

"Did he?" Billie took the tablets the girl gave her and went back into the head to swallow them with water. She didn't want to think about Roland's worry, or his care in taking out the sea urchin spines, a hazy memory now, but there.

"He wanted to put you in his room so he could watch you, but Mrs. Holloway wouldn't have it. She said it was too scandalous. He made me stay here to look after you instead."

Billie felt the way Maud watched her, as if she hoped Billie would reveal some secret about why Roland could possibly have felt it was fine to keep a single woman in his stateroom, but Billie was busy cursing him in her head, and she was in no mood to reward his indiscretion.

"Well, thank goodness for that." She looked down at her wrapped hand. "Did you do this?"

Maud nodded.

"Thank you."

"You've been asleep for a day."

"A day?" Billie was dismayed by the thought. "Have you been here the entire time?"

"Yes, but it's better than my room. It's noisy in the crew quarters."

"Ah." Billie had not thought to imagine Maud's situation before now. "You're the only woman among them, aren't you?"

Maud nodded and tapped her thigh, and Billie remembered the knife she kept there. "I have brothers. I know how to keep safe. I lock my door, and I put a chair against it that I stole from storage. No one can get in."

Brothers. It brought back a memory of Maud saying she had a brother who belonged to the Empedocles Society. Billie tried to rally the thought but, as before, couldn't make it make sense, and her headache made it worse, so she didn't try.

"Good. You'll let me know if you need help? If you need more protection? From anyone. Anyone at all."

Maud's eyes widened. Billie realized the young woman had not expected the offer.

"Matías said he would help you too. Remember."

"Matías is a man." Maud spoke with such disdain Billie couldn't help a laugh.

"Ask him for help anyway. He seems a good one."

"I—I burned incense for you too." Maud offered the information eagerly, as if the fact of keeping Billie's stateroom from stuffiness was of utmost importance.

Billie said, "Thank you," though honestly she wished Maud would stop, because the incense only made the tiny room feel closer and her headache worse, but the maid seemed so pleased that Billie didn't want to scold.

It was impossible for her to dress with her injured hand, and so she was thankful for Maud. She wasn't hungry either; the thought of food made her slightly ill, but Maud insisted on toast, and Billie was glad for that, too, when it eased some of her unsteadiness, though not all of it.

As she went up to the aft deck where the others already were, she heard the drone of James's voice as he read from the *Eurybia News*. The late-morning sun slanted beneath the canopy, and the rocky bluffs of the passing landscape looked stark and somewhat ominous, though Billie wasn't sure why she felt that way when she'd thought them gorgeous before. When the others saw her approach, James left off reading, and their expressions took on all shades and degrees of alarm. Seeing Roland there brought its own special nervousness, especially when he leaped to his feet and strode quickly toward her.

"What are you doing? Why are you out of bed?"

"I'm fine, as you can see. Thanks to your stellar care. And Maud's." She held out her bandaged hand for him to see.

Before she could stop him, he laid his hand against her forehead.

"No fever," she said, backing away. "I do have a headache."

"Your hand?" he asked.

"Hurts like the dickens. It's almost nauseating, in fact."

"You should sit down. Did you get something to eat?"

"You don't have to play nursemaid. Maud did that quite well already."

Something like satisfaction passed over his face.

Billie sighed. "You know I've been taking care of myself very well these past years."

"You're working as an assistant zookeeper."

"Well." She gave him a look, and he had the grace to look ashamed. She walked over to the others and sat, forestalling their questions by saying, "I'm fine except for my hand, which hurts a great deal. I doubt I'll be any good for a few days unless I can learn to do things with my toes. What have I missed?"

James shook out the paper he held. "I've been reading to everyone about the Scopes trial."

"Well, how appropriate. It seems we're all in the midst of an evolution craze."

"Everyone is certainly talking about it. I tried to get Oliver to go with me to the evolution debate in San Francisco, but he refused. Roland went instead," James said.

"I was going anyway," Roland said. "Fascinating."

"Why is it so fascinating?" Billie asked him. "You know the theory is proved as well as I. What needs to be debated about it?"

James glanced down at the *Eurybia News*. "In Tennessee, apparently a great deal. The judge allowed the scientists' testimony to be read, not in front of the jury, but as evidence for an appeal. Darrow put Bryan on the stand."

The infamous Clarence Darrow was the lawyer for Scopes's defense, and the equally famous Williams Jennings Bryan was the attorney for the prosecution. Two brilliant men, both blowhards in their own way, though Billie was surprised that Darrow gave Bryan more time to speak about the evils of teaching evolution in the schools. "Why?"

"To serve as an authority on the Bible, since they want it to be taught instead. So Darrow wants Bryan to establish the truth of it." James smiled.

"Darrow's made a fool of him, as you can imagine," Oliver said. "Asking him if he thinks God actually created the universe in seven days, in spite of the fact that geologists have proved the earth is millions of years old."

"What did Bryan say?" Billie asked.

"That the length of a day then might not have been what modern people think it," Victorine said idly. She put her hand to her eyes to shield them from the sun. "Of course, he's not wrong. God was busy *creating* things. If the orbit of the earth hadn't been established yet, then . . . well . . . a day could be anything."

Billie remembered her own questions as a child, her questioning of the Bible—the same question, as a matter of fact, her mother's answer the same as Bryan's. *"No one ever said how long a day was."* She'd accepted it then, but found it facile now.

James said, "By making Bryan admit that the Bible isn't literal, Darrow's damaged his argument that it's fact—that it can be used to teach creation. If it's not the absolute truth, and evolution, as you say, has been proved, then they would be teaching religion, not science. What do you think, Billie? Oliver believes whatever he needs to believe—"

"Excuse me!" Oliver protested.

"—and spiritualists believe that spirits evolve in spectral spheres. Isn't that right, darling?"

Victorine smiled. "That's the easy way to say it."

Billie's hand throbbed. She closed her eyes.

James probed. "Does God play a part in evolution? Or is evolution your religion, as Mr. Bryan complains is the fault of all scientists?"

Billie opened her eyes to find them all looking at her—except Roland, who was staring down at his hands. "Why don't you ask Roland what he thinks?"

Roland glanced up at her. "You know what I think. *Science* is only another word for *discovery*. Who knows what we'll learn next? Maybe something to prove the existence of God. And anyway, the Scopes trial is about law, not about truth. Bad law, maybe, but there are a lot of bad laws."

It was on the tip of Billie's tongue to say that for Roland, laws were things to be pushed out of the way when he found them troublesome, much like ethics, but that would be mean, and about this Tennessee law she didn't disagree, and more to the point, lately she'd been questioning some of the things she'd always believed about Roland, and so she remained silent.

"I'm not interested in Roland's thoughts. I'm interested in yours," James said to her.

"I believe that facts matter. There doesn't have to be a conflict between science and religion, because religion isn't based on facts, is it? But I suppose people need belief, and the two things can certainly coexist. It's forcing them together that causes a problem."

"Ah! You've quoted Clarence Darrow almost exactly!"

"Have I."

"Belief matters too," Victorine said quietly. "You have to admit it does. It's the reason we didn't stop at La Paz. Because the crew believes in something we can't fight."

"What do you mean, we didn't stop at La Paz?" Billie asked.

The others exchanged glances. Roland said, "We bypassed it."

"Oh? Why?"

Victorine leaned forward. "Do you remember any of your dreams, Billie, when you were delirious?"

"No." Billie didn't want to think of her dreams; the thought of them made her faintly sick. "Why did we bypass La Paz?"

"The crew was feeling mutinous," Oliver said darkly.

Roland explained, "Maud and Pollan overheard them talking about abandoning ship there. They view your incident as one more in a string of bad luck. After the swordfish, and losing the engineer, their superstitions got the best of them. James and the captain felt it best not to stop."

"We were afraid they'd go into town and not come back," James said darkly. "Better not to give them the chance."

Billie remembered Tomás's warning about the crew. She had not expected that she would be part of the problem, and yet there was something else to it, wasn't there? Something she tried to remember. Victorine was staring at her intently, and Billie remembered her sense that she'd been pushed into that sea urchin, though Roland had claimed there was no one around, and she'd seen no one, hadn't she? But it had felt so real, so hard, so *corporeal.* There had been a push. And her dreams . . . The ship was haunted . . . The swordfish and the sea itself wished them to leave . . . *You're not wanted here.*

Disquiet returned with force. Then the name of the island struck her. Espiritu. Espiritu Santo. Holy Spirit Island. "Did the crew say anything about Espiritu Santo? About my accident happening on that island? I mean, were there stories before about strange things happening there?"

"Are you talking about being pushed again?" Roland asked. "I told you, no one was around."

"You were out there alone. Maybe a wave . . ." Oliver speculated.

"The water was still," Billie said.

"Maybe it's the spirit I called the other night," Victorine suggested. "Are you feeling haunted, Billie?"

"Maud's been lighting incense in your room," Roland said to Billie. "I'm surprised you haven't stopped her. I never thought you liked it. The smoke."

"She thinks the room is musty," Billie said.

"Is that what she told you? She told me it was because the room was haunted."

His words sent a shiver down Billie's spine. She thought of the taps coming on by themselves, the presence she'd felt there. "She told you that? You believe her?"

"She said the sailors believe it too." Roland's gaze didn't leave hers. "I didn't think it hurt to let her do what she thought helped."

"The question is, do you believe her, Billie?" Victorine asked quietly. "Is the room haunted?"

Now Billie remembered what else Tomás had said about her stateroom, about an unsettled spirit being there. Emile's spirit.

Still . . . Billie shook her discomfort away. "How would I know?"

James coughed and reached for a cigarette. "Spirits aren't subtle."

"I've felt strange things in that room myself," Victorine said. "I went in there when you were on the island."

"You went into my room without my permission?"

"I wanted to see for myself if I felt anything." Victorine seemed completely unperturbed by the invasion of privacy. "Have you felt the presence there? Have you seen the ring of blood around the bathtub drain?"

"The . . ." Billie was speechless. "That's only a stain from the salt tap. When we go through the red water. I'm sorry I haven't had a chance to clean it . . ." The salt tap that turned on by itself. Tomás had said the red water came even when they weren't in it. "*It comes when it is called,*" he'd said.

"It won't come off," Victorine said bluntly. "I tried. You don't have to be frightened, Billie. Most spirits are benign. They *want* to communicate. Don't be afraid to share what you've seen. Or felt."

Billie swept them with her gaze. All of them—even Roland—watched her carefully. She didn't know what to say, because the truth was . . . what was the truth? How to explain, and what did Victorine mean, she'd felt the presence in her room? Billie tried to determine if Victorine's admission was a comfort or not. The woman's stare pierced her; Billie felt uneasy beneath it.

A gull cawed loudly in the sky above, breaking the silence, and Roland laughed shortly and said, "One can think anything possible out here. When even the land plays tricks on you, it's easy to believe in ghosts. You can hardly blame the crew for it."

James lit his cigarette and blew chemical-scented smoke into the air.

Oliver said, "I'm just wondering . . . with the engineer gone and the sailors discontent . . . even when Billie's healed, we can't risk stopping to collect her specimens. How long do we go on with this expedition if we can't do what we've come to do? Why not turn around?"

Billie felt a surge of anger at his casual dismissal of her project.

James said quickly, "Roland can collect for Billie until she's better. Her collection isn't the only reason we're here, remember. There's no reason we can't dredge, is there?"

Roland smiled easily and said, "No reason at all."

Oliver's eyes narrowed. "Really, James, it all seems a bit much. We've been beset on all sides. Why not just admit that this trip is a failure and go home?"

Billie watched with interest as James simply regarded his friend benignly and dragged on his cigarette. "Why, Ollie, we haven't come close to failure. We've only just begun. I promised Billie her collection, and she will have it. And more. What do you think, Billie? Do we have enough specimens to give San Diego a decent marine exhibition?" He looked at her and smiled.

The smile rolled over her uncomfortably. Before Billie could determine why it bothered her, Roland jumped in with "San Diego will have a marine exhibit to rival Vanderbilt's by the time we're done."

Now Billie remembered something, a vague, blurry something, words through a dream of pain. *"How long before she can use her hand?"* James's voice? It jarred unnervingly in a not-quite memory. *"We're going to need her . . ."*

Billie shifted her hand to relieve some of the burning pain. Victorine's gaze had not left her, and now she felt Oliver's, speculating, calculating. Icy cold traipsed down Billie's spine, along with the sense of portent she'd felt under the influence of gin. Something or someone had pushed her on Espiritu Santo. Some presence was in her room. Maud was lighting incense to keep away ghosts, and even Roland wasn't pooh-poohing the twin notions of bad luck and spirits, at least not completely. And she could not get rid of the niggling voice that had crept into her head and stayed there. *You're not wanted here.*

Chapter Seventeen

That night, Billie, needing the reassurance of the real, had the gangway put down. She sat on the edge of the step with a cluster of electric lights turned onto the water and waited. What came first were the heteronereis, the wormlike creatures, and free-swimming crustacea, a swarm of larval fish and crabs. She watched for a while, doing nothing, marveling, as she always did, at the quantity of life. The ship was at anchor, rocking gently in the current, but when she stirred the water with the edge of her long-handled net, there was the bioluminescence, too, that light from seemingly nowhere, a miracle light. Real life, not a ghost, though it might seem like it, so surreal, so unknowable to anyone who didn't know how to truly look. A mystery, but as Roland always said, only a mystery until you solved it.

Were ghosts the same, she wondered? Only a mystery until they were solved? What about voices in one's head? A call to leave, to go from this place, a warning that felt uncomfortably real?

A ribbonfish—transparent, gelatin-like—swam into the light. A squid darted after it, tentacles convulsing, the squid changing color as it trapped the fish, tangling it, drawing it in before the fish knew it was caught. Devoured. Gone in a moment, and so was the squid, propelling itself backward again, out of the light, gently now, like a balloon.

"Mr. Ely sent me to see to you."

Maud's voice startled her so that Billie nearly dropped the net. She looked over her shoulder to see the maid standing on the deck above. "Oh. Hello."

"What are you doing?"

"Collecting."

Silence. Then, "It's night."

"There are creatures in the ocean all the time, not just during the day."

"Yes, but . . ."

"Come see." Billie moved over on the narrow step and motioned for Maud to join her. She felt the maid's hesitation, and said, "You'll be perfectly safe. Nothing's going to jump up."

"They didn't tell you about the black demon?"

"What's that?"

"A shark as big as this boat."

"Well, I haven't seen him. Only some squid. Come look."

Maud scrambled through the gate and ventured down. Her feet came to rest on the step beside Billie, but she sat on the step above. Close enough.

"Look." Billie reached to focus the light better on the sea below.

"Mr. Ely showed me the . . . um . . . light from the plankton?"

"Bioluminescence."

"Yes, that. The other night. He said there were thousands of them."

"Millions. They're in every inch of the sea." Billie returned to looking as another squid propelled itself into view, and another one. "Mr. Ely said you lost two brothers to the sea."

Maud made a sound of assent.

"I'm sorry."

A small, sad laugh. "They knew the risks. Da says the sea is a cruel mistress."

"Maybe. But it's a fascinating one."

"I don't trust it. My other brother says this trip is a folly."

Holloway's Folly. Billie sighed. "Is this the brother with the Empedocles Society?"

"He wasn't *with* them. He only served the club. He was a waiter."

That explained the dissonance Billie had felt. "What did he tell you about it?"

"Nothing much. He was sworn to secrecy. But he said they did things like talk to spirits and study old books, and there was a room in back filled with jars of strange creatures. They had a two-headed calf. It was stuffed."

Billie had heard those rumors too. The reminders wearied her tonight. But now she understood Maud's position better, her vulnerability. A brother in service, a family in debt to Holloway—it only made Billie feel more protective of the young woman.

"What's that?" Maud asked, pointing to the water.

"A squid. See the way it moves? It squeezes water in and out. That's how it swims."

"It's changing color!"

Billie smiled. "Yes. That over there, that bubbly thing? That's a larval fish. Just born."

Maud went quiet. "There's so much."

"The whole sea. It's a community, like our cities. The squid eat these fish, other fish eat the squid, and those plankton? The ones with the bioluminescence? The whales eat those."

Maud sounded frankly disbelieving. "But they're so tiny."

"There are millions of them, remember? Enough to feed a whole species of whale. Blue whales eat plankton. So do whale sharks—that's probably what your 'black demon' is. The biggest animals on earth eat the tiniest."

"How do you know all this?"

Billie smiled. "I went to school, of course. I learned it. I study it."

"That's why you're here now," Maud said. "To collect these things. To study them more."

"Yes."

"You aren't collecting them now. Why? Does your hand hurt?"

It did, but that wasn't why. Billie glanced at the net she held. The bucket hanging from the step beside her was empty. She had come out here meaning to collect, though she hadn't thought of exactly how she would do that with only one hand, and frankly she hadn't made any attempt to bring in any of these creatures. She looked back down at the water, the community spinning toward the lights, staring at the lights, dazed by them. How easy to just sweep them up, plop them into buckets and then into the mixed formaldehyde called formalin, where they would exist in jars for the rest of time, ghosts of their previous selves.

That was what it was, she realized. She was tired of ghosts and uncertainty and talk of both. She wanted to look at the living, at the swirling, hungry, ruthlessly vast depths, to imagine teeming waters, things that could be touched, that could be studied and understood.

"It's all so alive," she said quietly.

"Doesn't it scare you to see so many things living there?" Maud asked.

"No," Billie said, thinking of the darkness Roland had lost Ángel to, that unexpected, unfathomable black. "Not seeing them is what would scare me."

San José Island had an otherworldly feeling to it, as if nothing lived there, as if nothing ever had. It was volcanic and quiet, the sea nearly motionless and flat around it, so the island itself seemed to skim the blue-black surface. Every now and then Billie caught a foul smell on the breeze, a sharp, sweet scent mixed with something rotting—the mangroves she'd hoped to visit and now could not. But it was the stillness that was so disquieting.

Behind her, the crew muttered as they worked on the deck. Matías couldn't keep the engines running consistently. Twice today they had died, which made dredging difficult, because each time the crew had to bring up the nets to keep them from tangling in the engines. Now, the nets were out again. Billie had just come up from the lab, where she'd spent the day, doing what she could with one hand—microscope work, mostly. She'd done some preserving in the aft hold, but she couldn't draw or dissect. Earlier, she'd been photographing in the forward hold, but using the darkroom was beyond her, and she'd had to leave that to Roland.

"I'm so sorry," she'd told him when she'd handed him that morning's film. "I know it's not your job—"

"I'm happy to do it for you, Billie," he said with a smile.

"But you'd rather be manning the dredge."

"We're in this together," he told her.

Except they weren't, not really, were they? He was keeping secrets, and she was well aware that if this fish was real and they caught it, he would push her aside as he always had, and she . . . well, what could she say except that she felt the aura . . . atmosphere . . . whatever you wanted to call it . . . on this ship more intently than ever. As if the wounds on her hand had made her more sensitive to the energies on the *Eurybia*. It made her uncomfortable.

"We're pulling the nets up!" Roland called to her.

Billie stood back as he and the crew hauled on the ropes.

Roland said, "The tidal current's pretty strong. I wish we were farther out, but if Matías can't keep the engines steady and we keep drifting closer to the island, this is the best we can do."

"There's nothing there. You can tell. No birds."

"Hmmm." He looked back at the dredge, lifting slowly into the air and lowering. The crew guided the cone-shaped net and its frame, coated with mud and seaweed and tangled now with shrimp and broken jellyfish, a few fish and a small shark, onto the deck. She could tell already it held nothing strange enough to be the *antorcha del mar*, at least as it was purported to be. The cook and the scullery boy were on deck now, too, with their pans to gather whatever would be good for eating.

Billie reached for an octopus snarled in the net and pulled it loose while it curled its tentacles around her arm, suctioning her skin. She had to get one of the sailors to help her loosen it to deposit it into one of the nearby collecting pans. Now, the net spilled wriggling shrimp, a few bonitos and skipjacks, which the cook quickly grabbed, crabs with bright-blue claws and parrotfish slapping their tails on the deck, gasping for air, all the colors pulsing and vibrant and then fading as the creatures died—their colors would never be so vibrant again, and Billie wished she could do something to save that color, something beyond drawing or photographing it, because the dying leeched it and the preservative leeched it more, but right now the color was stunning, it was alive.

But in the end, the haul was as disappointing as Billie had predicted. "The tide," Roland complained. "We're too close to San José. We need to be deeper."

The light was fading. Billie wiped sweat from the back of her neck. Her bandage was soaked, and the urchin stings and cuts burned. She stared down into the swarming water. "Deeper," she repeated. "Is that what your native stories tell you?"

He didn't bother to lie. "Yes. Before we left, we had men in the field gathering accounts. There wasn't much of a chance we'd find it here anyway. Most sightings have been farther north, between Point Lobos and Tiburón, but then I heard that someone was attacked by it here last year." He spoke so seriously.

"Wait. *Attacked?* You didn't tell me this."

"I didn't know it until Espiritu Santo. I talked to someone there before you fell."

She didn't argue the "fell." "You mean someone actually saw it?"

Roland hesitated. He rocked his head in that equivocal way he had. "Maybe."

"*Maybe* as in *yes*? Or *no*?"

"A goat had suspicious injuries," he admitted reluctantly. "They hung a few hammerhead livers around the farm, and it never came back."

"You mean a *goat* was attacked? So no one actually saw what attacked it? What did the livers keep away? The goat or its attacker?"

Roland gave her an annoyed look. "You know exactly what I mean. It's evidence."

Billie sighed. "You know what evidence would be, Roland? The fish itself, living or dead. Skeletal remains. Feces. Photographs. Actual data."

"Testimony is evidence, Billie," he pointed out.

She wanted to argue. But she couldn't, not really. Not after her talk with Tomás, or her own experiences in her room. It pained her in ways she couldn't articulate, even to herself, having to accept—or even acknowledge—things she would normally have scoffed at. But this place . . . Again she had that feeling of strangeness and truth overlapping, a sense of beauty in the undefined that was so alien to her logical self that she felt turned inside out. What was she to do with any of it?

A hoarse, guttural scream from the aft deck took her thoughts. Then a lighter scream—unmistakably Victorine. Billie and Roland both jerked to look. She heard the footsteps pounding across the deck, a flurry of Spanish, things crashing.

"What's that?" Roland asked.

She saw it in the same moment, a dark cloud that surrounded them almost as they spotted it, a giant, dense cloud of nasty, biting black bugs. The insects enveloped them, settling on Billie's head, her neck, any bare bit of skin, biting and stinging like tiny little bees.

She tried to dodge them. Impossible. They were everywhere, an overwhelming fog that covered the entire upper deck. She raced up the stairs to the closest shelter, the pilothouse, and nearly threw herself inside. Captain Rogers and six deckhands had crowded in there already. Only seconds later, Roland followed, cursing, brushing the bugs from his hair and his forearms as he slammed the door behind him.

"What the hell were those?"

One still clung to her sleeve. Billie pulled it off. It looked like a tiny black beetle. One of the sailors slapped it from her hand and crushed it.

The captain said, "I think they're from the island."

Billie looked out the window. San José Island was very near. The lone sandspit of the beach stretched before them. "Are we really that close? Or is it another mirage?"

"We're that close," the captain said tersely. "We're drifting again."

The tiny beetles swarmed on the pilothouse window. One of the deckhands said in Spanish that they were bugs from hell, and another said they were in hell already, so it was not far for the bugs to come, and another one said, "Son of a bitch I swear to God I am going home the minute I get to shore."

Billie didn't share this with anyone else, though she saw by the way the captain tensed that he understood perfectly. But then one crew member let out a sound of pure terror and dropped to his knees, covering his head with his hands, and another one called out to Santa Maria and began babbling a prayer, and when Billie followed his gaze, she understood why.

Another cloud rushed from the island, this one deeper black and larger than before, and with it came a rushing, swishing, weirdly fluttering sound she heard even through the men's prayers.

Roland said, "Christ."

Captain Rogers said, "What's that?"

Bats.

But bats like nothing Billie had ever seen or could have imagined. Bats crowding, bat wings flickering against the setting sun, so fast her eyes could not capture the movement, bats following the insects, swarming over the *Eurybia*. She heard screams from the other passengers in the saloons below. Billie's own heart stopped with both wonder and panic—*the bats chased the bugs*, she knew this, but fear wasn't logical, and she stepped closer to Roland. When he put his arm around her, she didn't move away.

Bats banged against the windows, blocked out the sun, encased them in loud, squeaking, flapping darkness. The noise was the creepiest thing about it, their little squeals, the leathery sound of their wings, the whoosh of them.

Two sailors threw themselves on the floor. One whispered a prayer. Another sang. One said in Spanish, "Where are the guns?" and his fellow answered, "What do you think to do, shoot them all? There must be hundreds," and after that they all watched in startled, terrified silence. It was like a nightmare, though Billie had never had a nightmare like this and had never imagined anything like this. She was not a bat specialist, but . . . wasn't this strange? Was this normal behavior?

It might have been five minutes. It might have been ten. It seemed like forever before the window cleared. As if called by some unseen force, the bats disappeared into pinpricks and were gone, leaving a clear view of the sun dipping below the horizon, striping the sky with brilliant fire that reflected gold on the blue-black water. Beautiful and somewhat terrible, too, in the aftermath of the bats. The world felt desolate and strange and somehow apocalyptic.

"Why did they do that?" Billie asked, her voice hushed in the weird silence that followed.

"You're the naturalist," the captain said.

"A marine biologist," she corrected. "I don't know about bats."

"They probably came from the mangroves," Roland said. "You can smell them from here. They followed the insects."

"But what brought the insects?" Billie asked him.

He only looked at her. Neither of them had an answer.

"It is San José," said one of the sailors.

"Not San José," said another one. "The *Eurybia*."

Chapter Eighteen

Oliver, Victorine, and James had taken refuge from the bugs and the bats in the main saloon. They looked shaken and sick when Billie and Roland came inside. Discomposed.

"I'm sure you all noted the bats." Roland attempted a weak smile.

"Is that what that was?" Oliver asked.

"They came from the island. They were after the bugs. Did you see them?"

Victorine held out her arm, which was covered by red welts. Roland showed her his, equally covered, with a grim smile. "But why?" she asked. "Why were the bugs here?"

"We don't know," Billie answered.

Victorine turned to look out the window. "Daddy used to say that each ship had a personality, her own destiny. I never believed that. Neither did Emile. But lately . . . this ship is changing my mind. You know, I never liked the *Eurybia*."

"That's only because of what happened to Emile," James said quickly.

She waved him off. "Even before that. It has a bad mien, don't you feel it? Any of you? I think it's angry. I think it holds spite."

Victorine's words seemed to shiver in a room that Billie already felt was unwelcoming.

Oliver sank into a chair. "Enough, Vic."

Victorine frowned. "I don't like that island either. I don't like the feel of it. What's it called?"

"San José. That's what Billie says too," Roland said.

Billie wanted nothing in common with Victorine. "It's purely an observation. It has no birds, that's all. A strange thing for an island in these parts."

None of them suggested going back on deck, though the evening air would be cooler there than it was in the saloon. The *Eurybia* had drifted even closer to San José with the stalling of the engines. Billie heard the chain of the anchor dropping—James straightened to attention as the generators came on.

"I guess Rogers has given up on the engines for tonight," Oliver said.

"I don't like being so close to that island," Victorine said, giving voice to everyone's feeling. "What if it happens again?"

James rose and turned on the little fan in the corner of the ceiling. It gave some relief, but not much. "We'll stay inside."

"At least the crew is afraid of the island too," Roland noted.

"Why does that matter?" James asked.

"Because none of them are likely to set sail for it." Roland went to the window beside Victorine and stared out contemplatively. "They were terrified. Even I thought it was terrifying, and I knew what was happening. They were crossing themselves and praying and jabbering . . . I don't know what they were saying, but it didn't sound good. Rogers wasn't happy, I know that."

"They'll settle down." James seemed unconcerned. "They don't get the rest of their pay until the cruise is done."

"I hope you're right," Roland said. "But . . ."

He didn't finish, and Billie heard his doubt and remembered the talk of the near mutiny at La Paz. She glanced at Oliver and knew by his grimly satisfied expression that he'd added James's lack of concern to his growing list of evidence that James was not seeing things clearly, that his obsessions had once again got the better of him. She remembered what Oliver had said that day in the lab—that James had gone mad and Oliver planned to take over the Holloway Foundation. Everything James said now justified Oliver's reasons—if the man needed justification, which Billie doubted.

"We can't let anything delay us now. Nothing, you understand? I don't care what the crew threatens—we're doing whatever we must to keep them on this ship until . . ." James trailed off as his intensity turned into a cough.

"Until what?" Oliver asked. "Dammit, James, you don't get to keep everyone a prisoner according to your whim. If the sailors want to leave, you have to let them. Otherwise it's kidnapping. You've taken this too far. And you're not paying them a penny more, do you hear me? If you do . . ."

"What? If I do, what?" James demanded. "You'll keelhaul me? You're acting like an ass, Oliver. Might I remind you that it's not your expedition? It's mine." He bent into a cough, his blond hair falling into his face and his whole body shaking with the effort to contain it, his frustration with it evident in a sudden burst of anger that had him striding from the saloon.

He would never stop, Billie knew. He would pursue this fish until it killed him, and he would take them all with him, and now she wondered if Roland, too, was determined to be so hell bound, and again, why he'd wanted to bring her along.

Billie found Maud in the supply closet. The maid's face was white in the dim light, her eyes black and huge, and she decided not to ask where the young woman had been during the attack by the bugs and the bats. It didn't matter. Maud looked frightened still.

Billie put her hand on the maid's arm. "Are you okay?"

Maud nodded tentatively. "I'm afraid they'll come back."

"They'll get the engines working again. Soon we'll be gone from this island."

The maid swallowed. She didn't look reassured. "Is there something you needed?"

"Only to see if you were all right."

Maud gave her a puzzled look. "You came looking for me just for that?"

How sad it was, that Maud should be so perplexed by simple concern. It made Billie wonder what the young woman's life had been. "Why don't you come with me? I want to check on the lab. I could use your help." For what exactly, Billie didn't know, but she would find something. The maid still looked half crazed; busywork might help.

Maud nodded and followed Billie to the lab.

Once they were there, among the books and boxes of slides and jars of chemicals, Maud looked around curiously. She pointed to the microscope. "What's that?"

"A microscope," Billie told her. "Have you never seen one before?"

"Mr. Ely talked about it, but I didn't know what he meant. What do you do with it?"

"It helps me look at things more closely," Billie explained, but she saw by the way Maud frowned at her that she didn't understand. "You remember the bioluminescence you saw with Mr. Ely the other night? The microorganisms? And the red water?"

"*Agua de sangre*," Maud whispered, crossing herself.

Billie couldn't help her smile. "It's not blood water. It's caused by tiny organisms—remember, I told you? Like the plankton that whales eat?" She went to the bucket of red water she had stored. It had been a few days, and some of the organisms would unfortunately be dead, but some would still be alive. "Let me show you."

She felt the maid's watchfulness as Billie prepared a glass slide with a droplet of the liquid, hoping that there would be enough life to show Maud an example, because Billie also saw the maid's wariness. If even one more person on this ship understood that there was no need for superstition, it would be better. It would . . . well, it would help Billie settle her own mind as well.

She went to the microscope and slipped the plate beneath the eyepiece, adjusting the focus. As she feared, plenty of the ciliate infusoria had died, but there, and there, thankfully, some moved.

Excitedly, Billie got off the stool and motioned for Maud to take her place. "Up here. Go on." She pointed to the eyepiece when Maud had settled herself. "Look into this. It's set for my eye, so it might not be the right focus for you. Turn this knob"—she took Maud's hand and directed it—"until you can see correctly."

Billie felt the young woman's hesitance. She thought at first Maud would refuse, but then the maid leaned down and looked into the eyepiece. She turned the knob one way, and then another, and then—

She jerked away. "They're moving!"

"Of course they are. They're alive."

"Alive? Out of the water?"

"They're still in water. This is just a droplet. Imagine how many there are in that bucket. In the sea outside. Millions. Millions upon millions."

Maud's forehead creased in a frown, but she turned back to the microscope. "Where are their eyes?"

"They have no eyes."

"Then how do they see?"

"With the little hairs on their bodies—they're covered with them, though they're hard to see with this microscope. You might be able to see them along the edges. They sense with them. These are the organisms that make the water red."

"But they're not red."

"When you have millions of them together, they are."

Billie felt the young woman's interest—or was it wonder? She hoped it was. She hoped the maid felt what Billie did whenever she looked at these creatures moving, living, reproducing. That sense of awe and amazement that such creatures existed, that she could see them in nature without truly comprehending their individuality and complexity until she looked at them this way. They made the water red, but they were so much more than that, and so crucial to the whole of the ocean.

Maud moved back from the eyepiece. "This is what whales eat?"

"Well, not these. These feed on bacteria, and tiny shrimp feed on these, and the whales and a hundred other creatures feed on the shrimp. Everything relies on everything else. The same way we do."

Maud went thoughtful. "And the *antorcha del mar*, what does it eat?"

She had brought the conversation back to legend, and Billie's heart sank. "I don't know what it eats, Maud. I don't even know if it's real."

Maud slid off the stool and regarded Billie with that direct dark gaze. "The crew says it's a monster."

"Those are stories. It's all just stories. Who knows what it really is? Who knows if it exists? I don't think we'll find it."

"But if you do?"

Billie shrugged. "I'll dissect it. Photograph it. Study it."

"What if it's as dangerous as the crew thinks?"

Billie laughed shortly. "They think the red water is dangerous, and I've just showed you that it's not."

Maud glanced at the microscope, and then away. Thoughtfully, she said, "Yes, that's true. I'm not afraid of the red water anymore. But . . . the crew doesn't really think the red water's dangerous either. They think it's a sign. They think you're the dangerous one."

"Why? Because I visited the galley when I shouldn't have?"

Maud shook her head. "Because your room is haunted. Why do you think I burn the incense there? To keep the spirit away."

Billie remembered Roland saying that Maud thought the room haunted. "Why would I be dangerous because I stay there? I don't understand."

"Spirits play tricks. They want to live again. They'll try to take over your soul. If this one takes over yours . . ."

Billie stared at her in disbelief. "My soul? Really?"

Maud nodded soberly. "Some of the crew believe it's already happened."

Stunned now—this was truly beyond comprehension—Billie said, "What do you think? Do you think I'm dangerous?"

"I'm not afraid of you." A little blustery, like a child puffing out her chest. "But I am afraid *for* you. You shouldn't stay in that room. There *is* something there. Whatever Mrs. Holloway called means you harm. It means us all harm."

Billie was uncertain what to say to that.

Maud reached into her collar and pulled out a cross on a cheap leather cord. She pulled it over her head and handed it to Billie. "You should wear this."

The gesture surprised Billie. It was touching that Maud was willing to sacrifice what was obviously precious to her. Billie didn't know how to say that she didn't believe in talismans, that God to her was something different from a presence that could be appealed to with a symbol or a prayer, that she couldn't in good conscience take what must be a comfort to Maud, as moved as she was by the offer. How to say it without offending?

Softly, she said, "You'd best keep it, Maud. I have my own defenses."

In Maud's gaze Billie saw doubt and annoyance, but Maud palmed the necklace. "You must keep burning the incense. My *abuela* used it to banish spirits. She swore by it. I'll give you more. And I'll pray for you."

"Thank you," Billie said, because what else could she say?

"If your eyes turn color—if they turn black—I'll throw you overboard," Maud went on.

"What?"

"It's a sign of soul possession," Maud said matter-of-factly. "You *will* be a danger to us all."

"Um . . ." Billie was taken aback. "Well, I don't want that. But . . . they're already brown, so make sure they're really black, and it's not just the light, please, Maud, will you? Ask Roland to check first. Please. I must insist on it."

Maud nodded. "Okay. I will." She slipped the cross over her head again. "Thank you. I feel much better now."

Billie was thankful for that, but as she watched the young woman go, their conversation stayed with her, uncomfortable and alarming. Her room was haunted by a being that meant her harm. Maud watched her for signs of possession. How long before the maid decided Billie's eyes weren't the right color, and Billie had that to try to explain as well as the other strange things that had been happening? The wind that had come out of nowhere and the dark ocean that had taken Ángel. The swordfish ramming the boat. The bugs and the bats. She'd made light of the strangeness of San José because she hadn't wanted to share anything with Victorine, but . . . no birds was odd. The island felt eerie, and Billie wanted to be far away from it.

She looked down at her injured hand. And then there was this.

Currents. A sudden wind. She'd lost her balance. It was hard now to remember. There'd been algae on the rocks.

Maybe.

She was rattled by the events of the day. Through the porthole, in the darkness, San José Island appeared more otherworldly than ever, a deeper void in the shadows on a night lit only by stars. She decided not to dine with the others; she felt on edge. Every sound made her jump. But she didn't want to go to her room either, and so Billie stayed in the lab until very late, her stomach rumbling with hunger, and looked at the organisms under the microscope until her eyes blurred and they'd stopped moving.

For the first time since she could remember, her work didn't reassure her.

Chapter Nineteen

By morning, thankfully, the engines were running again, and they escaped the hold of San José Island. The day was hot and the water deeply blue, and everything seemed better now that they were away. Even the stink of James's asthma cigarettes wafting from where he sat with Victorine and Oliver on the aft deck couldn't spoil Billie's relief to be gone from there.

She glanced toward Roland, who stood watching the wake of the dredging net off the side of the yacht. She was tired; the combination of Maud's pronouncements and Billie's own uneasiness had kept her from sleep. She'd worked in the lab until only a few minutes ago, when she'd come up for a breath of air, and now the sun worked its magic, and she found herself watching Roland and thinking of the night they'd spent together and wanting the reassurance of him that she knew was only an illusion, a memory of the old days, when she had trusted him and believed that they made the perfect team. How lucky she had been, to have love and desire and work so perfectly aligned.

Not real, she reminded herself. Just as his assertion that he would prove himself to her was an illusion. That she wanted to believe she could trust him—or that he was still a temptation—was a testament to how unsettled this expedition had her feeling.

"What are we doing?" James asked.

Billie turned from the rail to see that James had risen from the lounge to stare at the passing scenery. She had been too lost in her thoughts to understand what she'd been looking at, but now she saw that they'd come very close to the shore, close enough to see a valley opening up to the sea from the mountainous land, and what looked like a village at the foot of it. They sailed close enough that she could easily see a building with an arched roof and a dome, probably a church. It looked as if they were heading toward it.

James ran up the stairs to the pilothouse.

Victorine said, "We're not supposed to be coming into port here, are we?"

Billie heard the engine slow and Roland shouting for the crew to pull in the dredging net. Victorine was right; it looked as if they were coming into port. Billie knew of no plans for a landing today or any day until her next collection station—they still feared losing crew, and if they'd planned to come into port, they wouldn't be dredging.

She watched Victorine follow after James to the pilothouse. Only a few minutes later, Billie heard Victorine calling her name as the woman came back down again. Victorine looked worried. "Come with me, please, Billie. I need your help."

"My help?"

"The captain is missing."

Billie stared at her in confusion. "What do you mean, missing?"

"He's not in the pilothouse. The first mate is in charge."

"Okay . . ."

"You don't understand." Victorine's voice went low and urgent. "The first mate is *in charge*. He's taking us into Loreto. You speak Spanish. Come with me." Victorine grabbed her arm and pulled Billie toward the stairs leading belowdecks.

Still bewildered, Billie jerked her arm free. But Victorine's distress was real, and Billie followed her belowdecks, to the crew quarters, which were dim and hot, stinking of fish and sweat the closer they got to the galley. She heard shouting that grew louder as they approached; when they reached the mess, Billie saw a group of sailors with Captain Rogers among them.

Victorine looked disorientingly out of place among the crew in her light-pink mousseline. The scene became more disorienting still when Billie saw that Captain Rogers was arguing with several sailors, and that it wasn't just an argument. He was trying to leave, and they weren't letting him. She spotted Matías among the men, but not Tomás. Billie tried to catch Matías's eye, but he deliberately avoided hers.

"Captain?" Victorine asked.

He noticed them with a kind of grateful panic that alarmed Billie. "Mrs. Holloway—they're taking us into Loreto. I can't stop them."

The crewmen gathered around him turned to stare. All wore grim, determined faces. Billie felt the threat emanating from them. The anger, the fear. It was a mutiny. Even Matías? He'd seemed so reasonable. Again, she tried to signal him. Again, he avoided her.

Victorine said to her, "You have to tell them they can't."

"They can't what?" Billie asked.

"It's this cursed ship." Victorine rolled her shoulders. "It *wants* us to fail. Don't you feel it?"

"That kind of talk isn't helping," Billie whispered back. "They're just men, Victorine. They can be reasonable. What do you want me to say to them?"

"Tell them . . . tell them . . . let the ones go who wish to go. But the ones who stay will get double pay. Tell them that."

Billie scanned the faces. Some of the men understood a little English. Most of them watched her and Victorine uncomprehendingly. If Matías was among them, then Billie understood that their patience had run out. Whatever nonsense Victorine felt about the *Eurybia*, it was clear the men felt it too. Billie remembered what Maud had said last night, about the men thinking Billie herself was a danger. They didn't trust her, so she tried to seem calm and unperturbed as she translated Victorine's words.

"Mrs. Holloway," Captain Rogers protested after she finished, "Matías is one of those who wish to leave."

"Matías?" Victorine asked.

"The assistant engineer," Billie said quietly. She saw the moment Victorine understood.

"Ah. Can anyone else take over for him?"

The captain shook his head.

"Does he have a family?"

"Yes," Rogers said.

"Tell him I'll buy his family a house. I'll buy them chickens and a goat. Keep him here. *Tell him.*"

Billie translated. She added, "Please. We need you, and we will pay you to show you how valued you are. We will keep you safe. There is nothing to fear aboard this ship. How can we convince you of that?" Some of the men looked mollified, and she knew they'd stay. Others shook their heads; from others, there came a chorus of *no*s.

She motioned to the captain and said to the sailors in Spanish, "We will keep our promise to those who stay. But you must let Captain Rogers go. Someone needs to pilot us into Loreto. Unless you all want to crash on the rocks."

Victorine swayed. "Do you feel that?"

"Feel what?"

"That . . . that . . ."

Billie caught her just as Victorine lost her balance.

"I must sit down. I think I'm going to be sick," Victorine whispered.

Billie led her to a nearby campstool. The men dispersed; the captain raced out of the galley to take the helm again. As Victorine bowed her head, Billie heard the others murmuring as they left, some taking the deal, others not. She glanced up to see Matías looking steadily at her.

"Can I trust this?" he asked her in Spanish.

Before Billie could answer, Victorine said, "Tell him yes. Whatever he asks, tell him yes. I'll do what's in my power to do. James needs this expedition to continue. Therefore it must."

Only a few days ago, Victorine had wanted to turn back. Billie wondered what had changed her mind. To Matías, she said, "She says yes."

"Can I trust her?" he asked.

What to say to that? She hardly knew Victorine, and James Holloway did not have a reputation for honesty. How much like James was Victorine? How reliable were her promises?

But then, of course, Billie relied on James's promises, too, and the ones he'd made to her had been pared away by the engineer's death. Collecting stations down to three. She relied now on the dredging and trawling. If Matías left, Billie realized, the expedition was as much over, a failure. Her plans to revitalize her career, to make a name for herself as an expert on the Gulf's diversity, as much as over. Back to the zoo. To sea lion dams and algae and assistant zookeeper obscurity.

She had no choice but to reassure him.

So Billie said, "Yes," and hoped that she wasn't lying.

Matías nodded and left her and Victorine alone in the mess. The two of them and the hissing steam, the cook's snapping at the scullery boy from the galley. Billie touched Victorine's shoulder. "Are you all right?"

Victorine shuddered and raised her head. "Oliver is going to be very angry."

"Because you raised their pay?"

Victorine nodded. Then she frowned and stared off into the distance. "Didn't you feel it? The spirit?"

This again. Billie shook her head. "No."

"It was right here. I wish I knew what it wanted."

Billie said nothing to that. Her skin prickled at Victorine's words, but Billie refused to acknowledge it. "We should leave the crew quarters," she said softly.

Victorine put a tentative hand to her head. "I worry so. Have you noticed James? He's getting worse. He has so little strength. Has Roland said anything about it to you?"

"Why would he?"

Victorine gave her a look—knowing, shaming. That Victorine suspected something between Billie and Roland was obvious. Billie felt her own defensiveness keenly. But Victorine said only, "Ollie doesn't think this fish is real. He thinks James is crazy. It's convenient for him to think so, of course. He's been wanting to take over the Foundation for years, but if James doesn't find this thing, Oliver will use the expenditures on 'Holloway's Folly' as an excuse. He's been trying to get me on his side." Victorine lowered her voice to a whisper. "What was between the two of us is long over, and I . . . it's not . . . I'm not . . ." She shook her head as if to shake away her words. "What do you think, Billie? Is this quest just another one of James's fantasies? Is it a waste of time?"

Billie saw something in Victorine's eyes, some yearning, a hope . . . Billie's demurral caught in her throat. Victorine wanted this fish to be real, and Billie wondered why. She understood Roland—lured by a scientific prize, by ambition, by whatever the Empedocles Society had in mind. James she understood less well, except that he, too, belonged to the Society and financed its schemes. But why Victorine should care . . . And then Billie remembered Oliver's talk about James searching for a new cure, and with Victorine's comment about James losing strength, the hope in her gaze, it all fell into place.

"It would be a miracle if this fish exists," Billie said gently—the most she could offer. "Not to mention if it could perform miracles."

"I have to believe it can." Victorine rose. "Don't you understand? There's nothing left for me if I can't believe."

They lost six men to Loreto, which, after Ángel's death, left them with only nine crew, but at least Matías stayed. The next day, trawling, they brought up a sea turtle—good luck, according to the men, but the cook claimed it, and Roland and James gave it to him without consulting Billie. She was incensed. Even worse, the meat cooked up so black and foul it stank up the entire crew quarters and wafted toward the staterooms, and they finally threw it over the side.

Roland said, "We'll get you another one."

Wasting the lives of creatures reminded her of the pointless dynamiting on Cerralvo. "Why not capture ten or twenty?" she snapped at him.

"That's not what I meant," he snapped back. "Stop always thinking the worst of me."

Billie was taken aback at his words. It was true; she often did that. "I'm sorry. It's just—"

"Yes, yes, I know. I deserve it."

She said nothing, but his words stayed with her over the next days, troubling her. He *did* deserve it, that was true, so she didn't know why it bothered her that she thought it and he knew she thought it, but . . . he had done his best to help her so far on this cruise. She had to admit that. In spite of the fact that the collecting was solely for her research, he helped her and did the work when she couldn't because of her hand. And so . . . maybe she could give him a *little* bit of the benefit of the doubt.

Now, he seemed to be avoiding her, which bothered Billie more than she wanted to admit. It was fine when she'd been avoiding him—preferable, in fact. But now she felt his absence keenly. She missed his little flirtations and his sly glances and wondered if she'd pushed him past endurance—well, what did it matter? She'd divorced him, after all. She'd made her decision. Their relationship was over. If only she hadn't gone to bed with him again, she could feel fine about all this.

But . . .

They passed another extensive patch of red water, and this time Billie did not meet it with the same excitement. She found herself unsurprised when the stain at the bathtub drain grew—from eight inches to twelve—even though she did not run the saltwater tap at all. Only microorganisms, she told herself. She'd taken a sample and studied it under the microscope. She had no doubt as to what turned the water red. Still . . . that stain on the tub was the color of blood, and she wondered—*Was there more to Victorine's brother's suicide than just chloral and drowning?* She refused to ask. It would only be admitting . . . what? That there was something real happening that belonged to Victorine's *energies* and Roland's as-yet-unknown universes?

But she couldn't yet admit that. There must be another explanation. The tap must be leaking, though when she looked for the drip, she couldn't find it, and she never heard it. She tried to scratch some of the stain loose, to look at it under the microscope too. But nothing came loose, not even flakes beneath her fingernail. She tried to use the edge of a nail file, and got nothing. It was as if it had made itself part of the porcelain, which also was bizarre and frankly impossible. There was nothing to examine, no data to reassure her or create further puzzles. Nothing she could *use*. It was as if the very act of investigation meant to confound her.

She didn't sleep well. Restless, tossing and turning. She'd taken the bandage off her hand. It was still sore, and there were little black spots where the urchin barbs had pierced, but it was no longer swollen, and it was healing. The little room suffocated, and the incense Maud insisted on burning made it worse. Billie left the door open, and that didn't help. No air circulated in her room, and her dreams, when she remembered them, swam with shadows. The voice saying *You're not wanted here* hadn't returned, but it didn't have to; the eerie memory of it didn't leave her, and she didn't like the way Victorine looked at her sometimes, with a curious, searching gaze. One night Billie had come up onto the deck to try to sleep on the lounging platform, but it didn't help. The night air was sweltering and dewy, no better than in her room, as if whatever lay in wait there for her had followed her up top—*For God's sake, stop it!* What an absurd thought. Ridiculous. But it stayed. Last night Maud had asked her how she felt and if she prayed. The question had pierced deeper than it should. Billie had laughed it off, but she remembered it when she climbed into bed, and she couldn't help but wonder if maybe she should pray, though she felt like a bunny for thinking it. She hadn't prayed since she was a child; why should she start now? It was both hypocritical and unnecessary, a crutch she didn't need. At times she wondered if she was losing her mind. If not for the relief she found, and the material, logical, reasonable order her brain grasped so easily, whenever she worked, she would have feared she was.

She spent as much time as she could surrounded by what she understood—in the aft hold, where she dissected and preserved and kept company with dead things staring at her from jars or live ones in the aquariums, captured squids changing color and squirting ink and fish swimming idly about and contemplating her from behind the glass, or the fore hold, where she photographed specimens—and the lab, where she spent hours drawing and cataloging and making notes when her hand could manage it. Roland was frustrated and disappointed by what they took in dredging, but Billie was not, though as yet she'd found no new species, nothing better than the black holothurians she'd lost. Still, she didn't lose hope.

Three more days of dredging. On the second day they caught a small, chubby porpoise with black rings around its eyes. As with the black holothurians, she'd never seen its like, but when she raced to grab it, one of the deckhands scooped it up and threw it over the side before she could, and gave her a look that said, *Not that one.* On the fourth day she came on deck to find the net out, and only one deckhand watching. He barely acknowledged her when she stepped over. Seabirds had learned what the dredging net meant, and had taken to following the yacht, noisily cawing and diving, so obnoxious when the net was pulled in that they needed a crewman with a broom to beat the birds away. But right now, the birds stayed at a distance.

The day was brutally hot, and the heat irritated her healing hand. Not only that, but she was tired and irritated by Roland—or, more precisely, by his avoidance—and less patient because of it. The aft deck was abandoned, only the *Eurybia News* on one of the chairs, its pages limply stirring at a slight breeze. She didn't see any of the others; they were probably in one of the saloons, where there were fans, or napping in their rooms. Already, Billie felt the sweat at the back of her neck. She picked up the *News*. They were two and a half weeks out, and the Scopes trial had ended with Scopes pleading guilty after Bryan's testimony. The teacher had been fined a hundred dollars, and the law in Tennessee that made it illegal to teach evolution still stood. The trial had changed nothing.

A weirdly parallel world on the *Eurybia*, wasn't it? Billie thought, fanning herself. Everything hot and stupid here, too, here an evolutionary fish a man wanted desperately to believe in despite no proof or scientific fact, and there a fight over a proven scientific theory that people refused to believe because it interfered with their theology.

All because people with their own little fiefdoms had control and wanted to keep it. Incompetent men who triumphed so often over those more talented—not to mention women—that Billie had lost track of how many times she'd seen it. Men who felt so certain in their beliefs that they didn't hesitate to impose them on others. They were everywhere. Billie wondered sometimes how humankind had ever evolved, or if it would ever progress further, given the hold such men had on society. Always . . . always she reminded herself that evolution made no moral judgments. It applied equally to saints and monsters. Parasites evolved to be as complex as their hosts.

Billie was so deep in thought that she didn't hear the footsteps behind her, and when Roland said, "What are you thinking about?" she started.

"You scared me," she said, putting her hand to her heart with a little laugh. "Where is everyone?"

"Swimming." He nodded toward the other side of the ship. "Don't you hear them?"

She hadn't, but now that he'd said it, she did. Light laughter, splashes. She didn't know why she hadn't heard it before. "Swimming? What about sharks?"

"James put out a shark net. As long as they stay within it, they're safe."

"Why aren't you with them?"

"The pump on one of the aquariums stopped. I was fixing it. Why don't you go? You could use a break, I think."

Billie found herself surprised not just by the thought of Roland fixing one of her aquariums instead of swimming with their hosts, but also by his urging that she take a break. The familiar pull of resentment rose in her again. *All work and no play* . . . but Billie saw no judgment in his eyes. It was a casual comment, and it made her wonder when she'd last taken a break. When was the last time she had done something just for fun? Something that had nothing to do with her job?

She couldn't remember. Or yes, there had been that time when she'd gone out to a speakeasy with some of her neighbors. They had been mostly couples, and they'd spent the night drinking and dancing to a band playing in a little cave-like place in the storeroom of a farm stand. They'd had to have a code word to get in. It had all seemed very clandestine and risky, and that had added to its charm. Halfway through the night she'd noticed a stranger appraising her from the makeshift bar. He'd approached her with dark eyes and a drink in his hand. *"You're Billie McKennan, aren't you? I've heard about you."* A tease, a smile, a lingering exhale on his cigarette, and that gaze that had followed her all evening, until he'd had her in a corner, and . . .

She didn't want to think about it anymore. As with Oliver, she'd shoved the man off, but his persistence had troubled her. Understanding had come later, when one of those she'd gone with had said, "*Oh, yeah, Sid. He'd heard you were divorced, that's all.*"

Poor Sid had been disappointed that night, and so had every other man who'd approached her in that way since. After that, she'd mostly stuck to work. An occasional movie on her own. That was mostly it. She had no one to urge her to take a break. No one to say *All work and no play, Billie*. After a while, she'd forgotten how to play. She'd learned to be alone. She'd learned to focus on one thing: gaining back the career she'd lost.

Thinking of it now made her feel—what was that feeling? It was forlorn and a bit empty, and it was exacerbated by Roland's warmth beside her.

Loneliness. It surprised her to recognize it. She'd been lonely.

"You go on," he said again. "I'll call you if we find anything good."

But Billie didn't want to leave. Just standing here with him felt . . . nice, and she turned to say that, and ended up saying, "Trying to get rid of me?" and cursed herself when his gentle mood darkened.

Roland winced. "Have it your way."

Now that she'd said it . . . "It's just . . . you've been avoiding me."

He looked surprised. "You noticed?"

"How could I not, Rolly? You've made it very clear."

"I thought it was what you wanted."

"Hmmm."

"And it was easier."

"Easier than what?"

He looked down at her. In the bright sunlight his eyes were shadowed, but she felt that look shiver through her, that prick of desire.

"Oh," she said.

"You see? It just seemed better to keep my distance. For now, anyway. It's not what you want, and—"

"That's not exactly true. I just think it's best to—"

The birds circling the boat grew suddenly loud.

Roland frowned and glanced up. So did she.

There were more birds than usual. Crowds of pelicans and gulls. Terns dipped and swirled among them.

"*Señor!*" the deckhand called, frowning. "The dredge!"

Billie heard the creaking strain of the cable rope at the same moment. The net was too heavy. They'd got something big, or a load of mud or rock.

"Bring it up," Roland ordered.

The birds above went into a frenzy of squawking. She glanced again at the sky. So many birds.

The deckhand wound the rope, but it wasn't coming easily. Billie frowned and leaned over the railing to look, but the water boiled with the pressure from the rising dredge. There was nothing to see yet. She hoped the net didn't break or rip before they got it up.

"Maybe there's a shark caught in it," Roland said, but she heard an edge in his voice, one of anticipation. He threw a sideways look at the sky. "You might want to grab a broom, Billie. Looks like you're going to have to fight off some birds."

The moment he said it, the birds swooped down from the sky.

Chapter Twenty

Roland called out for another deckhand to help him and the other crew member to pull up the net. Billie grabbed the broom as the birds swept low. Their wings made a wind strong enough to blow off Billie's hat. She had no time to grab it; her hair blew in her face, blinding her. She beat at the birds with the broom, but they dived at Roland and the crew, who strained at the ropes. The birds screamed; she could hardly see through them, they massed so heavily, and then the ropes screamed, too, and something bumped hard, and the yacht rocked, but she couldn't see because of the birds. A group of them attacked her, forcing her to drop the broom. She stepped back with a curse. Roland and the crew still pulled; the dredge rose into the air, bulging, overloaded, the cone-shaped net dripping and swaying; there was a sound like a snap, and the net plunged to the deck hard, too hard. The *Eurybia* rocked again, rocking and then what felt like falling back.

Billie lost her balance and crashed to the deck. Roland shouted something—she couldn't hear it above the birds. One of the deckhands called out. Pelicans and gulls crowded the deck, sweeping in great arcs across, a swirling, crashing, diving cloud of motion, diving toward the fish tangled in the net. Except . . . no. It took a moment for Billie to comprehend they weren't acting like the birds usually did. A gull dived at her, its beak flashing in her face. She put up her arm to keep from being slashed. A pelican next. The birds weren't going after the fish. They were attacking the people on deck.

Roland shouted again. One of the sailors screamed. The birds were everywhere. Cawing in her ear, their feet in her hair, pulling, tugging. Billie curled into a ball, but she felt them at her shoulders, flapping against her, the sharp tips of their beaks scraping her arms and legs, her back through her blouse.

Then, a shot blasted through the air. Another. A third. She heard the thud of a heavy bird body hitting the deck beside her. Then the ship's horn—the long, deep, throaty blare of it. Once and again.

She felt rather than saw the birds scatter. Warily, Billie looked up. A dead pelican lay beside her; a cloud fluttered up and circled. Feathers dusted the deck like snowfall. Roland knelt a short distance away, blood streaking his cheek. The two crew members rose from where they'd thrown themselves. One of them grabbed the broom she'd dropped and raised it threateningly at the birds, which, except for a few braver ones, now mostly kept their distance.

Oliver stood nearby, soaking wet, wearing his bathing suit and bearing a rifle. "Are you hurt? Any of you?"

"No," Billie called. Roland came over and held out his hand to help her to her feet. "I've never seen birds do that." She looked toward the net, which was alive with motion, as it always was when they brought it out of the sea. At least most of it was, wriggling with crabs and smaller fish and the specimens they usually brought up. But part of it was still. Very, very still. A shark would be fighting the net. Anything alive would be fighting the net.

Roland, too, looked at the still mass in the center of the net. He moved toward it.

"Roland," she warned quietly. "If it's a shark—"

"It's not a shark." He pulled the net slowly, carefully, releasing gasping fish to flop freely, and one of the deckhands followed after, grabbing them to put into the collecting pans. The scullery boy appeared with his own pans to retrieve the ones for eating; Billie motioned for him to stand back. The sailor with the broom stood guard. Overhead, the birds circled, with now and then a lonely caw.

As if they're mourning, Billie thought, and then was surprised at the notion. She didn't like Roland getting so close to that still shark alone, so confidently—he was taking no precautions at all, and the thing was big and . . . and shinier than any shark should be. She squinted again, trying to see past the glare coming off it. She grabbed a grappling hook where it angled against the wall and started after him, ignoring the other creatures the net had gathered.

"Roland!" she called after him. "For God's sake, be . . ."

Her words died in her throat when he stopped short. She was only steps behind him, and she felt the wave of malevolence like a blow. Just pure hostility that stopped her in her tracks. Coming from where? Not Roland.

"You should come away," she said uncertainly.

Roland pulled the net back. The creature looked like nothing Billie had ever seen. It didn't move, and didn't attack, but neither was it benign. It stared at Roland as if it hated him; its gills fluttered and gasped, and yet it didn't flop and jerk the way the other fish did, and was it even a fish? It had a flat triangular head like a crocodile, though its nose was flatter and rounder. Eyes on the top of its head in the same way, but more centered and closer together. Its head was the size of Roland's torso, and the thing stretched probably nine feet long, that ugly head tapering into a long, sinuous body. It was also clearly lobe finned, with spade-shaped fins extending from short, bony limbs. Pectoral fins paired on either side, just beyond its gills, and pelvic fins near the lamprey-like diphycercal tail fin.

The sun touched it with fire, and every rainbow-colored diamond-shaped scale—blues and pinks, violets, golds, oranges, and a deep red-gold—glistened, and Billie couldn't help but think of the poison dart frogs with their bright colors and fatal secretions. An ugly, huge, misshapen fish in the most stunning colors, and she couldn't quite take it in, not the confusion of it, the simple contradiction of it.

The sailor with the broom made a sound of terror. "*El monstruo!*" he screamed, lunging at it, raising the broom to bring it down on the creature's head.

Roland shoved the man back. "No!"

The crewman stumbled and fell among the writhing fishes still caught in the net. He crab-walked backward in terror. His words strung together so quickly Billie could barely make them out, something about the monster and *get rid of it, get it off the boat . . . cursed . . . it will kill us all. Ella nos matará a todos.* No, not *it* will kill us all. *She* will kill us all. *She* will.

The other deckhand shrieked and ran off—*Bad news,* Billie thought. Within moments, the rest of the crew would know what they'd brought up in the net, and given the two sailors' reaction . . . it was likely to turn into a terrible situation.

James appeared, dripping in his swimming suit, pushing his way past, breathing hard as if he'd run a mile, almost staggering with his faltering breath, just as the creature's gills flapped in obvious distress. "Don't touch it! Don't you touch it! It's mine! Touch it and I'll shoot you! Do you hear me, Oliver! I want you to shoot anyone who tries to maim this creature!"

"Maim it?" Billie asked, finally finding her voice. "But . . ."

"Antorcha del mar." James's voice was softly reverent.

The creature pulsed with rancor so strong it made Billie nervous. Was she imagining it, or did the creature stare at her?

"Don't hurt it," James said again.

"It's a fish," she told him, trying to ignore her unease. "It's going to suffocate in a few minutes unless we get it into water."

Almost as she said it, the gills of the fish—if that was what it was—stopped moving. But not because the creature was dying.

Because it was no longer trying to breathe through them. It had two slits at the top of its head, behind its eyes. Billie had not seen them before, not until they began to expand, the way a porpoise's blowhole expanded when it breathed, or a whale's.

Lungs.

Good God, the thing was real. The legend was real.

Billie stared at it in stunned shock. James had been right. Roland had been right. The creature existed. The evolutionary miracle.

All the stories were true.

"Oh my God," she whispered.

Roland gave her a triumphant look. "I told you."

The creature blinked and raised its head.

It *raised its head*. Unlike any fish she'd ever seen. It twisted its head to look straight at her—*twisted its head*, which meant *articulating cervical vertebrae* of some sort; could it be?—and Billie's heart raced when it raised itself up on those fins. No, not fins. Legs. Short, stubby legs. Those fins . . . were there bones in those fins too? Were they proto-hands?

"Oh Jesus, Roland . . ." She barely breathed the words. "This . . . this is a . . . this is a discovery for the ages."

James nodded with self-satisfaction.

"You can't . . . you have to give this to . . . it has to be studied!"

James turned to Roland. "What's she talking about? Haven't you told her?"

"Billie," Roland said.

"We have an obligation . . ." She couldn't get the words out properly. The *antorcha del mar* glittered in the sun, its rainbow colors chasing each other, glowing with significance and power. Whoever brought this discovery to light would be celebrated forever; she would be a fool not to see that, but regardless, the search for knowledge required it be studied thoroughly. *Science* required it.

Roland took her firmly by the arm. "We'll talk about this later. For now, let's get it secured, okay? Tell the sailors to get it into the aft hold. It's too big to be moved easily. We'll have to bring the camera down there."

She looked at the deckhand cowering in terror and knew he wouldn't go near it. "They aren't going to touch it, Roland. They're afraid of it, remember? They think it's a *monster*. Besides, no one should touch it until we know more about it. Its skin might be poisonous. It might spit venom. We don't know."

Roland nodded. He met her gaze, forcing her to focus. "We'll have to anesthetize it here, then lift it in. We'll need a pulley."

"Yes, but—"

"We'll discuss the rest alone." He spoke in a low voice. "I'll need to explain."

"Yes, you will. You know what this means as well as I do."

"What *what* means?" asked James in obvious confusion. "Billie?"

Roland said, "Don't worry, James, we'll—"

"My God, what is that!" Victorine's voice came from beyond, shrill with surprise. "What on earth?"

Billie pulled away from Roland to see that Victorine had come up beside Oliver, who stood ready with the rifle. Victorine stared agape at the *antorcha*.

"This, my darling, is what we've been searching for," James said with a flourish. "The *antorcha del mar*!"

"Oh my!"

"Legend of the Gulf of California! Monster of the deep!" James rasped.

She gave him a look Billie could not read. "Monster? Why, it doesn't look like a monster at all! It's beautiful!"

"Some of the most beautiful creatures are the most poisonous," Billie warned her.

"Is that so?" Victorine asked. "Well, I simply must have a look at it."

"You'd best wait until we have it secured," Roland said. "Frankly, we don't know what it can do."

"Remember how nervous it makes the natives, Vic," James cautioned.

"Oh yes, well." Victorine seemed momentarily dissuaded. "But I can look at it when you have it in the hold?"

Victorine had not set foot in the hold, nor shown the least bit of interest in it, but Billie couldn't deny the fish was beautiful, and she remembered Victorine's hope and wasn't surprised that she might want to see it closer.

Billie glanced again at the creature. A miracle. A scientific oddity. The possible answer to a million questions about how life had come to be, how *humans* had come to be. She itched to get her hands on it. To examine it, to know it the way she knew the specimens she labored over every day. What was a marine exhibit when *this* existed? Studying this would change everything. *Everything.*

The *antorcha del mar* rolled its eye toward her, a steady glance, an almost human assessment. And strangely, bizarrely, impossibly, Billie heard the words from her dream. *You aren't wanted here.*

She shivered.

Then she turned deliberately away and hurried to get the chloroform.

Chapter Twenty-One

The crew refused to have anything to do with it; there was not one thing Billie or Roland could say to get any one of them to help—in fact, the men seemed to miraculously disappear the moment Roland went in search of aid. It took the two of them, clad in rubber gloves and ponchos to protect themselves from any secretions, along with a pulley system Roland designed, to get the creature into the tank in the hold, which they filled with seawater.

Billie finally peeled off her gloves, flexing her hand—mostly healed, only a little stiff—before she took off the poncho. "I can't believe it exists."

"I can hardly wait to get this back to San Francisco." Roland hung his poncho over the edge of a dissection table.

"Why, so every other scientist at the Academy can swarm over it? Thankfully we've a few weeks left of the expedition to start working on it before everyone else wants a piece—" She broke off when she noticed his look of distress. "Have I said something wrong?"

"Billie . . ."

"I hate it when you take that tone. It means I'm not going to like what you're going to say."

He exhaled slowly. "We're turning around now. We've got what we came for."

"What do you mean, we're turning around? We won't have enough time to do a full study on this before everyone else descends on us!"

"We're not doing a full study."

"What do you mean, we're not doing a full study? Of course we are. It will take us days just to take the photographs we need, and to do the drawings and the descriptions, not to mention the dissection—"

"We're not dissecting it."

She hadn't heard him correctly. She couldn't have. "We aren't . . . you mean . . . I don't understand."

Roland took a deep breath. "I mean we won't be doing any dissection. That's not what it's for."

"Then what is it for?"

Roland's mouth tightened. "It's for James."

Billie remembered then, James's shouting on the deck not to maim the creature, not to hurt it. *"Touch it and I'll shoot you!"*

She struggled to keep her voice steady. "What are you saying, Rolly?"

"He funded this expedition for this purpose. The *antorcha del mar* belongs to him, Billie. We have to do what he says." He wouldn't look at her as he spoke, and Billie's temper erupted.

"Isn't studying it what he wants? Isn't that why he wanted to find it? What does he mean to do, keep it as a trophy?" The thought was horrifying. "That's not science! How are we to know anything about it if we can't dissect it?"

"We're to keep it alive and paralyzed."

Billie stared at him in confusion. It *was* to be a trophy. "But why? How can I possibly study it that way?"

"I need you to study it that way," he told her. "Take blood and small tissue samples for microscope work. Do preliminary studies. You can do drawings if you want. Photos. Things like that. But there's a bigger point to this."

Everything he said was ridiculous. Billie worked to keep her voice even. "Roland. The water in the tank doesn't circulate. It's not even piped. How did you intend to keep this thing alive?"

"It doesn't need water to breathe," he pointed out.

"That doesn't mean it doesn't need it to live! It may need it for its skin or its circulatory system or . . . or . . . a hundred things. So it can breathe on land. So it can survive out of water. For how long? I don't know, and I can't know until I examine it. Neither do you. You're the herpetologist; you know this as well as I do. We'll have to change that water every day."

"That's why I have you, to make these determinations. Anyway, we're on the ocean. It shouldn't be too hard."

"For you and me to exchange gallons of seawater every day? No crewman is going to help us. Not only that, but what does it eat? How will we feed it?"

"Fish, I assume. Goat."

Billie laughed at the absurdity. "Goat. I didn't realize we had goat aboard."

"We'll keep it chloroformed. It won't have to eat."

"You don't know that. We don't know how its metabolic system works. It might starve. How long will it take us to get back?"

"A week, maybe."

"Or more, given our engineer. What else might it need? Roland, are you even thinking?"

"Billie." He let out his breath, came to her, and gripped her arms. "You're the one who's not thinking. This is why James brought you aboard. This is why you're here. Not to establish a marine exhibit in San Diego. *This.* You can bring back your career with this. All you have to do is play along."

"Play along," she repeated, pushing away from him. "What is this really about, Rolly? Why does James need this thing? Why is he so desperate to keep it alive and in one piece?"

"We need to study its lungs. Its gills. I can do some of it. But I need your expertise too. I can't do it alone."

"How am I supposed to study its lungs without cutting into it?"

"As best you can."

Billie snorted. She glanced toward the fish, the bubbles of its sleeping breath in the water. Everything Roland suggested was absurd. The worst of it was that she didn't know why, or why it should matter. The discovery of the *antorcha del mar*—and they really should come up with a better name for it, a scientific name—could turn evolutionary theory on its head, and all Roland wanted her to do was study its breathing system. Why?

Then she remembered what she should never have forgotten.

"The Empedocles Society," she said with a sigh. "Dear God, Rolly, please tell me this isn't to do with some bizarre Society cult-worship thing."

"It's not a cult."

"What do you mean to do? Attach the lungs of this thing to James or something?"

He made a face. "You know better than that."

"Do I? Or maybe you plan to say a couple of prayers, burn chicken feathers? Sprinkle holy water? Whatever it is, it isn't science! You want me to *waste* this discovery on *that*? No. No, I refuse to do it. I won't. How is it supposed to help me, or science in general?"

He stepped closer, close enough that she felt the burn of his intensity. "Listen to me, Billie. You've got it half right. James is looking for a cure for his lungs. That's why he's spent a fortune searching for this fish. There are men in the Society, surgeons, who think that if they transplant cells from its lungs, or its gills—or maybe both—into his, it may work. There are other parts involved, too, but that's the gist of it. Do you understand?"

It all fell into place—Victorine's concern, Oliver's machinations, Maud's fear. James did intend the fish to be his cure. This was why he'd been so determined to continue. But to predicate it all on some bizarre Society ritual . . . "How exactly do they intend to do this?"

"James found an ancient text—"

"An *ancient* text? Don't tell me it's a *magical* text."

He waved her comment away. "It involves some serums and a ritual, yes, but it's based on science."

"Whose science? Ancient Greeks'?" She couldn't keep the scorn from her voice.

"Billie—"

"That . . . that's crazy."

"Is it? Think about it. Discoveries are made every day by taking such risks."

"Yes, but—"

"It's not just a whim, Billie. I need you to analyze its blood, take tissue samples, do all this *without doing harm*. That's crucial. There are others who need to see it first. There are plans. Help me with this, please. If you do, I'll make sure you're credited in the papers that are published. I promise it."

So intense. So much in those hazel eyes. Billie found herself quieted in the same way she had been moved by Roland in the past. It wasn't his charm or attractiveness that had won her in those days, she remembered, it was this . . . this way he believed in the things he believed. It was hard to say no to him. It was hard to walk away.

"This is all just for James," she clarified.

A nod. He didn't look away. He held her with those eyes.

Billie said, "What has he promised you?"

It was the most important question, and Roland didn't answer it. He stepped away; he turned away. "Will you do it? It will be good for both of us."

Billie was silent. She'd heard those words before too. *"It will be good for both of us."* Roland's promises. "Because what's good for you is good for me, is that right?"

He looked puzzled. "Yes, of course."

"We're not married anymore, Rolly," she said quietly. "Even when we were, you never really thought of what was good for me apart from you."

"It was true by definition. You were my wife," he said, still puzzled.

That was the problem, she realized. It had always been. She was only an extension of him, and that was why he hadn't seen the publication of those articles under the name R. W. Ely the same way she had. He had apologized, but he hadn't understood; she saw that now. He had never understood how much it mattered to her, because he had never seen her as separate.

She wondered if he saw it now.

"I won't do it," she said. "You study this fish on your own if you want, but I won't be part of this."

"Billie." His voice went low and urgent. "You have to. This is why we brought you. I vouched for you. I need you. You help me and I'll help you. You want your career back? I'll give it to you."

She laughed shortly. "You don't have the power to do that."

"But I will," he insisted. "If this works—"

"Ah, I see. What's he promised you? Your own lab? A lab at the Holloway Foundation? Maybe even your own academy?"

Roland was silent, so she knew her guess was correct.

"Of course. I should have known."

"I'll bring you on."

"As what? An assistant, the way I was before?"

"Whatever you want," he said. "Name the position. It's yours."

Billie met his gaze and held it. "Whatever I want."

A quick nod. "Remember the study we planned? The crocodiles of Sinaloa? I can get it funded. We can do it."

They'd worked for years to get that study off the ground. He had to know how it tempted, and she knew Roland well enough to know that he meant it. He respected her science. He respected her research. He wanted this badly. Badly enough to try to wring this promise from her when he knew he was asking her to betray her principles. He was asking her to hand over what she'd learned about this creature to one man. One very rich, very determined man. To hell with the rest of the world. To hell with the good that such a discovery could do.

When she thought of it that way, it was not so tempting. But she considered the creature, and the things she could learn, and in the end, Billie believed that she could find some way to have everything she wanted. She could find a way to change Roland's mind. She *would* change his mind.

"Okay," she said.

That evening, Billie sat by the tank and watched the *antorcha del mar*, which remained mostly unmoving but for the slight jerk of its fins and the current from its breathing. She wondered if it was dreaming, and what it might be dreaming about. The camera still stood on its tripod after the flurry of photographs Roland had taken. Now Billie made notes on the capture, the depth at which they'd caught it, and the landscape and location, and tried to imagine the ocean bottom where they'd found it.

Already the creature's colors seemed to have faded, but that might be the harsh hanging lights, which were designed for dissection; they seemed to blast the color from everything.

Earlier, she'd thrown bonitos into the tank. Two dead and one alive. The live one wouldn't last long in the still, unoxygenated seawater, but Billie didn't know which the creature might prefer to eat if it woke and was hungry. Was it a scavenger or a hunter? If the tale about the goat was true, she would say hunter, but she hadn't enough physical evidence to make that assumption. Maybe the goat had tried to attack it. Maybe the fish had simply been defending itself. Billie studied the fins. No claws, nothing retractable. She studied the teeth. Sharp, razor-like in front, and in the back teeth for grinding—maybe omnivorous?

And yes, the creature was female, according to Roland, who knew amphibian sex determination better than she did. She hadn't doubted it, given the things she'd heard from the crew.

"Where have you been hiding, my beauty?" she murmured as she made notes. "How have you eluded us for so long?"

Send me home.

Billie jerked back on her stool, dropping her pencil. The voice had been loud in her head. She glanced around, but no one else was there. Only the gurgling aquariums, the jars holding her specimens, fish eyes staring blankly at her.

You don't belong here.

The same voice from her dreams. The spirit, as Maud or Victorine would say. It had followed Billie here, into the hold. She stilled, waiting to feel its presence, that shift in the air. But the hold felt just the same.

She looked at the creature. No, it couldn't be the fish. The chloroform had knocked it out. It couldn't speak to her. The voice from her dreams predated it. A spirit, a fish . . . both impossible. Was this what it felt like to go insane? Was it that impossible things felt so real?

The *antorcha* stirred. The live bonito swam around the tank, seeming confused, sending flashes of reflection from the lights through the water with every movement.

"Okay," Billie breathed. She closed her eyes for a moment to calm herself. The day had been long and full of emotion. "Well." Billie picked up her pencil. Her hand trembled, and she clenched her fingers to still it. Despite Roland's intention to keep the creature chloroformed, she had meant to let it wake, to see what it would eat, which fish it would choose, the living or the dead, but she found herself discomfited, ill at ease, strangely afraid.

She put the notebook and pencil aside and dosed it with chloroform once again.

Chapter Twenty-Two

That night Billie's dreams were roiling and anxious and angry, and she couldn't find herself within them. Voices—*Leave here; you don't belong here; send me back*—

Slap!

A hard strike to her cheek brought her startling awake to stare blindly into the darkness. It took her a moment to discern that the crashing, groaning, and shrieking sounds she heard were a storm, and not the rage from her dream, but the burning sting of flesh against flesh remained—that was not a dream. Her cheek hurt. She stumbled from her berth only to be thrown to the floor by the ship's abrupt pitch. The wind howled; water slammed against the hull.

Billie clung to the floor and crawled to turn on the light, but it didn't work. The power was out—now she realized she couldn't hear the generators. Her cheek burned from her dream—her *dream*, how absurd. The *Eurybia* rocked; she tried to get to her feet and couldn't keep her balance. She had to get out of this room. Billie dragged the blanket from the bed, staggered to the door, and twisted the knob in panic. It didn't budge.

It was locked. She must have locked it without paying attention. But . . . Billie had never locked it. There wasn't a key. Only her grip on the knob kept her from falling as the ship heeled and rolled. Billie kept a desperate hold. She wiggled the knob, then wrenched it harder, now jerking it. The door did not budge. She kicked it, then pounded on it, hot now with fear and panic, sweating with it.

"Hey!" she screamed. "Hey! Someone! Anyone? I'm locked in! Hey!"

The storm raged; something crashed against the porthole. Billie turned to see, but the curtain was drawn, and as far as she could tell, the porthole glass held. She turned back to the door and pounded again.

"Help! Someone!" She twisted the knob and jerked on the door. "Someone! Please!"

The door simply wouldn't budge.

Billie's heart raced. Her cheek still burned. She stepped back from the door. In the darkness she saw only shadowed shapes within the bedroom, nothing more. She took a deep breath, trying to calm herself, and tried to determine what to do. Wait it out. At some point, someone would wonder what had happened to her. Regardless of the storm, if she didn't show up for cocktail hour, surely they'd send someone to look for her. Or if Roland had a question he couldn't answer about the *antorcha del mar*, he'd have no choice but to search her out. There was no reason to panic. She wouldn't stay locked in here for long.

Then the *Eurybia* rolled so far on its side that it threw Billie back against the berth. The lotions on her dressing table cracked together and scattered onto the floor. The sound of rushing water—very loud—pouring water. From the head. From the taps. Pounding onto the porcelain of the bathtub. There was no light, but Billie knew what she'd see. Bloody water.

The hair rose on the back of her neck. Her panic resurged. She lunged for the door just as the taps shut off, but she didn't wait to investigate. She yanked on the doorknob, and miraculously, bizarrely, as if it hadn't been resisting her the last ten minutes, the door opened, jerking from her grip to crack against the corner of the wardrobe.

Billie raced out, crashing against the opposite wall of the companionway in her haste, tripping blindly in the direction of the stairs. She had just reached them when she saw a mass of shadowed motion plunging down, heard a grunt of pain. Billie stopped short.

She recognized the grunt and the shadow.

"Roland?"

"Roland, are you okay?" came Victorine's voice from above. She, too, sounded panicked. "Roland?"

"I'm okay, I'm okay," Roland said, struggling to his feet against the pitching of the ship. He reached out, grabbing for Billie, sounding relieved when he said, "There you are. Come up to the saloon."

Billie's own relief was overwhelming. She grasped the edges of the blanket around her and followed him up the stairs, into the flashlight-lit main saloon, which was disorienting in its mess, upturned furniture and mostly darkness and the stink of vomit and . . . tank water? Billie could swear she smelled the creature's tank up here, or no, the smell came from Victorine, who stood anxiously waiting at the top of the stairs. When Billie moved away from her, the smell faded too.

But in the howl of the storm and the ship's dashing and rocking, Billie forgot the smell quickly. Oliver and James, James's valet Pollan, and Maud were already there. The curtains had been pulled back, but she saw nothing but rain-dashed, impenetrable darkness. Crashing sounds came from above; a rope lashed against the window. A commotion from the dining saloon, the crash of tureens falling. The ship pitched; Roland tumbled into the hutch, and Pollan fell, sprawling with a grunt. The champagne-glass-shaped cigarette lighter hurtled to the floor, spilling naphtha. The oily, noxious stink of the fuel filled the saloon, mixing with that of vomit. Billie thought she saw seawater outside the windows, but she didn't believe it. The ship couldn't possibly be that far on its side.

"Are we going to sink?" Oliver moaned.

"I'm sure Captain Rogers has everything under control." James sounded very calm.

Again, the ship rolled. Oliver sank his head into his hands. "Dear God."

"Throw up again, Ollie, and I'll toss you overboard." James staggered and caught himself on the anchored settee.

The froth of water—rain? Sea?—beat against the glass. Billie had never seen a storm like this.

"I do believe we're going to sink," Pollan said.

"We aren't going to sink," James asserted. "Everyone calm down. The storm will pass. We've been blessed. We found the fish. Nothing's going to happen to us."

Pollan groaned. "Are you sure? How can you be sure?"

No one answered that.

The ship careened; books crashed to the floor. The freestanding furniture—the two armchairs, the coffee table—slid until it caught on the rug. Something cracked hard on the skylight above. The *Eurybia* shuddered as if under a great strain. Maud lost her balance and fell, sliding into the wall.

Billie said, "Maud!"

"I'm okay," the maid said.

The ship hurtled directionless through the rain and the wind, or so it seemed. Now and again Billie heard muffled shouting from below, but the engines remained silent. If the crew had a way to control the *Eurybia*, she couldn't imagine what it was. But James and Victorine seemed unperturbed, and they owned the ship, and so . . . Billie tried to reassure herself.

They remained in darkness but for the beam from the flashlight that bounced at every bump. Pollan looked as if he wanted to melt into the floor. Oliver's jaw set so tight he appeared made of steel. Maud huddled in a corner, knees to her chest like a child, watching them all with wide dark eyes that seemed to consume every stray bit of light. Roland sat stiffly and alertly, and Billie stayed as close to him as she could without crawling into his arms, which frankly she half wished to do. She had never been so glad of his warmth and stability, and it wasn't just because the ship sounded like it might break into splinters at any moment. The storm only added to her already heightened sense of disquiet.

She could no longer deny her experience. A room was not sentient. It did not have a will. It didn't invade one's dreams with voices that ordered one to *leave this place*. It didn't warn, *You don't belong here*. It didn't burrow into one's consciousness.

No, a room was not sentient. But something within it was. And that something was complicated now by the presence of the fish, because she'd heard the voice in its presence. What kind of spirit was this? Where had it come from? How did she research a ghost without everyone on board thinking she had lost her mind—unless she actually had—which she could not afford, especially now, when she had to convince both Roland and James that their plan for the fish was ill-advised.

The ship shuddered.

Assuming she survived the storm, which seemed more unlikely by the moment.

The wind's banshee-like howls squeezed through the cracks in the door, sending shivers over her skin. Billie curled more tightly into her blanket and stared up at the storm-painted skylight, which had grown so dark with the night and the clouds that the painted scene seemed only shadows upon shadows.

Victorine, who had slumped in one of the chairs, straightened. "Did you hear that?"

"A particularly loud gust," James agreed.

"No, not the wind." Victorine frowned. She rose and stumbled to the window to stare out into the darkness, clutching the edge for balance. "A voice. A scream."

"I think it was just the wind, Vic." James sounded inestimably tired.

The flashlight beam wavered and dimmed.

"You should turn it off unless we need it," Roland advised James. "The battery is dying."

"Then we'd be in darkness," Oliver protested.

"We'll certainly be in darkness if it's dead," Roland said. He pressed his arm against Billie's. "Okay?" he asked softly.

"Not a bit," she answered.

"We're not meant to end eaten by sea worms, Billie." He kept his voice low, just between them.

But she wasn't sure she believed him, and when the *Eurybia* shook so that Billie felt it in her own bones, she wondered how he was so certain. Was it only that same faith that James had, the belief that now the *antorcha del mar* was in their hands, nothing could go wrong?

Such hubris, wasn't it? How had Roland not felt the hostility of the thing?

As if in answer to her thoughts, the wind battered the skylight so heavily Billie flinched. The ship groaned as if it were being torn in two.

Victorine stumbled back to her chair. As she passed, Billie once again caught the scent of the tank water. Had Victorine been in the hold? It didn't make any sense, and because it didn't, Billie dismissed the thought. But it made her think of the hold, and the tank, and whether the creature remained secure there. The tank should be deep enough, but with the ship rolling so . . . Not only that, but the jars weren't secured, though the aquariums were. All the specimens . . . she imagined them falling to the floor, the jars breaking, the mess and the loss, and along with her fear came despair. What would be left? Anything at all?

You'll be lucky to survive this, she told herself wryly. There was no point in worrying over losing specimens when she might not survive to care about them. She remembered the words of the crew, of Victorine. The cursed ship. Yes, it did feel cursed now. She stared at Oliver curled in a fetal position on the floor, seasick and frightened, and then looked to James, who sat in a chair, watching out the window, looking unconcerned and unrattled, and she thought again of hubris, her own as well. This was what came of dynamiting the shore, harpooning manta rays, shooting dolphins. Of dragging creatures aboard in nets so roughly that jellyfish and holothurians and starfish were mangled and useless. Of tromping about in the shallows to gather living things only to plunge them into jars of formalin. As if it were possible to garner even the slightest bit of knowledge about such a vast community, to gain even the slightest dominion over such a foreign place. And yet, always, for her, there was the questing, the need to know, to understand.

And now, this moment, on this ship being tossed about by a sea that seemed vengeful and angry and more alive than ever, Billie realized that it had never occurred to her before that the sea might betray her. Men, yes, but never the sea.

Chapter Twenty-Three

Billie didn't sleep. None of them did. But as the storm lulled, and the *Eurybia* settled into a steady, rhythmic rocking, she fell into a mesmeric half-awake, half-trance state. None of them spoke. They all stared out the windows as the darkness faded and the sun rose first into gray and then into pink-gold that glittered through the raindrop-marked glass. Until a pelican glided by, she hadn't noticed how hard she'd leaned into Roland, that she'd rested her head on his chest and his arm was around her, but the pelican seemed to eye her as it streaked past, breaking her from her trance. Billie straightened, pulling away from Roland's warmth, understanding fully that the storm was over.

James said hoarsely, "Everyone okay? No one injured?"

There was a murmur of assent.

"I should see what the damage is." He rose like one who'd been still too long, creaky and bent, and cleared his throat.

Before he made it to the door, someone else came through it. The first mate, who looked exhausted and unhappy. "Captain wants to see the commodore."

"Is everyone okay?" James asked him. "The crew . . . ?"

The first mate shrugged, turned, and went back out.

James gave them all a tired glance and followed, saying, "Pollan, bring coffee to the deckhouse."

Pollan leaped to his feet.

Roland roused from the settee. "I should go with James."

"Why you?" Oliver asked.

"No one's stopping you from coming," Roland said, and the two of them disappeared outside.

Victorine uncurled herself from the chair they'd righted and lodged against the hutch. "I suppose I should see to everything."

"Would you like me to fetch you some coffee, ma'am?" Maud sat up from where she'd been stretched out on the carpet beside the turned-over coffee table.

"I'm not sure of the state of things." Victorine paused at the deckhouse door and looked over her shoulder at Pollan. "Forget what James said for now. Let the crew settle a bit before we get back to normal. If there's going to be such a thing." She went out.

"I should check on the hold," Billie said.

"Would you like me to come with you?" Maud asked.

Billie was surprised at the offer, and gratified by it. She didn't know what to expect in the hold or whether it was safe, so she shook her head. "Thank you, but let me see what it's like first."

Maud came up beside her. "Last night . . . in your room . . . did you . . . was there any trouble?"

Billie tried to read the maid's expression. "What do you mean, trouble?"

Maud met her gaze hesitantly, as if she were afraid to ask, but had to. "You know what I mean. The spirit."

It wasn't something Billie wanted to discuss. She remembered the maid telling her that incense and praying would protect her from bad spirits, and Billie wished she hadn't dismissed that advice so blithely now that she could think of no other explanation for what had happened to her.

But she only asked, "Maud, do you know if there's a key to my room?"

Maud raised a brow. "A key? I don't know. I've never seen one. Why?"

"No reason. Just wondering."

"Would you like me to ask for one? Is there a reason you want to lock your door?"

Billie shook her head. "No, no. Of course not. As I said, I was just wondering."

The engines were silent, and so were the generators. Billie grabbed the flashlight from where it lay abandoned on the floor, and went down the stairs, past the stateroom level, to the hold, each level growing darker and hotter. Rather like descending into Dante's circles of hell, she thought wryly, and then couldn't quite banish the thought. She switched on the flashlight, which only seemed to add a freaky, eerie aura to the ship's innards, and when she reached the door to the hold—open, which was strange; she was sure she had closed it when she'd left, but maybe the storm had forced it open—the aura seemed creepier than ever. Billie couldn't help shivering as she went into the deep darkness, which the narrow beam of the flashlight could not possibly illuminate.

The scent of formalin was overpowering. It had been strong before. Now the pungent smell filled her nostrils, making it hard to breathe. Billie's heart sank at what that must mean, and as she shone the flashlight around the laboratory, her worst fears became manifest. The saltwater tanks were intact, thank heavens, though the circulating pumps were still. But the jars . . . some of them remained on the shelves, but most had fallen to the floor and broken, and in the beam of the flashlight she took in the mess. Broken glass, flaccid sea cucumbers, the severed tentacles of octopi amid shards, dismembered starfish, the crushed shells of clams and crabs and other crustaceans. Smashed snails . . . much of the last weeks' work destroyed. The slime of guts and pools of formalin everywhere.

Billie wanted to cry. All gone. All her carefully cataloged specimens. She'd photographed most of them, but there was still so much to study, so much to describe . . . It was all she could do not to sink to the floor in despair. There was nothing left to establish a marine exhibit at the zoo, but more than that, the real reason she'd come on this cruise, her dreams of a groundbreaking paper . . . She had no option left but the *antorcha*. Her career depended on it now. Everything depended on it.

Then she saw the wash of seawater around the tank.

She had expected that some would splash out during the storm. The ship had rocked so. But this . . . there was so much that the puddle of it nearly reached where she stood. Billie raised the flashlight, running the beam along the sides of the tank, and saw the tarp was undone. Not just at a corner or here and there, where she might have expected one or two ties to break, but an entire side. As if it had been untied. It had been thrown back upon itself, leaving a section of the tank uncovered.

Billie hadn't done that. Roland never would have done so. Someone else had been in the hold. Someone had untied the tarp.

Cautiously Billie made her way through the pools of formalin and broken glass toward the tank. She was still barefoot, so she went carefully. As she approached the tank, the formalin mixed with the seawater, and it felt strangely . . . slimy?

Billie glanced down. There was something viscous there, something slippery. She frowned, turning the beam of the flashlight to her feet, searching for the source. Nothing, but . . . was that a bit of iridescence she saw? Like oil, or . . . ? She couldn't make it out. The light was too dim, and she wasn't sure that the dim light itself hadn't created the slight rainbow effect. Billie bent down to feel the liquid on the floor, rubbing her fingers together. Yes, she definitely felt a kind of slime separate from the tank water.

She straightened, puzzled, and stepped closer to the tank to peer in. The side was wet. Well, of course, how could it not be? The water had clearly splashed over the side. The level of liquid in the tank was much lower; they would have to replenish the seawater quickly. She looked back to the *antorcha del mar* to see just how much it would need.

Billie shone the flashlight beam on it, and . . . she could have sworn it moved in response to the light. A swipe of the fin, a current in the water as if the fish moved toward her. Billie stepped back. It was awake. But when she looked again, the fish was still, its rainbow colors glimmering in the faint light, incredibly beautiful, even though the colors had indeed faded, and the flashlight could not hope to capture how stunning it was. She played the beam over it, checking it for any damage. Those bony finlike appendages, the triangular head as large as her torso, the eyes staring into space, turning toward her to look, to meet her gaze, to peer into her soul, to ask who she was, where she had been—

For God's sake.

Billie swallowed hard. Then she noticed the living bonito was gone. The two dead ones remained. The creature had eaten the living one while she was gone. During the storm. How intriguing. So it liked live food. She wondered how it had captured the tuna, and cursed herself for not being here to witness it.

Ah, well, at least the *antorcha* had not been damaged. Billie would have to get more seawater for it as soon as possible, but the fact that it was alive was a blessing. It would be the mother lode if she could keep it out of the Empedocles Society's hands. She got the chloroform, and when she dosed the fish once again, it didn't move or try to avoid her. She wasn't sure now that she'd seen it move earlier. Another mirage, just like the many others she'd seen. She was exhausted. The storm had worn her out.

Send me home.

Billie jumped. Quickly she reached for the edge of the tarp and pulled it toward her to fasten it in place again, surprised to find she was shaking. She clutched the flashlight beneath her armpit as she quickly knotted the ropes. Her knuckles brushed the side of the tank, and she felt . . . slime.

Billie paused, perplexed and uneasy. She hurriedly finished fastening the tarp, and then shone the flashlight on the side of the tank. That same faint iridescence she'd seen on the floor. She swiped her finger through it. Slippery. Thick. Where the hell had that come from? That, too, she'd felt on the floor.

There wasn't much she could do to investigate until the lights came on, and she should report all this to Roland, who would want to examine the slime—he was the expert in it—and, too, Billie's uneasiness had gained hold. She wanted to get out of the darkness. She hurried to the stairs and closed the door of the hold behind her. All she could smell was formalin-scented tank water. On her hands, on her feet. The slime left a sticky residue. After last night, the last place Billie wanted to be was her stateroom, but she wanted to wash off the feel and the smell of the hold, and that won out over her reluctance. Besides, she wanted to change from her nightgown before she went on deck to see what other damage the storm had wrought.

But she was nervous, and the already-close companionway seemed to narrow as she made her way down it, the mahogany and the darkened sconces making it feel as if the corridor stretched on and on before her. Impossibly, too, it seemed as if the stink of the hold grew stronger the farther she got from it. Billie's nose twitched, she sneezed, and the motion sent the flashlight beam bouncing over something—a lump of shadow in the corridor past her stateroom door, nearer the engine room.

Strange. Billie pointed the flashlight toward it. The beam caught a rubber-soled shoe.

A rubber-soled shoe attached to a very still foot.

The hair rose on the back of Billie's neck, and a terrible sense of dread swept through her. The only thing that kept her from retreating to the safety of her stateroom was the fact that her stateroom was not the least bit safe. She took a deep breath and approached the mass of shadow.

It was a man. A sailor. One she recognized.

Matías, the assistant engineer, his eyes opened wide in what looked like shock—or no, fear. It was fear.

He was very dead, and the smell of formalin and tank water fogged the companionway around him. When Billie looked down, she saw she stood in a pool of it.

Tank water, with an iridescent glow.

Chapter Twenty-Four

Billie raced across the deck. From the corner of her eye she saw Victorine at the rail. Billie heard her hostess call, "Billie, what is it?" but she didn't stop. She nearly leaped the stairs to the pilothouse, unable to contain her panic.

She found James there, going over the *Coast Pilot* with the captain.

"Matías," Billie blurted out breathlessly. "He's dead."

James and Captain Rogers looked up, equally blank.

The door opened behind her. Victorine stepped inside. "What's happening?"

James said, "Matías?" as if he couldn't remember who that was.

"I don't understand," Captain Rogers said.

The images crowded Billie's head. The body. The pool of tank water. The smell. "He's dead. I found him in the corridor outside the engine room."

"You should sit down. You look like you might faint," Victorine said.

"I don't faint," Billie snapped, too unsettled to be anything but blunt.

"What happened?" Captain Rogers demanded. "How can he be dead?"

"Who the hell is Matías?" James asked.

"The assistant engineer."

"Dead? Then who—"

"No one," the captain said. "No one else knows anything about the engines. What happened? Where is he?"

"Where's Roland? And Oliver?" Billie asked.

"Checking the supplies," Rogers told her. "Show me to Matías."

"This way." Billie led the way from the pilothouse, and the rest of them followed her belowdecks. By the time they got there, other sailors had discovered Matías. They gathered where the assistant engineer lay sprawled in the corridor outside the engine room.

"It's almost like a movie, isn't it?" Victorine said. When Billie frowned at her, Victorine explained, "The look on his face. It doesn't seem real."

It was true, it didn't. It was a comically unreal expression of fear, in fact. Billie had the urge to kick him, to rouse him, to demand that he stop playacting. The flashlight beam only made the effect worse.

The other sailors spoke Spanish and Italian, high-pitched, panicked talk. The atmosphere felt fraught and dangerous. The captain spoke in a calm, reassuring voice, but it didn't seem to make any difference. And the smell . . .

Tank water and formalin, just as in the hold. Billie couldn't deny it. She remembered last night when she'd thought she smelled it on Victorine, and just as she had the thought, Victorine asked, "Had he been in the hold?"

Everyone went quiet.

Captain Rogers looked at her. "What do you mean?"

"Don't you smell it? The—what's it called?" She looked at Billie.

"Formalin," Billie said quietly, glancing at Victorine. "Formalin and tank water." So Victorine recognized the smell, which she wouldn't have if she hadn't been there herself. What did it mean that Victorine had been in the hold? Had she been the one who'd untied the tarp?

The captain glanced down at the floor. He had been kneeling by Matías, and now he rose. "Is that what that smell is?"

Billie nodded.

A flurry of speaking among the sailors. Accusations. Troubled glances at her. She remembered Maud's comment that they thought she was possessed. A few of them crossed themselves. Billie spoke harshly to them in Spanish. "I had nothing to do with this."

"What did you say?" James asked.

"That I had nothing to do with Matías's death. I only found him."

Captain Rogers scowled. "Where did all this liquid come from?"

"I have no idea. I found him this way," she said.

"You were in the hold," he said.

"I've just come from there," she agreed.

The captain's expression hardened. "Miss McKennan, I'm afraid this all looks a bit suspicious."

Billie couldn't hide her frustration. "What reason would I have to kill the assistant engineer, Captain?" Billie asked. "Without him, I can't get my collection. Besides, I'm the one who reported it."

"That could be to throw us off," James said, though he seemed uncertain.

"I didn't kill Matías," Billie insisted. "We don't even know how he died. And anyway, you may want to ask your wife where she's been, James, since she stank of this same smell last night during the storm."

Victorine made a sound of protest.

James looked at Victorine with a frown and asked, "You . . . you weren't in bed last night, were you? When the storm started. Where were you?"

"I told you, I couldn't sleep."

"Yes, but . . . where were you? You weren't in the stateroom."

"Why would I kill Matías?"

For a moment James seemed nonplussed. Then he put his hand to his forehead. "God, I don't know. I don't understand what's happening here. I guess . . . you've never liked the idea of the Society's involvement in this."

Victorine stared at him in obvious disbelief and hurt. "And so I would kill the assistant engineer? Really, James, you've gone too far.

I want your cure as much as you do. Now you've got your fish, and we're going home. I'm perfectly satisfied. Not only that, but I've communicated with Emile's spirit."

"Emile?" James looked surprised.

"Just last night, in fact. He came to me."

Now this, on top of everything else. Billie caught Victorine's sideways glance. She was profoundly aware of the crew's silent watchfulness. *No,* she thought. *No, please don't let her make this worse.*

James scowled. "When? What did he say?"

"Who's Emile?" Captain Rogers asked.

"Her dead brother," Billie said.

Captain Rogers seemed confused. He gestured toward Matías. "Obviously this needs an investigation." He told the crew to take the body to the foredeck; in response they looked mutinous. Rogers ordered, "Pronto!"

Some of them backed away, shaking their heads, disappearing down the companionway toward the crew quarters. Two men let out heavy sighs and moved forward to lift Matías.

"We'll need a neutral person to examine him," the captain said as he watched the men lug the assistant engineer down the corridor toward the stairs. "Do you think Mr. Ely can do it?"

Billie protested, "Roland's no more a doctor than I am. He's a herpetologist."

"Surely he can tell how the man died." The captain gave her a hard look.

"Is Roland really neutral?" Victorine asked.

Her husband looked puzzled. "What do you mean?"

"He and Billie have a past. Or perhaps a present," she told him, and then, to Billie's surprise, said, "Don't you, Billie? I've been wondering since San Diego what it is. Maybe you'd like to tell us?"

Billie stared at Victorine as coldly as she could. "I don't know what to address first. The idea that you're talking to your dead brother or that Roland and I have some kind of . . . of game going."

"Do you?" James asked. "How well did you know Roland before this trip?"

Billie squirmed. The urge to tell the truth struck her hard, but it would be a mistake, she knew, especially now. The time to say it had long since passed. Now it would only be construed as a conspiracy. "We're fellow scientists. I worked with him at the Academy once."

"You did?" James looked surprised. "He should have told me that. Why didn't he?"

She probably should not have said it. "I suppose he thought it unimportant. Every scientist in California has worked with the others at one time or another. There aren't that many of us, you know. There would be no reason to tell you unless he thought it was a mistake to hire me. Which I promise you it was not."

"Hmmm." James considered her. "I'm wondering about that."

"The only mistake you're making, James, is in not letting us properly examine the fish. There's no real way to do that without dissecting her. We'll never understand if we can't. She's a marvel—surely you see that. An evolutionary miracle. The world should know about her. The things we could learn from her—"

"*Her?*" James asked at the same moment Victorine said, "You can't cut it!"

The woman sounded almost desperate.

Billie sighed. Another protest to fight. "Yes, she's female. And I can't properly see how her respiratory system works if I can't cut into her."

James said, "The fish isn't to be harmed. Do you understand me, Billie? Roland is in charge of it. Anything that happens to it goes through Roland first."

"Of course," Billie said shortly.

"And, Vic, as for Emile . . ."

"I'll speak to you about it later," Victorine said tightly. "Alone."

James shook his head and stalked away down the corridor, leaving Billie alone with Victorine. Billie crossed her arms over her chest, feeling the residue of stickiness on her fingers, drying now, flaking, reminding her of real questions, of important ones. "Were you visiting the fish, Victorine? Did you undo the tarp last night?"

Her hostess lifted her chin in defiance. "If I did?"

"It let too much water splash out. It's going to be hard enough to keep the fish alive long enough to get it back to San Francisco. I can't afford to let anyone make it harder. I don't imagine your husband wants that either."

Victorine nodded. "I'll be careful next time."

"It may be too late, and I'd rather there wasn't a next time. You should leave the fish to me and Roland."

Billie was surprised by the desperation that flashed in Victorine's eyes. "I can't. I can't do that."

"Why?"

Victorine seemed reluctant at first, but then she said, "My brother . . ."

Billie was growing heartily tired of Emile Coustan. If Victorine mentioned the supposed spirit in the chintz room, Billie thought she would scream. The morning had been enough. She didn't want to talk about this now. "What does he have to do with the fish?"

Billie felt Victorine's hesitation, a reluctance. "Emile's spirit spoke to me through it."

"What?"

"I know it sounds crazy," Victorine said. "But I heard him. I did. It was Emile's voice."

Victorine had heard the fish speaking too. Out loud, or as a voice in her head? Billie suppressed the urge to laugh when she realized she was actually considering the question. It was impossible, wasn't it? A fish was not a sentient being. Billie knew that. A fish was not telepathic. A fish could not speak or project its feelings into anyone's head. *Send me home. You don't belong here.* What about the voice from Billie's dream? What was that? Victorine's spirit? Maud's ghost?

Billie felt on precarious ground. She couldn't simply deny what she'd heard herself, or what she thought she'd heard, and yet . . . this place was so strange. "How do you know it was Emile's voice?" she asked weakly.

"Don't you think I know my own bro—" Victorine broke off. "Wait a minute, you're not surprised I heard the fish speaking to me, are you?"

"Victorine, I—"

"You hear it, too, don't you? Just as you felt his spirit in your room. I knew it!"

The woman's eyes shone with triumph and vindication, and desperately Billie tried to quell Victorine's fervor. "Honestly, I don't know what I'm hearing or feeling."

"Yes you do. You just don't want to admit it. You know he's here. You understand! You'll help me, then, won't you? You won't cut into it, will you? Not until I know . . ."

"Know what?"

Another pause. "The answers."

What was true, what was not . . . Billie could barely force out her voice. "What answers are those?"

"I don't know," Victorine acknowledged. "I don't know what Emile's trying to tell me. I don't know why he's sought me out now. For two years I've been calling him. He's never deigned to contact me. Until now. What did he say to you?"

Billie didn't want to answer. She didn't know what to make of any of it. Victorine heard the voice, too, and while Billie had thought Victorine's talk of spirits delusional, now they were experiencing the same thing, which Billie could no longer easily ignore unless she wanted to call herself delusional, too, which she didn't *think* she was, but . . . it was all so confusing. Billie didn't interfere with people's beliefs, unless they interfered with science the way the Scopes trial had. But she had also never given them the same respect that she'd given science—how could she, when such things as faith healing and speaking in tongues and miracles could so easily be explained as hysteria? She had never experienced anything like that until now, and now . . . she could hardly believe how real it felt.

Real enough to be *real*? She couldn't quite accept that, even as everything in her insisted that the voice she heard was not an illusion, or madness, or hysteria. What of her growing sense that it was somehow connected to the expedition? That she needed to listen because it mattered greatly?

"It says we don't belong here," she said quietly.

"Really?" Victorine looked surprised. "Why would he say that, when he's come to me now? At this time? Here in this place?"

Billie proceeded carefully. "Maybe you've . . . wanted so to see your brother that you've misinterpreted things."

Victorine's eyes flashed with irritation. "Or maybe you have. Who has more experience speaking with spirits? I don't fault you—it takes time and skill to learn how to speak to them. They can be . . . elusive and . . . and, well, obscure. I worry that he's come to warn me . . ."

"Warn you of what?"

Victorine hesitated as if she didn't really want to say it, but then a determined look came into her face. "Of this cure. Truthfully, I didn't really expect we would find this thing. But now that we have . . . I want so to believe, but James is right when he says I've never trusted the Empedocles Society. They're the ones who planned this whole expedition. You know that too?"

Billie nodded.

"James has pursued some . . . frightening ideas before. The micropoisons almost killed him. Living only on air . . . well, you can imagine. I have to admit I'm afraid. He's so convinced this is the answer. He promises me it's scientifically sound. Is it?"

Billie wanted to mention her own doubts, but what did she really know about the studies or the procedure or this ancient text? Roland had told her so little. "You think Emile's spirit is a messenger?"

Victorine nodded. "I believe that's why he's here now. I believe he'll tell me whether to go ahead with this experiment." A soft laugh. "I can't fault you for your skepticism. It's all quite a shock at first when one first begins communicating with the dead. But you'll give me time to find out, won't you? You'll follow James's instructions? You won't disobey him?"

Billie took a deep breath. About one thing, Victorine was right. Something here needed to be explored. They'd both heard *something*, and Billie wanted to know what it was and what it meant. "For now, I'll do what James wants."

Chapter Twenty-Five

It wasn't until later that day that Billie saw the damage the storm had done. Lifeboats had been wrenched from their launches. One lay smashed on the deck, its planks ripped asunder; the other was nowhere to be found. The large launch that had taken them and the motorcar into Todos Santos had also been lost. The wicker deck furniture was thrown and scattered over the deck, much of it broken. Though the player piano remained anchored in its place, its music scrolls were tossed from their cupboard and lay sodden, unrolled and trailing across the boards, flapping, limp and torn, some still in their boxes, most not. Broken glass, cushions strewed about and soaked by the rain. The canvas canopy had ripped from its mooring in two places, sagging sadly and raggedly over the platform lounge, dripping water and dangling broken strings of lights. The wraparound settee was the only thing still in any kind of normal state, its upholstery littered with bits of seaweed and feathers. Bottles of whiskey, gin, and champagne rolled back and forth with every motion of the ship.

The sea was red. Not red because it reflected the pink of the sky, but red. Only microorganisms, but it didn't matter how often Billie told the crew—she didn't miss how the sailors crossed themselves, or their wary glances at the sea as they moved about the deck setting things to rights. The *Eurybia* drifted in a pool of red; Billie could not see beyond its boundaries to any blue. Not only that, but she could see no land either, not even the hazy outlines of mountains. They seemed to float in the middle of nowhere. But they couldn't be that far from somewhere, could they? The maps she'd seen showed no place in the Gulf of California that was more than a hundred and fifty miles wide.

Beyond the seabirds swooping and cawing, the day was eerily silent, the water without a ripple. The birds seemed to watch the ship as if it were a wounded creature they waited to devour. It was unnerving.

Roland told her quietly, "Rogers says we've been blown a great distance. We can't get any instrument readings until we get the engines or the generators running again, but he thinks we're north of Ángel de la Guarda Island."

"Ángel de la Guarda? But . . . that means we were blown past Tiburón and Las Ánimas. How did we get through that channel safely?"

Roland shrugged. "It's a miracle we didn't wreck. James says it's because we're blessed."

"The fish."

Roland nodded. "The fish."

"What are the chances the generators will work soon?"

"You tell me. I'll take a look, too, but I'm an expert at aquarium pumps, not ship parts." His gaze softened. "You okay? After all that with Matías?"

"At least you don't think I killed him."

"No. You're dangerous, but I wouldn't call you the killing type."

"How complimentary."

Roland grinned. "Maybe you're only dangerous to me. Have you checked on the fish today?"

Quickly she told him about the conversation with Victorine.

"Is she joking?"

Billie raised a brow. "Have you not been paying attention? Of course she's not joking."

Roland exhaled heavily. "We need to keep her out of there, Billie."

"I'll do my best. Maybe you should speak to James."

The next day, when Captain Rogers asked for volunteers to take the skiff and go for help, so many of the crew wanted the job that they drew straws. The winners were as happy as if they'd won a prize. They had, Billie supposed, and wondered if they really would send help when they reached shore, because who knew how far shore was? No one could see it. It might take them days with the skiff's faulty motor. They might not get there at all. None of the crew cared. They wanted off the *Eurybia*. She didn't blame them. After Matías's death, the only thing keeping them aboard was that there was no way off the ship except the skiff. Without the assistant engineer, they were stranded. The generators weren't yet working, and though some of the crew were working on it, no one knew how to get them running.

The sun beat down, the water was red, and the ship didn't even drift. It just sat there, even without being anchored, as if something held it into place. Billie went on deck to watch those who'd won the lottery go.

Oliver and Roland huddled around Matías's body near the deckhouse. Roland was examining him, but Maud told Billie the crew already had a theory. "Fear," she said. "They think his heart stopped in fear."

"Fear?" Billie asked.

"The spirit. The monster."

"It's not a monster. It's just a fish. A very special fish."

Maud considered her. "How special?"

"It could change the science world," Billie told her.

"It surely changed Matías," Maud said.

Now, as Maud came to see the sailors off, Billie saw how the maid rubbed the cross around her neck, and wondered if any of the crew actually mourned Matías, or if Maud did. Billie had liked the man for his reasonableness, his offer to help Maud, and his willingness to stay on the ship in return for benefits to his family, and she was sorry he was gone. She wondered if James would still give them the promised house and goats and chickens now—well, she could make sure of it, couldn't she? She would remind him. It was the least she could do for the part she'd played in keeping him here.

Billie went to the rail, where she and Maud and the captain stood to watch the four sailors descend the gangway into the skiff. The men nearly bounced with relief and excitement while those left behind growled their resentment and discontent.

"Don't forget us, Aldo," called one of them.

Aldo waved his hand and laughed. "I won't, I promise!"

The remaining crew called out goodbyes in Spanish.

"If you don't come back, I'll curse you!"

"May God curse you if you don't return!"

The words made Billie uneasy.

Captain Rogers handed them a canvas bag of supplies and said in Spanish, "I don't know our exact coordinates. We're somewhere north of Ángel de la Guarda. Send whoever you can as soon as you can."

The men nodded and settled into the skiff.

"Can you trust them? Do you really think they'll return with help?" Billie asked the captain quietly.

Captain Rogers shrugged. "Return? No. Will they send someone? Maybe. I'm not even sure how far they have to go. By my reckoning, we're miles from any land. Mostly I want them off the ship before they start a mutiny. I have more faith in the radio once the generators are up."

"You think the generators are going to work?"

"There's no reason they shouldn't." The captain spoke reassuringly. "It's just a matter of getting some spooked sailors working in the dark."

Billie wasn't reassured. She'd heard the talk of those spooked sailors, and the cursed *antorcha del mar* on board, and Victorine's talk of Emile's spirit speaking through it, only added to their fears that an unsettled spirit already lurked aboard and had possessed her. She doubted much repair work would get done—unless the captain could convince them that the radio was the fastest way home.

One of the sailors in the skiff untied the rope leashing them to the *Eurybia*, and they cast off. Aldo started the outboard motor, which in its usual stubborn way choked, gurgled, and sputtered its way into life, guttered and died, and had to be thwacked several times before it started again.

They were several yards away when one of the others stomped his foot on the floor of the skiff and called something out to his fellows, which Billie couldn't hear over the sound of the motor. They didn't wave or even acknowledge the *Eurybia* as they sped off over the red sea, toward whatever help they had promised to find, and Billie knew the captain was right. They wouldn't return. All those on the ship could do was hope that the men would send others to rescue them.

Then the skiff's engine sputtered again.

"That engine," Billie said, shaking her head.

The curses of the sailors carried easily on the still air. Aldo yelled obscenities at it and pounded it.

"Aldo's always been able to coax it to life," the captain said, but he was tense, Billie felt it.

Just as he said it, the motor growled. It got them a few more yards before it died again, and restarted—the same old game.

But the skiff didn't look right. Had it always sat so low in the water? Billie told herself it was just the weight of the men and supplies, but still . . . she didn't like the look of it.

True to form, the motor died again. This time, instead of trying to restart it, the crew in the skiff began furiously throwing something out of the boat. Over and over again, cupped hands, water—

The skiff was sinking.

Captain Rogers saw it at the same time she did. He shouted in Spanish, "Start the engine! Come back to the ship!"

For an answer, he got a chorus of shaking heads, *no no nos*. The men kept bailing, bringing out the pails they'd stowed in case the journey outlasted their water. But the skiff was sinking fast now, faster than they could bail. Aldo tried to start the motor, but the water had nearly reached the gunwales. Even if they could get the outboard started, they would not make it back with the boat.

"Good God," Billie muttered. In Spanish, she called to them, "Swim back!"

They ignored her. She heard Maud's small gasp. The maid rubbed the cross of her necklace and stared straight ahead, muttering. Praying.

Now it was clear that the only choice was for the men to leave the skiff and swim back. But when the captain yelled for them to do that, the sailors ignored him, and Billie understood then that they wouldn't. They were refusing. They were too frightened to return to the ship. *Cursed ship*. The *antorcha del mar*. The skiff had sunk below the surface, so it looked as if they were suspended in the red sea. *Agua de sangre.* Blood water.

Then she saw the sharks. The first one came quickly, its dorsal fin slicing through the water. Then another. Maud shouted in panic, "Swim! *Tiburones!*"

Captain Rogers ordered one of the deckhands to get the rifles and called to the men in the skiff, "Swim for the ship! We'll keep the sharks off with the rifles!"

The sailors now treaded water. Their supplies floated around them. But the men weren't swimming for the *Eurybia*. They only stared at the *Eurybia*.

"What are they doing?" Billie asked the captain. "Why aren't they moving?"

The sharks circled closer.

Two of the deckhands returned to the railing with the rifles, lowering them to aim. They shouted to their friends in the skiff, "We're ready! We'll shoot them before they get to you! Come on!"

The men in the water did nothing. They did nothing, and Billie knew. With dawning horror, she knew.

They would rather die. They would rather die than return to the *Eurybia*.

Captain Rogers spoke wonderingly. "My God."

Maud made a strangled sound.

One of the sailors in the skiff lifted his face to the heavens. Praying. He yelled out to his friends at the rail, "I'm not coming back while the monster is on board!"

"We die here or we die there!" shouted another. "What does it matter?"

"If you love me, shoot me! Sweet Mother Mary, God forgive us both!" said the first.

One of the sharks attacked the man on the outside. He screamed.

Another one shouted, panicked. "Now! Juan, please! Shoot!"

Billie felt the hesitation of the crewman. His hand flinched on the rifle. She wanted to cry.

Maud said, "Please, God. Please save them."

Captain Rogers said, "Do it."

Billie couldn't bear to watch. When the men at the railing fired, she closed her eyes. The screaming silenced, and she turned away when she heard the thrashing of the sharks so she didn't have to see the red of the sea actually turn to blood.

Chapter Twenty-Six

"I think it was heart failure," Roland said, looking unconvinced. "From fright, maybe? I can't find any physical wound."

"Keep that thought quiet," Captain Rogers said grimly. "It will only feed the fears of the sailors after what happened today." He looked at James. "I suggest you throw that fish back into the sea."

"That fish is the whole reason for this expedition. No one else is going to risk the same fate as those men." James seemed so smugly certain. "These sailors aren't leaving the *Eurybia* now, fish or no fish."

Billie didn't wait to hear more. She fled to the hold. The formalin-scented darkness now held the fetid, nauseating underscent of rot. The heat made it worse. After the grisly scene she'd just witnessed, the smell of death, the feel of it, seemed to be everywhere. She tied gauze around her nose and mouth to filter it out as she set a flashlight on its end as illumination, but the makeshift mask didn't help much as she cleaned up the mess, and before long she had a throbbing headache.

There was so little left. She still had her notes and the photographs, so it wasn't a complete loss, and a few jars survived, and what was in the aquariums—as long as they got those circulating pumps going again—but there wasn't going to be a collection for the San Diego Zoo. That wasn't Billie's concern now. San Diego didn't matter. What mattered was the *antorcha del mar*, and what could be learned from it.

She unwrapped the gauze from her face and went to the tank, thinking about what Roland had said about this fish, what the

Empedocles Society—those crackpots—intended to do with this creature, the things James Holloway wanted to do. Holloway was delusional if he thought the Empedocles Society could give him back his health—for that matter, so was Roland. She was grateful to Holloway's delusion for getting her aboard this ship, but she hadn't known his real plan, and she felt she owed him nothing. Roland was misguided and blinded by ambition, but she still hoped to change his mind. The world deserved this discovery.

Billie untied the cords of the tank and peeled back the corner. The water was dangerously low. The fish breathed shallowly, but it was clear that it needed the water as much as she suspected. Its skin—that wonderful iridescent rainbow of colors—was not only fading, but also drying, scales flaking. It needed more water, but . . . they were marooned in a red sea now, and she wasn't sure how the microscopic creatures would affect it. Were they parasitic or not? She would have to take samples first, but even so . . . how much of a choice did they have? The water might damage the *antorcha*, but not being in water might kill it.

She went to the supply box of syringes and grabbed one. Studying its blood would give her some answers, anyway, but when she sat on a stool next to the tank, she was struck again by the miracle of the creature, the fins that weren't fins at all, or not *only* fins, but short little legs, and the muscular tail with its rudder-like fin—the strength of it, the places this creature must have gone. What worlds it had known, undersea mounts and reefs swarming with life and the lands of Baja California, too, these islands all through the Gulf, if the stories were true. They'd found it in the depths, but where had it lived mostly? How much time had it spent on land? How strong were those jaws, and what would she find in its stomach if she opened it up? How intelligent was it? Oh, to get a look at its brain . . .

The creature's eyes flickered. Its tail flicked.

Let me go.

Billie jerked to her feet, dropping the syringe, nearly tripping over the stool.

"What? What did you say?" Her voice echoed eerily in the hold—it sounded so absurd that it brought home to her forcibly that she was speaking to a fish. A fish that only stared unblinkingly at her.

Send me home.

Billie swallowed. "Emile?"

Oh, that was truly ridiculous. Some voice might be speaking to her, but Billie didn't believe Victorine's notion that it was her brother. No, not at all.

This was all so . . .

The fish did not respond. Only silence around Billie, the pressing heat and stink of the hold. It was only the horror of the day making her imagine such things. The aftereffects of the storm, Matías's death, the sinking skiff, those poor men, the screaming and the shots and the thrashing sharks—she closed her eyes and took a deep formalin-scented breath, trying to force it all away. But when she opened her eyes again, nothing had changed. She rose and got the chloroform, and the creature only looked at her with unforgiving—*unforgiving???*—eyes as she drugged it into stillness. She would take its blood later, when her fingers weren't trembling so. She covered the tank with the tarp and retied the cords tightly, and when she'd finished, Billie sat there staring at the smooth expanse of rubber.

You don't belong here.

Her startled movement sent the flashlight crashing onto the floor. Billie fumbled for it. When she found it, she worked the switch. It didn't turn on. Frantically she tried again. Nothing. The flashlight was dead. She was in darkness.

You are a scientist, she told herself, but reasoning didn't work in the face of her panic. Billie raced for the door and went blindly up the stairs, away from the hold, to her stateroom, and closed the door. She heard nothing, no sound at all, no one moving about. The dead ship was preternaturally quiet. She leaned back against the door, trying to quiet her breathing. One breath, and then two, but when she closed her eyes, she saw the terror in the eyes of those sailors sinking into red water. She heard the screaming, the shots of the rifles. She saw the fish's eyes flickering, the languid motion of its tail.

You don't belong here.

Her skin crawled.

Suddenly she felt as if she were being watched. She slid her hand behind her back to the doorknob and turned it.

It didn't budge.

In the head, the tap creaked as it turned on. The rush of water.

This is not real. It's not real.

Billie turned around and wrenched on the doorknob with all her strength. "Open, you son of a bitch," she snapped. *"Open."*

She tugged, she pulled. Finally, she kicked. The doorknob gave way with a clatter, tilting at a strange angle. Billie jerked on it until the latch gave and the door opened. She fell into the hall, banging into the opposite wall with full force, just as someone came down the companionway.

"Billie?"

Roland.

She rushed at him, nearly bowling him over as she crashed into his chest. She felt his arms come around her, a solid, indomitable force, and all she could think was *Thank God, something normal*, and only then could she breathe again.

"What the hell?" He tried to hold her away so he could see her face, but she clung so tightly he couldn't. "What's going on?"

"I—I can't . . ." she murmured into his chest . . . *Explain.*

"It's time for cocktails. Put something on. Let's get you a drink."

She laughed. Her voice sounded hysterical even to her own ears. "Cocktails. Of course. A cocktail will solve everything."

"James wants to discuss—"

"Four men died. They were eaten by sharks."

"Five men," he said quietly. "Five men. You're forgetting Matías."

"Of course." She rested her forehead against him. "Five."

"Go on." He gave her a little push. "Get dressed. Then you can tell me what made you dash into the hall."

Billie shook her head. "I'm not going back into that room."

In the companionway, it was dark. She wouldn't be able to see his expression, and she didn't try. But she felt his hesitation, and his concern. "What happened?"

"I was . . . locked in."

Silence. Then. "Okay."

"It's the second time it's happened."

"There must be someone here who can look at the latch."

"Yes," she said. "There must be."

"Billie." His hands were still on her arms; he hadn't released her. "What is this really?"

"I was just . . . I was just cleaning up the hold. So much lost. The *antorcha* needs more water. It's drying out. I don't know if the *agua de sangre* will hurt it . . ." She trailed off, realizing she'd used the Spanish phrase, *blood water*, without thinking. The phrase of superstition, of stories.

"The captain's going to radio for help as soon as we get the generators going." Roland was reassuring, certain. But he hadn't heard what she'd heard—assuming she'd really heard it.

She hesitated, not knowing what to say to him. What should she say? That she was beginning to believe the ship was as cursed as Victorine and the crew said? That she didn't think she was crazy, but the fish spoke to her and to Victorine? There had been tank water on the floor around Matías, and slime. The same slime on the side of the tank. The slime on the *antorcha del mar*. But the fish was paralyzed. It was paralyzed.

You don't belong here.

"Emile's spirit spoke to me through it."

"Those sailors chose death over returning to the ship," she said finally. "They chose *death*, Rolly."

"Superstitions—"

"It was superstitions that brought you here. You and James. So don't dismiss them now. You can't believe them only when they're convenient."

He laughed shortly. "I'm hearing this from *you*? Billie McKennan, Miss Science-Above-All?"

She gripped his arm. "There's something happening on this ship. I didn't want to admit it, but there is. I can't go back into my room, and the fish . . . and Victorine . . . She's strange, but she's not wrong, not quite."

"What are you saying?" Roland sounded confused, which wasn't surprising, because Billie was confused herself.

"I don't know. I don't know." She shook her head as if that might somehow clear it. It didn't, not a bit. "I just know I can't go up there and have cocktails as if nothing has happened. I can't go back into my room. I can't . . ."

"That scene today upset everyone," Roland said.

Billie snorted. "Not enough to disrupt cocktail hour."

"Liquid courage."

"If you tell me next that they're going to dance their cares away, I will hit you."

Roland sighed. He put his arm around her shoulders, pulling her tightly into his side. "Come on, let's avoid them all for tonight. You can stay in my room."

Billie stiffened. "Naturally you think that's a good idea—"

"There are two berths. I'm not suggesting anything untoward. Unless—" At her glare, he sighed in resignation. "Get a change of clothes, and—"

"I'm not going back in there."

She felt rather than saw his quizzical look. "You're really serious?"

"You go," she said. "Fetch my trousers from the end of the bed, and my overblouse. Don't close the door."

"This isn't like you."

"I don't know what's like me anymore," she said. "Please."

She felt his reluctance as Roland stepped away, and she watched warily as he did as she asked. She didn't know what she expected—a force throwing him against the wall? The taps turning on? The door slamming shut?—but none of those things happened when he went into her room. In the gray light coming through the porthole, she saw him taking up her trousers, her blouse, calling to her, "Anything else?" and since nothing seemed to be haunting him, she told him to grab a pair of knickers and an undervest from the dresser, and one of her lotions from where the storm had scattered them on the floor, and was surprised that she felt no sense of shyness about it, though why should she, really? They'd been married, and after the other night . . .

He came out without incident. Her rayon underthings glimmered in the faint remains of the light.

"You didn't feel anything odd?" she asked.

"Like what? What have you been feeling? Is this to do with Victorine's supposed spirits?"

She took her things from him and followed him down the companionway, shadows upon shadows, to his stateroom. He opened the door and ushered her inside. Clearly he'd cleaned up after the storm, because the brush and shaving items on the dressing table were neatly laid out.

She set her things on the bed that was obviously not the one he'd been sleeping in, and tried not to let the memories of the night they'd spent together intrude, though they were heavy in the air between them.

He sat on the other bed, his hands between his knees. He was indistinct in the blooming darkness, but she felt his attentiveness, his listening.

"I had nothing to do with Matías's death, I swear to you. I just came upon him that way, but . . . I've been hearing voices. Rolly. And I've been experiencing strange things I can't explain. I'm afraid I'm going mad."

"Voices?" he asked. "What kind of voices?"

"In my dreams."

"Oh, your dreams. Well, everyone does that."

"Not like these. They're so loud and so real. It's not like a dream."

"What do they say?" Roland didn't sound convinced.

"That we don't belong here. That we should leave. It's angry."

Roland paused. Then, "Do you recognize the voice?"

She shook her head, and then realized he might not see the gesture in the darkness. "No. But it's violent. There's a presence in my room. It's thrown me against the wall. It's locked the door twice. It slapped me awake during the storm. And . . . the taps turn on by themselves. The water that comes out is red."

"Is this the seawater tap?"

"Yes! And that's what I thought, too, that it was just the red water from the ocean. But it comes out red no matter where we are. Tomás told me it comes when it's called. He implied that the spirit of the sea summons it."

"Tomás? Tomás the oiler?"

"Yes."

"You've been having conversations with the oiler about this, and you're only just now telling me?"

"It's not like that. He took it upon himself to tell me that the crew thinks my room is haunted, and the red water is part of the reason. Anyway, it's staining the tub. The stain grows wider and wider, and I can't scrub it off no matter what I do."

"Victorine's brother died in that tub, right?" Roland's voice was quiet, thoughtful. "Do you think she actually did raise a spirit?"

"I don't know," Billie said. "But there's one other thing. I told you Victorine believes her brother's spirit is speaking to her through the fish. I would have said she was mad, but . . . there is something in my room, Rolly. You know how you're always talking about this quantum physics research? That there may be universes we can't see?"

"You've always mocked me for that."

"Not for the theory itself," she corrected. "Because you use it as an excuse to justify your ambition."

"Come on, Billie—"

"You do, and you know it," she said. "Why else did you join the Empedocles Society? So that you could sweet-talk rich men into paying for your research. You're perfectly willing to study what they want as long as they fund your own studies. It's the whole reason you're willing to let James claim this fish when you know what a bonanza it would be to evolutionary science. Don't try to argue. You know I'm right."

"Let me think . . . oh, yes, I believe you've agreed to help me with that, haven't you?" Roland's voice dripped with irony. "You're the one looking for something spectacular to put your career back on track."

"That's rich, coming from you. Given that you derailed it."

"I don't need lessons in ethics from you, Billie," he said tightly.

He did, but as far as he knew she was on shaky ground, too, so she didn't belabor it. "It wasn't my point anyway. My *point* is about worlds we can't see. Maybe . . . maybe you're right. I don't know."

"Wait—let me write that down. What's the date? I need to record that you're admitting I'm right."

She couldn't even muster a wan smile. Billie rubbed her forehead, all at once exhausted. It felt as if it had been days since she'd slept. "*May be* right. I don't know if it's a spirit. But it's something. Even if it's not, we have to do something. What's left of the crew is ready to mutiny, and we're stranded. If we don't find a way to get moving again, the fish won't survive in that tank for long. The only way to learn what it can teach us may be to dissect it. Victorine will protest. She thinks it will destroy the communication she has with her brother."

"James won't allow it. The crew wants it off the ship completely," Roland said.

Billie winced. She couldn't bring herself to tell him that it was what the fish wanted too. How could she say that it was talking to her, telling her to send it home? To release it?

As if she could do that. As if she could ever let go of such a precious discovery.

Roland rose. He came to her and brushed his hand through her hair. She leaned into his calming touch, too tired to fight her need for his comfort. "You'll stay here with me. It doesn't matter what the others think. If we have to tell them the truth about what we are to each other, we will."

"No," she said.

"What does it matter now?"

"James already thinks we're scheming against him. Oliver too. It won't help either of us. Don't."

She felt him nod. "Okay. Look, why don't you go to sleep?"

"Honestly, I'm afraid to. The voices."

She detected a touch of amusement in his voice when he said, "I'm here. I won't let them touch you."

She didn't really think he could keep them at bay, but she was tired, and she was willing to let him try. She sighed. "Tell me again how we might be able to prove the existence of other universes. Your quantum physics."

Roland laughed softly. "Other universes. I must be hearing things too."

"Ha ha. Now you're mocking me."

"'There are more things in heaven and earth, Horatio, than are dreamt of in your philosophy,'" Roland quoted.

"Exactly," she said. "After all, look what we've found. A miracle."

"A miracle," he agreed.

It wasn't until Billie was drifting off to sleep that she wondered if he was only humoring her, or if he thought that she'd gone crazy or that it was all a dream, or if he believed anything she'd said at all.

Chapter Twenty-Seven

The morning was already hot and still, and the sea was a chalky, brick-like red that also had a faintly fetid smell, which made Billie remember the deaths of the crewmen yesterday. She pushed the thought away, not that she would ever be able to forget it.

A jungle of broken wicker and lifeboat was piled in the corner of the deck. The canopy had been jerry-rigged into a weak semblance of its former self, the jagged tear partially mended with twine, the rest of it secured with rope. Half a string of lights had broken, and the rest dangled desultorily, looking sad and bedraggled.

None of them looked much better. Victorine had pinned her hair into a messy knot at the back of her head. Roland had dark circles beneath his eyes. Oliver appeared jaundiced. James coughed into a tea towel embroidered with the *Eurybia* crest and eyed a manta ray off the side of the ship that periodically jumped into the air and plunged again into the deep red of the sea.

"It's as if it's mocking me," he said irritably once his coughing stopped.

"I'd think the last thing you would care about now is a damned manta ray. Let's just pray to get this over with," Oliver said, equally irritably.

"Get what over with, exactly?" James asked.

Oliver frowned. "What?"

"You said: Let's get this over with. What are you talking about?"

Victorine, wanly beautiful in aqua chiffon fringed in gold, picked at the innards of the torn lounge cushion. "He means getting home, James, of course."

"Yes, of course that's what I mean," Oliver said.

James frowned. "I can tell you're plotting, Ollie. Trust me when I say you're wasting your time. When we get home, I'll be cured, and I'll end your scheming once and for all. The fish—"

"The fish won't survive to San Francisco unless we start back soon," Billie noted dryly.

James turned to Roland. "Is that true?"

Roland shrugged. "The tank wasn't built to hold it for long. We need to change the water, but Billie doesn't know if the microorganisms in this red water will harm it or not."

Billie said, "It would be best if we could dissect it. Then we could keep it in formalin, and—"

"No! Absolutely not. It must be complete for the procedure to work."

Oliver shook his head. "Do you understand how insane you sound? I had hoped the cure you were obviously seeking was a sound one. Now I know it's as stupid as I suspected. Those people in that society are misguided, James. You really think a bunch of stupid Latin spells and incense can save you?"

"It's not just that," Roland explained patiently. "The cell transfer is based on well-studied hypotheses."

Billie snorted. "Untried on any living creature before now."

"This won't kill me," James said serenely. "It will work. I know it. How can you deny that we've found a creature that shouldn't exist? We found the legend. God is with us this time."

Victorine leaned forward intently. "Don't you understand? We've both found what we've been seeking for so long. How can it be anything but a sign?"

Billie felt a wave of sympathy for Victorine, but also impatience. Billie wished she could just come out and say that she thought the procedure was as likely to kill James as to save him—more likely, in fact—but she didn't. They wouldn't listen anyway, and honestly Billie wasn't certain what was true about anything anymore. James and Victorine were so supremely confident. How did one fight that? They had that attitude of rich people who had never been told no. How nice to be so wealthy, to be so certain that you could pay people to agree with you.

Let me go.

The voice came on a whisper of sound, a hush of the breeze.

There was no breeze, though when Billie heard it, she saw Victorine swipe at her cheek as if brushing away a stray hair. She wondered—did Victorine hear something too?

"When does the captain think the generators will be working again?" Victorine asked.

"He doesn't know," James said. "They should have been up by now."

Victorine rose. "I think I'll fetch my book."

"Ring for Maud," James said.

"I wish there was some ice," Oliver said dourly. "I would love something cold."

"No refrigeration either," James said cheerfully.

"The rest of the food will rot soon too," Oliver noted.

"As you so memorably said once, we have the sea as our larder." James gestured widely, taking in the landscape, nothing but red sea and hot blue sky.

"How much fresh water is there?" Oliver asked.

James coughed. "Don't be so glum. There's enough to last until help arrives."

"What if that help doesn't come for weeks?"

You don't belong here.

That assertive voice. That troubling voice.

Billie pulled herself off the chair, unable to ignore it. She glanced at Roland. "I'll be right back."

"See if there's any lemonade, won't you please?" Oliver asked.

"Why don't any of you ring for Maud?" James asked irritably. "Why did I bring a maid if neither of you uses her?"

Billie had meant to check the *antorcha del mar*, but now there was Oliver's request to see to first. The echo of the voice still rang in her head as she went to the crew quarters. With the *Eurybia* stranded, and no fans or the ventilation from a cruising wind, the interior stank dizzyingly of oil and diesel and sweat and fish and, again, that faint scent of formalin.

When she got to the galley, Maud was there, talking to the cook, who once again looked unnerved to see Billie.

"Is there something I can do for you, miss?" Maud asked.

"I was just seeing if there was more lemonade for Mr. Stanton."

"You should have rung for me."

"Oh, to hell with proper etiquette," Billie said, ignoring Maud's obvious startlement at her curse. "It seems rather precious right now to insist on it, doesn't it? After all we've been through?" She noted how the maid stared at her. "Are my eyes still brown?"

A grin played at the corner of Maud's mouth, though she didn't give in to it. "Yes, I think so."

"Thank God for that. You said you hadn't worked for the Holloways long, Maud?"

Maud nodded. "Only on the ship."

"So you don't know Mrs. Holloway well?"

"No."

"She's never given you any orders about me?"

"To dress you," Maud said. "To help you."

"I don't mean that. I mean . . . Did you lock me in my room the night of the storm? Have you done so since? Did she ask you to?"

"No!" Maud blurted out. "You know that's not me. I told you you should be praying. It's not playing games."

Billie glanced at the cook, who busied himself at the stove. "What is it you think isn't playing games, exactly?"

Maud stepped away from the galley and motioned for Billie to follow her. There was no real private place on the ship, but just now, the mess was empty. "You know what I mean," Maud said quietly. "I told you. The spirit."

"Did Mrs. Holloway tell you that?"

Maud laughed weakly. "I don't need her to tell me what I know in my bones."

Maud's answer unnerved Billie. She asked, "You're convinced it's a spirit. You don't think it could be something else?"

"Like what?"

"I don't know." Billie didn't want to ask the next question, but she did it anyway. "Would a spirit . . . would there be voices?"

Maud stepped back in obvious alarm. "Do you hear voices?"

Billie felt oddly nervous—suddenly it mattered very much what Maud might think. "Maybe. Yes, I think so."

"Then you must pray with me, miss. With Mrs. Holloway too. We need all the power we can."

"I'm not sure," Billie said.

"It's a call for help to something bigger than us. To God. The ship is cursed. It's been cursed from the start. It's not something you can ignore. Bad luck is a sign. You have to pay attention."

"You've been listening to the crew."

Maud shook her head. "No. I mean, yes. They feel it too. But I don't need them to tell me what I know. You know it too. I know you do. Some things are beyond explaining, don't you see? They're things we know without having to explain. Haven't you ever just felt something to be true without knowing why?"

Her intensity shook Billie in a way she didn't understand. Maud's belief felt so real and pure and clean. Billie tried to grasp it, to hold it, and couldn't. It reminded her of Roland's belief, though his wasn't religious in nature. His certainty, his faith in possibility. Billie stared at the young woman in surprise. She had not expected this. "Who are you? I mean really? Who are you?"

Maud seemed confused by the question. "No one. I mean, I'm just a girl, miss."

"No one's just a girl and nothing else," Billie said.

Maud looked surprised by Billie's words, and then thoughtful.

Billie said, "I have to check on the fish. Could you bring Mr. Stanton some lemonade?"

"There's none to be had. Can I come with you? I'd like to see it."

"I've work to do there," Billie said.

"I won't disturb you. I just want to see what all the fuss is about."

Why not? Billie nodded and motioned for the maid to follow.

Neither of them spoke as they left the galley.

Billie wondered if Maud was right, if bad luck was a sign of something. Billie would have said bad luck was a quantifiable thing, cause and effect. Discover the cause, and one could stop it. The engines kept breaking down not because of bad luck but because Holloway had hired an inexperienced crew. The crew believed the ship was haunted not because it was but because they'd been told the story of Emile's suicide on board, and Victorine had made it worse by trying very publicly to call his spirit.

Yes, cause and effect.

Yet Billie couldn't deny that there was something to what Maud said, the idea of intuition, of knowing something without knowing why. Billie herself knew that intuition often played a part in both exploration and experimentation. Too, there were the voices Billie heard that Victorine also heard, and the strange events Billie had experienced. So now she had to ask herself: What was bad luck, really? What was the unexplained?

She grabbed a working flashlight from the pantry and motioned for Maud to follow her. Billie meant to take the creature's blood and some tissue for Roland to look at and compare to that of his other amphibian studies. She didn't see any harm in letting Maud see the fish, but Billie refused to let anything disconcert or distract her today.

A few men worked in the generator room, but the engine room was dead empty. Just past them both, she slipped on something on the floor. She caught herself with a hand on the wall. The floor was weirdly slick. It was too dark to see what the substance was. Billie put out a tentative foot. It wasn't just in one spot. There was more of it. Some kind of spill. It felt slippery enough to be oil.

"Be careful," she told Maud. "There's something spilled here."

"What is it?" Maud asked, slowing.

They were opposite Billie's stateroom, and the door stood open, which was strange. She never left it open. Billie glanced inside. Her room was faintly lit by the light coming through the porthole. Enough to set a shine on the glimmer trailing over the floor, the path of something wet, something shiny, that led from the door into the room. Not oil, but . . . *What?*

Billie's nerves tingled. She traced the trail with her gaze—from the door into the hallway, the same slickness beneath her feet. She very deliberately didn't mention it to Maud. No need to raise any alarm. Not yet. Carefully, she led the way farther down the hallway. The trail continued, slippery and smelly too. With every step, a smell grew stronger—formalin and tank water, the same stink that had lingered around Matías's body, the same liquid.

"What's that smell?" Maud whispered.

In the maid's voice, Billie heard her own nervousness. More than nerves now. Dread crept over her as the slimy trail led down the companionway to the steps to the lower level of the ship.

The hold.

The door to the hold was open; there was only darkness within. She switched on the flashlight and stood for a moment, letting her eyes adjust. Her skin prickled, and the hair on her arms and the back of her neck stood on end. The light glimmered on a trail that led to the tank; the mucusy scum reflected the glow like phosphorescence.

The *antorcha*? It had escaped? Impossible. The sides were too high; there was the fastened tarp; the creature was anesthetized, and yet . . . the trail was irrefutable.

Slowly, Billie approached the tank. She heard the soft pad of Maud's step behind her, and held up her hand to halt the young woman. The flashlight beam jiggled in Billie's hand; she was apprehensive; she couldn't keep it steady. The tarp had been untied and pushed aside. *Victorine.* It was Billie's first thought. Victorine had been down here again. She'd left the tarp untied again, too, regardless of Billie's warning, and probably it had been Victorine who had tracked the water up the stairs and to . . . Billie's room? But why? How had the slime got there too?

None of it made sense, though Billie kept trying to make sense of it. Not only that, but the *antorcha* seemed to glow weirdly.

"Oh, what's that light?" Maud asked in an awed tone. "Is that . . . is that it? How beautiful!"

"Wait here," Billie instructed. She went to the edge of the tank and stared down at the *antorcha*, and that light . . . She, too, felt awestruck by its beauty. How splendid it was, how she inexplicably ached for the creature, overwhelmed by how much it missed the sea and how much it longed to be back swimming among the reefs and the seamounts, to be free in that beautiful, fantastic ocean.

That longing consumed Billie until she saw the body in the tank beside it.

Aqua chiffon, floating like wings in the water. Victorine, face down in the tank, still as death.

Chapter Twenty-Eight

"I don't know," Billie said as they all gathered around the tank, everyone who had come running when she'd sent Maud to fetch them. "This is how I found her. Maybe she fell in."

James stared blindly at the tank. "Get her out of there."

"Of course. Right away," Captain Rogers said. "I'll get some of the men."

"I mean now. I can't stand to look at her that way." James let out a sob. "My beautiful Vic."

Oliver put his arm about James's shoulders, looking as if the world had just collapsed around him. "There must be an explanation for this."

"An accident, undoubtedly," Roland said.

"Was it?" Oliver glared at Billie, who was taken aback by his venom. "Don't you find it strange that Billie happened to find both Matías and Victorine?"

"Are you accusing her of something?" Roland asked tightly.

"I'm just making a connection," Oliver said.

"The only connection to be made is that it's Billie's job to study the fish, and Victorine is here in the fish's tank," Roland said. "Matías was found outside the engine room, where he works. That it's next to Billie's room, I'd say, is coincidental."

Oliver's glare didn't let up. "Of course you would defend her, but I'd like to hear from her."

Billie sighed. “It’s as Roland said. I came down to study the fish, and I found her. Maud was with me. You can ask her.”

“Don’t worry. I will,” Oliver said darkly. “Where is she?”

“No doubt recovering from the shock,” Roland said. “I told her to get a drink from Pollan.”

James began to sob loudly. “Get Vic out. For God’s sake, get her out.”

Captain Rogers and Roland leaned into the tank to drag Victorine free. Oliver pulled James away into the darkness. Billie watched with a sick sense of sorrow. James was bereft, that was easy to see, and watching Victorine’s limp body, with the dripping aqua chiffon draping her limbs, was a special kind of horror. To see someone you’d known, even if Billie hadn’t known her well, this way . . . it held its own kind of awfulness. Billie thought of Victorine’s worry over her husband, and her hope for him. But Billie hadn’t told any of the others about that, not what Victorine had told her, not the trail that had led from Billie’s room to the hold, nor the slime she’d seen in it, and her fear about what it meant. None of them had noticed it in the rush to get to the hold, even if they’d slipped on it, and she had been careful not to bring it to their attention. Until she understood it, she wanted no one rushing to conclusions about how the slime had got there or her connection to it.

She looked at the fish, still paralyzed, motionless in the tank as the two men removed Victorine’s body. She’d checked it over and over again. The chloroform kept it asleep. It couldn’t have left the slime. But if it hadn’t, what had?

As they took Victorine out of the hold, Billie trailed the others. She didn’t miss the frightened looks of the crew they passed, and she knew the rumors that would sweep the lower decks now. Maud had witnessed the entire scene. How would that change the stories? Or would it?

James was in no condition to listen to Billie, but she corralled the captain and Roland as soon as she could. “The crew is going to blame the fish for this,” she told them. “We’ll need to protect it. I don’t know what they might do.”

“Mutiny is likely,” Captain Rogers said grimly.

"There are so few of them," Roland said.

"More than there are of us."

Billie said, "They could gather against us and throw the fish overboard."

The captain took a deep breath. "They might not stop at that. They blame you all for bringing it aboard. There's still Matías's death to reckon with, and those men . . ." He trailed off, bringing a fresh vision of the men in the skiff into Billie's head. "Maybe it would be best to get it off the ship before it puts us all in danger. Maybe Mrs. Holloway's death was an accident, but that doesn't explain Matías. That won't be lost on the crew."

Firmly Roland said, "We need to band together to stay safe. Billie, you're staying with me. No arguments."

She didn't try.

Captain Rogers said, "Can we throw the thing overboard?"

She thought of the voice. *Send me home.* It argued with her own need. To simply let such a thing go without study . . . How could she do that? She shook her head.

Roland said, "If we do, James Holloway will die. This is his best chance of a cure. So no. He won't agree. We need to protect the fish and ourselves."

Of course James wouldn't agree, but whether Roland agreed with him, Billie couldn't tell. After all this, what mattered to Roland? The greater good, or a cure for James? Billie hoped it was the former, but it was impossible to know from his words.

"I think it's a mistake to keep it aboard," the captain said.

"Argue with James," Roland told him.

The captain nodded and went grimly off. Billie turned to Roland.

"There was a pool of tank water around Matías," she told him. "Before I found Victorine, there was a trail of it from the hold to my stateroom."

Roland frowned. "What?"

"And slime, too, Rolly. Slime from the fish. If you'll notice, it's dying. We can't keep it alive for much longer. We have to get moving. We can get more water in the tank, but I'm worried about the infusoria. If they're parasitic, the water could do more harm than good. It could also affect the *antorcha*'s organs and its tissue, which—"

"Wouldn't be good for James," Roland finished. "Yes, I know."

"I can only know how it affects the fish when or if it does. I'm just saying it's a risk. It might be too late anyway. If we could just dissect it—"

"Don't start."

There was her answer. It was still James who mattered.

"Okay, but . . . but for God's sake, explain that trail to me. Explain how the tank water got on the stateroom level. *Explain* it."

"You're sure it's anesthetized?"

"Are you?"

Roland pushed his hand through his hair, obviously as troubled as Billie was. "Yes. Yes."

"Are there other amphibians you can compare it to? Anything like it? Anything that can . . . maybe jump? Or climb?"

"If it could jump, Billie, don't you suppose it would try to escape? Why go back to the tank where it's dying?"

She laughed shortly. "How big is the brain of an amphibian?"

He went thoughtful. "I'd compare it to the hellbender, I suppose, but they absorb most of their oxygen through their skin, so . . . not really the same. Like a giant salamander, you know, but . . ."

"Can they *jump*? Or climb?"

"Not the way you're talking about. Why would it leave the tank, anyway? Why would it kill Matías? *How* would it?"

"Venomous secretions?"

Roland sighed. "The hellbender does have those, to keep off predators. Okay, I'll look at the slime. But you're talking premeditation, Billie. Thinking and strategizing. For a *fish*. One that's *anesthetized*."

"I'm only asking questions," she insisted, because Roland was right—none of this made sense. There were too many *whys* here, and all of them were based on how intelligent that creature was. They had put it out with chloroform—could it be pretending? Could it climb from the tank? Could it target someone? Matías? Victorine? Why? She remembered the malice she'd felt when they'd caught it. "We've got to learn more about it. I'm going to look at its blood. You're looking at tissue and slime. We have to get more information before the crew decides to kill us all in our sleep. Maybe we should set a guard on it."

They stood near the rail. At a sound behind them, they both turned. James, Oliver behind him, came racing up. James's face was red and misshapen from crying. Oliver looked angrily determined.

"You're scheming, aren't you? I know you are! You mean to cut it up, to steal it from me! I know what you want!" James's face contorted with anger. "Both of you! The answer is no! Roland, if you make a single cut into that fish, I will have you arrested! I will have both of you arrested!"

Billie saw Oliver's clever eyes glow with anticipation at James's rage and knew he was the one scheming. She said, "I don't think there's a law—"

"I will *destroy* you," James threatened. "You'll be nobody. Just another stupid woman."

She didn't expect the anger that swept her at his words. Billie opened her mouth to say *Go to hell, you bastard,* but Roland touched her arm, stopping her.

"No one's touching the fish," he said calmly to James. "It was only a suggestion to help keep things under control. You're overwrought, my friend. It's understandable. To lose a woman like Victorine, in such a way . . . believe me, we all understand. Let's stop all this talk of schemes and betrayal, shall we? You want another cigarette? I sure could use one."

Billie felt her own anger ease. Admirable, the way Roland defused things; she'd forgotten that about him, too, the way people liked him and so listened to him. She felt the way it worked on her, and she saw how it worked on James, how James reached for his package of cigarettes. Oliver's expression she couldn't read. He turned to look at the landscape. She followed his gaze to the red water, the way it seemed to stretch its fingers into the horizon, and before her eyes it seemed to separate, to slide into a landmass, dun red, hazy with mist, a landmass where there had not been one before, and Billie's heart raced with confusion and then excitement; for a moment she thought they were saved, though how to get there—it was not far, but far enough—but then she blinked and it was gone. Just another mirage, just red water now reaching into a misty horizon, and as if to laugh at her, a manta ray lifted itself from the water, shedding droplets from its wings, and sailed a good distance before it dipped again, no mirage that, just a reminder of how obsessive was the man who'd hired her, how impossible it was to fight him.

Yet they were all in danger if she didn't.

She didn't sleep that night. Roland's room didn't have the feel of her own; there was no presence, no watchful eye, and yet she felt their danger and couldn't sleep for it, ever alert for the sound of—what? What was she waiting for? The footsteps of the crew or the sliding, crawling sound of a supposedly paralyzed fish that shouldn't be able to climb or even move? She didn't trust the crew, and she didn't trust the *antorcha*, and that was the worst part, that she had somehow attributed malevolent intent to a fish chloroformed and dying in a tank of seawater, but her mind—such a logical and reasonable thing always—kept winding back to the trail of slime, the slime on the side of the tank, the pool around Matías, the stink of it on Victorine the night of the storm, and Billie had been trained to ask questions.

Was the fish sentient? Could it speak to her? Had it spoken to Victorine? Was the *antorcha*'s voice the one they'd heard? The voice Victorine had attributed to Emile's spirit? Billie remembered when the men had pulled in the *antorcha del mar*, the rancor emanating from it. Even if she denied that, it was hard to forget the legends about it. The stories of attacks. The fear.

What of the presence Billie had certainly felt? The one Maud claimed was a ghost or a demon, or . . . who knew what? Billie had felt it even before they'd brought the fish on board. She wasn't prone to hallucination, and yet . . . she couldn't deny that something had thrown her down and locked her in the night of the storm. Was it related to the *antorcha* or separate from it? Was it a spirit or something else? It, too, had a voice. It, too, had invaded her dreams even before they'd captured the fish. *You don't belong here.*

Billie felt as if she'd landed inside a story where different rules existed, where the laws of physics and chemistry and biology had been thrown out the window, leaving her flailing for understanding. Nothing worked the way it should. She had never been one for fairy tales—what was she missing?

Roland breathed softly in the bed beside hers. He hadn't tried to touch her—both of them were too wound up for that, though she half wished he lay beside her now. But she hadn't suggested it, and he'd fallen asleep quickly and seemed untroubled by dreams. She envied him that. How easily he seemed to adapt to uncertainty. That faith he had that he would eventually find the answers he needed, his conviction that the unexplained was simply the unexplored. The universe would reveal itself to them in time, if they simply kept investigating.

What had Maud said? *"Haven't you ever just felt something to be true without knowing why?"*

Billie had always tended to attribute such things to subconscious knowledge. That was logical and reasonable, explainable. But what if it wasn't? What if it was something else?

In the end, she had no choice but to come back to the voice, to the question of the fish's intelligence. Did it *think*? What did it perceive? She wished now that she had stepped past her own prejudices to ask Victorine what the fish had said to her. Victorine had been puzzled when Billie revealed what it told her. So what had Victorine heard?

Was it communicating via some kind of telepathy? Was that possible? Or was it only a weird kind of self-knowledge, as Billie had always thought about intuition? Was it only a fear she'd felt subconsciously, a sense that the Gulf was dangerous, and they were doing things to harm it with their clumsy collecting, that they had taken something too valuable from it, something they couldn't possibly yet understand, and her own subconscious was saying, *Put it back; leave it be; you don't know what you're doing*?

Was she responding to her own fear with hallucinations telling her to walk away? Or perhaps . . .

What did she trust? Facts or what weren't yet facts? She thought of William Jennings Bryan on the stand in Tennessee and Darrow's questioning and the way she'd asked questions of her father when she was a child. Bryan believed the Bible literally, but perhaps being too literal was also Billie's Achilles' heel. She believed the literal truth of what science knew now, but she had not opened her mind to what it might know twenty years from now, fifty, a hundred, of what it *could* know, of what *could* prove to be true. Roland was right: Science was the search for the unknown; they learned new things constantly; facts were always evolving—quantum physics showed that. If she lived to be ninety, what would the world have discovered about the living and the dead that might explain the presence she felt in her stateroom, or if Victorine could have called a spirit? What would be discovered about the sentience of fish?

Another sobering thought, and one that set her mind afire. There was so much to know, and she couldn't afford to deny anything, especially now, when everything felt so dangerous. She had to do something about it. She couldn't ignore the danger, not to herself or anyone else. Maybe the fish wasn't doing the killing, but *something* had killed Matías and Victorine, and this ship was certainly cursed by *something*, even if it was superstition, incompetence, and bad decisions. It had to be acknowledged. It had to be reckoned with. If James Holloway wasn't going to do it, Billie would.

The only question was how.

Chapter Twenty-Nine

The heat intensified. It beat down upon the ship, oppressive and stifling. The red sea simmered, and they floated in the middle of a dreamlike nothingness. No land in sight, nothing to anchor them, no touchstone. The crew threw molding oranges and grapes overboard to attract fish and then netted those they caught to fry: skipjacks and groupers, tiny little fish the size of anchovies that fried up delicate and crisp. James was right; the sea was their larder, and the cook used diesel and the ruined wicker and lifeboats to light fires in the stove to cook with, and warned that fresh water was getting low. What remained was stale. James said there was plenty of gin, and he and Oliver drank a fair share of it.

The next morning, Billie woke to find that the crew had caught a hammerhead shark. While she watched, they clubbed the thing to death.

"What are you doing?" she asked, but they only glared at her and didn't answer, not even Tomás, who looked red eyed and too intense. His expression made her nervous, but she couldn't tear herself away from the bewildering sight of the crew going at the shark with knives, splitting the thing open, spilling blood all over the deck, and fighting off the birds swooping down to grab pieces of carrion. It wasn't long before Billie understood their intention.

Roland came up beside her. "The liver."

She nodded, watching as they cut the organ loose. The sailors lifted the rest of the carcass over the rail and dropped it back into the sea. The birds dive-bombed after it. Then one of the men cut the organ into pieces and handed it out to the others. She remembered the hammerheads on the beach at the Cape, all without livers.

"What will they do with it?" she asked in a low voice. "Eat it?"

Roland said, "I'm not sure. If I had to guess, given the things I've heard, I'd say they're using it as a repellent." He sounded troubled, and she felt it, too, the sense that they were borne along on a tide they couldn't escape. One of the men looked up at them with an expression so ugly she felt the force of it where she stood. Billie backed away, out of sight, and pulled Roland away too.

"Best to keep our distance," she cautioned.

When she went down to the galley, she caught the cook nailing his bit of shark liver to the doorway, where it broke and dripped in bloody bits down the jamb. He made no comment when he saw her, and he left the liver like that, in gory pieces dribbling over the doorway. The rest of the crew had done the same. There were pieces of the shark liver everywhere; the reek of it, the sticky drips of it, the blobs of it, gelatin-like and smelling of fishy rot, all through the crew quarters. Even, Billie saw, on Maud's door.

Billie retreated to the hold, which at least smelled of familiar stinking things. The fish was immobile, its colors more faded than ever. Even with only the flashlight she could see the webs of decay—slime, iridescent—trailing from it. Billie had thrown another live bonito in, but that fish floated, its gills slowly flapping, dying, too, and the *antorcha* had obviously made no effort to eat it.

Billie unlatched the hold hatch and threw it back to let in the light. It brought with it the stench of the red sea and the sultry air, but the hold was already so hot and foul it hardly mattered. At least she could see better. She put on a pair of gloves and reached for the box of syringes.

The creature's skin was thick and difficult to pierce with the needle; Billie had to change to a stronger, thicker one. Still the skin fought her. *Come on,* she urged silently, *let me know you.* The fish didn't move when she managed it the second time and filled the syringe with blood.

It seemed truly dosed with chloroform, and it looked terrible, a sickly version of its former self—it didn't seem capable of getting out of the tank, much less killing Matías or Victorine.

"Was it you, my pretty?" she murmured.

She went to the microscope, prepared a slide with the blood, and put it beneath the eyepiece. With the flashlight, she could approximate the microscope lamp somewhat, though it wasn't perfect. Billie looked into it and saw what she expected. The creature's blood didn't surprise her. Elliptical, biconvex red-orange blood cells with nuclei, lymphocytes . . . She grabbed her notebook and a pencil to make notes, and looked back again and saw . . .

Red blood cells shrinking as if they were sizzling, deforming as if they were *cooking*.

Billie frowned. Impossible. She twisted the focus knob, thinking she must have hit it by accident, but no, the cells still twisted and contorted, and more impossibly still, they liquefied into a thin pink homogeneous gel.

She grabbed the slide from beneath the eyepiece and let out a disbelieving laugh. What was this? What the *hell* was this?

Billie looked over at the tank. The water was still. So was the fish. She prepared another slide. The same thing happened. Another, and then another. She couldn't get a careful read on the blood because it wouldn't stay in one form. The cells melted and liquefied the moment she put the slide beneath the light.

Send me home.

Loud and insistent, but when Billie went to the tank, the *antorcha* was quiet. Asleep? Pretending?

There was nothing to fear, Billie told herself. Nothing. Yet gooseflesh pimpled her skin. She frowned and skimmed a small jar through the tank, collecting slime and some of the scales that had flaked from the fish. Billie was just screwing on the lid when she heard a noise at the door of the hold. Roland.

She turned, words already rushing out. "The strangest thing just happened—" She broke off when she saw it wasn't Roland but Oliver. "What are you doing here?"

"I came to see the thing," he told her. "And to talk to you."

Billie didn't like the look on his face, and she'd had her fill of talks with Oliver. She shoved the jar into her trouser pocket. "About what?"

"About James and his obsession." Oliver looked as if he'd been run over. His sandy hair was disheveled, and he was sunburned. She thought he might be drunk. "Do you believe that it's possible, what he says? That it can cure him?"

There was no point in lying. "No."

"Is it going to survive to San Francisco?"

"Probably not."

"Is it going to kill us all?"

Billie met his gaze. "You're asking me if a chloroformed, half-dead fish is responsible for the deaths on this ship."

"I think you know as well as I do that it is."

"I think you're drunk." She started for the door. He wouldn't move out of the way. "I need to find Roland."

"We're being picked off one by one," Oliver said. "Who's next? You? Me?"

"Please let me pass."

"Help me, Billie," he pleaded. "Let's throw this thing overboard or fill it full of bullets or something. I'll give you whatever you want. Money? A position on the board? Once I take over, you can name your price."

Yes, he was very drunk. He stank of whiskey. Billie pushed by him. He grabbed at her as she went up the stairs, pulling her blouse from where it was tucked into her trousers.

"Please!"

She jerked away, saying coldly, "Get hold of yourself, Oliver."

He cried out, "We're all going to die."

Billie raced as quickly as she could from the hold, looking for Roland. He wasn't in his stateroom. She found him on the aft deck with James and the captain, arguing about the shark's liver. They talked so loudly she heard them easily when she reached the deck.

"Let them hang it everywhere if it makes them feel better," Roland was saying.

"These damn superstitions are going to be the death of us," James said. "Plus the blood is ruining the woodwork. Vic would be beside herself. She took such pride in this ship."

"Get me a rifle and I'll take care of the damn thing right here and now," Captain Rogers said. "Then we don't have to worry about shark livers."

"Roland!" Billie called, interrupting them. "Roland, I need you right now."

He frowned and hurried over. "What is it?"

"Oliver's down in the hold drunk, and I just looked at the *antorcha*'s blood, and . . . you need to see this."

Roland threw a glance back at the others, but he didn't ask any more questions; he followed her. She went as quickly as she could through the dark corridor. When they got to the top of the narrow stairs to the hold, he stopped.

"Why is there so much water?" Roland asked.

He was right. Water spread over the floor to the bottom of the stairs, dimly lit by the sun from the hatch.

Billie took a careful step down. "I don't know. It wasn't like this when I left." She went fully into the hold, and stopped short.

The aquariums against the wall had exploded; water still drained from them onto the floor. The few fish that hadn't already died from the lack of working pumps flapped and gasped for air. Squid twisted in the puddles; crabs scuttled about.

And on the floor, curled in a fetal position, eyes rolled back in his head, his mouth open in a scream, lay Oliver.

Chapter Thirty

"What the hell happened?" Shock sharpened Roland's voice as he came up behind Billie. "Oliver?" He went to the man and turned him over. "Billie, he's dead."

Billie took in the devastation. She didn't want to look too closely at the water around Oliver, or whether there was iridescent slime. But she couldn't help noting the streams of an oil-like sheen. For a moment, she could barely breathe. "He said . . . he said it was picking us off one by one."

"What was?"

"The fish." She stepped to the tank. The *antorcha* was as she'd left it. It hadn't moved. The water in the tank remained as it had been as well. The water on the floor was all from the aquariums. She stared at the creature, her terror a tight thing she couldn't dislodge. "Oliver came to tell me we needed to kill it before it killed the rest of us."

"It's asleep," Roland said in confusion. He sat back on his heels and looked around. "Did Oliver do this? Did he smash the tanks?"

Billie would have liked to say that he had. It would have explained everything neatly. Oliver had come here, had smashed the tanks in anger, and they'd been too far away to hear it from the upper deck. Then . . . maybe he'd had a heart attack like Matías. She could pretend to understand it. Except . . . who knew what could have caused that look on his face? And the tanks didn't look as if someone had smashed them. There was no tool lying around that had been used as a weapon. There was that slime . . . "They look as if they just exploded," she said.

"What would have made them do that?"

"Without the pumps?"

Roland shook his head. He straightened and went over to the ruined tanks. "I don't know."

"He was drunk, Rolly. Very drunk."

"What else did he say?"

"He asked me if I thought the fish could cure James. I said no. That's all I really remember because I was on my way to find you."

"Yes, the blood. You said there was something about the blood."

"It liquefied, Roland."

He turned to look at her. "What?"

"I looked at it, and it looked normal—elliptical leukocytes, nuclei, everything I would have expected. Then the cells started to distort, and they simply . . . melted into a kind of gel. A homogeneous one."

"That's not possible."

"That's what I thought. But that's what happened. You cannot use this fish to cure James, Roland. There's too much here that's inexplicable. I think . . . I think it might be sentient."

He only stared at her, his expression unreadable. Finally, he shook his head as if he tried to shake loose his thoughts. "Sentient? Are you crazy?"

"I don't know, but—look at that water around Oliver. Is that slime? Do you see that?"

"What are you saying? That it's from the fish? That it poisoned him?"

"I don't know! I don't know. You said you'd examine the slime."

"I will. I will. I haven't had a chance. None of what you're saying is possible, Billie. How did it get out of the tank? It's neutralized by chloroform. Besides, the blood doesn't matter. It has the lungs and gills we need. We have to get it back to San Francisco. It's the whole reason—"

"Your own laboratory is the reason," she said. "Don't mistake it. Roland, the fish is dangerous. I don't know exactly how, but it is. We should dissect it now."

"No," he said.

"Roland—"

"We're arguing over the body of a dead man," he reminded her. "Let's get Oliver out of here."

"This is only going to make things worse," she warned him.

"I know that," he said shortly. "You're not to leave my side. You understand? Not even to use the head."

They grabbed Oliver together and hoisted him through the water, up the stairs, and into his stateroom, where they laid him on his bed. Roland rang for Pollan to fetch James and the captain. When James and Captain Rogers came down to see Oliver's body, it was clear James was in a state of shock. He was as pale and fragile as Billie had ever seen him.

"You found him?" he asked Billie, and she heard accusation in his tone.

"We found him together," Roland said. "I told you that. She was with me."

"When I left him, he was very much alive and railing about how we should kill the *antorcha* before it killed the rest of us," she said quietly.

James made a sound of dismissal. "He was drunk."

"Very," Billie said.

"He was worried for me."

She didn't comment.

"He was my best friend." James put his hand to his eyes. His shoulders shook as he started to cough.

"Let's get him wrapped in canvas. We'll put him beside Mrs. Holloway's body on the deck, but really both he and Mrs. Holloway should be given an ocean grave. It's what's customary . . ." Captain Rogers spoke respectfully, but James turned on him viciously.

"And watch my most beloved be eaten by sharks? No, I forbid it. Why aren't the generators working? Why isn't anything working? What the hell am I paying you for? We should be heading for San Francisco! They deserve a decent funeral and a decent grave!"

The captain took a deep breath. "Yes, Commodore. I'll have some crewmen come for him right away."

They waited until the sailors came to take Oliver. James followed them. When he was gone, Billie said quietly to Roland, "You're going to have to tell James that the fish is dying. You're going to have to tell him about the blood. You have to examine that slime now. You're the expert in it, not me."

Roland said nothing, but she knew by his posture that he was trying to think of some way around it, some way to delay. Some way to save it all. His dreams balanced on the precipice, she knew, everything he'd ever wanted. Even their danger wasn't enough to sway him. He was too close to his future. Roland had always been an optimist and a dreamer. She wondered what exactly she could say to make him walk away.

Honestly, she didn't know.

That night, Billie stood at the rail while Roland and James sat and smoked behind her. The heat had faded to soft warmth, and stars freckled the sky in cloudy swaths. In the dark, it was impossible to see that the water was red; it only looked dark and mysterious. Like something the Greeks would call *wine-dark*. Romantic sounding and beautiful, but now the setting also felt poisonous. Taut and suspenseful. Waiting. She hadn't returned to her stateroom except once to gather up more of her belongings, and Roland had come with her. Yet the presence hovering there seemed to have expanded now to encompass the whole of the Gulf of California. It surrounded them, inhabiting not just the ship but also the sea, and if it wasn't throwing her around and locking her in, it also wasn't setting her free—or any of them. She was as trapped as if she were behind a locked door. So yes, the beauty of the night was suffocating, and it felt fatal.

"Miss."

The voice came from behind her, quiet, sneaking into Billie's thoughts for so brief a second she thought the words were in her mind, that spirit again, and she started. But it was only Maud.

Billie tensed. "Oh, yes? What is it?"

"They're talking belowdecks." Maud's voice was low. "You should lock your door tonight."

"What are they saying?"

"They want the fish off the ship. They won't touch it. They're too afraid. But they're going to force you and Mr. Ely to release it."

Billie glanced back at Roland, who was only a shadow and a cloud of smoke next to James's cloud and shadow. "We have a rifle."

Maud said, "I don't think that will help."

Maud wasn't wrong, Billie knew. The only thing that could change their situation was the *antorcha del mar* itself. "I'm going to do something about it," she assured Maud. "I promise."

"I know it doesn't matter what I think, but . . . it wants to be back in the sea."

Billie was startled. "H—how do you know that?"

"I can just tell. She's such a beautiful thing . . . Remember when you said it scared you more to think of things not living in the sea?"

The night Billie had shown her the night ocean. Billie nodded.

"When I saw her, I thought of that. How she wasn't there and how it scared me to think she wasn't. I've been having nightmares about it."

Another inexplicable thing. Incredible. That whisper of instinct that had begun to nag at Billie when she and Victorine both heard the voice, that feeling that there was something deeply connective at work—the Gulf, the *antorcha*, the *Eurybia* bound in a way Billie could only barely grasp—solidified into a certainty. It shook her profoundly. "I see. Well. Thank you for letting me know. It does matter what you think."

Maud turned to go and then paused and turned back. "You also said . . . the other day you said no one is just a girl and nothing else, and I was just wondering . . . what did you mean?"

Billie understood what Maud was really asking. Billie recalled all those times when she'd been challenged, those quizzical looks, those questions about why she was so intent on pursuing an education, on needing answers. *"Why do you need to know such things? Shouldn't you be learning instead how to bake a pie?"* "Why are you on this ship, Maud? What debt does your family owe Mr. Holloway?"

Maud did not hesitate. "My brother is a fool." A glance over her shoulder, toward James. "He thought he could best the Society. He couldn't. No one can."

Billie remembered what Maud had told her about her brother, the bizarre rituals he'd seen, the room with the jars. Probably he'd tried a bit of blackmail and lost. He should have known better, known the kind of men he was dealing with. God knew she'd warned Roland often enough. "Why isn't he paying off the debt, then? Never mind—I know. Who else makes the sacrifice but the girl?"

Maud nodded, and Billie felt the maid's anger and resentment.

"You don't have to be the sacrifice, Maud. You don't have to be just the girl," Billie said slowly. "Not if you don't want to be. It's your life. You don't have to let rich men take everything away. I'm certainly not going to let Holloway dictate my life."

"It might not be him," Maud warned her. "The crew—"

"I'm not underestimating the crew, believe me. But I'm not letting them tell me what to do either." She felt rather than saw Maud's concern.

"Do you know what you're doing, miss?"

"I hope so."

That considering look, long and slow. Billie had no idea what Maud saw in her at that moment, and the night was brightened only by starlight, but the maid seemed to reach some kind of satisfied conclusion. Billie heard the young woman's sigh, and then Maud walked off into the night, and Billie felt . . . bereft—was that what the feeling was? As if she hadn't quite done what she needed to do, as if she was more alone than she wanted to be.

She looked over her shoulder at the bright ends of the cigarettes glowing in the darkness, took in the smell of smoke, the abrasive scent of James's special asthma blend. The two men were quiet, but she felt the tension in the air between them. She wondered what they'd been talking about, and just how frayed Roland's loyalty to James might be, or whether his ambition had been shaken at all by the deaths of Victorine and Oliver. How much was Roland comfortable sacrificing? In the end, would he sacrifice her, as he had before?

She'd had two years to think bitter and unkind thoughts about him, to blame him. But this cruise—not just the obvious fact that he still wanted her, but also his apologies, his willingness to stand up for her, to help her, which showed he still cared . . . maybe what had happened in the past was as he'd said, and she had been too angry to listen. Maybe he'd thought of her as an extension of himself because that was what all of society did, and no one ever questioned it. Had she ever tried to teach him to be better? She couldn't remember.

What if she tried now? What if he could learn—and she could too? She'd worn the last two years of bitterness as a kind of hair shirt, and for what? For whom? She'd let her anger make her a victim. She had become "just a girl." How much time she'd wasted.

Billie glanced down at the dull water. It seemed the red absorbed the light; there was no phosphorescence in this water. Not even the reflection of the stardust. She felt suddenly tired, and she threw an "I think I'll go to bed. Good night" to James and Roland and headed to the stairs, down into the ship's stinking, claustrophobic darkness.

Even though she knew the way by heart now, the confines of belowdecks felt labyrinthine in the dark, and it was so brutally hot, the air dense and dank with the foul stench of rot and fish and sweat, worse as she descended deeper into darkness. The presence that surrounded her above deck followed her here, too, enveloping her, pressing. The only reason to sleep down here instead of up top was that here there were doors that locked. Billie tensed at every sound; she glanced constantly over her shoulder.

When she heard the racing footsteps, her breath lurched. In panic, she flattened herself against the wall, hoping that whoever was behind her would pass, but there was so little room in the companionway, and whoever it was stopped only a few feet beyond her.

"What did I tell you about going nowhere without me?" Roland demanded.

Billie let out a sigh of relief. "I'm sorry. I wasn't thinking."

"Well, think next time. For God's sake. Come on. The sooner we're behind a locked door, the better I'll like it." He practically pushed her down the hall to his stateroom, and when they were inside, he locked it.

"Where did you get the key for this room anyway?" she asked.

"It was in the lock," he said.

"There wasn't one for mine."

"Maybe the ghost took it."

"Don't tease," she said.

"I'm not sure I am." The lesser darkness of night from the porthole made Roland a shadow, tracing his movement through the room. "What was Maud talking to you about?"

"She said the crew plans to force the two of us to release the fish tonight. They won't touch it on their own, of course."

Roland let out a breath. "Too afraid. I see. I think I'll keep watch."

"Did you know her brother? The one who worked at the club?"

He braced a chair against the door. "Danny. Yes. He was a waiter."

"Did you know he's the reason she's here?"

"What do you mean?"

"I *think* he tried to blackmail James. Maud is James's insurance policy."

A long pause. Then, "I didn't know that. I knew she was unhappy to be here. I've tried to watch out for her. I liked Danny."

It made Billie feel better to know that Roland hadn't been part of that, too, that his reasons for being around Maud were admirable ones. She wished . . . well, she wished that those admirable motives extended to other things.

He said, "Why don't you try to get some sleep?"

She watched as he picked up the rifle from its place on the dresser. She heard him check to make sure it was loaded. The rough clicking sound made her shudder, only because it made her think of what might happen.

"Rolly, I need to talk to you about something."

"Hmmm. A sentence that never ends well."

"There's only one way to keep everyone on this ship safe. Either we dissect that fish and learn from her or we throw her overboard."

"Bad choices, Billie."

"No, James is making the bad choices. You know it too. That fish is full of information, Rolly. Think of what we can discover and how she can advance science! And James wants to keep her all for himself."

She felt his hesitation.

She continued to press. "You know the procedure you're planning can't work. What happens when it doesn't? Do you still get your own lab? Your own academy? Or does James die, and you're stuck with nothing?"

"It's going to work."

"I ask again: Really? Roland, for God's sake, look what's happening around you. People are dying. The fish's blood doesn't behave normally. Her slime might be weaponized."

She saw his shadow move, the bulk of him, heard the squeak as he sat on the bed. He asked, "So what if we do this thing, hmmm? What if we cut apart this fish—or throw it overboard—and nothing stops? People still die? Then what?"

"Rolly." She sat beside him on the bed. The mattress was soft enough that she couldn't keep from falling into him. "You have always been the most brilliant scientist I know."

A soft laugh. A warm expulsion of air. "Next to you, you mean."

"No. I loved—*love*—the way your brain works. It just . . . the things you could do! Let me ask you this: What if we dissect it and find something remarkable in it that can help James? Something certain? Something that is real knowledge, not some arcane prayer and dance—"

"It's not a dance."

"You know what I mean." She touched his arm. She let herself relax into him and felt him tense and then ease. He rested his chin on her hair. "Something that could help not just him but all people with lung problems, because it's *real* knowledge? And you've just given it away for your own ambition. When instead this knowledge could make you famous and lauded and . . . and . . ."

"If this works, I'll also be famous and lauded." A pause. "Just . . . trust me on this, Billie. Please."

She took her hand away, drew away. "Oh, Rolly. You keep saying that, but how can I really?"

"How many times do I have to say—"

"That's not what I'm talking about. I believe you about the past, okay? I believe you. When I say I can't trust you, I mean I can't trust you to do what's best for the world and not for yourself. I can't trust you to know that they're the same thing. I want to. I do. You could be the very best, you know."

She felt him turn to look at her. She saw the glint of his eyes in the darkness.

"Billie, I'm trying to help you," he whispered.

"You can help me by being the man I know you are," she said.

Chapter Thirty-One

When the door rattled, Billie jerked awake at once. Someone pounded on it so hard the chair that bolstered it shook.

"Open up!" a man in the hall outside shouted.

A chorus of *Open up!* Some in Spanish.

Only then did she see that Roland was already up, standing near the door, the rifle in his hands. He'd done as he'd told her, and kept watch.

She sat up, backing against the headboard.

"Go to hell," he called out. "I'm not opening this door for you or anyone else."

"We'll break it down," the voice announced.

"I'll blow your damn heads off." Roland cocked the rifle.

"Roland," she whispered.

He motioned for her to get down. "Behind the bed," he said roughly.

Billie did as he said, her heart pounding in her ears.

"Care to try me?" he challenged the men behind the door. "Go ahead. Try me."

There was a flurry of talk on the other side, much of it loud enough for her to hear. Loud and panicked Spanish and bits of Italian. "Break down the door." "Yes, break it down!" "How many more have to die?"

Roland stepped back, aiming the rifle at the opening. "Get the hell out of here," he warned again. "You come through that door and I'll pick you off one by one."

"We don't want to hurt you," said a voice in Spanish—one she recognized. Tomás. "We only want you to throw the monster back into the sea before it kills us all."

Roland looked at her in question. Quickly she translated.

"No!" he shouted at the door. "No deal!"

Another flurry of talk. Billie looked around for a weapon of her own and spotted it—the flashlight on the dressing table. In a moment, she had it, heavy and reassuring in her hand. She ignored Roland's shake of the head when she went to stand beside him. "You're not doing this alone," she whispered.

"We don't want to hurt you, but we will if we have to." A tougher voice now. "Do as we say before we break the door down."

She didn't bother to translate for Roland this time. Instead she answered grimly in Spanish, "Do you want another curse on your heads? If you hurt us, that's just what you'll get. We're the only ones who can understand the monster." Let them stew in that for a minute.

One of the sailors on the other side of the door cried out in fear.

Roland looked at her. In a low voice he said, "I hope you're not making this worse."

She screamed as loudly and with as much force as she could. Roland jumped.

On the other side of the door, she heard their surprise; she felt their sheer panic. The scream had done what she wanted; it had fed into the nervousness and fear she'd heard in their voices, their confusion when she'd said, "*We're the only ones who can understand the monster.*" The corridor rang with their running footsteps as the sailors fled, shouting.

Billie let the scream die in her throat.

A low voice behind the door. "This isn't over." And then the heavy clomp of rubber-soled shoes down the companionway.

Neither she nor Roland said anything until the sounds faded. Then Roland loosened his grasp on the rifle and slumped, exhaling sharply. "Christ."

She sagged onto the bed, her heart still racing. "Thank God."

"What the hell did you say to them?"

"That they would have another curse on their heads if they hurt us, and that we were the only ones who could understand the monster."

"That scream . . ." Roland put the rifle aside and sat on the bed beside her.

"Banshee enough for you?"

He snorted. "It's the bee's knees."

They were both quiet, Billie trying to gain a measure of calm.

Then Roland said, "You heard what he said. This isn't the end of it."

"I didn't imagine so. But I doubt they'll be back tonight. I think you can go to sleep."

He ran his hands through his hair and moved to his bed, and again Billie felt as she had when Maud had left her on deck. Alone, bereft. The sailors' attempt had frightened her; she could admit that. She crawled again beneath the blankets. Already, in such a short time, they were damp and clammy again, and though the night was not cold, she felt chilled to the bone. Who knew what tomorrow might bring?

"Roland," she whispered.

For a moment he didn't answer, and she marveled again at his ability to slip so quickly into sleep, but then, "Yes?"

"Don't take this the wrong way or anything. I don't mean . . ." Billie paused, rethinking. This wasn't a good idea. But rationality was little comfort just now. "I don't mean I want . . . This isn't an invitation for . . . Will you sleep with me? Just sleep."

She expected a tease, a scoff. Instead, he said, "I'm here, Billie. There's no reason to be afraid."

A no, then. She was surprised at her disappointment. But she heard the creak of his mattress, the shush of his movement, as he came to her.

"Move over," he said quietly.

She did, her relief more potent than she wanted it to be. When he got in beside her and drew her back against his warmth, spooning her against his body, Billie could finally relax. The night was not so cold now, nor so perilous, and she was no longer alone.

Billie had hoped Roland would agree with her and say, *Yes, you're right, let's dissect the fish. To hell with James.* He hadn't, and that was a disappointment.

In the morning, that realization saddened her to the point that she could hardly speak to him. She knew he understood that something was wrong, but she couldn't help herself. The way he watched her as the morning broke through the porthole and she came out of the head, having washed with pink-stained salt water, that curious, almost hurt expression . . . as if he expected something important, or as if he believed something had changed . . . well, what could she say to him except what she did say?

"Thank you for last night. I appreciate what you did."

"You appreciate it," he said, obviously disappointed by her words. "That means what?"

She knew he was waiting for something honest. Some admission, or confession, and she couldn't make it, because nothing *had* changed, not really. "Have you thought about what I said? About the fish?"

"We're back to that again?"

"It matters, Rolly."

"Look, I—"

The shouting—or was it screaming?—stopped them both. It came from above deck, and it sounded like more than one person.

Roland ran to the door. "What the hell is it now?"

Billie's heart sank. She was desperately afraid that she knew what it was, and her only question as they dashed out of the room and up to the deck was *Who is it this time?*

It was at least easy to see where it had happened. The crew—what was left of it—gathered at the gangway side of the ship, where everyone had been swimming the day the *antorcha del mar* had been brought on board. Except there was no shark net there now to protect them, and the body floating in the Gulf now was not swimming.

Captain Rogers. There wasn't much left of him either. The sharks were already at him, tearing him apart. Billie took one look and turned away.

"What happened?" Roland asked. "Did he fall overboard?"

She didn't know whether to laugh or cry at such a question. Perhaps that was all it was. Perhaps Rogers *had* fallen overboard. But she doubted it, and then she knew it wasn't true when she looked down and saw the faint shine of mucusy residue on the rail.

"He was like this when we found him," replied one of the crew to Roland.

"Fish him up," Roland ordered. "For God's sake, at least get what's left of him away from the sharks."

Billie reached down and ran her finger along the edge of the deck. There, too, slime. She curled her finger into her palm, hiding the discovery from everyone, but when she looked up, she saw one of the crewmen watching her, and when his eyes narrowed, she knew he'd seen what she'd just done. She knew he knew. She grasped Roland's arm, hurrying him away.

"What is it?" he asked.

She opened her palm. The slime had smeared over her hand; it was hard to see now, but Roland was quick, and she heard his harsh inhalation.

"Does anyone else know?"

"I think so. Where's James?"

James was nowhere on the deck. Roland looked alarmed. "Where the hell is he?"

The dread that came over Billie couldn't be quenched. The captain was dead, and there would be no stopping the sailors from coming after her and Roland again, no matter what curses she threatened. James might be the reason they were stranded here in the Gulf of California, but he was also the owner of the yacht and the head of this expedition. Without him, who was in charge?

Behind them, the sailors shouted and argued with one another. She heard the splash of the hook and net as they went about fishing Captain Rogers out of the sea. The firing of a rifle made her jump—they were shooting at the sharks to scare them away. Billie felt sick.

To her relief, James appeared, coming from the pilothouse, smoking one of his foul cigarettes. He looked almost gray, his blond hair unbrushed. It looked as if he had slept in his shirt.

"Captain Rogers is dead," Roland said.

James nodded. "I know. Damned luck, isn't it?"

Billie was shocked at how lightly he spoke. "I think it's a bit more than bad luck."

He looked at her as if he was surprised to see her there. "What would you call it, Billie? We've still got the first mate. He can get us back to San Francisco."

She couldn't help herself—she laughed. "San Francisco? Are you crazy? We haven't got the engines running, and there's no engineer. The generators are dead. We're a floating ship of death with hardly any water left and no way to send for help. How exactly are we getting back to San Francisco?"

"A floating ship of death. Hmmm." James made a face and took a drag on his cigarette. "Well, now, that's very poetic. I didn't expect it from a scientist."

"James, I wonder if you're seeing this clearly," Roland tried.

"We've got the fish. Everything will turn out all right," James said.

The fish was exactly the problem. The slime on the railing . . . Had Captain Rogers gone to the hold, or was the fish mobile—and intent on killing them all? Billie met Roland's worried glance. "We need to start thinking about ways to save ourselves, James."

"The fish will save us. It will save me. It will save all of us."

Billie glanced over her shoulder at the crewmen hoisting the captain's torn body to the deck. "The fish won't survive the trip back to San Francisco if help doesn't come very, very soon. And we may not survive either if we don't do something."

James patted her shoulder with a small smile. "You need to have faith, Billie. You're very learned, I know, but I've discovered something recently, in my search for a cure. Vic kept telling me, but I never believed her. Now I do. Faith transcends all learning. Like William Jennings Bryan said during the Scopes trial. Remember? 'One miracle is as easy to believe as another.'"

With that, Billie was done. Done talking. Done persuading. "You're a fool, and I for one am not going to die for your foolishness," she said bluntly. She shrugged away from him, leaving both him and Roland to stare after her as she walked away.

Chapter Thirty-Two

She waited for night to fall. She watched as Roland put the chair to the door and checked the locks and hoisted the rifle. When he sat down wearily on the bed, she told him, "We'll both wake up if they come again tonight. You should get some sleep while you can. At least for an hour or two. I'll feel better if you do." She crawled into her bed, brandishing the flashlight she took with her. "And I've got my weapon at the ready."

He lay down on his bed, not releasing the rifle. "They didn't come until the middle of the night before."

"We'll hear them."

Roland was exhausted, she saw it in his face, and Billie wasn't surprised when he fell asleep within minutes. She also knew that even in sleep he remained vigilant. He had always been a quick riser, up and ready to face the day while she was still deep in her coffee. So what she meant to do now required stealth and silence. She wasn't sure it would work, but she had to try. There was, in fact, no other choice.

She waited restlessly, wide awake herself, until his grip slackened on the rifle and his breathing grew deep and even, a familiar rhythm. When she thought it was safe to move, she took the flashlight she'd brought into bed with her. Slowly and as quietly as she could, she got out of bed. She pulled a sweater over her nightgown, went barefoot to the door, and eased aside the chair—slowly, slowly, holding her breath and praying for no noise, no scrape against the floor. The lock was another thing altogether; Roland would wake even at a click. But the lock was well oiled, and the key turned without a sound.

Billie didn't breathe until she was safely in the corridor and she'd shut the door behind her. She'd done it. The swelling darkness gathered and crowded. It felt corporeal; she felt she was physically pushing through it as she made her way to the hold, and once she got there, the air there, too, felt as if she were enfolded in a moist, hot fleshiness. Hard to breathe in, hard to move through. She switched on the flashlight. The thin trail of light forced its way through the darkness. Billie went directly to the tank. Quickly she undid the knots on the cords holding the tarp in place and pushed it back.

She played the flashlight beam over the fish, which was chloroformed, motionless. The light picked up the fading rainbow, though those colors seemed still to shine and glitter, and Billie was caught again by the miracle of the thing, the absolute impossibility of it. She shone the beam into its eyes, which were unseeing, unblinking, and murmured, "What wonders have you seen, my beauty?"

The fish answered, *Set me free, and I'll show you.*

The voice was so strong in her head Billie started. But the fish, of course, was silent. The fish didn't move. She felt a surge of guilt that they had caught this thing and now must destroy it, but she stifled that. If she was right, the *antorcha* had killed Victorine and Oliver, Matías, the captain. There was science to consider. It might not help James, but there was so much to learn. She was doing what was best for the world, for everyone on this ship.

"I'm sorry," she whispered. Billie went to the shelves, where she grabbed scalpels and rubber gloves, forceps and pans. She readied a series of jars and mixed the formaldehyde. She prepared the chloroform, enough this time to put the fish out of its misery. When she had the equipment laid out, she brought over the cart with the camera and positioned it as best she could in the near darkness lit only by the flashlight. She was sweating both with the heat and with anticipation;

impatiently she tied back her hair with a piece of string and took off her sweater, then put on a lab coat over her rayon nightgown.

She had just pulled on a pair of rubber gloves, and was debating how best to lift the fish from the tank—it was nine feet long and huge, and she hadn't the strength to lift it. She hadn't thought of this. It meant that she would have to cut in the tank and lift it out piece by piece, which wasn't ideal.

Billie stood at the edge of the tank, a rag wet with chloroform in one hand, the flashlight in the other, trying to decide how best to approach it, when she heard a scrabbling sound behind her, a rush of footsteps. She spun around, afraid—she hadn't thought the crew would follow her here, given how afraid they were of the fish—and then her fear turned abruptly to tension when she realized it wasn't the crew at all but Roland.

"Dammit! I knew you'd be here! I knew it!" He sounded furious and also desperate. "Billie, what the hell do you think you're doing?"

"What needs to be done," she said.

"How can I protect you if you insist on going against James?"

"You know it's the right thing to do."

"You don't understand what a dangerous man he can be."

Billie laughed shortly. "You can help me or you can step away, but I'm doing this."

He stared at her, obviously torn. "Billie, please."

"This fish might hold the answer to every riddle about evolution," she said patiently. "I want those answers, don't you?"

"James will find a way to destroy you. He'll destroy us both."

"What will it matter if no one makes it off this ship? Who's going to be next, Roland? Are you going to help me or not?"

Roland closed his eyes. When he opened them again, he seemed not conflicted but determined. "Yes. Yes, you're right. I just hope . . ."

She couldn't help smiling with relief—and joy, too, at the knowledge that he had chosen her. "It will be worth it, I promise. You'd better put on a lab coat. I think it's going to be messy."

He did as she asked, and put on rubber gloves as she laid the chloroform over the *antorcha*'s nostrils and waited for its breathing to slow. *I'm sorry,* Billie said again, inwardly this time, counting until the creature stopped breathing, and then a few seconds more, just to be sure.

The decision was made. There was nothing James or anyone else could do about it now. The creature was gone. Billie shoved aside her lingering guilt—it wasn't as if she hadn't performed this same task a hundred times before—and forced herself to focus on what came next. When Roland came to help her wrangle the fish from the tank, she was reminded of all the times they'd worked together in the past. It was a reassuring comfort to fall into that rhythm again, to work without words, to simply know what he was going to do and to act in tandem with him, clumsily manhandling the slippery, stinking fish from the tank to the examination table. Its long tail flapped hard against the table; the mucus made it hard to keep it in place.

Roland stood on one side; she stood on the other. Roland picked up a scalpel and said, "Where do you want to start?"

"From the thorax," she said, pointing the blade.

He nodded for her to start. "Your turn."

It was a professional nicety; Billie appreciated it. She set the blade against the paler skin of the fish's throat and pressed. The skin was tough; it did not cut easily, and when she finally pierced the skin, the thin line of blood that rose—

Smoked?

Billie pulled back.

Roland said, "What's that?" He touched the blood with his gloved finger, jerked back, and bit off a curse.

"What is it?"

"It burned." He held up his hand. The blood had burned through the rubber of his glove. "What was it you said about the blood?"

Billie stepped back. "It liquefied."

"Into an acid," Roland said ruefully. "Keep going. But be careful."

Billie moved the scalpel through the fish's belly, down, pressing hard, cutting through what felt like cartilage as the blood now pooled from the wound, dripping, a thin trail of smoke rising, and—

Pain sliced through her hand so intensely Billie dropped the scalpel. It clattered to the floor as she yanked her hand back. The same hand that had been stung by the sea urchin, bleeding profusely now from a cut that sliced across her palm, through the rubber glove, as if the scalpel had turned on her and cut her.

But that wasn't what had happened.

"What the hell . . ." Roland sounded awed.

Billie looked down at the fish.

A fin. A new fin had emerged from the cut she'd made, glistening like a rainbow, sharp and red with her blood.

A flood of malevolence, the same she'd felt when they'd pulled the fish from the depths, the same that had enveloped her when she'd first looked into its eyes, gripped her now. It seemed to inhabit the hold, to take her breath, to raise the hairs on the back of her neck.

Billie stepped away from the examination table, holding her hand, dripping blood on the floor. She met Roland's gaze.

"*Monstruo*," she whispered. "They said she was a monster."

Send me home.

Impossible. She'd chloroformed it. It was gone. It was dead. It could not be doing this. And yet . . . it shouldn't have been able to do any of what it had already done . . . what she believed it had done . . . what the legends said it had done . . .

Billie looked down again at the fin that had not been there before.

The sides of the *antorcha* began to rise and fall. Breathing. The blood spurted from the wound she'd made as its heart began to beat again.

"Billie . . ." Roland warned in a whisper of a voice.

"I see."

"You chloroformed it, didn't you? You killed it?"

"I thought so. Yes, I . . . I know I did."

The *antorcha* squirmed. The new fin flexed. The cut she'd made began to knit.

An evolutionary miracle. So much to learn. *The unknown was only what science had not yet explored,* and yet . . .

Send me home.

Billie held Roland's gaze. "I . . . I . . . it wants to go home." Her eyes blurred; her chest felt tight. She thought of Maud's words—how it scared her to think of this fish not in the sea—and Billie saw the vision then, too, the horrible blackness devoid of the creature's light, the blackness Roland had seen surrounding Ángel, the engineer, and she wanted to—no, she *was* crying. She was crying. *What the hell is wrong with me?*

Send me home.

Roland said quietly, "I know. I understand. She doesn't belong here. It's okay, Billie. It's okay. Let's do it then, yes?"

She could only nod.

Roland went up the stairs and opened the hatch. The quiet night glistened with starlight. It wasn't until the air flowed inside that Billie perceived how thick and stale the air in the hold had been, how claustrophobic. The pulley system Roland had devised to lift the fish into the hold was still there, and now, avoiding the weaponized fin, they hefted it into the sling. It seemed to recognize what they were doing; it didn't fight them. The blood from the healing cut she'd made in the fish dotted the floor and vaporized with a hiss that seemed loud in the silence marked only by their footsteps.

They pulled the ropes to lift the fish out of the hold and into the air, where it dangled, a dark shadow against the spattered sky, and then lowered it into the water. She and Roland leaned over the rail to watch. Billie wondered if the wound she'd made would hamper it. She wondered if the *antorcha*'s time in the tank had sickened it past hope. Half of her believed the creature would float and then sink like a stone, but it didn't.

The fish floated free of the sling, and for a moment it was motionless, as she anticipated, and then . . .

"Look," Roland said.

It flicked its tail. It lowered its triangular head. Did it look back at her? She wasn't sure, she couldn't tell. What Billie did know was that it began to glow. It seemed to cast off the sickly pallor of the last days in the tank, and even in the dark, those rainbow colors flashed to life.

Then it slid into the water and disappeared.

Chapter Thirty-Three

They returned to the hold in silence. Billie bandaged her hand and Roland put antiseptic on his burned finger, and then they cleaned the examination table as if nothing strange had happened.

They left the tarp untied—there was no reason to keep it covered, and there was no point in hiding what had happened.

"You said . . . when I told you it wanted to go home, you said, 'I know,'" Billie said. "Why did you say that?"

Roland went very quiet. "I don't know. I just felt it. I did. I knew it was true."

That connection again.

He paused in shelving the cleaned scalpels. "You were right about everything you said, Billie. I think I just wasn't ready to hear it until now."

"You were right too," she told him. "Some things maybe we aren't meant to understand."

"*Yet*," he said with a small smile. "It's only that we don't understand them yet. One day we will. One day. Just . . . maybe not today. We never stop exploring until we do, Billie."

Billie realized suddenly that those were the words she wanted most to hear.

She'd wanted so much from this expedition. She had intended for it to solve all her problems. Instead, it had only shown her what small dominion she had over the sea—well, over the world—and created more uncertainty. It had only made her question everything she knew.

But maybe . . . maybe that was its purpose. The sea's lesson, the *antorcha*'s, was to take away her certainty. To force her to understand that she had been too rigid, too angry, too *sure*. To make her reexamine, to see things from a different perspective. It was as Roland said—the unknown was only the unexplored. It was true not just for science, but also for everything.

Together they went back to Roland's room. The rifle, the chair, all was as they'd left it, though the beginning of the night now felt a hundred years ago, and the events in the hold seemed like a hallucination, or a dream, or . . . Billie couldn't decide what it was. It made no sense, and there was no rationale that resolved it, and yet her hand throbbed beneath its bandage, and she felt calm as she hadn't since she'd stepped onto this ship, calm as if her future had been decided in a way she hadn't anticipated or thought to imagine, but it was just as she wanted.

She crawled into bed and watched him undress, a shadow in the darkness. It wasn't only calm that swept her now, but also relief, the knowledge that she'd done what the sea wanted, that they'd both done so. She said, "We did what was right, don't you think?"

Roland laughed quietly. It was sincere and deep, and it reminded her of their past, of the beginning, when discovery had been the thing that brought them together, that bound them. Before everything else—ambition, stubbornness, anger—had got in the way.

"Yeah, Billie," he whispered. "I do."

He came to her bed. When he crawled in beside her, she welcomed him. When he took her in his arms, she held him tight. He kissed her.

"What about this?" he whispered against her mouth. "Is this right too?"

"Yes," she whispered back, wrapping her arms around his neck, pulling him closer. "Yes."

The pounding on the stateroom door, along with the frantic "Mr. Ely! Miss McKennan!" woke them both.

Roland called, "What is it?"

Maud said through the door, "It's Mr. Holloway. He's . . . you'd better come."

"We'll be right there," Roland told her. He bounded out of bed and pulled on his trousers while Billie rubbed the sleep from her eyes.

"What do you suppose it is?" she asked.

"Another death?" he posited grimly.

"But the fish . . ."

"Come on, let's go."

Billie rolled out of bed and dressed quickly. There was no doubt about where James was; they heard the commotion on the aft deck before they'd got past the main saloon. Shouting and a babble of languages, Spanish, Italian, and English, all so melded together Billie couldn't extricate them, and she and Roland rushed up the steps into the morning.

James stood at the rail, against the vivid backdrop of the sky, which painted the oily stillness of the red sea a sickening magenta. The man was disheveled and raging, his face pink and the tendons in his throat standing out as he shouted at the crew gathered around him. "What have you done with it? Where is it?"

And Billie knew there was no new death. James had discovered already that the fish was gone. Roland stopped short; he'd obviously realized it too. He reached back for her and took her hand, but before either of them could do anything, James caught sight of them.

"You!" He jabbed his finger toward them. "It was you, wasn't it? I should have known you would betray me, you bastard. What have you done with it?"

The men turned as one mass to face them.

Roland didn't lie. Quietly, he said, "The fish was causing too much trouble, James. Surely you can understand that. People were dying—"

"Are you seriously telling me that you think that fish was *murdering* people?" James laughed, and the laugh became a cough that nearly turned him purple. When he recovered, he rasped, "I should have known not to hire a woman scientist. A woman scientist! Oliver warned me, and I didn't listen."

Roland stiffened. "That's enough, James."

Billie's anger surged. She stepped forward. "I don't have to take that from you, you selfish son of a bitch."

Roland pulled her back.

James said, "I promised you a new exhibit! I gave you everything you wanted! All this time, all you were doing was scheming against me!"

"You're corrupting science for your own ends," Billie snapped back. "You don't care about anyone else. You've made your riches from the world, and now you don't want to share. How sorry I am for you, you pathetic worm of a man. You deserve to lose everything."

"Damn you!" James grabbed a harpoon leaning against the harpoon gun beside him. He hefted it, his eyes wild, aiming it at her.

Roland said, "For God's sake, James, put it down!"

The crew dodged away en masse. One of them shouted, "Santa Maria!"

Another pointed at the rail: "Devil!"

Billie looked toward the rail—they all did—and, distracted, James looked too. The manta ray that flung itself from the water was huge, one of the largest Billie had seen yet, thirty feet wide at least, so big, and so close, that its wings nearly swept the rail. With a gasp of . . . fascination, joy, shock, James twisted, the harpoon still in his hand, to face it.

"My God, I have you at last!" he shouted. He threw the harpoon, and the creature simply lowered the tip of its wing—was it with intention, or an accident? Billie afterward could never say which—and propelled the spear away before it dived again into the water.

James stood too close to the rail, and he was already off balance from throwing the heavy spear. The rope of the harpoon caught his arm, tangling him. By the time they understood what was happening, the harpoon had dragged James Holloway over the rail. No one tried to help him. It happened too quickly for anyone to try.

The splash seemed to echo for a long time. For a moment, no one moved, and then they all raced to the rail.

Billie didn't know what she expected to see: James floundering in the water, James swimming to the ladder off the side of the boat, a man diving in to save him, sharks massing.

She saw none of those things. Instead, she saw nothing. Nothing at all. James Holloway had simply sunk into the Sea of Cortez, leaving not even a ripple behind.

But as everyone turned from the rail, Billie saw—or thought she saw—an intense glow come to the surface, and the snout of the fish, the *antorcha del mar*, emerge from the water. A moment, no more, and its eyes rolled toward hers, an acknowledgment, before it, too, sank back into the *agua de sangre*.

Chapter Thirty-Four

The next eleven days

They rationed the remaining drinking water; only a few swallows a day. They didn't go hungry; the rotted food was inedible for the passengers aboard the *Eurybia*, but it brought the fish in droves to the side of the ship, where they were easily caught. They'd burned the last of the wicker furniture and the lifeboat, and since it was so hot, they needed fire only for cooking, and the wood had lasted until now. When it rained—not often—they caught what they could in tarps and buckets. Billie and Maud woke early to soak up what dew they could from the ship's surfaces and squeeze it from sponges. It wasn't much, but even a mouthful made the job worth it.

They threw the corpses of Victorine and Oliver into the sea with prayers and a makeshift service.

There were no more deaths.

What was left of the crew, Roland and Billie, Maud, and James's valet Pollan had formed a small community. They ate together, cooked together, bathed in seawater, and wore rimes of salt on their skin.

Roland worked with the valet and one of the other crewmen who had some mechanical ability on trying to get the generators running again, but with no luck. It looked increasingly as if no one was searching for them, and no rescue was coming. They hoped for passing fishermen, but to no avail.

Billie spent the time doing what she could to salvage the expedition's purpose. She'd engaged Maud to help her organize notes and catalog specimen photographs. Assuming they were ever rescued, she would need whatever she could recover.

The organisms that caused the red water had either died off or moved on, because the day after James disappeared, the water had turned blue. Sometimes it was so clear they could see what seemed like fathoms down. Billie taught Maud how to identify the creatures they spotted.

"The world feels different now," Maud marveled as they watched jellyfish one day. "I'm tired of being scared of everything. I'm not going back to my da and ma and all that. They'd just make me marry a fisherman, and I'm not going to. No sense in arguing with them."

"What will you do, then?" Billie asked.

"Well." Maud gave her a shy look. "Seeing as how you and Mr. Ely are . . ."

Billie felt herself redden. She had thought they were discreet, but Maud had proved to be very observant. The young woman would make a good naturalist.

"I've been thinking," Maud went on. "Maybe you need an assistant or something like that? I could carry pails and keep organizing for you. I could do anything you wanted. Even be a maid, but I don't think I'm very good at it. I only know I want to keep learning about things. I don't want to be just a girl anymore."

The truth was that Billie didn't know what the future held for her either. The San Diego Zoo was not her calling. Roland's future was equally up in the air. He still had his job at the California Academy of Sciences, but the laboratory he had dreamed about was no longer in the cards—at least not one funded by Holloway. But like Maud, Billie felt energized. If they made it off this ship, if they had a future, it would not be the one she'd left behind. What it would be, she didn't yet know. "I'll see what I can do," she said to Maud with a smile.

The twelfth day after James's death, Billie sat on the aft deck under the canopy for what little shade there was, drawing a squid before it became their dinner. Roland sat behind her making notes about a sea turtle, his knee gently brushing her shoulder. Maud stood at the rail, idly throwing fish bones into the water, when she burst out, "There's a ship."

Roland glanced up, shading his eyes. "Just another mirage."

They had seen several. A group of revenue ships a week ago that had turned out to be a pod of whales. A landmass that had been . . . well . . . nothing. Haze that made distant mountains and small waves that became canoes and birds that were planes—the Gulf of California was only a dreamland, after all.

Maud turned to them with a frown. "Maybe." She turned back to her view of the sea. "I don't think so."

Roland made a sound of lazy disagreement.

"Come see," Maud urged.

From the forward deck, Billie heard the cry of a sailor. *"¡Un barco! Un barco!"*

She put aside her pencil and notebook and got to her feet, carefully avoiding the spread tentacles of the squid. They were all sunburned and languid, and she was used now to avoiding any movement. Movement meant being hot and thirsty, and Roland was right—this was no doubt just another mirage. But she went to the rail anyway to stand beside Maud, who pointed.

"There," the maid said.

Billie followed the line of her finger. At first, it looked like nothing, a bank of clouds, or haze, gray against the blue. Then she caught a sparkle of white, something glinting in the sun—a very good mirage, one of the best she'd seen, growing bigger as it approached, moving into itself, a stream of smoke trailing from a funnel painted red.

Billie blinked, expecting it to disappear before her eyes, the way they all did.

It didn't.

She blinked again.

It was still there.

"Um . . . Roland?" She twisted from the rail. "I think this might really be a ship."

From the forward deck came shouts and whistles. Roland walked over lazily. When he got there, he straightened in surprise.

"My God!"

The idea of it being a mirage dissipated in the next moment, when the ship blew its horn, when it seemed to be coming straight at them. Billie didn't know what to feel—shock, elation, relief, fear? All those emotions coursed through her, and none stayed. What stayed was numbness, a dumb sense of disbelief. Part of her, she realized, had thought she would die here, and maybe she still would. She didn't know who was on the ship, or what they wanted. They could be Mexican officials, they could be smugglers, they could be anyone, and the passengers on the *Eurybia* were so very vulnerable.

As if he read her mind, Roland headed toward the deckhouse. "We'd better get the rifles. Tell the crew, will you, Billie? Don't let them get too excited."

When she translated Roland's directions as he handed out the rifles, the crew listened, but it was clear they were bursting with hope. Billie couldn't blame them; so was she. "Wait until we see what they want. Don't stand down until I say."

By the time the ship reached them, the sailors looked, if not formidable, at least slightly threatening. Disheveled, sweating, rifles at their sides.

The *Mary Beth* pulled up beside them. It was a smaller boat than the *Eurybia*, but very well apportioned, with lifeboats and shiny brasswork and a group of well-dressed people standing at the rail, most of them holding drinks. Billie's mouth watered at the sight of that. Ice. They had ice.

"Ahoy there!" one man—the captain? The owner?—called out affably. He was a corpulent man who looked to be in his fifties. "You look to be in need of some help."

Another man, taller, wearing a uniform—this man obviously the captain—pushed his way to the front. His gaze scanned the flagpole, and then came again to Roland. "Is this the *Eurybia*?"

"Yes." Roland's voice held relief. "Yes, we're the *Eurybia*."

"Thank God, man—we've been looking for you for weeks!" the captain said. "Where's your captain?"

A quick glance at Billie, and then Roland said, "I'm afraid we lost him. I'm afraid we've lost . . . um . . . mostly everyone."

The corpulent man looked horrified. "Everyone?"

"We're all that's left," Roland said. "We were caught in a storm, and . . . we lost everyone to the Gulf."

The captain frowned. "Well, you had an inexperienced crew, I understand, and that was a monster of a storm."

Maud laughed. Everyone looked at her, and she lowered her gaze, seemingly abashed. "A monster, yes. But it was beautiful too."

The captain gave her a confused look, but said, "Well, I guess some people look for the positive. But I'll say it's been a terrible season. I've been sailing these waters for years, and I've never had so many mishaps. Storms and fogs . . ."

"We were attacked by a whale!" one of the women at the rail exclaimed. "A whale! Like in *Moby-Dick*!"

The captain grimaced. "True. Honestly, we were afraid we wouldn't find you. You know you've been all over the news. The lost Holloway expedition."

"Bigger than the Scopes trial!" said the corpulent man.

"Really?" Billie asked. "Well. That's something."

"Won't you all come aboard?" the corpulent man said. "I'm the owner of the *Mary Beth*. Gregory Holder, from San Diego, at your service. You're all most welcome, if you don't mind sharing quarters or sleeping with the crew."

"That would be a luxury at this point, Mr. Holder," Billie said.

"We're on our way back, and we can drop you there. I'm afraid there won't be room for your specimens . . ." Gregory Holder looked only slightly sorry.

Roland glanced at Billie. "Most of them were destroyed in the storm, anyway."

"We have the *Eurybia*'s location, and you can make arrangements to have her towed at some point, I suppose," said Holder, though who would do that was entirely unclear, given that the owner was dead and no one present wanted ever to see the *Eurybia* again.

Better to leave her to her ghosts, Billie thought.

"We'll get our things," Roland told him.

They dispersed to their rooms. Most of Billie's possessions were in Roland's. After she retrieved those, along with her sketchbooks and film, she went to the small chintz room to get what was left and was unsurprised to find that nothing there felt like hers any longer. Desultorily she scraped her lotions into her suitcase. She shook out a pair of trousers to fold them and was puzzled to feel something bulky in the pocket. She pulled it out.

A jar, filled with milky liquid, iridescent threads of slime. At the bottom, fish scales, small and diamond shaped, opalescent, glinting rainbow in the light coming through the porthole, as bright as any jewel, though they'd been faded when she'd collected them. She stared at them, remembering the day she'd discovered the *antorcha del mar*'s strange blood, how she'd pulled this sample from the tank for Roland, how she'd shoved it into her pocket in her hurry to escape Oliver and find Roland to tell him.

How those scales glowed for her now. Billie felt the weight of their beauty as a tightness in her chest, a reminder of the world she'd wondered about when she'd looked into the creature's eyes, the things it had made her feel, the way it had challenged her. *Where have you been? How do you exist?*

What do you think about?

So many questions. So many unknowns still waiting to be discovered. So much unexplored. And here, unexpected, some answers. Here, the future. Maybe.

It felt like a gift.

How tender she felt. How exposed. How open to the world in a way she'd never felt before.

She gripped the jar hard, her own miracle. She closed her eyes and breathed deep, waiting for the touch of the presence that had haunted her nights and her days in this room.

It didn't come, but she no longer doubted she'd felt it. Or that it had touched her once. Inexplicable, but somehow real.

Real enough to change everything she thought. *"There are more things in heaven and earth . . ."*

She slipped the jar into her suitcase and went to meet the others.

AFTERWORD

The Holloway expedition is inspired in part by William K. Vanderbilt's many cruises on his ships the *Ara* and the *North Star*, where he also collected specimens for the American Museum of Natural History, the Vanderbilt Museum on Long Island, and his private estate. These were serious collection cruises. While guests expecting luxurious seagoing vacations (including sportfishing, touring by car, and hunting) were always aboard, the yachts were also outfitted with the best in scientific equipment, including trawls, aquariums, labs, and scientists. One such collecting cruise is described in his *Across the Atlantic with Ara*, a travelogue of his summer 1924 expedition. More information on Vanderbilt's cruises is available at the website Yachts International: www.yachtsinternational.com/owners-lounge/vanderbilt.

The Gulf of California (Sea of Cortez) was not well studied at the time *The Vermilion Sea* takes place. The US Fisheries *Albatross* exploration of 1911 studied only the lower Gulf. The 1921 expedition led by the California Academy of Sciences focused on the flora and fauna of the islands in the Gulf. One of the most famous later explorations was that written about by John Steinbeck in *The Log from the Sea of Cortez*, where he and a small crew set sail in 1940 on the *Western Flyer* to explore the denizens of the Gulf. Steinbeck's philosophical musings on our relationship with the sea, and his notes on the alienating and beautiful features of the Sea of Cortez in particular, inspired Billie McKennan's character—and Roland's.

The collection techniques and procedures detailed in this novel, including the dynamiting, harpooning, shooting, and bottom trawling, are accurate depictions of collection at this time (as are the depictions of the sporting life of the rich and idle). Science of the future is built on the back of science of the past, and our current knowledge of the creatures of the deep has depended on such techniques—it was a long time before such procedures were questioned.

One note: I am not a scientist; I simply have an abiding interest in science. I am truly NOT a marine biologist. Much of the information for this book came from researching piloting books, exploration journals, and scientific papers from the era. Taxonomies change as information changes; thus, some of the scientific names for the creatures in the novel may not be the same as they are today, but they are as accurate for their time as I could make them. In some cases, I gave up finding the era-correct scientific name, and used the modern-day name. Please be gentle in your criticisms of my scientific faults—I did my best.

Women were in scientific fields like marine biology in the 1920s, and Billie's trials and the prejudices she encountered were common. Women rarely, if ever, moved up through careers in science in academic, industrial, or government fields. They remained in lesser positions, such as assistantships and junior faculty roles, regardless of experience or education. Getting an advanced degree in science was problematic enough, and even having a PhD did not guarantee employment. The lucky ones had male mentors and supporters. Even those more enlightened men, however, were not immune from taking credit for women's research or keeping those women in lower positions in order to take advantage of their work. Men, too, of course, are a product of their times, but not all found it an effort to share the credit. In any case, women were held to a different standard, and what one woman did reflected on all—if she did poorly, she was an example of her entire sex. If she did well, she was considered sui generis. In short, there was no way to win. For women scientists, the easiest and most successful upward movement professionally usually meant taking a position in an out-of-the-box or up-and-coming field like a zoo, home economics, or newly growing technologies that weren't so hidebound.

The 1920s were an interesting era, with much in common socially, politically, and culturally with the 2020s. The Scopes trial is a particularly resonant example. When Tennessee passed the Butler Act, which prohibited the teaching of any theory that denied the biblical account of human origins, including evolution, in public schools, it was only one of many school districts in the US looking for ways to censor and control curriculum. John Scopes, a teacher in Dayton, Tennessee, said that he'd taught evolution in his science class in order for the ACLU to set up a test case. The ACLU hoped that the case would ultimately bring to the Supreme Court a fight for individual liberty—it was *not* against religion. But while the trial encompassed many philosophical and cultural issues—parental rights, academic rights, religious freedom, censorship—the judge in the trial kept it very narrowly focused on the simple fact of whether John Scopes broke the law. The trial pitted two of the biggest attorneys and orators of the time, Clarence Darrow and William Jennings Bryan, against each other, which created a show that arrested the nation, and was the focus of radio broadcasts and newspaper and magazine articles. The testimony from the scientific community regarding proof of evolution was not allowed before the jury, and it soon became clear that the question the country needed to address—What exactly did society's obligation to educating its populace mean?—wasn't going to be answered. John Scopes had broken the law. He was fined one hundred dollars, and declined to take the case beyond the state supreme court, which upheld the anti-evolution law but freed Scopes on a technicality.

Yet laws have consequences, and this particular law meant that other states holding such fundamentalist views felt free to put their own limitations on curriculum through law, statute, or resolution. Not all of them could be tested. This happened mostly in the South and the West. Because textbook writers and publishers have a national market, and they worried about sales and didn't want to do editions for each region, they looked for a compromise. Evolution soon became not a "proven theory," but simply a "theory" or a "hypothesis" in textbooks meant for national distribution. Darwinism was a "belief" and an "interpretation" of the theory of life's origins. Thus entire generations have grown up learning and believing that evolution is unproven, which is simply not true. The theory has been proved over and over again. There are many factors involved, and it's more complicated than popular culture would have you believe, but such explanations are beyond the scope of this afterword, and I leave you to your own explorations.

Beyond that, the play and movie *Inherit the Wind*, which is based on the Scopes trial, highlights the trial as a war between science and religion, and though that was an aspect of it, it was also much more nuanced than that (see above: Individual liberty, church versus state, academic rights, censorship, parental rights, etc. were all at play here). It is also, in the way of most forms of entertainment about historical events, not quite accurate. For those wishing for more information on the Scopes trial, the books *Summer for the Gods* (updated version), by Edward J. Larson, and *Keeping the Faith*, by Brenda Wineapple, are excellent sources. Transcripts of the Scopes trial, which are fascinating in their bizarreness, are available at https://profjoecain.net/scopes-monkey-trial-1925-complete-trial-transcripts/.

While the practical effect of unpopular laws is that eventually they're ignored and unenforced in places where they become problematic—which is what happens when fervors die down in the fallow times before they resurrect themselves again—Tennessee's Butler Act wasn't repealed until 1967.

The *antorcha del mar* in the novel is not a real fish. However, it is based on a real fish. *Tiktaalik roseae* is a 375-million-year-old fossil fish discovered in the Canadian Arctic in 2004. It's the earliest fossil record found of a fish that ventured onto land, and thus an evolutionary "missing link." I've based much of the physiology of the *antorcha del mar* on *Tiktaalik*, including the proto-leg lobe fins, the eellike tail, and the triangular, alligator-like head. The rest is purely my imagination. There's a very cool video on YouTube by Professor Neil Shubin about the discovery of *Tiktaalik* for those who wish to explore further: www.youtube.com/watch?v=yvDQCa7rleI.

And finally, although there are many secret societies in this world, and one of them may indeed be named after the philosopher-poet Empedocles, the society in this book came purely from my imagination. In history, Empedocles not only was a philosopher and a poet but also had medical skills and healing powers. His works survive only in fragments (*On Nature* and *Purifications*), but my primary interest in him came thanks to his fascinating views on the origin of species, where he hypothesized that various limbs and organs were produced from the earth and joined together in different configurations, spontaneously creating, say, fish-headed men or man-headed fish, until natural selection figured out which combinations worked and which didn't, and everything was weeded out until species as we know them were perfected.

It was so perfect for the thematic nature of this novel that it felt serendipitous. Some things just fall so wholly and perfectly into your lap it's as if the universe is handing you a gift.

Beyond that, as always, I hope to get things right, and I research to the best of my ability, but any errors are purely my own. Mea culpa.

ACKNOWLEDGMENTS

First, thanks must go to everyone at Browne & Miller Literary Associates, for being exemplary in all ways literary agenting—and also extra kudos and eternal gratitude beyond the usual to my agent, Danielle Egan-Miller, and foreign rights agent, Mariana Fisher, because without them *The Vermilion Sea* would not exist. That was some brainstorming session, ladies—I salute you!

Thanks also to Danielle Marshall at Lake Union, who first cheered the novel; Chantelle Aimee Osman, who bought it and championed it; my editor, Marilyn Brigham, who loved it and contributed not just encouragement but also great ideas; and my developmental editor, Jodi Warshaw, who has always, always helped me make a book better. The kind of trust I have in her is invaluable, and after so many books together, she may now be bound to me in some magical unbreakable dependency. I hope so.

Thank you so much to the production team at Lake Union, also, which has always been dedicated, capable, and just the best. From the production manager to the copyeditor to the proofreader to marketing and publicity . . . you guys are the ones who make it work, and I appreciate it and never forget it.

Thanks once again to Spencer Fuller at Faceout Studio for another fantastic cover.

As always, Kristin Hannah is owed eternal thanks not just for being a wall for me to throw ideas and (sometimes) axes against, but also for forcing me always to be better. Kany Levine for reading and being honest and loving me even when I am impossible. Jayne Ann Krentz for saying "Horror lite, Megan!" and Christina Dodd for nodding along and the two of you for being great lunch and commiseration partners. Suzanne Selfors for just being there for me. Donna Smith Hursh for equally just being there and for amusing me and philosophizing with me every day. And last but definitely not least, thank you to Maggie and Cleo for making me glad to be alive.

ABOUT THE AUTHOR

Photo © 2024 C. M. C. Levine

Megan Chance is the critically acclaimed, award-winning author of more than twenty novels, including *Glamorous Notions*, *A Dangerous Education*, *A Splendid Ruin*, *Bone River*, and *An Inconvenient Wife*. She and her husband live in the Pacific Northwest with their two grown daughters nearby. For more information about Megan and her books, please visit www.meganchance.com.